D1593387

Collision of Lies

Also by John J. Le Beau

Collision of Evil

Collision of Lies

A Novel

John J. Le Beau

Oceanview Publishing

LONGBOAT KEY, FLORIDA

ISBN: 978-1-60809-045-7

Published in the United States of America by Oceanview Publishing, Longboat Key, Florida
www.oceanviewpub.com

2 4 6 8 10 9 7 5 3 1

PRINTED IN THE UNITED STATES OF AMERICA

All statements of fact, opinion, or analysis expressed are those of the author and do not reflect the official positions or views of the CIA or any other U.S. Government agency. Nothing in the contents should be construed as asserting or implying U.S. Government authentication of information or Agency endorsement of the author's views. This material has been reviewed by the CIA to prevent the disclosure of classified information.

—Publication Review Board, CIA

For my daughter Angelika, whose discerning eye and thoughtful words make her a wonderfully helpful critic and editor, as well as her father's unending joy.

Acknowledgments

A number of subject matter experts were kind enough to contribute thoughtful ruminations, suggestions, and information that greatly enhanced the texture and the content of this book. This is a work of fiction, but hews as closely as possible to the real world in many matters of detail so as to provide credible atmospherics and technical accuracy. Meriting special note are:

Detective Chief Superintendent (ret.) Keith Weston, QPM, formerly of the Metropolitan Police, New Scotland Yard, London, who, after retiring from the police, was a senior research fellow at Cranfield University. He is currently the director of Keith Weston Consultancy, Ltd. in the United Kingdom. In December 2001, Keith was the law enforcement official directly engaged with the Royal Navy in the maritime interdiction and boarding of the *MV Nisha*, suspected (falsely) of carrying a chemical weapon bound for Great Britain.

Dr. Michael Allswede, D.O., is Clinical Professor of Emergency Medicine at the Oklahoma University School of Medicine. An internationally recognized expert and lecturer in the fields of chemical and biological threats as well as crisis response, Michael knows his poisons, and was most helpful in contributing creatively toxic input.

Colonel Olaf Lindner, commander, and several officials of the GSG 9 *der Bundespolizei*, the elite and rightly fabled German federal police unit, who explained their international mission, challenges, and capabilities while exhibiting, in addition to their peerless professionalism, great kindness and generosity as host and tour guide in their impressive headquarters

A salute and sincere appreciation is extended as well to the invariably collegial and patient Oceanview publishing team for once again turning a manuscript into a book.

Collision of Lies

The rhythmic sound of waves accosting the solid-metal hull of the ship mingled with the deep hum of powerful diesel engines, creating a baritone polyphony. The sound drifted out from the vessel but was quickly muted in the vastness of the ocean. The night sky was cloudless, the shimmering black expanse of the sea humbled beneath an endless canopy of stars. A brief burst of light and motion interrupted the nocturnal tableau as a comet displayed a fleeting trace across the indigo darkness, and was gone.

Closer to earth, a breeze eased over the rolling water and swept the thick hair of the solitary figure standing on deck, his frame concealed behind a corrugated metal container at the rear of the vessel. The man glanced over his shoulder to confirm that he was alone. Satisfied, he huddled deeper into his dark wool watch coat and retrieved a rectangular object from a capacious pocket. He held the object in front of his chest with one hand and pushed a large red plastic button with the other. Instantly, a row of three small lights blinked awake on the device, orange at first, but turning bright green in a few seconds. The man nodded to himself and pushed down on a silver oval at the center of the device, aware that this engaged the transmit mechanism.

As unseen as a soul, a burst of enciphered text launched from the electronic tool and raced silently upward toward an orbiting communications satellite far above the Atlantic, invisible in the distant heavens. The burst transmission was completed in seconds and its owner pressed the red button, which caused its tiny lamps to flicker briefly before returning to electronic sleep.

"I thought so," a voice from behind the man spat in guttural German.

Before he could turn, the man holding the electronic device felt a probing point of pressure against his coat, followed an instant later by the sensation of a long, sharp object penetrating the fabric and then his stomach. A bass cry of panic erupted from his throat, but a beefy hand slammed over his mouth, splitting his lip and silencing him. Wide-eyed and trembling, the man felt the hard object withdraw swiftly from his punctured abdomen, trailing blood, fluids, and pain in its wake, only to be slammed into him again, and then again.

"You stupid, stinking bastard," the assailant hissed as he drove the long screwdriver into his victim a fourth and then a fifth time. The man's straining, jerking resistance ebbed away with each blow, replaced in under one minute by the passive, heavy slackness of death. The transmission device was released and fell heavily to the deck as the victim's muscles relaxed involuntarily and his dead hands opened.

The man holding the blood-slicked screwdriver in a firm grip was squat and powerfully broad, and he hitched an arm solidly around the corpse to prevent it from falling. Breathing deeply with the exertion, and taking one halting step at a time, he moved his cargo of deadweight toward the rust-streaked metal rail above the ship's propellers. He flung the murder implement into the heaving water and then eased the blood-seeping cadaver over the side, head first. Gravity was his ally and accomplished the rest. The lifeless form fell through the darkness into the effervescent turbulence below and, in an instant, vanished from the visible world.

Expelling a long breath, the attacker watched the motion of the waves for a moment and noted the uninterrupted progress of the vessel on its course. He surveyed the scene and, with a grunt, retired below deck, returning moments later with a large bucket of water. He splashed the water along the spot where the murder had transpired, flushing tendrils of blood over the side. Stooping, he retrieved the communications device and studied it, turning the object in his hands. His brow furrowed. There were no visible markings on the instrument, nothing indicating its purpose or place of manufacture.

Of course not, he thought. His survey of the device completed, he tossed it over the side. There was now no remaining trace of the violence that had transpired mere minutes ago.

The man turned his gaze toward the sweep of the stars, stretching away into infinity. He observed them clinically, without emotion, unmoved by any sense of wonder. He thought only of what would happen next.

The disappearance of his victim would not be noticed until morning. With the absence of a crewman discovered, the ship would be bound to follow established regulations and conduct a cursory sweep of the area. No trace of the vanished crewman would be found, of course. By the time the search commenced, the body would have been ingested by a variety of aquatic denizens.

Following standard maritime procedures for a "man overboard" situation after the search maneuvers, the ship would radio its next port of call and report the incident. There would be a formal investigation once the vessel docked, but it would be pro forma. In instances of this sort, the governing presumption was that there had been an accident, or possibly a suicide.

There was nothing to hint at foul play. With a nod of satisfaction, the man pulled his jacket tightly around his muscular frame and trudged off to the warm cabin that awaited him, his gait accommodating the familiar roll of the ship.

Now a mile in the ship's wake, the corpse, weighed down by its heavy wool coat and leather work boots, sank slowly into the silent black depths, arms plaintively outstretched. A large fish hit the left hand tentatively, and then again with more purpose, tearing away a piece of soft flesh near the thumb. As the body continued its unanimated descent, a democracy of other fish followed, large and small, making further incursions on the corporeal integrity of the recently deceased. Eventually, a cluster of tiger sharks moved in, scattering the lesser-finned diners before them. Their dull eyes surveyed the carcass with primordial purpose to ensure that it represented no danger. Moments later, the man who, ten minutes previously, had stood aboard the

ship was ripped by serrated rows of slashing teeth into several uneven pieces and devoured in voracious gulps, until nothing remotely
human remained.

INNSBRUCK, THE TYROL, AUSTRIA

The jutting, uneven peaks of the Nordkette range turned a diffuse,
ethereal red as the sun surrendered its domain to the stealthy en-
croachment of a summer's evening. The *Alpengluehen*, the "alpine
glow," as it is called by inhabitants of the mountainous terrain, suffused the Austrian landscape with pastoral tranquility. A sure-footed
clan of mountain goats clattered along the narrow purchase of a cliff
and paused, permitting the final trace of the day's solar warmth to ca-
ress their sides. They sniffed the air with flaring nostrils, detecting
the familiar fragrance of enzian and other alpine flowers. Still,
somber cloud banks were gathering from the south, signaling that
the warm, sunny days were about to end. In the valley far below the
magically lit summits, the ancient city of Innsbruck prepared for
evening, the first strings of streetlamps winking on, an illuminated
necklace laid upon the terrain.

There was much to drink and every reason to drink it. Exquisite
white wines from the steep, dark slopes of the Wachau valley on the
Danube, and enticingly hearty reds from the rolling hillside vine-
yards of Burgenland. Rich, malty monastery beer handcrafted by the
Benedictine monks of Salzburg competed with drier but full-bodied
Austrian pilsner from the little town of Hirt. Renowned apricot,
pear, and plum schnapps from Dolsach, East Tyrol, also provided
steady refreshment to the jostling, laughing phalanx of customers at
the open bar.

Red-and-white Austrian flags hung from the exposed rafters
above the cavernous room of giddy celebrants. For centuries, the
structure had served as a stable for dairy cows but, a decade removed,
had been converted into an elegant reception hall for occasions such
as this. The antique, exposed timber had been carefully restored and
the rough stone walls painted ochre. A circular cherrywood bar oc-

cupied the center of the room, an array of tables on one side and an expansive dance floor on the other. Subtle lighting illuminated the scene, providing a soothing display of light and shadow. An over-sized, deeply veneered oil-on-wood painting of a stern-faced farm woman leading a herd of cattle to pasture provided the dominant decorative motif.

Georg Forster surveyed the scene and felt physically warmed with contentment. He was warmed as well by the excellent Williams brandy that he had been dispatching at an impressive rate for the past hour. This was a night to celebrate—they had all earned it, not least himself. In a bow to popular tastes, he bit into a warm pretzel, savoring the salty taste. A plump, well-attired woman with protruding teeth waved from the bar and he raised his schnapps glass in salute. He did not recognize her. But then he could not be expected to know all of the local party functionaries who had contributed to this unexpected electoral victory. That they would know him, on the other hand, was self-evident.

Georg Forster had founded the Nationalist Defense Front Party, *Nationalistische Verteidigungs Front Partei*, and had successfully or-chestrated its rise from humble, rural roots to national prominence in Austria. The welcome results of the elections two days ago meant increased power for him personally, too. Having acquired 25 percent of the total votes, Forster would be invited to Vienna from his party base in Innsbruck, and given an important post in the ruling coali-tion government. He smiled broadly at the realization that his plans to eventually rule Austria were proceeding flawlessly.

A rotund, balding man in a well-tailored charcoal loden suit ap-proached and vigorously pumped Forster's hand. Forster knew him as a businessman and financial donor from Kufstein. "Thanks for your excellent support, Hans. Your generosity played a big role in this winning campaign. I'll never forget that."

The businessman looked at Forster earnestly through wire-rimmed glasses. "It's the least I could do, Georg. I'm behind the scenes; it's you and the other party candidates who are in the fight. I expect you'll be fighting for us in Vienna now."

Forster clapped the shorter man on his shoulder. "Right. And it is a fight, no need to be dainty. Unlike the other parties, we are going to smash some political furniture and push Austria where she needs to go. There is no shortage of enemies we're facing, Hans."

The balding man nodded, his features assuming a brooding cast. "Enough enemies, all right. Immigrant criminals, Gypsies, Slavs, North African beggars. We've become a dumping ground for that trash. Now, maybe, we can turn things around. Show those outsiders there's no welcome mat for them here." He glanced up at Forster for confirmation.

Forster straightened his tall frame and placed his glass on the bar. "Don't worry, Hans. I founded this party to purge Austria of unwanted elements. We won't bow and scrape to Israel, either, apologizing for what allegedly happened during the war. And acting as if it were yesterday instead of ancient history. Times are changing. That's why our message resonates and why we did so well two days ago. Austria is for Austrians of Aryan blood. We still have to be guarded in how we say that, but people understand what we stand for."

The smaller man nodded. "Georg, the people I represent are behind you one hundred percent. You can count on our help, silent as it may be. You know what I mean."

Forster reached again for his glass and drained the contents in a quick gulp. "I do know what you mean, Hans. And I—and the party—need that support. In fact, I'm driving to Germany in a few hours for a private session with someone there who is also providing some quiet support."

Hans beamed. "Excellent. We'll talk again, in a few weeks. In the meantime, enjoy your victory."

Forster smiled and wagged a finger from side to side. "*Our* victory, Hans. I'm enjoying *our* victory."

The businessman chuckled and disappeared into the swirling anonymity of the crowd, his presence replaced by the tall, regal figure of Forster's deputy, Anton Hessler, his face handsomely ascetic, every hair in place.

"Congratulations, Georg, this is all due to you and you alone.

You organized the perfect campaign." Hessler raised his wine glass in a salute.

Forster laughed lightly. "Thanks for the sentiment, Anton, but that's not true. You played a pivotal role with your connections and advice. We're a good team. Of course, now that we have a role in government, not just the opposition, we'll have to exercise more caution in our dealings and, shall we say, choice of behind-the-scenes associates. But that's the price of power, and worth paying. You and I will map out our strategy in the next few days."

Hessler nodded, his face an untroubled field of agreement suffused with a benign smile.

From across the expanse of the hall someone began to sing the hymn of the Nationalist Defense Front, *Unser Blut ist Rein*, Our Blood is Pure. Forster joined his untutored voice to the boisterous chorus and discreetly checked the pearl-faced Rolex at his wrist.

NEAR GARMISCH, STATE OF BAVARIA, GERMANY

The night sky was alive with a frantic display of flashing lights that invaded the darkness like a swarm of angry, illuminated hornets. A line of police cruisers, ambulances, and fire trucks was strung along the rural Alpine road in an uneven chain. Rain pounded ceaselessly and with loud insistence on the vehicles, turning the shoulders of the road into an oozing, primordial morass. Kommissar Franz Waldbaer thought that it sounded much like an insane person playing steel drums.

The German detective surveyed the scene, one hand clutched around a Styrofoam cup of strong, black coffee. He noted the skittish choreography of the assembled officials. The wooded area was alive with uniformed policemen, volunteer firemen in orange coats, and first responders sloshing here and there, their forms jammed deep into parkas and raincoats. It was cold at this late hour, and Waldbaer saw the exhaled breath of his associates hang in the heavy air like apparitions. All in all, Waldbaer considered with a long, low sigh, it was not a very good place to be on such a night.

An atonal symphony of radios crackled around him as Waldbaer worked his way to the crash site. He was feeling considerably put out. His shoes were wet and clotted with rich Bavarian earth. Water had insinuated its way inside the leather, soaking his socks and making him vastly uncomfortable as he walked. He longed to be inside somewhere, preferably back in the bone-dry, well-heated, and refined surroundings of the Elmau Palace concert hall he had so recently vacated, several kilometers away. The gentle strains of Haydn's chamber music were now quite forgotten. Waldbaer frowned and duck-walked forward in sodden shoes, moving toward the battery of floodlights up ahead, anticipating the unpleasantness he would find there.

The wreck was so complete as to be nearly surreal. In the brutally unforgiving illumination of police lamps, Waldbaer made out two wheels splayed out at improbable angles, the tires collapsed. What had once been a sturdy Mercedes sedan roof was now a series of uneven metal waves, driven down almost to dashboard level. The chrome grill was missing and the trunk had popped open and hung drunkenly and precariously attached to the black chassis. Shatter-resistant glass lay everywhere. *Mein Gott*, Waldbaer thought to himself.

The ruined Mercedes was occupied. Waldbaer could see a single form wedged inside the collapsed front seat, tangled and broken between steering wheel, brake pedal, and the deployed, white remnants of the air bag. There was no possibility that the driver was alive. Waldbaer noted with the eyes of the trained observer that the body was clad in a tweed jacket and beige trousers. The trousers were profusely stained with blood. The Kommissar also saw a shock of tousled, thick brown hair, but the man's features were mercifully concealed from view. The angle at which the head rested told Waldbaer that the driver's neck had snapped with the impact of the crash. The seat belt still girding the man had been of no utility in a wreck of this magnitude.

Two firemen wearing white-painted World War II-style German helmets were working on the corpse, trying to determine the best way to extract it without further damage. Nearby, a tall, balding man, as thin as a windhound, was moving away from the car, carrying a thick leather satchel and wearing a frown. Medical doctor, Waldbaer concluded, and moved to intercept him.

"*Gruess Gott,*" Waldbaer intoned as he approached the man. "I'm Kommissar Franz Waldbaer. I expect you're the first physician at the scene, *ja?*" Waldbaer extended his hand, which the other man shook with a vigorous motion.

"Quite right, Herr Kommissar. My name is Doctor Robert Garning. I'm the duty physician at the accident ward in Garmisch hospital. The fire department brought me here to confirm that the victim back there is dead. He is. Death was instantaneous. Never had a chance. We'll autopsy later, but it seems clear that excessive speed was the main culprit, combined with this lousy weather."

The doctor slowly rubbed a hand on the back of his neck and shook his head from side to side. "People never learn that a car is a dangerous weapon." The doctor looked directly at Waldbaer with eyes as pale blue as a robin's egg. "Something else. I probably shouldn't say it yet, until the autopsy has been conducted. But between us, Kommissar, the body smells of alcohol. I'm sure the deceased had been drinking. How much, I can't guess, but it could be a contributing factor. Anyway, keep that between us."

Waldbaer signaled his agreement with a slow up-down movement of his head. "Right. Just between us. Look, this isn't my case anyway. It belongs to the traffic police and they're welcome to it. I happened to be near the scene and stopped to see if I could provide assistance. But thanks, *Herr Doktor,* I appreciate your candor." The gaunt physician nodded again, smiled, and vanished into the downpour like a specter.

Nothing more to do here, Waldbaer concluded. He turned to leave and was confronted by a large figure in a black leather police jacket and white peaked cap who effectively blocked his path. The set of the policeman's features was obscured by the darkness, but the suspicious tone of his voice was evident. "And you might be?" he asked Waldbaer.

Waldbaer smiled coolly and without humor, drew out his kommissar identification card and passed it to the policeman. The face beneath the white cap examined the laminated document perfunctorily and returned it, his other arm offering a brief saluting gesture.

"Sorry. We do get accident voyeurs poking around sometimes. Look, Kommissar, we have it all under control. Traffic accident; no wonder in this damned weather. Driving too damned fast, more than likely, and couldn't make the curve. Hardly a matter to occupy the homicide boys."

Another uniformed policeman appeared from the curtain of rain and whispered something to his taller associate. "Are you certain about that?" the first man asked.

"Ja, no doubt about it," came the mumbled reply.

Waldbaer listened impassively, conscious again of his wet feet and wanting to return to the relative comfort of his Volkswagen.

The shorter policeman splashed off the way he had arrived a moment before. The remaining officer moved a step closer to Waldbaer. "Well, Kommissar, we have a development that might interest you. It seems the crash victim is Georg Forster. You know that name? The Austrian right-wing politician. A popular guy with our cousins across the border, at least in some quarters. It doesn't change anything; it's still a car accident. But this will make the papers and television, for sure. I expect word will leak out soon. Keep that quiet for the moment, Kommissar, if you don't mind. I have to notify next of kin and Austrian authorities."

Waldbaer considered the news and ran a thick hand through his rain-slicked, graying hair. He articulated his words slowly. "Georg Forster. Of course. He made a name for himself with his anti-immigration politics. Everybody thought he was about to move up to an important post in the Austrian government after this last election. Nobody counted on a car wreck to end his career. This will be a shock for a lot of people, count on it. I wish you and your colleagues well dealing with the media feeding frenzy this will spark. I mean that—no schadenfreude from me. Still, you can thank God it wasn't homicide. Imagine how the press would react to Forster as a murder victim—and in Germany, mind you."

The tall policeman let out a low whistle and arched his eyebrows under the brim of his service cap. "You're right, Kommissar. The present circumstances are bad enough. Have a pleasant ride home."

Waldbaer snorted, aware again of how unpleasant the evening was as an unwelcome stream of cold water trickled down the collar at the back of his neck. He waved a hand at the policeman and strode through the clutching mud toward his car, squinting his eyes against the onslaught of flashing lights. He drained the last of his coffee, shoving the empty cup into his jacket pocket so as not to pollute the accident scene.

Well, he thought, an episode to remember in my dotage. Having been at the site of the crash that killed the much-publicized, controversial Georg Forster. He shook his head sideways as he sloshed through the terrain. A senseless death, more senseless than most. He always regarded murder as an affront, but traffic accidents he found profoundly depressing in their own way. Many accidents, Forster's included, represented the triumph of bad judgment to a lethal degree. What impulse possessed someone to speed in inclement weather on unforgiving, serpentine alpine roads? Had Georg Forster behaved with a modicum more prudence, he would be alive. Glancing through slaps of water, Waldbaer made out the silhouette of his car in the distance. He moved more briskly and encircled a hand around the key in his pocket, aware that his trousers were now sodden to the knee. In this weather, it would be a tiring ride back to his home in Gamsdorf, a good hour distant. Neither the rain nor his temperament betrayed a sign of lifting.

VIENNA, AUSTRIA, TWO DAYS LATER

The cacophony of multiple conversations echoing through the high-ceilinged chamber muted quickly as the newly appointed leader of the Austrian Nationalist Defense Front stepped from behind a wall of blue curtains and took to the podium at the center of the conference room stage. The seething crowd of journalists and television crews, by nature an undisciplined lot, knew when silence was re-

quired. They took their seats, the only sound now the subdued whirr
of video cameras and the squeak of an overtaxed folding chair.

With one hand adjusting the podium microphone, Anton
Hessler seemed well-suited to his role as NDF chief and successor to
the recently deceased Georg Forster. Hessler's angular, granitic features were solemnly set, his thick graying hair brushed straight back
from his forehead. The fine fabric of his navy blue wool suit fell well
over Hessler's athletic frame, the white shirt underneath it starched
to crisp perfection. An Italian tie of black silk complemented the
broad black armband on Hessler's right sleeve. Camera bulbs flashed,
capturing the image of mourning combined with resolute determi-
nation.

Hessler launched directly into his remarks. He stared straight
ahead and spoke without notes. "The sudden and tragic death of our
founder Georg Forster has hit the NDF like a hammer blow, and it
will take considerable time to recover. As all of our supporters know,
Georg Forster was the center of our party, and now we have lost that
center, brutally and unexpectedly. We grieve for our loss and for his
devastated relatives. May a merciful God accept his soul."

Hessler paused a moment, the muscles in his cheek revealing a
slight tic. "Austria can be assured that the NDF did not die with its
beloved founder. The party that I have been asked to lead as Georg
Forster's successor will continue the fight to preserve Austrian identity and honor. The NDF is Georg Forster's living legacy. We who
mourn him will pay homage by implementing his policies and assuming a growing role in the affairs of state. No one should doubt
this, or doubt that the NDF will guarantee and protect Austria's future. I am certain the NDF will not only survive the grievous loss of
our comrade, but will, based on his work, grow and prosper as Austria's most courageous political voice."

The speaker grabbed at the podium with both hands and he drew
himself up a degree, his voice becoming more emotive. "And now
permit me to reveal a truth that Austria deserves to know. A truth
some would doubtless like to remain hidden. The NDF possesses in-

formation that makes it clear that Georg Forster did not die in a simple traffic accident. No. Georg Forster was murdered. Murdered for his political beliefs. As we will soon be informing the law enforcement authorities, Georg Forster was killed by operatives from Israel."

The silence in the room disintegrated, replaced by a surprised roar of exclamations and questions. Most of the assembled journalists had jumped to their feet, some frantically trying to move closer to the speaker.

The penetrating, high-pitched voice of a young female reporter sounded out above the aural chaos. "What is your evidence for this assertion, Herr Hessler? Can you demonstrate that Forster was murdered?"

Hessler searched out the source of the voice, looked the woman in the eye and arched a brow. "We can prove murder," he intoned. "I will take no further questions today, so as not to detract from the propriety of the mourning period. We will have more for you later. Thank you." Turning on his heels, Hessler strode out of sight, concealed by the curtains at the back of the stage.

Reporters slammed into one another, absent any pretense of civility as they headed for the conference room doors, intent on filing this extraordinary story.

MUNICH, GERMANY

Waldbaer sat on a varnished bar stool in the subdued light of the Paulaner im Tal and watched as the televised image of the impeccably clad Anton Hessler made his revelation. It was an astounding announcement, whether or not it was true. The assertion that the state of Israel had murdered an Austrian politician would guarantee a furor of international publicity and diplomatic activity, regardless of whether the allegation possessed factual merit. Without more information, Waldbaer did not know what to believe. He did know that it was up to Hessler to prove his accusation. If he could not, Hessler might face legal prosecution for incitement, defamation, or another similar offense.

"Politicians," Waldbaer muttered, taking a long sip of the frothy Paulaner Pilsner from a tall, fluted glass emblazoned with the profile of a cowled monk.

"Excuse me?" the bartender in a black bow tie inquired from nearby.

"Nothing," Waldbaer rejoined sourly, not wanting to call attention to the fact that he had been talking to himself. He had just concluded a mandatory one-day course on police relationships with the public at the Munich city hall, and simply wanted to enjoy a quiet beer before driving back to Gamsdorf.

With a slight start, Waldbaer realized that his cell phone was issuing its familiar ring tone from Mozart's "A Little Night Music." He fished the phone from the pocket of his herringbone tweed jacket. He had bought the jacket twenty years ago, and was no longer able to button it. This he ascribed to an obscure shrinkage process caused by dry cleaning. "Franz Waldbaer," he half-sighed without prelude.

"Good, I've reached you, Waldbaer," a nasal voice replied from the phone's speaker.

The detective grimaced, aware that his interlocutor was his immediate supervisor, the colorless careerist Hauptkommissar Streichner. Waldbaer thought it inconceivable that Streichner had good news to convey. "Yes, Herr Streichner, you have surely reached me," Waldbaer grumbled, drumming thick fingers against the bar top.

"Very fine," the slightly tinny voice said, a touch of hesitation evident. "Well, it's like this, Waldbaer. An Austrian politician named Hessler has just made allegations that another Austrian political fellow, Forster, was murdered."

"I saw the press conference broadcast," Waldbaer replied.

"Good. That makes it easier. Well, since Forster died in German territory—Bavarian territory in fact—we're going to have to conduct a homicide investigation." The voice braked to a stop for a moment and then resumed. "Or, more precisely, we have to conduct an investigation as to whether a murder was committed, and if it was, launch a homicide investigation."

"Right," Waldbaer said absent enthusiasm, suspecting where the conversation might be heading.

"Yes. I recall, Waldbaer, that you were at Forster's crash site because you were traveling in the area at the time. That area falls within your Upper Bavaria jurisdiction. I want you to handle this incident for us. You already have a claim because you were physically present where Forster died."

Waldbaer cursed silently and brushed his hair back from his forehead with the swipe of one hand. "I would rather not do that."

Streichner did not immediately reply, but instead issued a series of fretful, mildly feral noises. A few seconds later he found his voice. "I understand you're busy, Kommissar. And I am fully sympathetic, believe me. But the fact is there is no one else free at present who can handle this with your degree of professionalism. After all, this is a case with international ramifications. And the Austrian police have already been in touch with us. You'll need to coordinate with them tomorrow morning. I sent the contact information forward to your office in Gamsdorf."

"The Austrians don't know me. It will be all the same with them if someone else takes this case."

Streichner cleared his throat. "Well, actually, I've already given them your name."

Waldbaer could picture the despised Streichner with his thick bifocals halfway down his long nose chattering on the phone with some Austrian official, trying to appear proactive and decisive. Still, Waldbaer realized there was nothing he could do. He had been given a legitimate order by his idiot of a superior, who had already locked him into cooperating with the Austrian police service. He thought of Marcus Aurelius's *Meditations*. Accept the things you cannot change, or something to that effect.

"All right, Hauptkommissar. I will get in touch with our Austrian cousins tomorrow and see what should be done. But if you'll excuse me, I'm halfway through a conversation with a Paulaner monk, and it's a conversation I'd like to finish."

"Of course," Streichner said rather cheerily, clearly uncertain what Waldbaer was talking about. "One more thing, Waldbaer. With the international attention on this case, both of us could benefit career wise. If it's properly handled, of course. My regards to the friar."

Waldbaer was about to reply that he didn't much care about career intrigues, but Streichner rang off. Staring at his half-consumed pilsner, Waldbaer concluded, with a brooding premonition, that the next morning was unlikely to provide him much joy at all.

GAMSDORF, UPPER BAVARIA, GERMANY

The morning dawned overcast and cool for midsummer, but the sulking gray that hung over and partially concealed the Bavarian Alps suited Waldbaer's temperament. Parking his Volkswagen on the main plaza of the market town, he trudged the hundred feet to the police station, concealed in the basement of the town hall like an unpresentable relative sequestered from the rest of the bureaucratic family. As he thumped slowly down the unadorned concrete steps, his kneecaps issued a series of clicks. He wondered what that meant. Nothing good. Another sign of the machine running down.

When he threw open the double doors to the bay area, he mumbled an indifferent "*Guten morgen*" at the four police officers engaged in quotidian tasks. Without commentary, he filled a relatively stain-free porcelain cup at the still-wheezing coffee machine and trundled the few steps to his office, shutting the door behind him with force sufficient to suggest that he would not welcome disturbances.

Waldbaer took a sip of coffee, placed the cup on his worn cherrywood-veneer desk, and sank into the familiar contour of his leather chair. He saw that his secretary had placed a yellow piece of paper at the center of the desk. He sighed, rubbed at his eyes, and picked it up, knowing what information it contained. As anticipated, the block writing provided a name and phone number for the Austrian police official working the Forster case. Waldbaer squinted at the name and drew the piece of paper closer. *S. Reiner*; the phone number beneath the name had an Innsbruck area code. No time like the present. Waldbaer picked up the receiver of his desk phone and punched in the sequence of numbers.

"Innsbruck police presidium," a woman's voice informed him. Waldbaer grimaced at having to deal with a secretary.

"*Guten morgen.* Please connect me with Herr S. Reiner. This is Kommissar Franz Waldbaer calling from Gamsdorf, Bavaria, on an urgent matter."

"Apparently so urgent that you've started by making an assumption, Herr Kommissar. This is Sabine Reiner, but frau rather than herr. No matter, but you might note that police investigation is no longer solely a man's world. At any rate, it appears that you and I will be working together on the Forster case."

Waldbaer did not like being lectured and felt momentarily flustered. Still, he decided against making a riposte. "Yes, Frau Reiner, it's about the Forster matter. I was at the crash scene moments after his death, and so I've been asked to run the investigation."

The female voice offered a brief, almost whispered laugh that Waldbaer did not fancy. "Not so fast, Kommissar. You might be running the investigation from the German side, but I can assure you I am not one of your subordinates. I have been charged with the Austrian investigation, and I look forward to our working together on an absolutely equal footing."

Waldbaer rolled his eyes and mouthed words that he would never utter in polite company. "Don't worry, Kommissarin. I am aware this will be a joint German-Austrian police matter. Or Austrian-German, if that makes you feel better. Whatever. The point is, we need to sit down together to decide how to proceed and share whatever information we each have so far."

The Austrian police detective made a sound that suggested concurrence. "Agreed, Kommissar Waldbaer. We need to talk soon. When can you get to Innsbruck?"

"I was actually thinking that Munich would be a better place for an initial discussion."

"Innsbruck."

Waldbaer tapped his fingers against the desktop with some force. "Forster died in Germany, Kommissarin Reiner. If this was in fact murder, the crime was committed here, and Munich is nearby."

"Innsbruck."

"Munich." Waldbaer found that he had raised his voice, a loss of conversational discipline in which he seldom indulged. He struggled to moderate his tone.

"If you come to Innsbruck, Kommissar Waldbaer, I promise you a thorough briefing on Forster's background and our findings to date, with everything laid out for your review. I can also promise you a very fine Meinl coffee and even a warm apple strudel. Consider it a symbol of Austrian hospitality." The voice had assumed a more cheery lilt but there was a trace of iron beneath the surface.

Waldbaer judged that he could afford to lose this minor skirmish and then insist on subsequent meetings on his terrain. "All right, I accept, no need to prolong this further. We need to get on with things. Tomorrow morning is what I recommend, say ten o'clock. In Innsbruck."

The Austrian policewoman signaled her satisfaction and Waldbaer feigned indifference. Contact instructions were passed and the two parties rang off after an exchange of pro forma insincerities.

Waldbaer pushed himself back from the desk and sank more deeply into his cracked leather chair and thought of Austria. Perhaps small countries are like some small people, he mused. Inferiority complex, thin-skinned, and bellicose. After all, Austria, once a powerful European empire, had in more recent times been reduced to a tourist attraction, a living *Sound of Music* tableau. Maybe they feel a need to assert themselves, he thought, as compensation for lost glory. Frau Reiner would probably meet him in some kitschy folkloric costume complete with edelweiss broach, and dissect his words for any incipient sign of misogyny. Despite the strong coffee, Waldbaer felt tired. He did not anticipate an enjoyable stay in Innsbruck.

The next morning broke flawlessly sunny, promising a warm afternoon. The sky was a porcelain blue above the rugged peaks of the Karwendel chain of the Alps that separated Upper Bavaria from North Tyrol. Waldbaer drove his diesel Volkswagen Passat with restraint along the two-lane road that slipped past Mittenwald and curved its way to the Austrian frontier. He took his time, feeling in no hurry to reach Innsbruck, still unhappy over the prospect of having to work the investigation jointly with an easily offended Austrian policewoman. What was the American phrase he had heard? High maintenance. Precisely. Waldbaer nodded his head and grunted. *Well, I can deal with her,* he concluded. He opened the glove compartment and extracted a music disc of Alfred Brendel playing Beethoven sonatas and slipped the CD into the player. As the first piano notes of Moonlight filled the car, Waldbaer felt his mood lighten. He would not permit Kommissarin Reiner to ruin his day.

He drove over a bridge crossing the Isar River, which meandered through the wildflower-laced, alpine countryside on its way to Munich some seventy miles distant. The smooth, newly resurfaced road was braced by dense pine forest on both sides, gray stone peaks soaring to seven thousand feet in the background. A moment later he passed the spot where Georg Forster's life had so precipitously ended. As Waldbaer anticipated, there was not a trace of the accident visible. The cleanup squad had performed its task admirably, almost preternaturally, the ruined Mercedes towed away to the police garage. The storm had swept away the traces of oil, blood, and debris.

Waldbaer reflected for a moment on the transitory nature of human life. It seemed strange that as complex a creature as man should be so vulnerable, but there it was. He pushed this line of thought away before it threatened his current contentment. Waldbaer concentrated on Beethoven's composition, brought to melodic life by the accomplished pianist. A road sign advised that he was crossing the border from Germany into Austria, and Waldbear began mentally preparing for his meeting with the prickly Frau Reiner. He switched gears and pedaled the brake, the car making the steep descent of the Zirler Berg mountain, the verdant contours of the Inn valley visible far below.

THE APPROACHES TO HAMBURG HARBOR, NORTHERN GERMANY

Riding low in the water, its hold filled with bone-white Asian rice and an uninvited entourage of well-fed if unsated rodents, the *Condor Fury* navigated the final approaches to its off-loading dock in the Hanseatic port of Hamburg. After weeks at sea, the freighter, built in South Korea and of Belize registry, had on the final leg of its voyage transited the North Sea and steamed up the broad sweep of the Elbe River toward its destination. The water surrounding the freighter was a swirling gray soup flecked here and there with viscous traces of oil, which was illuminated by an anemic-yellow dawn. A host of gulls trailed the vessel, voraciously observant for any trace of edible jetsam.

Fifty-eight-year-old Horst Zellmann had communicated with the Hamburg harbormaster and faxed a goods security certificate, the bill of lading, and other required documentation to the appropriate office in the port. From his place on the bridge, he surveyed the skyline of the city of Hamburg in the distance, noting the distinctive brick profile of the old Michl church steeple and the familiar lines of the Blohm und Voss ship repair wharf. Zellmann pushed his smudged captain's hat higher on his forehead and scratched at his three-day-old stubble.

A long voyage from Hong Kong behind him, he savored the thought of spending several nights in the Atlantik Hotel, drinking prodigiously of tart North German pilsner beer in the smoky harbor pubs, and perhaps purchasing the services of some young Polish girl in the Saint Pauli section of town. Of course, first there was work to be done. The *Condor Fury* had to be unloaded and the holds cleaned and prepared for the next consignment. Most importantly of all, he had a phone call to make.

Zellmann checked the Mueller+Blanck cargo software and then shifted his vision to watch the unloading activity of the wharf-side cranes for thirty minutes before turning over responsibility to his first mate. "Everything is on track. I'll be back later," he said with a touch of gruffness, "I have things to take care of." As ship's captain he owed no one any further explanation.

Then he zipped himself into a blue parka, left the ship behind, and walked a half mile from the harbor toward the old center of the city. It was blustery and the air was wet and clammy; *typical Hamburg weather*, he thought. As he walked, the raw seediness of the harbor area gave way to a more refined mix of commercial and residential buildings.

Crossing a busy intersection at Ost-West-Strasse, Zellmann moved at a deliberate pace to the broad, cobblestone plaza in front of the handsome, brown-hued old Rathaus, or city hall. A steady stream of pedestrians crisscrossed the plaza and Zellmann stood for a moment until he spotted what he wanted. A bank of six yellow public phone booths. Most were unoccupied, the captain noted with contentment, a side effect of the proliferation of cell phones.

Zellmann traversed the plaza, his figure darkened by the shadow of the looming city hall watchtower. Entering a booth, he pulled the glass-paned door shut and extracted a folded snippet of paper from his worn wallet. He checked the time on his wristwatch, waited two minutes, and entered a series of Hamburg telephone numbers with his stubby, work-scarred fingers.

Two miles away from the city hall, a phone rang to life in another public booth on the banks of the Alster lake, in the elegant Poeseldorf district. A tall, blond-haired man in the booth allowed the phone to ring a few times before lifting the receiver, his antique sterling cufflinks glinting above his gloves with the movement. "Commendable punctuality," the man said in precise High German.

"You said to call at ten o'clock," Zellmann's less-cultivated voice replied.

"Quite right. It would appear your journey was uneventful."

"It was. Everything is as it should be. Which means we can proceed as you planned. Unless there are changes on your end."

"No changes at all," the man said cheerily. "Everything will go ahead as discussed previously. We bring the items from the warehouse in two days. You will be there personally to receive them and take the necessary precautions. *Alles klar?*"

The captain repeated the refrain. "*Alles klar*. Don't worry; I know what to do."

The man in the lakeside booth laughed lightly, glancing at a pedestrian couple that passed by arm-in-arm, their adoring focus on each other making them oblivious to his presence. "I'm sure you do. I am aware of your quality. By the way, when you check your bank account next, you will notice the deposit of a considerable sum. Half of what we discussed, the remainder to be paid once you are underway again."

"Thanks," Zellmann said, a snicker in his voice. "That's welcome news. I intend to have some expenses shortly, of the female variety."

The blond man winced at the crudity of the remark, but kept any trace of disapproval from his voice. "Quite. Well, then, enjoy your stay. I'm looking forward to a successful transaction. All the best." He replaced the receiver and exited the phone booth, taking the waterside gravel path through the lush Alster Park, his hand-sewn shoes carefully avoiding the unwelcome deposits left by flocks of Canada geese. The man, tall and spare of frame, brushed a kid-gloved hand through his curling hair and buttoned and belted his Burberry trench against the damp breeze drifting in from the Elbe. He gave a passing glance to a white water taxi and a small sailboat moving lethargically on the expanse of the Alster, and headed back toward his nineteenth-century brick townhouse, half-a-mile distant.

Everything was falling into place. The *Condor Fury* had arrived on schedule, which meant the consignment would not have to wait long in the warehouse, where it might be subject to chance inspection by the authorities. Zellmann was confident that they could violate German export law with complete success. He shoved his hands deep into the pockets of his trench and picked up his gait, whistling softly as he went, the tune snatched up and devoured by the wind driven in from the flat North German plains.

•   •   •

Zellmann shoved the telephone booth door open with a grunt, looked about, and headed with a rapid, shuffling gait toward the harbor. He had a voracious longing for a currywurst and french fries with mayonnaise, and knew just the fast-food stand to visit on the water at Landungsbruecken. As he walked, he considered the conversation he had just concluded. Satisfactory. He had decided not to mention the little episode involving the piece of human shit he had tossed overboard off the African coast. It would just lead to hand-wringing, second-guessing and might even scotch the whole transaction if his conversation partner was weak in the nerves department. Better to keep the information to himself. After all, done was done and it wasn't as if he had any choice. Snitches were a problem these days. Every customs agency was trying to identify narcotics shipments, weapons shipments, and support to terrorist organizations.

Well, whoever the piece of fish bait had been working for would only be able to find out that their man was reported missing, presumed overboard. They would have their suspicions, but no proof of foul play. After a while, their interest would disappear just as surely as the corpse itself. Zellmann wondered which authority might be interested in the *Condor Fury*, and why. Interpol, perhaps? Maybe a random check of freighters on that route? He shrugged to himself; it was fruitless to speculate. But with the spy silent, whatever inquisitive party was involved would focus on other suspicious vessels. Of which there were many underway on the high seas. With a smirk, Zellman pulled his frayed denim collar closer to his bull neck against the cutting dampness and picked up his pace.

INNSBRUCK, CAPITAL OF THE PROVINCE OF TYROL, AUSTRIA

Like any city with over a hundred fifty thousand inhabitants, Innsbruck was a maze of streets, bridges, and tunnels. Waldbaer had visited Innsbruck several times, but always only briefly, and had no real feel for the place. He dutifully followed the precise directions provided over the phone by Kommissarin Reiner. He drove past the old

Olympic ski jump as he entered the downtown area and headed for the police station in the Wilten district, an area that had been home to the Roman imperial military a millennium ago. He passed the elegant facades of shops and boutiques that lined Theresienstrasse and made a series of turns that took him onto less trafficked streets. Finally, Waldbaer located the white-on-blue *Polizei* shield affixed to a four-story office building in need of painting. He found an empty space and parked his sedan, sighing as he contemplated his pending conversation with Frau Reiner.

"*Gruess Gott* and welcome to Austria," a woman's voice greeted him as he locked his car.

Waldbaer turned to see a petite form in a navy blue business suit and vanilla blouse. The woman had pageboy-cropped red hair and high-cheeked features that Waldbaer assessed as not unpleasant. She looked about forty, he judged.

"Frau Reiner, I expect. *Gruess Gott.* I'm glad to be on time. It's our German obsession with punctuality. Anyway, your directions were perfect." He reminded himself to smile.

"A policewoman surely ought to be able to give clear directions, Kommissar. At any rate, let's go inside my office. I have the coffee and strudel that I promised."

Waldbaer nodded, mumbled agreement, and followed a step behind. He had the unhappy sense that his pert Austrian counterpart was a take-charge type. Need to be courteously assertive at the right point, he noted to himself, this would be a German-led investigation in fact, if not in name. Finding the appropriate point to get this bilateral working arrangement into proper repair would take a bit of finesse, he realized.

Frau Reiner led the way up a winding stone staircase, its surface smoothed by time. "This seems to be a building with some history," Waldbaer said conversationally, as they headed for the top floor. Waldbaer did not like climbing stairs. There was a reason elevators had been invented.

Frau Reiner flashed a very white smile at Waldbaer and nodded. "The building is three hundred years old. It was the residence and commercial office of a merchant who shipped goods on the Inn River, which is just past the park over there. He made lots of money. The place stayed in the family for over a century. It was eventually sold and went into slow decline. The military used it to store munitions during the Empire, when Franz Josef was Kaiser. The police acquired it as a station house after the First World War. We've been the inhabitants ever since, for good or ill."

Waldbaer decided to forego a remark on the wisdom of storing munitions in the center of a city. A moment later, they reached the top of the stairs, walked a few steps, and entered through a beige-painted hardwood door with a bronze nameplate identifying it as Frau Reiner's. Waldbaer surveyed the spaces and concluded with dismay that the office was considerably more representational than his own in Gamsdorf. The claw-footed desk and high-backed chair looked both venerable and valuable. The window behind looked out over downtown Innsbruck and the imposing North Group mountain range in the distance, its peaks already tipped with snow. A collection of well-tended flowers in terra-cotta pots cluttered the windowsill.

Instead of the police calendar and topographical map that graced Waldbaer's office walls, Frau Reiner had two lithograph prints in gold frames and an oil painting with an elk at its center. No bow to practical police work here, Waldbaer concluded with disapproval. His judgment was reinforced when he cast a glance down at the Persian rug covering much of the parquet floor. A brace of delicately carved chairs and a couch surrounding a low coffee table completed the décor. The coffee table held a pewter coffeepot, two cups and saucers, and what was unmistakably an *apfelstruedel* on a tray. Hospitable, if a bit precious for police work, Waldbaer thought.

"Let's sit, shall we?" Frau Reiner said with an Austrian lilt, pointing Waldbaer to the plush, slightly faded couch.

He sat a bit too heavily and the couch registered a sharp, creaking objection. Need to lose a few pounds, Waldbaer reminded himself. He folded his hands below his chest, feeling slightly uncomfortable. "Thanks again for this reception," he said.

Frau Reiner flashed another iridescent smile. "No reason investigative work can't be conducted in a civilized manner, Kommissar. We can discuss the case as easily with cup in hand as without, I imagine." She poured and then cut two precise pieces of strudel, passing one to her guest. "So, I suppose the best place to start is with a simple question. What have you officially concluded is the cause of death of Herr Forster?"

Waldbaer let his eyes contemplate the strudel as he spoke. "I have a copy of the written report in my pocket for you. But it's straightforward. Forster died from massive internal injuries resulting from losing control of his Mercedes navigating a curve in inclement weather, at night. The technical niceties are in the document, but the crash was so severe that some of Forster's organs were literally moved around in his torso from the injury. He was driving too fast for that road under any circumstances. About ninety kilometers an hour, maybe a bit more. Very unwise, but there is something else." Waldbaer forked a bite of strudel into his mouth.

"That something else being?" Frau Reiner leaned forward attentively.

"Forster had been drinking. The autopsy determined that he had an alcohol level of two-point-one. In fact, if he left from Innsbruck, it's surprising he drove as far as he did before he crashed. He managed to make it up the Zirl Mountain in that condition, a feat in itself. The alcohol impaired his visual judgment on the road. Tragic, but, as you're certainly aware, not uncommon."

The woman placed her cup and saucer on the coffee table noiselessly and stood, brushing a hand at her skirt. She walked to the window, her back to Waldbaer, and stared out over the cityscape. "His alcohol level was above the legal limit. He was intoxicated by any standard. You're certainly right, Kommissar Waldbaer. Alcohol leads to poor judgment, which leads to dangerous driving, which, coupled with rain and darkness, resulted in traumatic death. All very clear. But it doesn't suffice for the investigation. We still have questions to resolve."

Waldbaer moved a hand to the inside of his sports coat and withdrew a folded sheaf of papers in an envelope emblazoned with the Bavarian police shield. He took a sip of coffee before responding. "Given the prominence of the victim, we've ordered a follow-up autopsy by the chief medical examiner in Munich, just to make sure nothing was missed. I'll see that you get the results when they're available. There might be loose ends to tie up, I agree. But it seems fairly transparent that this was an accident, don't you agree? Regardless of the melodramatic assertion made by Herr Hessler in his television speech."

Frau Reiner turned from the window, hands clasped behind her back, and faced Waldbaer, this time offering no smile. "I expect we'll get to judge the worth of Hessler's remark soon, Kommissar Waldbaer. We are expected at his home in Mutters in an hour. It's a mountain village above Innsbruck, about fifteen minutes from here."

It was Waldbaer's turn to stand, and he winced as a brief pain shot through one knee with the motion. "This is unexpected. I wish I'd known in advance, I could have prepared some questions."

Frau Reiner unclasped her hands and spread them in front of her. "Sometimes spontaneity keeps us fresh, Kommissar. I'm certain that an investigator of your experience will know what to ask. The main point for us is clear-cut. Does Hessler have any factual basis to back up his Israeli murder claim? I will tell you this: Hessler might be distasteful to a lot of people outside of his right-wing circle, but he isn't stupid. He's a trained lawyer, which should mean he is cautious about what he says."

Waldbaer nodded reluctant agreement. "Undoubtedly. But I'll tell you right now that if this were Bavaria, I'd have Hessler in front of my desk. He should come to us, not we to him. It's psychologically important."

A fleeting trace of Frau Reiner's smile returned. "I know about those things too, Kommissar. But sometimes it's best to study a creature in its natural environment, don't you agree? Visiting his home might give us a better feeling for the man."

Waldbaer again had the grating sensation that he was being lectured on police work by someone younger and less experienced. "Done is done. We'll follow through with the interview you've arranged. In the future, though, I'd appreciate it we discuss forays like this in advance."

"Of course," Frau Reiner said with a brief deferential nod of her head.

Waldbaer felt appeased. Less happily, he also felt manipulated.

MUTTERS, ABOVE INNSBRUCK

A white-coated modern apartment house rose up in front of them, the structure seeming to erupt from a surround of rich, meticulously manicured grass. Although Waldbaer was traditional in his architectural tastes, he found that the design did not offend. There was considerable style to it, and more importantly, grace, a commodity infrequently considered in the buildings of the late twentieth and early twenty-first centuries. There was much glass, to take advantage of the sweeping mountain views and the red tile roofs of Innsbruck far below.

Frau Reiner gestured toward the structure. "Herr Hessler resides in the penthouse. I understand that it occupies the entire top floor."

"Not cheap, I expect," Waldbaer muttered as he unfastened his seat belt. He had driven them in his Volkswagen.

"No, not cheap. But then, Hessler has always been associated with money. His law practice was very successful, and his father did quite well in commerce."

"And his wife, what's her background?"

"Hessler is unmarried, no children. He's a lifelong bachelor."

Waldbaer filed the snippets of information among the mental index cards stored in his head.

The two police officers walked along an orderly white-pebble path to a set of double black iron doors that opened onto a spacious lobby with a shining Italian marble floor. A gleaming stainless-steel elevator was located across the expanse, braced by two lush ferns in terra-cotta planters. The lobby was spare of decoration, resulting in a clinical asceticism that Waldbaer regarded with little joy. Modern interior design, he thought, often seemed hostile to beauty.

As they walked toward the elevator, Waldbaer's eyes were drawn to an immense, frameless oil painting affixed to an otherwise bare wall. The painting consisted of a series of bright red and orange splashes flung randomly against a textured jet-black background. He had no idea what the image was supposed to represent, if it was supposed to represent anything at all. Waldbaer noticed that Frau Reiner's eyes were drawn to the artwork as well. "Horrible stuff," he allowed.

"Do you think so? I find it rather charming. At least it's not one of those unimaginative, dusty, rustic village scenes."

Waldbaer had no objections to rustic village scenes, but decided to remain a cipher to the Austrian.

They entered the spotless elevator, and Frau Reiner pushed a button marked P for penthouse with the red nail of her fingertip. The doors whispered shut and the elevator ascended at a stately pace, a recorded female voice enunciating the floor numbers as they passed. Waldbaer found this touch a bit too precious and shook his head slightly from side to side. Frau Reiner smiled.

"Penthouse," the anonymous female voice exhaled, and the elevator doors slipped open onto a gray marble-floored anteroom. The detectives stepped out, moved past a potted fir tree and toward a carved oaken door, incongruously rustic in the modern surroundings. The wooden door opened with a slight creak and Waldbaer and Reiner were confronted by a tall, austere figure garbed in a silk burgundy morning coat and patterned yellow ascot. The effect was not to Waldbaer's liking, but he had long ago learned to conceal his prejudices from others.

"I am Anton Hessler," the figure announced, a trace of theater evident in a rich voice trained in public speaking. "I expect that you are the police who called earlier." Hessler stepped aside and with an outstretched arm bid the pair to enter his chambers.

Sabine Reiner extended her hand. "I am Kommissarin Reiner,

and this is Kommissar Waldbaer. Thank you for your time, Herr Hessler."

Hessler nodded in perfunctory acknowledgment and led the detectives down a hallway into a large living room embraced by a high, carved-wood ceiling and Italianate ochre walls. The front of the room was almost all glass and faced onto the deep valley and the sprawl of Innsbruck far below. The sleek, modern profile of the Bergisel ski jump, built on the site of the 1964 Winter Olympics, was visible in the near distance. It was a striking view, and the room had been constructed to highlight it.

Waldbaer studied the space, his detective's brain recording it in a series of mental snapshots. Hand-fitted redwood floor in perfect condition. Solid, crafted antique furniture, most of it probably eighteenth century, contrasting pleasantly with the modern architecture of the building. A series of small stone sculptures adorning various end tables. They were oddities, with vaguely human forms, but with the hook-beaked, wide-eyed heads of owls. A clutch of couches and chairs, dressed in exquisite fabric, arranged upon a red-and-blue silk Persian rug. Indirect lighting built into the wood-veneered ceiling. All very tasteful in a studied sort of way. Several large charcoal sketches decorated the walls, their black-and-white images probably chosen so as not to compete with the polychrome, panoramic view. "Male figures in motion," Waldbaer muttered, half to himself.

"Yes," Hessler responded, arching his eyebrows. "All of them are of my own modest composition, I'm afraid." He smiled diffidently in a practiced show of self-deprecation. "Not worth a thing, of course, but I find that sketching relaxes me on those rare occasions when I have sufficient time to indulge the pursuit." He gestured toward the couches and his guests took their seats side-by-side, Hessler sitting across from them. He did not offer refreshments.

Waldbaer glanced at Frau Reiner and gave a barely discernable nod, signaling that she should take the interrogative lead.

"Herr Hessler," she began, "as you are aware, we're here to investigate the recent death of your political colleague Georg Forster."

"You mean the investigation of his murder?" Hessler replied.

Frau Reiner spread her small hands in the universal symbol of suspended judgment. "That is what we will try to determine, whether the cause of death was accidental or not. Let me say that at present we have no evidentiary suggestion of murder. We are advised by the coroner that Herr Forster's death was fully consistent with the result of a car wreck at high speed. That only relates to the immediate cause of death, of course, and doesn't take account of whether the car accident was caused, somehow, by another party." She sat back, her hands clasped loosely in her lap.

Hessler grimaced and let his eyes drift toward the windows and distant Innsbruck. "Georg was killed. I meant what I said during my press conference, and you are most certainly both aware of my statement at that time. Georg fell victim to Israeli agents. He was murdered by the Mossad."

Waldbaer leaned forward and felt his belt tug at his too-ample abdomen, an unwelcome development of the last few years. "You are going to have to prove that to us, Herr Hessler. If you have information about the supposed murderers, now is the time to tell us. Every detail that you possess." Waldbaer fixed his host with an unblinking stare that conveyed no malice but did not offer friendship.

Hessler nodded and fluttered an adjusting hand for a second at the folds of his ascot, as if checking its contour. "Quite right. Of course I will tell you everything you need to know. Let's start this way: the Israeli government despised Georg. That's a matter of public record. The Israeli administration was constantly condemning him, calling him a Nazi and anti-Semite. He wasn't, of course, he was just a true Austrian nationalist. Israel saw Georg and the party he founded as an implacable enemy and they were determined to get rid of him."

"Facts, please, Herr Hessler," Waldbaer breathed, seeing the Austrian Kommissarin nod in agreement.

Hessler crossed his legs and his arms simultaneously and snorted dismissively. "Well, first start with the Israeli public statements and their unsuccessful efforts to get Austria to outlaw the party and to ban Georg's political writings. What do you call that in police work?

Motive, I believe. And now for something you don't know. For months before he was killed, Georg felt he was under surveillance, that he was being followed. He was certain it was the Israelis; who else would it be? There were one or two men, Georg told me, and he saw them time and again at a distance, sometimes on foot, sometimes in a car."

Frau Reiner nodded and glanced quickly at Waldbaer before returning her eyes to Hessler. "That is certainly interesting, Herr Hessler. Did Forster mention this development to anyone other than you?"

Hessler shrugged with arched eyebrows and a hint of petulance. "I don't know; I can't be sure. I was his main confidant in the party. It's possible he mentioned this to someone else. The important thing is that Georg *did something* to check this out."

"And that would be?" Waldbaer interjected.

"Georg hired a private detective to substantiate his concerns. You can talk to the detective; he's here in Innsbruck. I have his written report here, the one he prepared and gave to Georg. Georg passed it to me for safekeeping, probably in case anything might happen to him. I expect that you will agree that it provides the proof of Israeli involvement that I've spoken of publicly. Please, have a look." Hessler picked up a manila folder that had been lying on the coffee table in front of him and passed it to Frau Reiner.

Waldbaer moved to her side and squinted at the typed paper that the kommissarin extracted from the folder. Still, he could not make out the letters. With a terse grumble, he shoved a hand into the pocket of his jacket and pulled out a pair of reading glasses. He hated to wear them and resented that his eyes betrayed his ability to read without assistance. The glasses grudgingly affixed to his face, all became clear as he read over Frau Reiner's shoulder.

The memo was headed with the name, address, and phone number of the private investigator, Herr Norbert Engel. Short paragraphs of text followed, explaining that Engel had been engaged to determine whether Georg Forster was under active observation. Engel

conducted discreet countersurveillance over two weeks, including
weekends, following Forster on his normal rounds. Engel established
that Forster's instincts had been on the mark. The right-wing politician was being followed. Engel determined Forster was being tailed,
usually by one middle-age male, and occasionally two, respectably
dressed. Engel had not attempted to confront them and had kept his
distance so as not to reveal that the hunter was in fact the hunted.
The men appeared to be professional and knew what they were
doing, never getting too close to the quarry. Engel had taken photographs with his cell phone camera, but the men evidenced no dis-
tinguishing characteristics at long distance. The private detective
observed one surveillant on two occasions following Forster's car in
an automobile. Engel was in a vehicle a few cars behind them. He
had been able to make out the license plate and recorded its number in the memorandum.

Frau Reiner was the first to speak. "Well, it would seem that we
have something here, Herr Hessler, and you can be sure we'll check
out the license plate. But this does not prove that the men were Israeli."

Hessler curled his lips in a self-satisfied smile. "Next page, Kommissarin."

Frau Reiner flipped the vanilla paper over and discovered one
more sheet underneath. She and Waldbaer sighed simultaneously as
they perused the text. Engel had on one occasion, two weeks before
Forster's death, noted that the usual surveillant was accompanied by
another person. Engel decided to get closer. The two men had been
following Forster on foot through the old pedestrian zone of Innsbruck. Forster entered the train station there and the men followed
him into the building, but did not risk exposure by going with him
to the tracks. The two men remained in the main lobby of the station and consulted the schedule board, trying to guess Forster's likely
destination. Engel remained in the lobby as well. As the two men
were absorbed with the schedule, Engel walked past them at close
range. He was within earshot of them for a few seconds. They were

not speaking German. Although the content of their remarks was a mystery to him, Engel recognized the distinctive sound of the language. It was Hebrew.

Hessler was still smiling and regarded his guests with the look of an owl noting with interest the scampering of field mice. "So, you see? There can't be much doubt that Georg was being tracked by Israeli agents. Presumably they waited until they had an opportunity to kill him undetected. They probably ran him off the road near Garmisch that night."

Frau Reiner returned the sheets of paper to the manila folder and placed it in her voluminous leather handbag. "We'll need to retain this for the moment. And we'll contact this Herr Engel, to be sure. Your information is certainly useful, and troubling, Herr Hessler. But if I were you, I wouldn't go around publicly stating that Israel arranged for Forster's murder. That's going too far; murder is not demonstrated by this report, only surveillance. Is there anything else you might have for us?"

Hessler considered and steepled his long fingers. "No, I can't think of anything else, other than what I've told you. I have great respect for the police, and I'm certain you'll be able to demonstrate Israel's role and maybe even find those involved. You can rely on my help whenever you might require it."

Waldbaer sensed that the interview had reached its end and wanted to get moving on the information from the private investigator. With a nod toward Frau Rainer, he addressed Hessler.

"Thank you for providing us with your information. We'll pursue it, as my colleague mentioned. We may need to speak to you again, depending on where things lead. Tell me, Herr Hessler, were you at the Nationalist Defense Front celebration here in Innsbruck on the night Forster died?"

Hessler moved his gaze to the ceiling and rubbed a hand slowly at the back of his neck. "Yes, I was there, Kommissar. Actually, I didn't speak to Georg for long though, there was an absolute crush of people who wanted to congratulate him and I thought I should let them. Had I only known I would never see him again . . ." Hessler's voice trailed off into a low sigh. "Well, the rest has been in the newspapers. He enjoyed the celebration and our election victory and spent some time mixing with his supporters. He left directly from the event for Germany. I suppose we will never know why. He never made it past Garmisch, as we all know."

Waldbaer made a sympathetic noise in his throat and continued, "Did you notice what and how much Herr Forster was drinking that night?"

Hessler sat erect and glared at his interlocutor. "Georg certainly had a few drinks. This was a huge victory and the mood was celebratory. I didn't notice what he was drinking. Georg appreciated a fine wine, but I expect his social drinking tastes were rather catholic. A mixed drink on some occasions, a beer or a schnapps, perhaps, with our working-class supporters. But he was no idiot. As a politician in the public eye, the last thing he would do is drive drunk."

"You're right. It would seem that the last thing he did, in fact, was to drive drunk." Waldbaer knew that the remark was too barbed, but he had not cared for Hessler's slight to beer drinkers.

Hessler narrowed his eyes and regarded Waldbaer. "I trust you have the facts from the coroner to back up that remark, Kommissar. Let me say this: Georg would not have climbed into his car if he thought that he had too much to drink. Never. There was too much at stake. If his blood-alcohol ratio was above the limit, it must have hit him later while he was driving. Maybe he was tired; the campaign was draining, I can tell you that. When I last saw him, Georg Forster did not seem intoxicated. But who knows? Might the Israelis have been diabolical enough to infiltrate the celebration and spike his drink?"

Waldbaer decided to leave it there. He glanced at his Austrian partner, and she gave him a nod.

Frau Reiner rose and extended a hand to Hessler. "Thank you. We've concluded our business, I expect. We'll be on our way."

Waldbaer rose as well, wincing at a certain stiffness in his knees.

He buttoned his jacket and had taken a step toward the hallway when Hessler addressed him. "Herr Kommissar. I note you have an accent. I take it you are not from this part of Tyrol?"

Waldbaer allowed a thin smile to trace across his worn features and fixed his eyes unblinkingly on his host. "I'm not from any part of Tyrol, Herr Hessler. Not from Austria at all, in fact. Perhaps I should have mentioned it. I'm from Germany, more specifically, from Bavaria. We're conducting a joint investigation with our Austrian colleagues because Forster died on our territory. His journey started in Innsbruck and ended in Garmisch. Both of our police departments are involved."

Hessler said nothing in reply, gave an almost imperceptible, deferential bow, and showed the two inspectors to the door.

HAMBURG, NORTH GERMANY

It was a raw day and, although it was not raining, the air was saturated with a penetrating moisture, propelled by a clammy wind. Horst Zellmann, captain of the docked *Condor Fury*, pulled his black nylon jacket tightly around his fireplug frame and zipped it. His eyes, still bloodshot from the liquid excesses of the previous evening, took in the rapid movement of the slate-gray clouds scuttering above his head. Coming in from the northeast, he noted unhappily. Russian weather. It would probably stay foul for days. Not a bad thing, then, to have to spend most of his time inside the massive warehouse that sat stolidly at harbor side. At least it was warmer inside the bare cinder block walls, and the brute structure, even with its bay doors open, blocked the assault of the moist wind.

There was much to be done in the warehouse during the day and Zellmann was there to supervise it. It was a task for which he was being generously reimbursed with funds additional to his captaincy fees. He was determined to see that things were done properly, which meant avoiding problems with German customs officials. Zellmann's thoughts were momentarily splintered by the pounding behind his forehead and he fished in his jacket for the plastic bottle of aspirin, popping one into his mouth. He chewed at the pill, winced and considered for a moment, then consumed a second tablet. He would stick to brandy tonight, he counseled himself, and avoid the temptation of whiskey. It was the black-haired bitch in the strip bar who started him on the whiskey. More money in it for her, no doubt. He intended to demonstrate more discipline tonight, although he realized that such prudent resolve always seemed to vanish once he swallowed his first drink. He shook his head in fatalistic self-rebuke and trundled toward a container truck parked near the middle of the warehouse.

Three men in jeans and heavy sweaters huddled together at the back of the vehicle, immersed in discussion. All were crew from the *Condor Fury*. Zellmann joined them, nearly slipping on a slick residue of old oil.

"What is it?" he grunted. Two of the men were tall Nigerians who spoke broken German. Zellmann's question was directed to the third man, a solid, crew-cut-maned native of Frankfurt named Udo.

Udo frowned and looked at Zellmann through eyes too small for his face. "We're trying to work out how to secure this stuff once it's on board. If we're going to run the Cape, we can hit rough weather. The goods look sensitive. We'll risk damage if we don't work this out right from the start."

Zellmann hacked and spit some aspirin-tinged phlegm off to his side. "It's simple. Everything stays in the containers, the one from this truck and the other containers that will follow. It's like anything else; the containers get lifted up by crane and stored in the hold. We aren't placing them on the open deck, so they shouldn't get banged around, no matter what the weather is like."

Udo shook his head from side to side. "Won't do, Captain, not good enough," he said in a guttural voice. "Too much spare room inside the container. A loose fit is all right for transport on the autobahn cross-country, but not good enough for the open sea. You just have to look in there and you'll see what I mean." The tall man gestured with his thumb to the open doors of the Volvo container truck behind him.

Zellmann moved to the vehicle, placed his hands on the lid of the container, and peered inside. His eyes took a moment to adjust to the semidarkness within. He made out a series of rounded shapes swathed in blue plastic packing material. Each shape was about as tall as a man. There was considerable free space between the curved objects and Zellmann knew Udo was right; the equipment would move and bang around if they encountered rough seas.

"Shit," he mumbled as he turned back to the three men. He rubbed his hands together for a moment before speaking. "All right. Let's fill the container with extruded pellets, make it tight so those things don't move. Udo, there must be packing material around here. Find what we need; have them bill the *Condor Fury. Alles klar?*"

Udo nodded his square head in agreement. "*Klar.*"

The issue resolved, Zelmann plunged his hands into his pockets and strode away, surrendering the relative warmth of the warehouse for the biting and sullen outdoors. He had an appointment at dockside, next to the *Condor Fury.* He did not want to be late.

Minutes later he was standing at the quay watching his ship heave gently on the controlled waves of Hamburg Harbor. His eyes took in the decaying, whitened remains of a dead flounder near the ship and the outline of the Blohm and Voss ship works across the water. He noted the comings and goings of various tugboats and water taxis on their journeys. He returned his gaze to his ship and studied its faded white bridge and the lines of incipient rust along the prow. Not pretty but seaworthy, he concluded, satisfied. Zellmann tugged up the sleeve of his jacket and studied his watch. His visitor was five minutes late. He glanced down the wharf and squinted; a car was approaching from the distance.

The burgundy Audi that moved toward him at moderate speed was like the ship, he thought, not attractive, but sturdy. He was happy the visitor's car wasn't a flashier model. He did not want his brief rendezvous to attract attention. The Audi pulled up next to him and came to a stop, and Zellmann could hear the steady idling of the engine. "Let it run," he said to the driver, "this won't take long."

The driver nodded and exited the vehicle, extending a hand to Zellmann as he approached. Zellmann shook it perfunctorily. Stupid little ritual, he thought. "Glad you could make it," he said, "I think we can arrange some business."

Zellmann studied the visitor's eyes and detected interest. Good. Not that he expected problems. The Audi driver, a man named Hacker, was a third cousin of his and they had gotten together occasionally over the years. Frequently enough for Zellmann to have determined that his visitor was not above taking cash for discreet favors. Hacker was a customs officer for the harbor authorities.

Without prelude, Zellmann extracted a thick white envelope from his jacket and waved it in front of his distant cousin. *Bait the fish*, he thought. "Here's what we're talking about today. I have an important consignment of equipment that I need to load and ship without lots of paperwork. Don't worry, it's not guns or explosives or crap like that. I wouldn't want to chance getting you into trouble."

Hacker smiled with a display of tobacco-stained teeth. "Your familial concern is touching, Horst."

Zellmann managed a brief laugh. "Whatever. Really, this is just industrial stuff. Hi-tech equipment and my client doesn't want to screw around with all the damned export certificates. So, I want to get it on board nice and simple without inspection difficulties. The bills of lading will appear to be in perfect order and the consignment listed as drilling equipment. Clear, so far?"

"Perfectly," Hacker replied, not taking his eyes off the envelope clutched in Zellmann's hand.

"Good. I want to be able to give you the paperwork and have you take care of everything that needs to be done. And absolutely no inspection, no matter what strings you have to pull. I want this to be smooth. Inside the envelope you'll find six thousand euros in fifties. Clean money."

Hacker rasped out a low, avian cackle. "Money is always clean, Horst, you know that."

"What I mean is, these are banknotes with no history. Nothing traceable."

Hacker's deep-set eyes devoured the envelope and he bit at his lower lip for a second. Zellmann noted that his cousin had not shaved this morning.

"Listen," Hacker said, extending his hands in a supplicating gesture, "I sure want to help and I think I can arrange this just fine. But it's risky, clean bills or not, I'm taking a real chance, Horst."

"Six thousand euros," Zellmann repeated. "Not one cent more. Six thousand euros buy a lot of risk."

Hacker fidgeted for a moment and looked past Zellmann at the looming form of the *Condor Fury*, tied securely to the pier. "Okay. It's a deal. I can take care of it. Just for you, our being related and all."

Zellmann smiled without warmth at his underachieving, corrupt relation, but was satisfied. "Good choice. You look more impressive when you're in uniform, by the way. You should shave more often, we don't want people thinking you're anything less than a respectable official." Zellmann held out the envelope, and Hacker snatched it like a wino going for a bottle.

"All right. I'll call you when we're ready to load, so you can monitor everything. No need for you to hang around here any longer, we don't need anybody to see us together."

Hacker wagged his flabby, stubbled chin in agreement and pressed the thick envelope of cash deep into the recesses of his trouser pocket, before sliding back into the Audi. A moment later he was gone.

Zellmann still felt a subdued roar banging somewhere in his head but now felt considerably better. Things were moving as they should. And soon enough he would be in motion as well, physically propelled with oceanic rhythm on the gray Atlantic waves far beyond German jurisdiction, with a sensitive cargo concealed beneath the stained and abused deck of his vessel. A crooked smile formed on Zellmann's blunt-featured face. Perhaps a touch of whiskey might be in order this evening after all.

GAMSDORF, BAVARIA

Waldbaer noted the uncharacteristically suffocating humidity in the air as he locked his forest green Volkswagen, unbuttoned the collar of his shirt, and pulled down on the knot of his tie, loosening its clutching hold on his throat. It had been a long workday, and he felt the need to unwind, to sit and think matters through. He walked a few yards along a sidewalk canopied by thick-trunked linden trees, their foliage shielding the sun. Reaching the Alte Post, Waldbaer entered through the venerable oaken door propped open with a crumbling piece of brick.

A hum of conversation greeted him as he crossed the threshold. The familiar rustic Bavarian surroundings were sparsely inhabited this evening, as it was a weekday. He glanced over the rows of white-clothed, empty tables, searching for a familiar face. There was none. He found no member of his *stammtisch*, that informal circle of a few friends who congregated here regularly. Too early, he concluded, with a glance at the wood-framed clock affixed to one wall beneath an oil portrait of a solemn King Ludwig the Mad, the most popular exemplar of Bavaria's vanquished royalty. No matter. He would have a beer alone and run through the day's events.

Waldbaer seated himself at the table where he and his comrades usually met and waited for the dirndl-clad waitress to finish drying glasses behind the long wooden bar. He knew from experience that it would be futile to try to attract her attention; she would appear in her own good time. He began to run through the next required steps of the investigation. As a first matter of business, the allegations of Hessler and the private investigator Engel would have to be confirmed or refuted. Frau Reiner had promised to interview Engel in Innsbruck tomorrow morning. Waldbaer would have preferred to conduct this session himself, but decided that a division of labor made sense. He would concentrate on the German angle. But what was the German angle, exactly?

The broad-faced, unsmiling waitress suddenly loomed above him, her graying hair pulled back in a bun that looked painfully tight. She studied her customer, her expression caught somewhere between neutrality and lack of amusement. Waldbaer supposed that she had served him food and drink hundreds of times within these walls, invariably absent any display of friendliness.

"A dark wheat beer," he pronounced, and, his familiar invocation issued, the woman muttered a subdued grumble and lumbered off on thick legs that betrayed no hint of ankle.

Waldbaer returned to his thoughts. The German angle. Forster had died about twenty kilometers inside German territory. Aside from examining the crash site again, what evidence was there to collect? There was nothing to suggest Forster had stopped between Innsbruck and the place of his death near Garmisch. Waldbaer recalled that the fuel tank of the savaged Mercedes had registered over three-quarters full. Forster had probably gassed up in Innsbruck before his trip, obviating any stop at a gas station so soon after his journey began. Waldbaer would have his colleagues check the three or four gas stations on the German side of the border on the route to Garmisch, but he doubted this would provide any result.

The waitress appeared again on her ankleless pillars and placed a tall, half-liter glass of Franziskaner wheat beer on the table with a thud, before wandering back to the bar.

Waldbaer took a sip of the tart, unfiltered drink and wiped a trace of foam from his lips with his sleeve. Was there *anything* on the Bavarian side of the border that might be of use in determining what happened to Forster on that lethal night? Waldbaer had driven the same route from Innsbruck just an hour ago, and he ran its features through his head in a series of recalled images, like a film advanced at rapid speed. He closed his eyes for a moment and saw again the steep climb from Innsbruck over the pine-lined Zirl Mountain pass, with its uncompromising switchback curve halfway up the incline. A series of tiny, undistinguished farm villages flashed by thereafter, the road eventually skirting the ski resort of Seefeld and its splendid alpine surroundings before the last stretch of Austria surrendered to the sovereignty of its German neighbor at the border town of Scharnitz. On the German side of the border, long, solemn rows of pine braced both sides of the road. A few gas stations and homes dotted the landscape. Lush open meadows hosted bovine and equine occupants. And at the end of a long stretch of straight, black-surfaced road, a gray metal police camera box. Waldbaer slapped his hand flat against the tabletop with enough force to stir more foam in his beer glass. The waitress looked up sharply from her place behind the bar, disapproval evident on her thick features.

Waldbaer dismissed her silent censure; here was something solid to check. The camera box, placed near the road to automatically register any cars violating the speed limit. Forster had been exceeding the speed limit that night. Indeed, excessive speed was the direct cause of his death.

Presuming Forster had been traveling at high speed before the immediate accident site, his image would be contained within the camera apparatus. Waldbaer would have the film retrieved first thing in the morning. He knew that the resolution of the cameras was quite high and that a flashbulb activated to provide visibility at night. The captured images were intended to display with unshakable accuracy the license plate of the offending vehicle, and the face of the driver as well, to make any proffered denials impossible.

And, if Forster had in fact been followed, the image of his speeding pursuers should have been recorded as well. If, on the other hand, there was no photographic evidence that Forster was being pursued, that would eliminate any suggestion that the Austrian politician had been forced off of the road. For once, Waldbaer mused, technology might prove useful. Smiling, he placed both hands reverently around the glass of wheat beer before him and resolved to arrive at his office especially early in the morning. An additional thought occurred to him, adding further to his celebratory mood. There was an international phone call that he could profitably make.

McLean, Northern Virginia, USA

Robert Hirter felt early-morning energy pulse through his body. He sipped a second cup of rich Italian coffee and stretched his legs, Adidas-clad feet planted firmly on the gray tile of his kitchen floor. The cloying humidity that defined Washington in summer did not reign at this early hour. Hirter had finished his morning run along the suburban streets of his neighborhood and was preparing to shower and

change before the drive from his town house to work. Work, in
Hirter's case, meant activity in the sequestered, heavily guarded compound of the Central Intelligence Agency, located a few miles away
off of Route 123.

Hirter enjoyed the profession of intelligence operations and
looked forward to what the day might bring. He was currently assigned to the Counterproliferation Center and involved in an operation covertly tracking a lieutenant of the notorious Pakistani
nuclear proliferator, A. Q. Khan. Khan himself had been previously
exposed and defanged in a CIA campaign during the tenure of CIA
Director George Tenet years previously. But Khan's acolytes had escaped arrest, and were attempting to sell their nuclear know-how to
unsavory potential buyers.

The case involved East Asia, and Hirter was in touch with a
string of CIA case officers from Hong Kong to Bangkok. He and his
comrades suspected a North Korean angle, but first had to put together a complex puzzle of evidence and rumor before they could establish what Khan's man was up to. It was hard, exacting work with
an uncertain outcome, and it engaged Robert Hirter thoroughly. He
expected the overnight message traffic waiting for him in his Langley office contained results from the surveillance and covert photography of Khan's man in Indonesia.

Hirter's contemplations were interrupted by the jarring ring of
the phone attached to the wall near the kitchen table. He frowned
and registered concern; it was unusual to get a call this early in the
morning unless it heralded some problem, professional or personal.
Hirter moved the few steps to the phone and lifted the receiver.

"Robert Hirter."

A guttural laugh barked in reply. "Excellent, Herr Hirter, glad to
see you up so early. It's six hours later where I'm sitting."

A smile traced across Hirter's even features as he recognized the
voice. "Well, well. Kommissar Waldbaer. Haven't heard your Bavarian accent in quite awhile. *Servus.* You sound well."

"I am well, Herr Hirter. Some aches and pains, to be sure, but still fit enough to earn a living as a detective. And you, I trust, are also well?"

Hirter pulled up a kitchen chair and let his lanky frame fall into it. "Quite well, Kommissar. Busy, but I like that. Still, I suspect you didn't ring me up to inquire about my well-being. Am I right?"

Hirter was treated to another deep, brief rumble of laughter. "Always so direct, you Americans. But that's fine with me. Listen, Hirter, I want to ask a favor. I'm looking for information, unofficially. I don't want to go through channels, not yet."

It was Hirter's turn for mirth. "Ah, yes, Kommissar, I understand entirely. That's your trademark, isn't it? I believe you once called it 'the little path of the services.' Okay, let's see whether I can help. What information are you looking for?"

"*Ja.* Actually, I'm looking for background on an Austrian politician. A recently deceased Austrian politician, to be exact. The name is Georg Forster. You might recognize it; I don't know how much publicity he received in the States."

Hirter nodded to himself and ran a hand through his thick brown hair. "Forster. Right-wing guy? Controversial? Something of a populist and in the press a lot for making provocative statements? I sort of recall someone like that, but not much more."

"Very good, Hirter, glad to see you keeping up on European news. Forster was all of the things you just recited. What you might not know is that Forster's brand of populism resonated well in Austria. He adopted an anti-immigration message that won him a considerable share of the vote in the last elections. He was, as you Americans like to say, going places. Sadly for Forster, he died in a car accident in Bavaria a few days ago. The investigation landed on my desk."

Hirter considered. "I can't imagine that I can dig up any information on his car accident that you don't have, Kommissar. Is it something else you're looking for?"

"Yes, Herr Hirter, something else. It's a principle of mine that you can't launch an investigation without understanding the victim, and in this case, I confess, I don't. I only know about Forster's public persona. I know next to nothing about the real, flesh-and-blood man who died in the collapsed steel of a Mercedes on a wet mountain road. I need to know more. Maybe your employer has, shall we say, acquired background on Forster. After all, he was an important politician, and I recall that some of his statements were not exactly favorable to U.S. policy interests. Could be Forster has a file with your people."

Hirter released an extended sigh. " Kommissar, you recall from our past dealings, I expect, that I can't pass classified information without getting all sorts of permission on this end. I have to talk to people."

"That's what I'm asking, Hirter. Talk to your people; use your charm. See what you can give me. Between us, I could care less how your agency got the information. I don't care if you recruited some Austrian to spy for you inside Forster's political party. I don't even care if you recruited a German citizen as a source; that's not my concern. I'd be happy to receive any background you can provide. What made Forster tick? Were there threats against him? Do you know whether he was hiding anything from public view that could be damaging to his political career? Did he have rivals within his party? That sort of thing."

There was a momentary pause on the line as Hirter considered. "Okay, Kommissar. Let me see what I can do. Give me a day or two. I'll get back to you."

Waldbaer made an approving sound. "That's all I ask. Call anytime. I'll be waiting." The German rang off.

Hirter secured the wall phone in its mount and stared out the picture window of his town house at the suburban street. Waldbaer could be right, he thought, CIA might have a file on a character like Forster. What details might be authorized for passage to a Bavarian detective was quite another story. Hirter noticed that the sky outside was a hazy, pale yellow. It promised to be a hot and humid day in the Washington area and Hirter's mind recalled, for a moment, the infinitely more comfortable weather he had enjoyed in the Bavarian Alps during his first encounter with Waldbaer. He returned his thoughts to the Virginia present and bounded up the stairs for a shower and to change into a summer-weight suit, the garb most suitable for another long day at CIA headquarters.

GAMSDORF, BAVARIA

Sabine Reiner found an empty parking place in front of the Gamsdorf City Hall, the building housing the police station and Waldbaer's office. The available space was tightly braced by two green police cruisers, but Sabine deftly maneuvered her BMW into place on the first attempt. What will this meeting bring, she wondered as she entered the curiously turreted, blue-painted building.

Moments later she was seated across from Waldbaer, the detective's heavy, scarred desk occupying the intervening space between them. Sabine sat bolt upright, her back arched straight, in counterpoint to Waldbaer's slumped form, which seemed to merge with the contours of the oversized leather chair. Waldbaer had provided them both with mugs of coffee, the ceramic of which, Sabine noted, had been less than robustly cleaned.

"You will find this photo interesting, I expect, Frau Reiner." Waldbaer pushed a large black-and-white print across the table to his business-suit-clad Austrian visitor.

She held it in both hands and considered the image. "My God, Kommissar, that's Georg Forster. He's driving the car he died in. This is clearly a traffic camera photograph. When was it taken?"

Waldbaer laced his hands into a ball and rested his chin against it. "It was taken the night he died. In fact, if you consult the time registered at the bottom of the photo, you'll see it was taken about fifteen minutes before the estimated time of the accident. The camera activated because Forster was speeding."

Sabine simply nodded and continued to evaluate the police camera's *memento mori*.

"There's more," Waldbaer said. He pulled a second oversize photo from a yellow folder on his desk and handed it to her.

"I'm not really sure what I'm looking at," she replied.

Waldbaer grunted in understanding. "Look at the registered time on this photo, too. This car was clocked speeding less than a minute behind Forster's. I think Forster was being tailed, that's how it looks."

Sabine studied the second photograph more closely, moving it slightly to deflect the glare of the ceiling lamp above. "There is a man in this car. There's enough detail to show that he looks pretty earnest. And the license plate is of Austrian registration, from Kufstein."

Waldbaer smiled. "The registration number is the one I read to you over the phone yesterday. Were you able to trace it?"

It was her turn to issue a slight smile. "Indeed," she said brightly. "It's a rental vehicle. Kufstein is just a few kilometers across the border from Germany, not far from Rosenheim. I have a copy of the rental agreement. The person who rented the car used a German driver's license with a Munich address." Sabine pressed open the flap of her Italian leather handbag and extracted a sheet of paper, handing it to her host.

Waldbaer hunched forward over his desk and squinted at the document. He grabbed his cup of coffee and took a long draw. "David Kirscheim. Date of birth makes him forty-three years old. The street address in the Grunwald section of Munich looks real, but we'll check. This won't take long." Waldbaer pulled himself up from his chair with a sigh and stretched; a fleeting look of concern clouded his face as he heard his elbows crack. With a fatalistic shake of his head, he left the office for the duty officer's desk, leaving his visitor to sip her coffee in solitude.

He returned through the battered office door ten minutes later, an intense cast to his features.

For a moment he remained standing, leaning on the edge of his solid desk for support. He glanced at Sabine and then his gaze moved off, focusing on some point unseen. "Now this is interesting, Kommissarin. David Kirscheim is a true name. He's real, birth date matches too."

"Wonderful," Sabine interjected.

Waldbaer held up a hand to delay her commentary. "David Kirscheim is accredited to the Israeli Consulate in Munich as second secretary of mission. No mistake."

Sabine's exuberance vanished. "Oh, God."

Waldbaer moved his chin up and then down a single time. "Not what we expected. But true, nonetheless. Kirscheim is on the diplomatic list. He's been at the consulate two years. Born in Haifa. Fluent German speaker; his father was a Holocaust survivor."

Further conversation was interrupted by the shrill ring of Waldbaer's desk phone. Waldbaer pulled the receiver to his ear. "Hello, Hans," he muttered. There was the distant sound of a voice on the other end, and Waldbear nodded affirmatively, at junctures intoning, "Ja, gut."

After issuing a perfunctory goodbye, Waldbaer replaced the receiver heavily. He looked directly at Sabine, his eyes sharp and focused. "It gets better. That was Hans, a friend of mine in Munich police headquarters. He's in the section responsible for the security of the diplomatic corps in the city. According to Hans, the police list Kirscheim as an undeclared intelligence officer working under diplomatic cover. Probably from Mossad, the Israeli external service."

Sabine swept a hand through her dark red hair before replying. "An Israeli intelligence officer. He traveled to Austria from Germany and rented a vehicle. And the same vehicle was pursuing Forster's car, both of them driving above the speed limit, on the night Forster died."

"Yes," Waldbaer said.

She continued. "This would seem to confirm what Hessler told us. On the other hand, why would an intelligence officer out to kill someone go about it in true name? Wouldn't he employ false identification?"

Waldbaer shrugged and pulled at his shirt collar. "Maybe not. Consider. Kirscheim travels to Austria from Germany and figures no one is watching him, a fair assumption on his part. He conducts surveillance on Forster with a rented automobile. Why does he rent a car? Because his Munich car would have diplomatic corps license plates, which he wants to conceal. An Austrian registration blends in. Wisely or not, Kirscheim is not planning on being discovered. The last thing he would consider is that he would end up being photographed on a rural alpine road by the police, who eventually trace the rental registration back to him. Seen that way, what Kirscheim did isn't so unreasonable."

Sabine pursed her lips and arched her eyebrows. "Perhaps, Kommissar. Herr Kirscheim nonetheless made a mistake. Especially if he was, as Hessler believes, involved in causing Forster's death that night."

Waldbaer exhaled a breath slowly and bent his head to inspect his scuffed walking shoes. "Well," he said after a moment, "putting someone under surveillance isn't the same thing as murder. I'm sure neither one of us wants to jump to conclusions, Frau Reiner. In fact, my suspicion is that if Kirscheim was planning to kill Forster, he would have done things differently. Made sure there was no way it could blow back on his government and cause an enormous diplomatic incident. But that's supposition on my part."

Sabine waited to see if Waldbaer had more to say, but he did not, and she broke the intervening silence. "So, we've confirmed that the Israelis fit into the picture. What do you propose we do next?"

Waldbaer rubbed a hand slowly along the bridge of his nose and regarded his guest with a look of mild suspicion, uncertain whether the note of deference was sincere or feigned. "Simple. We have to talk to Kirscheim and assess what he says about that night. He's at the Israeli Consulate in Munich, not that far from here."

Sabine raised a finger in the air for emphasis. "That doesn't seem simple to me. Kirscheim is an accredited diplomat. He has diplomatic immunity. He can refuse to talk to us and the Israeli Consulate can choose to be unhelpful. It's frustrating, but that's how it works." She fixed the German detective with a fatalistic look.

Waldbaer returned her stare. "You're right, for the reasons you say. Something else, too. If I want to speak with a foreign diplomat, I have first to coordinate with the Bavarian Ministry of the Interior and let them know what's up. There's a protocol for these things. Nobody will like this, because it transforms a clear-cut police case into a political furor. No percentage in that for anyone. But I don't see that we have much choice. The trail leads to Kirscheim and nowhere else."

Waldbaer paused in his soliloquy and walked an abbreviated pattern behind the hulking mass of his desk, like a dog on a leash. He stared off in the distance, lost in his cerebrations until he punched a fist into his open hand. "You know, Frau Reiner, if we play this right, Kirscheim might choose to talk to us. Voluntarily. We want to know what he has to say, right? Whether or not he can be subjected to legal prosecution is a separate matter, and, frankly, out of our hands. Maybe we invite him to an informal chat, letting him know we fully understand his privileges and status. Let me think of a workable approach. I'll call him when I have my strategy in order and try to set up a meeting for tomorrow."

Sabine stood. She smiled at Waldbaer, but that sentiment was not reflected in her eyes. "I wish you luck, perhaps it will work. Of course, you know any interview you are able to arrange in Munich will have to involve me."

Waldbaer's eyes narrowed. "I don't think that's necessary, Frau Reiner. No need for you to drive to Munich. I can handle it on my own and report the results to you by phone."

She arched her eyebrows. "No," she said, absent elaboration.

"We don't know Kirscheim," Walbaer insisted. "He may feel threatened if two people meet him rather than a more casual one-on-one arrangement. And you coming from the Austrian police might make it all too international for his liking. Not to mention that he's from the Middle East, with all of their traditions. Could be that he's a misogynist. He might not want to talk with a woman around."

Sabine walked a step closer to the kommissar and looked up into his brooding, baggy-eyed countenance. "I suppose we'll have to take our chances, won't we? And as far as not wanting a woman around, there wouldn't be a misogynist in the room aside from Kirscheim, would there?"

"Frau Reiner. My only concern is the progress of this investigation; you can rely on that. If you feel so strongly, I won't object to your presence in the session with Kirscheim."

Sabine nodded, her smile now exhibiting a certain warmth. "Well done, Herr Kommissar. And I'm sure you meant to invite not just my presence, but my participation in the interview."

Waldbaer raised a hand and let it fall limply, in a gesture heavy with defeat.

Munich Autobahn, Germany

The A8 autobahn to Munich from the south had been free of both accidents and congestion, for which Waldbaer was grateful. The seventy-minute ride from mountainous terrain to the capital city of Bavaria had been accompanied by brilliant sunshine and the heroic strains of Richard Strauss's *Alpine Symphony*, the harmony of nature and music permitting him to consider again how best to question Israeli Second Secretary David Kirscheim. Waldbaer was pleased at how he had persuaded the reluctant Kirscheim to accept an interview. He had played the Israeli gently, avoiding direct confrontation and emphasizing the value of safeguarding Israel's reputation.

That had been the key, Waldbaer was certain. "Herr Kirscheim," he had said in his telephone conversation, "the last thing either one of us wants is for this matter to reach the press and sully Israel's image. If you decline the interview, as is your right, the matter moves to another department of my government to handle. They may choose to declare you persona non grata, which I understand is permissible under diplomatic protocol. Once that happens, the press will be all over it. Drawing the most sensational, damning conclusions, of course; that's what they do. If you consent to talk to me and a colleague, discreetly, we can prevent that unpleasantness."

The detective smiled with self-contentment. It had worked perfectly with Kirscheim, who was clearly eager to avoid an international scandal. A moment later, Waldbaer willed the smile from his features. Smugness, he counseled himself, was an impediment to professionalism.

Arrangements for the meeting had been kept simple. They

would meet in Via Veneto, an Italian restaurant not far from the Israeli Consulate, an informal dining establishment Waldbaer had visited in the past. It had several virtues. The restaurant was convenient for Kirscheim, making it easier for him to accept the venue. It was low profile and anonymous, suiting all the parties involved. And it provided a pleasant atmosphere, underlining the voluntary, non-hostile tone Waldbaer desired to communicate to the diplomat.

Waldbaer drove past a yellow sign indicating that he had crossed into the Munich city limits. He stole a glance at his wristwatch and saw that he was making good time. By agreement, Frau Reiner would meet him inside the Via Veneto. They would have about half an hour together to compare notes before Kirscheim's scheduled arrival. That would suffice, Waldbaer was certain, still wishing he could run the investigation on a unilateral basis without the intrusion of his Austrian counterpart. Still, Frau Reiner, though occasionally abrasive, was not the amateur he had initially anticipated. She was professional in her own way, if too concerned about her status in the investigation. He raised his eyebrows and emitted a fatalistic sigh; no percentage in fighting what can't be changed. He pulled off the autobahn onto the Munich Ring and moved with the ebb and flow of traffic toward the ancient stone spires of the city center and his rendezvous.

MUNICH, CITY CENTER

Frau Reiner had preceded him. She sat at a small, round table toward the back of the restaurant, at the end of the long marble-topped bar near doors opening onto a walled cobblestone terrace awash with vines. The effect was a pleasant conspiracy of urbanity and rusticity. Frau Reiner spotted the detective as he entered the restaurant and beckoned him with a subdued wave and generous smile.

Waldbaer smiled in return, a bit idiotically, he realized, before arranging his features into a more brooding repose. "We have plenty of time before he arrives," he said, opening the dialogue.

Frau Reiner moved her chair a degree, making way for Waldbaer's solid frame. "I can see why you chose this place," she rejoined.

"He'll feel comfortable. At least, as comfortable as someone can be who's being interrogated."

Waldbaer looked pained. "Interviewed, Frau Reiner, interviewed. That's how we want Kirscheim to see things. And in fact, interrogation suggests that we possess a power we don't have. Kirscheim can leave any time and that's it for us. We need to persuade, not coerce."

Frau Reiner settled her face on top of steepled, manicured fingertips. "Kommissar, don't worry, I am as aware as you of our limitations. And I know how to conduct this type of questioning. Your expectation that I am a novice in these matters is a misapprehension, I assure you."

Waldbaer let his gaze drift toward the courtyard. "No need to argue the point. We will doubtless conduct this session properly. I think we should put our cards on the table at the outset. Courtesy doesn't translate into wasting time. You have the rental car agreement?"

Frau Reiner patted her leather handbag in affirmation.

"Good," Waldbaer replied. I have the photos from the traffic camera. With luck, that will cut through any dissembling the second secretary might be tempted to engage in."

A tall waiter in starched white shirt and burgundy bow tie arrived at the table, his complexion and bountiful black hair suggesting that he was well suited to the ethnicity of the restaurant. "*Buon giorno,*" he said, confirming his origins. He proffered a menu but Frau Reiner waved it away politely, ordering a cappuccino. Waldbaer asked for a liter bottle of mineral water.

As the waiter departed, Waldbaer returned to the conversation. "I'd like to get Kirscheim to confirm he was following Forster. That accomplished, we can ask him why. If he clarifies that point, we press him to convince us that he wasn't involved in Forster's death. Provided we win his confidence, we could learn a lot in the next hour."

Frau Reiner nodded, her hair shimmering slightly in the subdued light. "One problem with that. If he was involved in Forster's death, you don't seriously expect him to come clean, do you?"

Waldbaer swept a hand slowly over the smooth surface of the table and lowered his eyes. "No. I don't expect a man with diplomatic immunity to walk in here and confess to a murder just because we inquire. But if he did do it, for personal reasons or on orders from his intelligence service, I think we'll get a hint. Most people aren't comfortable liars. Something gives them away; intonation, the story they are fabricating, body language, something. Nothing we could bring to court, but Kirscheim is not going to court anyway. You and I might spot the lie." He poured some mineral water into his glass and took a long gulp.

Frau Reiner glanced out at the rush of vines and lifted her chin a degree.

Waldbaer found that she had a pleasant profile, like the women in a Botticelli painting.

"Herr Kommissar, what you say makes sense. But don't forget. Kirscheim is a professional Mossad officer. He's trained in deceit. I'm not sure what we'll get out of him."

Waldbaer frowned and nodded. "We'll try our best, Frau Reiner. Remember, we are as professional as Kirscheim is. And there are two of us; not bad odds."

The frosted glass front door to the restaurant opened with an audible protest and the pair looked up simultaneously. Two men in dark business suits entered, their arrival accompanied briefly by the sounds of the urban street, until the door shut firmly behind them. The first man was thin and nearly bald, his companion shorter and stockier, with a full head of wavy hair. Waldbaer focused his gaze on the first man. "That's Kirscheim," he mumbled, "just like in the traffic photo."

Frau Rainer nodded assent and raised an arm slightly at the new arrivals.

Kirscheim unbuttoned his suit jacket and made his way to the table. His companion moved in the opposite direction, finding a stool at the bar that offered a clear view of the proceedings.

"He has backup," Frau Reiner whispered as Kirscheim made his way toward them. "No doubt another Mossad man. They don't trust us."

"Prudent of them," Waldbaer allowed as the Israeli arrived at their table.

"You are Kommissar Waldbaer?" the balding man inquired in a surprisingly falsetto voice.

"Yes, Herr Kirscheim, that would be me," Waldbaer replied, standing. He pulled his laminated police identification from his jacket. "And this is a colleague of mine, Frau Reiner." The detective pulled up a chair for the diplomat and both men took seats.

Frau Reiner interjected before Waldbaer could converse further. "Your friend at the bar is welcome to join us. I presume he is an associate of yours from the consulate." Her voice was solicitous but communicated quiet authority.

The Israeli blushed, the rush of color making visible where his hairline had once been. "No, that's not necessary. He's just here to ensure that this wasn't a terrorist ruse. We have to be careful about the Palestinians. Hezbollah has operatives in Munich."

Waldbaer spoke next. "Well, Herr Kirscheim, be that as it may, our conversation today is on quite a different topic, as I mentioned on the phone."

"Yes," the Israeli said quietly, his stiff frame betraying his discomfort.

Frau Reiner leaned closer to Kirscheim and spoke in a near whisper. "Try to relax. We aren't about to handcuff you. We want to give you the opportunity to clarify some points. This talk is as much to your advantage as it is to ours."

Kirscheim's lanky body seemed to uncoil a degree. *Nicely done, Frau Reiner*, Waldbaer thought to himself.

"Let's get you something to drink," Waldbaer enjoined, signaling for the waiter, who was serving customers from behind the bar. The Italian appeared a few moments later and Kirscheim ordered a cola.

Waldbaer pulled a manila envelope from inside his jacket and deposited it at the center of the table. "Herr Kirscheim, I'd like you to explain a few things about your recent travels."

Kirscheim stared at the envelope quizzically.

"Recent travels to Austria," Waldbaer continued, his voice even, almost soothing. "What can you tell us about that?"

Kirscheim swallowed and looked at Waldbaer directly. "It's been busy here lately. I haven't been to Austria for a while. Not for months."

Waldbaer sighed heavily, and Kirscheim turned his attention to Frau Reiner. She fixed him with a slight smile that communicated disappointment. Reaching into the generous spaces of her leather handbag, she withdrew sheets of paper and without preamble passed them across the table to the Israeli.

Kirscheim's wide eyes devoured the documents. Scarlet coloring returned to his visage.

"Rental car agreement," Frau Reiner intoned. "From Kufstein, Austria, as you can see. And signed by you much more recently than a few months ago."

Kirscheim made eye contact with her but said nothing.

Waldbaer lightly rapped his knuckles on the tabletop. "So, Herr Kirscheim, one foray into fiction is sufficient. Of course you were in Austria, recently. You rented a vehicle there. Why?"

The conversation was clearly not to Kirscheim's liking, and Waldbaer feared for a moment that he would stand up and leave. But then Kirscheim began to speak, stress evident in his high voice.

"All right. I was in Austria. As to why, it was official consular business. I'm not permitted to provide details. Diplomatic privilege. I assure you it was nothing criminal."

Waldbaer and Reiner exchanged glances. Waldbaer continued his query. "Official consulate business. You mean intelligence business, yes? Mossad business."

Kirscheim darted a hand to the knot of his tie. "Draw whatever inferences you want, Kommissar. I'm an accredited second secretary of mission here. But let's say, hypothetically, that I'm an intelligence officer. It wouldn't make any difference. What I said remains true. My presence in Austria was official business and not of a criminal nature."

A waiter, stockier than the first, appeared with Kirscheim's cola and placed it on the table before wandering off.

Frau Reiner joined the conversation. "Fine. You say it was nothing criminal, but you aren't at liberty to provide details. Maybe we can help." She glanced quickly at Waldbaer who gave a covert nod. "Did you rent a car in Austria in order to follow someone?"

Kirscheim put his elbows on the tabletop and rubbed at his temples. He breathed in deeply and took a long sip of his drink. "What makes you think that?" he replied after a moment.

Waldbaer's baggy eyes bored into the younger man's. "That's not an answer. As I said earlier, Herr Kirscheim, if you don't give us some minimal cooperation, I won't be able to stop public consequences from transpiring. It's up to you."

A fatalistic look possessed Kirscheim's features. "My mission did involve observing an individual, yes. But only that. That's no crime, at least not in Austria. It was only observation."

Waldbaer let his frame ease back into his chair. "Maybe we're getting somewhere."

"Who was it?" Frau Reiner asked, striking a relaxed pose.

Kirscheim's jaw tightened as he weighed his words. "A political figure of interest to my government as a possible threat to Israeli interests. An Austrian. That should suffice for your purposes." He stared at Waldbaer, vainly seeking confirmation.

A dry smile crossed Waldbaer's face, but with no humor reflected in his eyes. "How about this? You rented the car to conduct surveillance of Herr Georg Forster, chairman of the Austrian Nationalist Defense Front. How does that sound?"

Kirscheim looked beaten and his facial muscles seemed to go slack. He looked at the tabletop, which still held Waldbaer's manila envelope. The Israeli toyed with his beverage glass and said nothing.

With a sideways look at his partner, Waldbaer picked up the envelope and unsealed it, pulling out the traffic camera photos. "So, Herr Kirscheim, it's showtime," he muttered, passing the Israeli the photo of Forster in his Mercedes. The Israeli took it with trembling hands. As his eyes focused on the image, Waldbaer noted that sweat began to bead on Kirscheim's forehead, unsummoned and unwanted. After permitting the diplomat a moment to consider the image, Waldbaer slipped the second photo into his hands. Kirscheim surveyed his own image and moaned softly, unaware that he was doing so.

Frau Reiner drummed her manicured nails against the tabletop in a slow rhythm. "Now would be a good time to offer clarification, Herr Second Secretary."

Kirscheim glanced over at the bar, where his compatriot was hunched over a cup of espresso, watching their table intently. He returned his gaze to Frau Reiner. "I didn't kill Forster. That just happened; the slick road, I guess. I saw the car lose control and swerve off the road, that's true. I didn't stop to help. That would have raised too many questions. I was conducting surveillance to see where he was going. My government was interested in knowing who his contacts are in Germany. I've already said more than I should."

Waldbaer's voice was a low rumble, like a volcano threatening to erupt. "You might not realize it, Herr Kirscheim, but you've already said enough to make it clear that you did break the law that night on the road to Garmisch. You left the scene of an accident and failed to offer the possibility of first aid to the victim. Those are criminal offenses in Germany."

Kirscheim's eyes were imploring. "It couldn't be helped. If I got involved it would turn up the connection to my government, and that violates our rules."

Waldbaer pulled himself a degree closer to Kirscheim, intruding on his space. "Look around. Does this look like Tel Aviv? Your rules don't matter here. My rules matter. Your actions that night were wrong—legally and morally." Waldbaer stared silently at his subject for a moment and then slowly eased away. "All right. We aren't about to prosecute you, and you'll have to live with not having rendered assistance." Don't push too hard, the detective counseled himself. "Although, to be honest, nothing you might have done could have saved Forster's life. He was dead within seconds from massive internal injuries."

Frau Reiner's lighter voice joined the conversation. "And where does this leave us?"

"A good question," Waldbaer said. "Let's see what Herr Kirscheim has told us and what he can confirm. You admit you rented a car in Kufstein to follow Forster?"

Kirscheim nodded assent.

Reiner interjected a query. "You then traveled to Innsbruck to begin surveillance of Forster. Where did you start watching him?"

Kirscheim eyed the ceiling briefly before replying. "Initially at his home, to pick up the target. I parked up the street, saw him leave the house, and followed his Mercedes to the victory rally across the city in the Wilten section. I didn't go into the hall, just remained in the parking lot with his car in view. When he left the rally, I followed at a distance. It was dark by then."

Frau Reiner continued. "And then?"

"I followed Forster as he drove out of town. He took the highway past the Innsbruck airport and headed toward Seefeld. The weather turned lousy, visibility decreased. Forster crossed the border into Germany. I stayed on his tail, but at a distance, so as not to arouse suspicion. My people had information that he'd be meeting German contacts that night, and it looked like I was proving the information correct. I wanted to identify his backers in Germany, but that was not to be."

Waldbear took up the questioning, now that the narrative had crossed the frontier into Bundesrepublik Deutschland. "Describe what happened next as clearly as you can."

Kirscheim's hands tightened around the cola glass. "Everything seemed fine. It was raining hard, and Forster was driving above the speed limit. I sped up too, to keep him in sight. We weren't driving dangerously fast though, in my estimation. We'd been driving at the same speed for about twenty minutes. Suddenly, as he rounded a broad curve, Forster's car swerved. In a second the Mercedes had left the road and slammed into the forest. I could see his headlights illuminating scrub growth, and then the car disappeared into the pines. I was stunned. I didn't know if Forster was dead or alive, but

I knew he wouldn't be visiting anyone that night. I turned around and drove back to Kufstein. I returned the rental car and took the next train to Munich."

Waldbaer crossed his arms over his chest, the fabric of his jacket bunching at his shoulders. "Why did your government care about Forster enough to observe him? And where did you get information about his supporters in Germany?"

"Israel regarded Forster and his party as a security threat. Forster was an anti-Semite and in contact with some of our enemies internationally. As to where we got our information, that I won't reveal. That has to do with intelligence sources."

Frau Reiner moved the discussion in a different direction. "You said Forster's car swerved, and he left the road. Had he been driving erratically?"

Kirscheim frowned. "No. His driving was all right. Too fast for the weather conditions, as I say, but not horribly so."

"Thank you," Frau Reiner said softly. "Is there anything else that you can tell us that would seem relevant? The sooner we clear up this case, the better it is for you, Herr Kirscheim."

The Israeli looked Frau Reiner in the eyes. "Only to say one more time that I didn't kill Forster. I didn't force his car off the road. I wish he had lived and led me to his German contacts. My mission failed."

It was Waldbaer who called the proceedings to a close. "We'll consider what you've told us. You've been forthcoming, under the circumstances. If we need you again, I'll let you know, but that's all for the moment. At this stage, I think we can keep this out of diplomatic channels and prevent any further details, including your surveillance of Forster, from reaching the media."

Kirscheim offered his hosts a tentative smile. With a mumbled goodbye he left the table, collected his associate from the bar, and exited the coffee house.

"I think he's telling the truth," Frau Reiner allowed to her companion.

Waldbear emitted a brief, grumbled laugh. "Not the whole truth,

I'd wager, but the truth nonetheless. I don't think he killed Forster. And we have nothing to suggest that he did, no matter what Hessler says. Surveillance is one thing, murder quite another. The problem we have, Frau Reiner, is that we still don't know what happened that night. And Forster and what he was up to is more of an enigma than ever."

CENTRAL INTELLIGENCE AGENCY HEADQUARTERS,
LANGLEY, NORTHERN VIRGINIA

The sun could be felt, but not seen. Waves of invisible heat reflected up from the cement sidewalk and the air was thick, moist, and tropically oppressive. The sun was concealed behind an obscuring mask of pearl-hued sky that would collect into brooding clouds as the afternoon matured, unleashing the usual thunderstorms by evening. Robert Hirter and fellow CIA Case Officer Caroline O'Kendell were nearly done with their walk around the CIA compound, a thirty-minute, noontime routine.

As they neared the main, glass-doored entrance to the headquarters building, they paused by the bronze, life-sized statue of Nathan Hale, whose visage stared stoically straight ahead, hands bound behind his back. Carved into the round plinth of the statue were the last words ascribed to Hale, "I regret that I have but one life to lose for my country." Hale was a CIA totem, a young American Colonial espionage officer who had been discovered and hanged by the British in the War of Independence. His short life and dramatic death provided both inspiration and a cautionary tale to more contemporary practitioners of the covert craft.

Caroline, garbed in a lightweight, pale-yellow linen suit, rested a hand on the pedestal. "So what did our Bavarian kommissar friend actually ask you to do for him, Robert?"

Hirter held his light-blue, seersucker jacket loosely over his shoulder and admired, as he so often did, the contour of the entirely feminine face before him. He smiled, recalling his conversation with the Bavarian earlier that morning. "Waldbaer was being his usual sly self, not seeming to ask for much, but, really, trying to get me to provide him information he shouldn't have access to. I have to see what I can do, if anything."

"What does he want to know?"

"More who than what. It seems Waldbaer is investigating the death of an Austrian politician who died in a car wreck in Bavaria. A right-wing populist named Georg Forster. Maybe you've heard of him; he made the news over here occasionally because of his provocative, in-your-face style. Waldbaer wants to know if the CIA has anything on the guy. Information on his character, lifestyle, secrets he might have had, dubious contacts."

Caroline nodded in understanding. She brushed a lock of damp hair from her forehead, a victim of the humidity. "I get it. Well, the place to go is Europe Division. I have some friends there, if it helps. Still, I don't know that they'll permit you to pass information to a Bavarian cop." She shook her head in mild amusement, causing her small gold earrings to glitter.

"I think I have a way to prompt some cooperation. It's true we're not inclined to just clear and pass along classified information to Waldbaer. What I'm thinking of is quid pro quo. Think about it a second. Forster is killed in a car wreck. But I checked the Internet before I drove in this morning and it seems that his political party claims he was murdered. By the Israelis."

"What? That's explosive stuff, Robert."

"Precisely. And our rumpled friend Waldbaer is leading the investigation. I would think CIA would be interested in getting the inside track on that, not just because we deal with the Mossad, but because so many of our foreign policy interests involve Israel and Europe."

Caroline moved away from the sculpture and resumed the slow stroll toward the headquarters lobby, her companion at her side. "You want headquarters to authorize passage of information in exchange for Waldbaer giving us privileged insight into whatever his investigation reveals."

"Great minds think alike, Caroline. Maybe I can work a deal with Europe Division. Not that I can get too involved in this Forster thing myself. If our side decides to go forward with Waldbaer, I'll pass it off to someone else. I'm busy enough trying to track A. Q. Khan's acolytes."

Caroline laughed softly as the couple entered the cool, air-conditioned expanse of the lobby, one marble wall punctuated with rows of carved stars, each one representing a CIA officer who had fallen in the line of duty. "Well, Robert, make sure to count me out too. You have your proliferation duties, and I'm fully employed on the international terrorism account, thank you. Not that I would mind seeing Munich again."

Robert pulled on his suit coat and adjusted his striped Dior tie, smiling down at the more diminutive woman. "Okay, see you after work. Remember, there's the retirement get-together at Clyde's tonight." They parted, each heading to their separate offices. Outside, the sullen Virginia sky continued to darken.

NYMPHENBURG, A RESIDENTIAL AREA OF MUNICH

The day broke clear and crisp as the morning fog lifted over the Nymphenburg canal, its long, straight course lined on both banks by the sweeping branches of stately trees, many of them over a century old. Behind the trees and well-maintained streets, the canal was braced on both sides by the proud profiles of impeccably maintained noble homes, most dating to the mid-nineteenth century. The district was one of Munich's most distinguished and most desired, located like an elegant courtier at the foot of the Nymphenburg Palace, an architectural jewel of the baroque, surrounded by an expansive park once the exclusive preserve of Bavarian royalty. The eventual triumph of more democratic sentiments had, in more recent times, made the park accessible to the general public as a place of leisure.

David Kirscheim shut the heavy oak door to his home behind him, giving it a solid tug to ensure that it was locked. He unfastened the bicycle chained to the wrought-iron railing and pulled on a bright turquoise helmet, carefully seating it on his nearly hairless head and adjusting the black nylon chinstrap until it was snug. It was Sunday and he looked forward to biking along the quiet length of canal and then taking the side streets to the shady, pastoral Hirschgarten, one of Munich's largest and most popular beer gardens. Unlike many native Munich residents, Kirscheim was not one to drink beer in the morning, but he did intend to enjoy a tall glass of ice tea with a slice of lemon.

He set off down the somnolent street, most of its inhabitants clearly sleeping late on their day off. Minutes later he reached the grassy bank of the canal and turned left, cruising under the protecting boughs of thick-trunked trees at its edge. He glanced for a moment at the elegant, glimmering white-and-yellow form of the Nymphenburg Palace in the distance, an appropriately royal-blue sky presiding above it. The sprawling symmetry of its form spoke of an age of power and pride, wealth and the whims of kings. The placid water of the canal and the exquisite refinement of the view removed his cares, and Kirscheim let the despised name "Forster" slip away from his contemplations. Hunched over the handlebars, Kirscheim proceeded along the canal at a leisurely pace; no pedestrians or automobiles marring the pastoral scene at that early hour.

He felt his body slam forward at the same time that he registered a loss of control of his bicycle. Something was suddenly, wildly wrong, and the bike fell swiftly sideways as he tumbled over the handlebars and connected hard with the pavement. He felt as if a fist had punched through his back and lodged in his chest. A heart attack, he wondered briefly, aware that these things happened even to people in excellent condition. His arms now shaking spasmodically, Kirscheim pulled himself to his knees, feeling suddenly and enormously faint, his vision marred by a moving pattern of dark spots. Staring down at his formfitting, blue Lycra shirt, he saw with horror that a broad, dark stream of blood was coursing from the middle of his chest. He could feel its propelled, pumping warmth covering his abdomen and coursing thickly down his legs.

"Oh no, no," Kirscheim managed to articulate once, before his eyes lost focus and his vision shut down. He pitched forward, slamming back into the pavement, his supine, bloodied, athletic form still shielded from the sun by the venerable, gnarled elm branches high above.

Lake Starnberg, Bavaria

Waldbaer bit with voracious purpose into the mustard-covered brat-wurst and savored its satisfying, meaty flavor, so dear to Teutonic tastes. As he chewed the thick sausage, the detective gazed at the shimmering lakeside scene spread out before him. A silent fleet of swans and mallards cruised close to shore, alert for any stray morsel that might be tossed into their midst by the virtuous among men. A hundred meters out, an impeccably white catamaran slipped past, driven at moderate speed by the alpine breeze captured in its emerald-green sails. Waldbaer watched a white-haired, tanned, and shirtless man aboard work the lines, adjusting the canvas expertly to increase the velocity of his voyage. Retired and not without means, Waldbaer assessed, a brief trace of longing coloring his thoughts.

Perhaps a kilometer away, a two-deck tourist ship regally crossed the quiet expanse of water on its way to Tutzing, the next village along the shoreline. Tutzing had once been home to Elisabeth, the striking young beauty of noble birth who, through marriage, became Empress "Sissi" of Austria in the late nineteenth century. Waldbaer's eyes noted as well the backdrop to the lake, the distant necklace of the Bavarian Alps, the Zugspitze the highest summit to be seen, its soaring mass of stone rendered deep blue by the optic vagaries of sun, weather, and space.

Another bite of sausage concluded, Waldbaer turned back to the festivities in the park behind him. Occupying a wooden gazebo, a small brass band of middle-aged men in lederhosen played a *laendler* with hearty enthusiasm and moderate skill to the milling crowd. Several hundred people present eddied around stands selling fresh pretzels, sausage and chicken, and beer. The children moved as if with magnetic attraction to a large, pink tent dispensing gummi bears and chocolate-covered fruit. Above it all, a broad white banner was fastened with nylon cords to two trees, its message embla-

zoned in red block letters. DAY OF THE OPEN DOOR—BAVARIA'S PO-
LICE: YOUR FRIEND AND PROTECTOR.

"Waldbaer!"

The strident voice was familiar.

"Hauptkommissar Streichner, what a surprise. *Gruess Gott.*
Didn't expect to see you here, I must confess."

"Save your confessions for the clergy, Waldbaer. I would have
expected to find you in my office given what happened this morning." There was no humor evident in the eyes distorted to owl-like
dimensions behind thick spectacles. The Hauptkommissar's tall,
avian frame was garbed in a gray business suit, a sure sign that he
had arrived at the social outing directly from work.

Waldbaer nodded his head slightly and swallowed the last remnant of sausage and roll. "You mean the Kirscheim murder, of
course."

"Yes. What else would I mean but the shooting of the Israeli
diplomat David Kirscheim right on a Munich street? I was in my office expecting you to arrive any minute and provide a full report. I
called your mobile but couldn't raise you. Just by luck, one of the
uniformed officers recalled you saying a few days ago that you intended to visit this little festival here. Of course, I couldn't believe
you would stick with that plan under the circumstances. I came here
as a last resort, and what do I find? You with a sausage instead of a
report. We have an international incident on our hands, and you
just stand here eating."

Waldbaer arched his dark eyebrows a degree. "Yes, eating. And
drinking, I might add. I intend to have a Hacker-Pschorr beer in a
moment. You couldn't reach me because I left my phone in the glove
compartment of my car. I wanted to think without interruption."
An unwise rejoinder, Waldbaer knew, but he couldn't resist.

Hauptkommissar Streichner reacted predictably to the verbal
foray. "Waldbaer! This is hardly the time for your insouciance. Entirely inappropriate, under the circumstances. I expect you have
some explaining to do. After all, I put you on this Forster investiga-

tion in the first place, and now this." Streichner buttoned and then unbuttoned his jacket and tugged at his patterned tie, nerves forcing his hands into random bursts of motion.

Waldbaer decided to provoke the despised Streichner no further. He acknowledged the limits imposed on his behavior by rank and propriety. "Hauptkommissar Streichner, permit me to clarify things. You do not have a report from me because it is too early to report anything other than the basic circumstances of Kirscheim's death, which you already know. The pathologist is still examining the corpse and won't provide any conclusions for hours yet. Furthermore, I visited the shooting scene in Munich before I came here. Not much to see, by the way. No one has come forward as a witness and I doubt there were any, given the hour and location of the killing."

Streichner shook his head sideways. Waldbaer noted that Streichner's color was slowly reddening from the neck up.

"Waldbaer, you could be back in the city now, going door to door through the Nymphenburg neighborhood, trying to locate a witness."

Waldbaer took care to keep his tone measured. "Yes, I could do that. But that is not what a kommissar is paid to do. I instructed two policemen to survey the residents in the area. If they uncover information of value, I'll go back and conduct an interview. But I'm quite certain no one saw a thing at that hour. I doubt anyone heard a thing, either. I surmise that a silenced weapon was employed."

Streichner calmed his fluttering a bit. "Why do you think that?"

Waldbaer began a slow stroll toward the beer tent, Streichner moving along at his side. "I think a silenced weapon was employed because this was most surely a professional murder. I am certain that Herr Kirscheim was not killed in a robbery attempt; he was not the victim of some casual but lethal crime. There is nothing to suggest this was a crime of passion. The circumstances suggest strongly that this was a crime of calculation. As such, the killer would have taken every precaution to protect his own identity and facilitate his escape." Waldbaer stopped a moment in his tracks and fixed Streichner with a disarmingly innocent look. "You do follow what I am say-ing?"

To Waldbaer's immense internal delight, the hauptkommissar exploded. "Of course I follow you, Waldbaer! I didn't get to my po-sition because I'm an imbecile! Don't patronize me." With effort, Streichner calmed himself. "Anything else?"

Waldbaer resumed his deliberate walk toward the beer stand. "Not much, yet. We'll know a bit later today what caliber of weapon was employed to kill the Israeli. We will probably be able to figure out where the shot was fired from. I suspect, but cannot yet prove, that the killer kept his distance. Probably fired from fairly long range, using a four-power scope or something. I wouldn't be surprised if his firing position was inside a vehicle, maybe parked on the other side of the Nymphenburg canal."

"What makes you think that?"

They had arrived at the beer dispensary and Waldbaer placed his fleshy hands on the rough wooden counter, nodding at the bartender to pour him a draft. "I think that the killer takes a professional view of his craft. Firing from inside a vehicle, a van maybe, provides su-perb cover in a residential area. Remember all of the publicity about a sniper in Washington, D.C., years ago? He killed several people before detection. He fired from inside a vehicle. These people learn from one another, they study what works. As I say, those are my ini-tial thoughts."

A half liter of blond beer capped with an inch of foam was placed in front of him, a stream of white bubbles sliding down one side of the glass. Waldbaer smiled, placed three euro coins on the counter, and took a long sip. He was pleasantly aware that Streichner was ob-serving him through narrowed, disapproving eyes.

"So, Waldbaer, what next?" Streichner crossed his arms in what he intended to be a display of authority.

Waldbaer's eyes regarded the beer rather than the hauptkom-missar as he replied. "The forensics from the murder scene won't help much. We'll resolve this case through old-school investigatory

work. This murder was committed for a reason. I doubt it's coincidence that the victim played a role in the Forster investigation.
There is a link somewhere. I have to find it. With the help of an
Austrian colleague, for better or for worse." He lifted the glass once
more to his lips and heard again the calling of the eternally hungry
gulls circling over the lake nearby. His superior, he was pleased to
note, had been reduced to granitic silence.

CENTRAL INTELLIGENCE AGENCY HEADQUARTERS,
LANGLEY, NORTHERN VIRGINIA

The "green line" internal network phone on Robert Hirter's desk
emitted a subdued buzz. The telephone occupied the only part of the
cherrywood veneer desktop that was not obscured by stacks of an-
notated cables or finished intelligence reports. Hirter rolled his
wheeled office chair a degree closer to the desk and reached for the
receiver. "Proliferation section," he intoned automatically, "Robert
Hirter here."

The voice on the other end began with a stifled cough. "Mr.
Hirter, I'm glad I reached you. My name is Aaron Foote, over in Europe Division. I understand from a message on my screen that you've
developed a certain interest in the late Austrian politician, Georg
Forster. I thought maybe you could elaborate a bit on the nature of
your interest."

Hirter leaned back into the yielding contour of his chair and
studied the white ceiling tiles and stainless-steel water sprinkler
above his head. "Sure. Your info is correct, Mr. Foote, as far as it
goes. I put in a request for background information but with the
caveat that I'm serving as middleman for a query from the German
police. This isn't a formal liaison matter. This is more an informal
query from a German police detective who worked with the agency
a while ago on another episode. His name is Kommissar Waldbaer
and he's in charge of investigating Forster's death. It's not my call to
determine whether or not the agency can cooperate with him, but I
did want to advise Europe Division of the request and get things in
the proper channels. Over to you."

Foote laughed slightly. "We should talk face-to-face. And call me Aaron. Herr Forster and his activities are certainly not an unknown commodity over here. I can fill you in. As far as passing our stuff to a German police official, well, that will require further discussion. You know this detective personally?"

"I do," Hirter replied, "fairly well."

"Is he trustworthy? Willing to play by our rules if we find a way to provide him some, shall we say, privileged information?"

Hirter considered a moment before replying. "He's trustworthy and honorable. I can vouch for that personally. Willing to play by our rules? If our rules are sensible to him, sure, and if it doesn't compromise his sense of professionalism. He knows how to be discreet. But he's an informal contact, not a recruited agent. As I say, he dealt with us on an important case once before and things worked well, despite what was an unorthodox arrangement."

"Okay, that's fair enough," Foote said. "Listen, my day is completely owned by a liaison visit from the chief of the Czech external service today. Tomorrow looks pretty ruined too. But if you have time for a drink at the Vienna Inn after work tonight, I can at least outline the Forster story and the reason why the agency kept an eye on him."

Hirter found himself intrigued. "Great idea. The Vienna Inn is good, let's say around six. You can't miss me. I'll be the only guy wearing what my girlfriend describes as a truly hideous, purple-and-red Jerry Garcia tie."

"Sure couldn't ask for a better covert recognition signal."

BAKU, AZERBAIJAN

The interior of the vanquished airport on the outskirts of the capital city was draped with the austere and worn look of the Soviet era. Overhead lights provided severe illumination, as if the corridors and gates of the terminal were gigantic surgeries. The rows of glowing tubes emitted an ill-tempered hum, and some flickered in sporadic malfeasance, testimony to the prevailing indifference of maintenance. The once whitewashed walls and columns had faded to an unappetizing pastiche of sour vanilla and gray, betraying the accretions of dust, grit, and handprints. The air in the enclosed spaces held a trace of the rancid, the accumulated result of years of cheap tobacco, human sweat, and the perpetually garlic-laden meals of the airport employees.

Vestigial evidence of the frowning Soviet era were provided by the Azeri airport officials as well. Their uniforms had undergone a modest change of insignia, but the poorly tailored style remained much the same as in Cold War days, to include the oversized military-style saucer caps of the customs officers. Bored, poorly paid, and sullen, the customs officers wielded their Entry Approved stamps like weapons. The lines of arriving passengers were cast in the role of supplicants, hoping to appear sufficiently harmless and obsequious to pass through the stern official gauntlet. The queue lengthened as more passengers arrived, and the customs men studiously took their time dealing with the human cargo.

The businessman knew the routine well and would have none of it. Without a glance at his weary fellow travelers—it was two in the morning after all, the normal arrival time for all flights from Western Europe—he pushed to the head of the line, wordlessly elbowed a sunken-cheeked elderly woman out of the way, and placed his passport directly on the shelf of the customs booth. The black-mustached, narrow-eyed face behind the smudged glass glanced up at him suspiciously. "You must fill out visa application, other paperwork," the official grumbled in a guttural, broken English, fluent enough to communicate contempt.

The businessman replied in Russian, evenly but with an undertow of irritation. "You'll find everything you need inside the passport."

The customs officer let his glance slide down to the passport on the counter before him. "*Germanski,*" he said, his mouth hanging slightly open in a display of bad teeth.

The businessman nodded abruptly, impatiently. "Yes, clearly. German."

With a slight nod of the head, the customs man reached for a cup of black coffee at his side, took a slow sip, and stared at the passport, as if determining whether to open it. A moment later, his hand snaked slowly across the counter and retrieved the document for closer appraisal. Flipping open the burgundy document cover with a practiced motion, the official confronted a wedge of crisply folded euro notes. He glanced again with more interest at the man before him and drew the passport and its contents below the counter. He counted the bills rapidly. Five hundred euros.

"I presume that you find the paperwork quite in order?" the businessman inquired.

The official nodded quickly and just as quickly placed the visa into the passport. "Have a nice stay," he allowed.

"I doubt it," the businessman breathed, leaving the customs booth behind and heading for the waiting line of taxis outside.

The predawn air was raw and fresh and the businessman breathed in deeply to purge his system of hours of cloying, recycled air. Like a shark detecting minute, distant sounds, the man noted a slight trace of sea scent on the moderate breeze. The source, he knew, was the Caspian Sea fronting the capital city of Baku, his destination. The Caspian was less saline than the oceans, the visitor recalled, but was a saltwater body nonetheless. The businessman moved with his single piece of carry-on luggage toward the jumble of taxis, nodding curtly to the potbellied, balding driver of a nearby Fiat. The driver scrambled from his slouch at the side of the cab and reached for the teal-green textile pouch that his passenger held by its handles. The businessman waved him brusquely away.

"I'll hold onto this myself," he grumbled in Russian.

The driver nodded deferentially and opened the back door of the vehicle for his passenger.

"Take me to the Hyatt Regency," the visitor said. "I know where it is, so don't play games."

Moments later, the Fiat moved with a subdued purr along the

impressive broad new highway which carved an ebony slash through the rolling countryside from the airport to the center of Baku, several kilometers distant. Bright streetlamps illuminated the way. The highway had been built by oil revenue, the visitor knew, and was meant to facilitate more commerce for Azerbaijan. The thin diet of Soviet Communism had been eagerly pushed aside by the Azeri government; a voracious appetite for profit had taken its place. *Well, that's what it's all about, isn't it?* the visitor mused. *Turning a profit is the first imperative.*

Along the sides of the highway, more streetlights came into view and here and there their monotonous sameness was punctured by a neon sign advertising a hotel or restaurant. They were approaching the sprawling, modern outskirts that surrounded the ancient walled city that hugged the contour of the coast. Proletarian apartment complexes of poured concrete and no distinction passed by, silhouetted now by the suggested glow of an incipient dawn. The highway ended suddenly and the taxi crossed through an intersection with a blinking yellow light. The buildings were taller now, but most remained dark, the majority of Baku occupants still asleep.

Turning a corner, the taxi entered a tree-lined street and coasted up the parking apron of a rectangular building with a softly lit lobby. An illuminated sign identified it as the Hyatt, one of two in the city. The businessman paid his fare and provided a generous tip, grateful that the driver had not attempted to engage him in conversation. He clutched his piece of luggage, and quickly checked the lobby as he entered through automatic glass doors. There was only a young, overly cosmeticized woman at the check-in desk and a yawning, bow-tied porter leaning against one wall next to a large potted palm. The visitor relaxed a degree and moved to the check-in counter. If all went as it should, he would be flying out of the dreadful Baku airport at this time the next morning. In the meantime, he would permit himself a few hours of sleep followed by a cold shower to clear his head. He would then head to the rendezvous location near the old city, a place providing both physical security and anonymity. The man nodded to himself as he considered the plan. Security and anonymity were the two requirements for a transaction like his. Precisely because his activities were highly illegal, the businessman was intent on concealing them beneath the veneer of an everyday encounter. He could not prevent himself from smiling. If only the German authorities knew what he was up to, he would be occupying far less satisfying quarters than the Baku Hyatt.

Town of Vienna, Northern Virginia

The narrow interior of the Vienna Inn was boisterous and crowded with life, the normal condition of the establishment during late afternoon and early evening. Groups of men and women huddled around vinyl-topped tables in animated conversation, occupied with the culinary pleasures of chili dogs and plastic baskets of onion rings. The drinks selection was limited, and popular preference ran from white wine to India pale ale. A large television screen attached to one wall was tuned to a sports channel. A number of waitresses in polo shirts, generally young and attractive, navigated the floor, carrying short-order grill food from the kitchen.

Robert Hirter was seated at the bar, which formed the beating heart of the establishment. The bar occupied the center of the floor space, forming a large rectangle. Seemingly without pause, two tee-shirt-clad women behind the bar dispensed beer and soft drinks from an array of taps.

From his bar stool perch, Hirter surveyed the surroundings. The patronage of the Vienna Inn was truly egalitarian. He noted a clutch of lawn service Salvadorans in sweat-stained baseball caps and short-sleeved shirts laughing over a Spanish-language witticism, while a more restrained trio of men in silk ties and business suits traded stories nearby. He noticed a few faces vaguely familiar from the corridors of Langley, about four miles distant. The place was something of an agency watering hole. There were some retirees as well. Hirter recognized the lean frame and countenance of Mike Sears, a former CIA nonofficial cover officer who had left a successful agency career to become an equally successful leadership consultant. Although he would have fit seamlessly into the more sophisticated surrounds of the refined restaurants at nearby Tyson's Corner, Sears was a fixture at the Vienna Inn.

Hirter's attention moved to the door, where a tall man with receding curly hair had just entered from the parking lot. The man had his hands in the pockets of a blue blazer, and he studied the figures arrayed along the long bar. The newcomer's gaze halted at Hirter's brightly colored necktie.

"Hi, I'm Aaron Foote," the curly-haired man announced a moment later. "Your cravat description identifies you as Robert. I expect I'm a bit late, Beltway traffic on Route 123 was worse than I had figured. Let me get a drink and we can talk about the late, lamented Georg Forster."

Hirter signaled agreement and, following a necessary prelude of small talk, the conversation migrated to the deceased Austrian politician. Hirter ordered an Old Dominion ale.

"Aaron, you suggested on the phone that Europe Division kept a file on Forster. Is that just the normal stuff we would retain on any European politician of note? You know, biographical facts and such?"

Foote swirled the glass of white wine on the bar in front of him, and contemplated its shimmering depths. "Yes and no. Sure, we have a bio file on Forster, but there's more. You know something about Forster's politics?"

Hirter shrugged. "Not much. I know from television that he was a populist politician. Founded his own political party in Austria, I recall. It has an anti-immigrant platform, sort of rightist. Forster made controversial remarks on occasion, maybe to get publicity, not unknown for politicians."

Foote nodded and grinned, taking a modest sip of wine. "All true. Bravo, Robert. But we came up with more. Not all at once, mind you, but over time."

"Just gossip?"

Foote shook his head sideways. "No. Fairly solid information. Some of it from our friends in Austrian Intelligence. What they told us off the record was interesting enough for us to put discreet unilateral surveillance on Forster. We learned a few things. Enough, at any rate, to monitor Forster's movements actively. And his connections."

Hirter considered. "Okay. Are you able to say why Forster's activities were interesting from an intel perspective?"

"You mean to share with this German detective conducting the investigation? Well, we can permit you to pass along a few things, without revealing our sources, of course. I'll send you a tear line memo tomorrow, but I can give you a summary now. Georg Forster was not just a right-winger in the Austrian context, he had neo-Nazi sympathies and contacts. He played cards and socialized with some aging, unrepentant SS officers, and we acquired an audiotape of him in a ranting anti-Semitic private monologue with that crowd. The sort of thing he always publicly denied.

"That recording gave us clout to use against Forster, if we ever needed that. If we chose to release the tape through intermediaries, concealing the fact that CIA was involved in the chain of acquisition, it probably could have ended his political aspirations. People might be inclined to support someone mildly anti-Semitic, but it's a different matter to endorse a guy singing the praises of the Third Reich to a circle of former SS officers.

"We discovered something else through our surveillance. Forster had, shall we say, a fairly intense, unadvertised interest in very young men. Despite having a wife. And Forster's manner of finding male liaison was sordid. He spent an inordinate amount of time in select public men's rooms in Vienna. We have a photo or two which, if unedifying, are incontrovertible on this point."

Hirter took a draw from the glass of amber, malty ale. "So, the issue with Forster was his covert neo-Nazi associations, right?"

Aaron Foote pursed his lips, brow furrowed. "No, that's just background; it told us something about Forster's true political leanings. But, really, the Nazi stuff was an internal matter for Austrian politics. It didn't have much to do with U.S. security interests. We found out that there was more to Forster than National Socialist affections. This is where it gets interesting. Our surveillance team followed Forster on a number of his trips in Austria and Germany. Forster had a network of business connections that set off alarms in Langley. We weren't able to acquire all the details of what went on in these business meetings, but we do know what products these companies produce.

"Technologie Impex, GmbH, in Germany, produces sophisticated centrifuges our proliferation people judge to be dual use, sufficiently precise to be of utility to a nuclear program. Forster was a part owner and linked to another European firm, Verbindung Ost KG, in Vienna, which has ties to small companies in Moscow and Saint Petersburg run by former KGB officers. These firms, in turn, have been linked to illicit crew-manned weapons sales in the Middle East. In brief, Forster seemed to be up to his neck in financial deals that had little to do with Austrian politics. Deals our proliferation colleagues found troubling."

Hirter loosened his tie and unfastened the top button of his shirt. "Forster had dubious connections. Maybe making money privately for himself, maybe to fill the coffers of the party he founded. Were these associations illegal, Aaron?"

Foote splayed his hands flat on the bar, surrounding his wine glass. "What we don't know, Robert, outweighs what we know. We don't have a smoking gun on any illegal activity that he was engaged in. But Forster was involved with several companies that produced dual-use items or had a record of clandestinely selling weapons to rogue states. And that's not all.

"Forster set up front offices in Austria for some of these firms. Forster knew Austrian law and business. He set up shell companies in Vienna and Innsbruck to facilitate international transactions by tainted firms. This permitted new, unsullied companies with western addresses to cover some Russian-based activities. Which facilitated playing fast and loose with end-user certificates for shipments to and from the Middle East. In short, Forster was helping dirty firms conduct their business with unsavory clients." Foote paused and took a sip of wine, savoring it.

Hirter nodded. "And for all of these helpful activities, Forster was presumably compensated by his content, criminally inclined clients."

"Just so, Robert. Very well compensated, we expect. But the story doesn't end there. We think Forster's travel as a politician provided him cover to serve as a sort of salesman in countries he visited. We've assembled a list of Forster's travel destinations over the last few years. It makes interesting reading for the suspicious minded.

"Forster visited China in a well-publicized trip to try to open markets there for legitimate Austrian products. What is not generally known is that Forster quietly made a side trip from Beijing to Pyongyang, North Korea. We suspect he was facilitating a deal to provide European-produced high-tech items for the North Korean nuclear weapons program. Forster was pretty active internationally. We know he traveled to Syria, Iran, and Venezuela, among other destinations."

Hirter twisted the ale glass in his hands and nodded. "I get it, Aaron. Forster was no pillar of altruism. I'm sure whatever you can approve for passage to Kommissar Waldbaer will be appreciated by him. But there's another question we haven't addressed. In view of his activities, do we know whether anyone was out to kill Forster? Seems like he ran in circles where that sort of thing could happen."

Foote glanced around the room to ensure that no one seemed to be following their conversation. Satisfied, he pulled a degree closer to Hirter and lowered his voice. "Fair point, Robert. Forster accumulated some enemies. We're sure the South Korean Intelligence Service was monitoring him; they were worried about his Pyongyang connections. Separately, we were in touch with a source who claimed Forster had pissed off a Ukrainian crime syndicate by moving in on their turf, whatever that means. The Ukrainians can be a nasty bunch. But this is just an allegation from an untested source who offered no proof."

Hirter took a small sip of pale ale and wiped his lip before speaking. "Interesting. Anything else?"

Foote's eyes followed the passing form of a lithe ponytailed waitress and he spread his hands on the bar and studied them. "One other thing. We've collected technical intercepts indicating Mossad had an active interest in Forster. Remember, he was accused of anti-Semitic leanings and was dealing with Syria and other countries in the Middle East. That sort of profile would put Forster on Israel's blacklist, I expect. But I haven't seen anything to suggest they would go so far as killing him. That would be risky business. Murdering an Austrian politician in the heart of Europe is rather different than dropping a missile in the lap of some Hamas guy in the Gaza Strip. Forster's party is making that claim, I know, but you can't prove that by any information CIA has developed. Anyway, anything I've said you can give to your German police friend, on an informal basis of course."

"It sure gives him something," Hirter replied. "Look, Aaron, here's what I propose. I'll call Waldbaer and tell him to expect the passage of some authorized information. I presume you can free up one of our officers in Germany to courier a written memo to him in Bavaria?"

Foote smiled with a flash of even teeth. "We could do that. But why not serve as the courier yourself? I can get you Europe Division clearance. You know this kommissar personally. That puts you in a better position to dialogue with him, and we aren't forced to expose one of our officers. You're probably going to tell me you have too much going on to travel to Germany. But, hell, you can be there and back within three days."

Hirter regarded Foote with a careful gaze. "You know, maybe that's not a bad idea. I have to square it with my proliferation superiors, but I don't think a brief absence will upset them. So, that's a tentative yes, pending authorization." Hirter admitted to himself that he felt pleased with the prospect of a few days back in pleasant Bavarian surroundings.

Foote loosed a small laugh. "Okay. Europe Division will cover your travel costs, just to make this easy. But there's a price."

"Which might be?"

"Make the information flow a two-way street. Pass along what I've told you to the police detective. But pump him for information too. If Forster was murdered for political reasons, that's something Europe Division would like to know. Especially if the German authorities are inclined to keep the information secret to avoid an international dustup."

Outside of the Vienna Inn, the sky was turning an angry gray-black, and the air was heavy with moisture, heralding a thunderstorm that would drench the countryside and its inhabitants, without repelling the humidity even a single percent.

BAKU, AZERBAIJAN

The Azeri morning arrived yellow and hazy over the broad Caspian Sea as a moderate breeze crossed the water and passed into the ancient city. The wind forced away the stale air along narrow streets of faded ochre buildings, and held at bay the pungent urban accretions of diesel exhaust, spoiling fruit, and decaying sewer pipes. The sun was a vague, spectral presence only, concealed behind obscuring layers of haze.

The German businessman exited the taxi, addressing the driver in Russian and advising him to return in exactly ninety minutes. He felt a first drop of rain against his forehead as he turned and made his way up crumbling concrete steps to the Persian restaurant. The establishment occupied a small hillock overlooking the sea on one side and the solid, venerable walls of Baku fortress on the other. He frowned as more drops of rain struck lightly at his face and a raw wind picked up. The restaurant location was not his idea, but that of his contact.

The German's proposal for a meeting at the Hyatt had been declined. "Better to put some distance between where you're staying and where we converse," the contact had said. Probably prudent in view of what they were up to, despite the disagreeable weather and the cheating taxi drivers.

A thin, bearded Iranian waiter in a buttoned, tieless white shirt opened the smoked-glass door as the German approached. The waiter, with an earnest, long olive face and a meadow of black hair combed brutally back, bowed slightly and placed a hand over his chest, signaling welcome. Insincere little shit, the businessman thought, saying nothing. His eyes scanned the dark interior of the establishment until he detected a flash of movement. Barely illuminated by the dim lamps, a stubby hand was raised in the air, beckoning. The businessman did not gesture in response but made his way to the table, the Iranian waiter trailing in his wake.

"Hello, Jahanghir," the German intoned in Russian.

The large, seated shape that was Jahanghir smiled and hissed agreeably through a picket fence of teeth, some of them glittering with gold. Jahanghir Karimov was large boned and overweight, his rambling bulk stretching the fabric of a beige suit. A broad face took in the German visitor, with heavy-lidded eyes that were almost Asian. A trimmed salt-and-pepper goatee contributed to an overall exotic effect. The Azeri's head was closely shaved and bullet shaped.

"A hearty welcome to Baku, Herr Tretschmer," Jahanghir said, signaling the waiter with a shake of the head to leave them alone. The Iranian bowed and disappeared into the shadows of the restaurant. "You look well. Your trip, I presume, was uneventful?"

"Yes," Otto Tretschmer replied absent emotion, "just the way I like it. A quiet trip without anyone paying me attention. And a quick trip as well. By the way, I leave here on the two a.m. flight to Frankfurt, which means my stay will be just over twenty-four hours. A short stay shouldn't attract notice." It was true, of course, and Tretschmer knew it was also what Jahanghir wanted to establish, that was the real intent of the seemingly innocuous question.

The Azeri shifted his bulk in his chair, oblivious to its protesting squeak. Fatty hands folded on the tabletop before him, he regarded the German through hooded eyes before speaking. "A short stay is all that is required. We can conclude our business over some quite passable Persian food. There is a fine, spiced lamb dish I will point out to you."

"All right. But let's talk about the important details before we get the waiter back here, shall we? I want to make absolutely sure we're both working toward the same understanding."

Jahanghir shrugged, studying the oversized rings on his fingers. "As you wish, Herr Tretschmer. Let's get to the most important point. I've brought the sample with me, as you requested. It's here, in the bag by my side, for you to take with you. I took the liberty of enclosing it within a ceramic souvenir of a Baku mosque, to avoid any problem with customs officials. That probably eases your mind."

Tretschmer nodded and murmured approvingly. "Very good, Jahanghir. That's what I was hoping to hear. As for customs officials, I know how to deal with the ones here, and I've never been subjected to a search upon arrival in Germany. I've done my part for you as well. Your payment will reach you via a *hawala* money transfer, using *hawaladars* here and in Kuwait. All I need to do is make an innocuous cell phone call when we're done. One quarter of the funds immediately available after I leave here with the sample, and the rest to flow the same route once my people confirm the quality of the sample. I believe that is the arrangement we agreed to previously?"

Jahanghir unfolded his hands and spread his thick fingers on the tabletop. He was wearing four large rings; two on each hand. "Of course, my friend! We trust each other. That's the arrangement, and it's a good one, simple and safe. We'll discuss the details, but first let's refresh ourselves." The Azeri signaled for the Iranian waiter, who immediately appeared from the shadows. The waiter bowed and asked Jahanghir something in Farsi. The Azeri answered at some length in the same tongue, pointing occasionally to the vinyl-bound menu proffered by the Iranian. As the Azeri gestured, Tretschmer noted the butt of a pistol and a shoulder holster under Jahanghir's jacket. The waiter rapidly penciled a few notations on a pad of yellow paper and withdrew, bowing again in a display of deference.

"I have taken the liberty of ordering for both of us. A local red wine and the roasted lamb specialty. You will enjoy it, trust Jahanghir on this."

"Absolutely." Employing the words "trust" and "Jahanghir" in

the same sentence was not, however, something that he would ever
seriously entertain.

GAMSDORF, BAVARIA

The plangent, echoing clang of church bells in the distance announced that it was six in the morning, the beginning of another
working day for farmers, bakers, and the parents of schoolchildren
who were even now being roused from their sleep under protest. The
orb of the sun had worked its way above the sharp peak of the
Hirschgipfel, or Elk Summit, to the east, suffusing the pastoral countryside with a delicate gauze of yellow.

Waldbaer had been up for an hour, had showered, and, combed-
back hair still damp, was dressed for the day in a well-worn loden
trachten jacket of hunter green. The jacket, he noted with mild con-
sternation, buttoned more tightly than it had a few years ago. The
deep, bass notes of the bell continued to spill from the steeple in the
village center, echoing across the expanse of the valley, disappearing
finally into the dark forests of pine that embraced Gamsdorf on all
sides.

Standing in the small tangle of garden behind his stucco home,
Waldbaer sipped coffee from a gray ceramic mug that had belonged
to his father, watching thin wisps of steam rise and vanish into the
brisk alpine air like departing souls. Waldbaer felt dampness insinu-
ate its way into his shoes; the dewy grass of the lawn was long and
needed mowing, a task he seldom found time to perform. After a
final, fading peal, the church bells fell silent.

Waldbaer recalled that he had seen the massive bronze forms of
the two bells close-up, long ago, as a teenager. The original bells that
had served the church for over a century had been confiscated by
the Reich during the war and melted down for munitions. Replacing them had been expensive, especially for a rural Bavarian village
in the hardscrabble days after World War II. Years of parishioner do-
nations had finally resulted in the purchase of substitute bells from
Innsbruck, Austria. There had been a festive parish celebration, and

Waldbaer, young, lanky, and vigorous, assisted the men of the village in hoisting the bells with heavy ropes to their place in the steeple of Saint Andreas. He wondered again at the fascinating phenomenon of time, that relentless, dispassionate force that changed all things. He sighed into his coffee mug, wondering where that lanky, vigorous youth had gone.

The investigation bothered him. It was a frustrating puzzle; there were a number of pieces on the table, but they refused to fit together. Taking another sip of coffee, Waldbaer laid the pieces out in his mind. First Georg Forster. Indisputably dead, but murdered? Not clear. Another piece of the puzzle: Forster was without doubt being followed by an Israeli Intelligence officer at the time of his death, certainly ominous, but not *necessarily* lethal in intent. Yet an additional piece: Kirscheim, the Israeli who admitted to tailing Forster, was now himself dead. Murdered in broad daylight with a single rifle shot. By whom? That piece of the puzzle was missing, too. And where was the motive for either death? Missing as well.

Two men dead within a short period. Linked together by surveillance. Forster the observed and Kirscheim the observer, both of them travelers that rainy night on the road to Garmisch. Waldbaer narrowed his eyes and rubbed his creased forehead. Linked deaths, that was the key point. He was a skeptic when it came to the notion of coincidence.

Waldbaer was startled from his contemplation by a tinny musical tone emanating from his jacket pocket. Wondering what a call at this early hour presaged, he pulled a sleek Siemens cell phone from his pocket and flipped it open. Coffee cup in one hand and phone in the other, Waldbaer grumbled his name into the receiver, hoping not to hear in reply the irate voice of the loathsome Hauptkommissar Streichner.

"Kommissar Waldbaer, hello and *servus*, Robert Hirter here. Hope I didn't wake you."

Waldbaer smiled to himself, relieved. "Not at all, Hirter. A dutiful policeman needs to rise before the wicked awake. It provides us an advantage over the machinations of the malevolent. But speaking of time, it must be midnight in Virginia. What prompts you to call at such an hour? Insomnia?"

"No, Kommissar, just some fast-breaking developments. Are you still interested in the Forster case? If you are, I might have some interesting details for you."

"*Wunderbar*, Hirter. I was just thinking about the Forster matter. Feasting on more information is precisely what I need to sate my hunger at the moment. How do you propose that we work this?"

Hirter gave a subdued laugh. "I propose a moveable feast. I'll bring you the information I've assembled, in person, day after tomorrow. My people have authorized my travel. You can decide what you want to tell your police higher-ups."

"At the moment, I needn't report a damn thing," Waldbaer said. "Let's regard this as a friendly, informal visit and see what you can deliver and we'll move from there. Day after tomorrow, you say? That would be the direct flight from Dulles arriving in Munich early morning. I'll book you a room in Gamsdorf for a few nights. I presume I can use your true name?"

Hirter laughed again. "Simple will do. True name is fine. I'll reserve a car at Munich Airport and drive to Gamsdorf; I remember the route to your office."

Waldbaer considered a moment. "No, that won't do. It's too prosaic a start for your trip to Bavaria, Hirter. The weather is projected to be good the entire week. So, we'll meet in the beer garden of the Alpenblick, I expect you recall that past venue."

"Consider it done, Kommissar."

"One more thing you should know about before you arrive, Hirter." The detective described the Kirscheim episode to the espionage officer.

"And something else, Hirter, before I forget. I am forced by necessity to partner with a representative of the Austrian police. Here is what you must decide. Are you willing to share the information intended for me with a third party? And are you willing to reveal youself to an Austrian kommissarin? From Innsbruck, named Kommissarin Reiner?"

Waldbaer shrugged in resignation, the fabric of his rustic jacket gathering at his shoulders. "Not my choice. A political necessity given that Forster was a prominent Austrian who died on German territory. What do you CIA people call these collaborations—a joint operation?"

There was a pause on the line as Hirter considered. "That complicates things a bit. I didn't know this investigation involved the Austrian police. Headquarters hasn't cleared this information for them. If you think she's discreet and can keep a secret, I can request she be cleared. It can be done quickly on my end, since this is an informal exchange."

Waldbaer sighed into the receiver, the sound conveying resignation. "Clear her, Hirter. I'll make sure our charming policewoman from Tyrol follows the rules."

Arrangements made, the conversation moved to inquiries about Washington weather and American politics. The dialogue concluded, Waldbaer slipped the phone back into his pocket and finished his now lukewarm coffee in one prodigious, satisfying gulp. His spirits had lifted, reflecting both Hirter's good news and the steady rising of the sun, with the resultant explosion of colors as the alpine valley illuminated spectacularly, like a pastoral scene in an endless stained-glass window.

CENTRAL INTELLIGENCE AGENCY HEADQUARTERS,
LANGLEY, NORTHERN VIRGINIA

Caroline O'Kendell walked with purpose past the CIA souvenir store near the cafeteria, the heels of her Italian shoes resonating along the gray tiled corridor and her shoulder-length dark-auburn hair shimmering with each step. Without breaking pace, she glanced for a moment at the wares displayed in the shop. White ceramic coffee cups emblazoned with the CIA logo, tee shirts featuring the U-2 high-altitude spy plane, agency baseball caps, sweats, and even cuff links. She smiled to herself; blatant self-advertisement seemed peculiar for an espionage organization that valued secrecy.

Seconds later, Caroline turned a corner, walked past the credit union office, and headed to a bank of four stainless-steel elevators. A handful of other CIA employees were waiting as well. Caroline buttoned the jacket of her charcoal-gray business suit, glanced at her wristwatch, and mentally ran through the points she wanted to make in the meeting scheduled to start in four minutes. After a short breath of time a soft tone rang out, the doors to an elevator opened, and Caroline and three men entered. Caroline placed a manicured finger on the button for the sixth floor. As the elevator ascended, she considered again Robert's most recent remarks. *See what the Israel Desk might offer. Explain the authorization we have to participate in the Forster investigation and bring up the Israeli diplomat murdered in Munich, something they must know about. Might be a useful conversation.*

With a breath of sibilance, the metal doors of the elevator opened at the sixth floor and Caroline stepped out. She turned left, knowing where the Israel section was located. Moments later she stood in front of a locked vault door and pressed a buzzer for entry. A metallic click signaled that the door had been opened from inside and Caroline strode in. The vault was large, the space divided with mathematic precision into a series of shoulder-high earth-tone cubicles. Colored topographical maps of Israel and the West Bank were taped here and there, and Caroline noted a high-resolution satellite photograph of what appeared to be a military installation. She could make out a blue-and-white Israeli flag draped across the hood of a truck.

A head popped above a cubicle at Caroline's side. "Can I help you?" a middle-age woman with a mass of henna red hair inquired.

"Hi. I'm looking for Saul Morgenstern. He's expecting me."

The woman nodded and lifted a cardigan-clad arm above the cubicle, pointing. "You're in the right place. Saul's office is at the back of the vault, straight ahead." The woman disappeared again behind the wall of her office fortress.

Caroline followed the directions and in a few seconds found herself at the threshold of a windowless office, the door open. She rapped her hand lightly on the door, and the man seated at the desk within raised a head of thinning hair. The face below the vanishing hairline was long and thin, the countenance interrupted by wire-frame glasses and a thin brown mustache. The rest of Saul Morgenstern was clothed in a navy blue suit that seemed too generous of cut for his spare frame. Caroline introduced herself and entered the office, where Morgenstern gestured for her to take a chair in front of his desk.

"Caroline, what can I do for you? Does this have to do with terrorism? Because if it does, I'll have to ask one of our Hamas or Hezbollah specialists to join us. They know more about the bad guys than I do."

Caroline shook her head twice from side to side and smiled slightly. "No, Saul," she replied, indulging the CIA penchant for routinely dealing in first names with colleagues, "this isn't a terrorism inquiry. It's about Israeli Intelligence, Mossad specifically. We're looking at the recent shooting death of an Israeli diplomat, allegedly Mossad, in Munich."

Saul leaned back in his chair. "Uh-huh. I'm aware of that incident. I have to ask, are you interested in information for internal agency use or passage to foreign liaison?"

Caroline considered and nodded. "That's your call. It's your information, so we'll play it your way. Optimally, it would be great if we could share whatever you have with the German police, or more precisely, with a trusted contact in the German police who understands how we do business. And with a single associate of his from across the border in Tyrol. But if your preference is to keep this within agency circles, we can do that too."

Saul removed his glasses, closed his eyes, and rubbed at his nose. "Okay, Caroline. Our equities with Mossad are always a sensitive topic, and I'm reluctant to go higher and ask for authority to pass memos to the Germans, or to any foreign service for that matter. So, let's avoid that. I'll tell you what we know—and what we believe—about the Kirscheim killing, for your background information. If your people want to orally transmit that information in a general form to your German contact, I can live with it. But no official memo, no mention of sourcing, and no acknowledgment of attribution to CIA. Fair enough?"

Caroline leaned forward in her chair and offered a full burst of her radiant smile. "More than fair, Saul."

"All right then." Morgenstern pulled himself back to his desk and placed sharp elbows on its veneered surface, hovering over the piece of furniture like a bird of prey protecting its nest. "Let me tell you a story, Caroline."

BAKU, AZERBAIJAN

The cold drizzle had not abated as daylight ebbed and the jumbled streets of the city fell by degree into darkness. Streetlamps flickered on at the appointed minute, but much of the city remained untouched by artificial illumination. The last dinner customers of the evening, an elderly but prosperous Azeri couple, had departed the Persian restaurant an hour ago. Soon thereafter, the cook and a dishwasher left together in animated conversation, using the front door, which was the only point of entry and egress.

Jahanghir waited with controlled impatience inside his Mercedes, parked on the street several yards away from the place where he had dined several hours before. He had selected a parking place on a slight hill, providing an unimpeded view of the restaurant. Snippets of movement and spots of light behind the windows told him that someone still remained inside. Jahanghir reached into his suit pocket, extracted a breath mint, popped it into his mouth, and waited. He had time.

Minutes later the interior lamps of the restaurant went out and Jahanghir stepped carefully from his vehicle, shutting the door quietly without locking it. As expected, there were no passersby on the street at this late hour. Jahanghir moved slowly and with deliberation into a strip of fully dark, unclaimed and weedy space between the restaurant and an empty storefront building, a picture window of which hosted a placard marked, in Azeri, COMMERCIAL PROPERTY TO LEASE.

From his concealed position in this patch of urban detritus, he continued to survey the restaurant's front door. He detected a sound before he spotted motion; the heavy door of the restaurant being opened, swinging in on rusty hinges, and closing again with a resounding thud. This was followed by the unmistakable tinkle of keys and a metallic exclamation as a lock was engaged. Now, in the dim ambient light, Jahanghir made out the shape of the man he had been waiting for. He opened his mouth and hissed in wordless satisfaction, still tasting the stinging freshness of the breath mint.

The Iranian waiter was always the last to leave the restaurant. The successful proprietor seldom visited, leaving it to lesser beings to see to the boring routine of gastronomy. The waiter tugged once on the door to ensure its security and, satisfied, brushed both hands through his hair, and turned to the concrete stairs leading to the sidewalk. He pulled his dark wool coat around his spare frame against the chill, and bowed his head a degree to keep raindrops from his eyes. His second-floor apartment was fifteen minutes distant by foot, and he headed away from the sea, toward the familiar, looming urban structures in the distance. His route took him directly past the weedy lot where his former luncheon guest was now standing, unobserved. As he walked, the Iranian waiter considered again that it was time to find more rewarding and lucrative employment, the restaurant was a dead end to all but its owner.

Jahanghir smiled as the waiter approached along the sidewalk, mere feet away. Perfect. Carefully and without a sound, not even the slight creak of Russian leather, Jahanghir lifted the automatic pistol from the shoulder holster under his jacket. He felt the weapon's familiar heft. With two hands wrapped in a tight embrace around the wooden butt for maximum stability, he aimed the barrel and its attached silencer at the approaching shape. At such close quarters, he knew that he did not need to fire at center of mass but could go for the cranium. He lined up the weapon with the approaching Iran-

ian's head, now just three feet away. At the precise instant when the
waiter's head intersected the line of fire from the barrel, Jahanghir
pulled back slowly on the sensitive trigger and let his wrist absorb the
recoil as a nine-millimeter Parabellum round punched into the target's temple, burrowing deep into the pulsing brain. Oblivious to the
end, the waiter pitched wordlessly backward, arms thrown wide, and
slid to the sidewalk.

Jahanghir replaced the pistol in its retainer without hurry and
surveyed the street again to ensure that no one else was in sight. He
stepped over to the waiter's body and assessed the scene. Dead. Even
in the very limited light, he detected white, open eyes, and noted
with satisfaction a spreading puddle of blood around the head. The
modest entrance wound was obscured by the prevailing darkness,
but Jahanghir could well make out the massive exit trauma. No need
to loiter, he counseled himself and moved purposefully to his parked
Mercedes. Climbing in, he placed the keys in the illuminated ignition, disengaged the emergency brake, and coasted down the hill
several yards before turning on the headlights.

He was satisfied with his evening's exertions. Something about
the waiter's demeanor had set an alarm bell to ringing in his head
during the luncheon. The man seemed too observant, too present,
always hovering in the shadows. Was he reporting to someone? To
the Azeri Internal Service? Or to the Iranian Pasdaran, perhaps? Did
the waiter know something of Jahanghir's activities with the German? Of course, it could all have been entirely innocent, his suspicions unfounded.

Jahanghir was aware that he might have killed someone who
represented no threat at all. He shrugged, turning the steering wheel
and rounding an intersection surmounted by a huge statue of a
woman throwing off shackles, the symbolic act captured in stone.
Well, he had to go with his instincts, something that had kept him
alive in a sadly uncertain world. If the Iranian waiter was innocent,
so what? After all, people died every day. But if the waiter was an informer, that danger had now been forever eliminated. And the stakes
at hand demanded that he take no chances. Jahanghir released a

long breath through a row of teeth heavy with gold and relaxed in the plush comfort of the heated leather driver's seat.

FRANKFURT AIRPORT, GERMANY

As he had anticipated, there were no difficulties with the *Zollpolizei*; German customs. He had simply walked down the broad aisle marked NOTHING TO DECLARE and regarded the uniformed customs officer with a bored, imperious glance. Without further ceremony, he strolled through the automatic doors that led out of the arrivals security area and into the bustling labyrinth of a terminal lined with magazine stores, souvenir concessions, and coffee shops. Otto Tretschmer was entirely self-confident, and was convinced that this attitude communicated itself to others, to his enduring advantage.

Now safely back on German soil, Tretschmer had only to catch the next train to Hamburg and proceed as planned. Things were moving as they should. He smiled and adjusted the knot of his Italian silk paisley tie. He had acquired precisely what he wanted, and without complications. Unappetizing as it was dealing with the repellant Jahanghir, Tretschmer was a realistic man of commerce. He was reconciled to dealing with an entire demimonde of his social inferiors; this was simply the price of business on the edge, where risks were considerable but potential profits enormous. His suitcase with its concealed cargo secured with a firm grip, Tretschmer took the escalator from the teeming airport arrival terminal to the train station located below ground.

Safely delivered to the underground station, he stepped from the escalator and consulted the overhead timetable for the next express Deutsche Bahn train to Hamburg. It would arrive in twenty-seven minutes and, this being Germany, would undoubtedly be on time. There were only a handful of other passengers lining the track. He found an isolated spot to stand, and considered what remained to be done. First, he would secure in a safe place the item Jahanghir had provided him in Baku. That done, he would get in touch with that other dreadful but necessary contact, Horst Zellmann, who, it was to be hoped, would be sober. They needed to determine when the *Con-*

dor Fury would be ready to sail, once the consignment had reached Hamburg. And then, of course, there was the status of the consignment itself to check on. At least, Tretschmer's partner for that aspect of the transaction was someone civilized. Ensuring that the special goods were in functional condition was the cornerstone of the entire venture.

Some minutes later, two intensive headlamps appeared like miniature suns in the center of the pitch-black tunnel to Trestchmer's left, accompanied by an increasingly insistent rush of wind and the protesting whine of several sets of brakes. The businessman watched the sleek red-and-white aerodynamic form of the ICE train slide by, its progress slowing by degree, until it moved at magisterial pace before coming to rest. Tretschmer glanced along the long, spotless caravan of wagons until he found the one with a numeral denoting first class. He stepped inside, noting the art deco interior, and smiling in anticipation of his arrival in the distant hanseatic port city, bringing him a step closer to the immense profits to be realized by trafficking in illicit and deadly commerce.

INNSBRUCK, TYROL, AUSTRIA

Frau Sabine Reiner most assuredly did not intend to subordinate herself to the "I'm in charge" conceit of Kommissar Franz Waldbaer. It was so typically and infuriatingly German, she thought, Waldbaer's unquestioning assumption that he was the lead investigator and everyone else was predestined by the natural order to play a supporting role. This self-focused Teutonic propensity was, she reasoned, no doubt strengthened when the other party involved was Austrian, not to mention an Austrian female. She considered further, lining up additional negative Germanic traits like prisoners before a firing squad. Germans had an annoying tendency to patronize their co-ethnicists across the border, regarding their Austrian cousins as charming but a touch dull-witted, pleasant but unimaginative, well-meaning but inept. In German eyes, the endearingly rusticated Austrians were all apple strudel and edelweiss. Well, she concluded, not with Sabine Reiner, and not with the Forster investigation. She had already pushed back at her Bavarian counterpart's disposition to be in control, and it was time to assert herself again.

Waldbaer had been operating independently the last few days and had politely fobbed her off, on the specious grounds that the Kirscheim murder was a purely German affair and one he could not, "unfortunately," as he put it, actively share with the Austrian authorities. Of course, Waldbaer had asserted with unctuous and annoying solicitude, he would subsequently share any information that seemed even marginally relevant to the Forster matter. There was little she could do about the kommissar's gentle intransigence, not directly. But, two could play that game and she intended to move ahead in Innsbruck on her own steam.

Which was why she now found herself sitting in an unmarked police Audi on a quiet and unremarkable side street of that city. Unremarkable except for the fact that she had discreetly followed Anton Hessler to this location twenty minutes previously. It was, at least, something she could accomplish without the presence of the gruff Bavarian. A bit of surveillance locally to see what sort of contacts Hessler enjoyed. This was her third occasion following Hessler over the past two days. His first venture from his mountainside dwelling had been utterly ordinary, a trip to a Billa supermarket and on to an exclusive wine store, followed by a brief stop at a Bank Austria branch office. Hessler's second excursion the day before had been equally banal, a journey to the Innsbruck office of the NDF on Theresienstrasse, where he had remained for two hours, departing with a sheaf of party propaganda material under one arm.

Today, her anonymity aided by drizzle and a thin gauze of fog, Sabine had parked in Mutters early in the morning, a half kilometer from Hessler's apartment, and waited to see if his burgundy Jaguar sedan would leave the underground garage of his residency. She had not been disappointed. Oblivious to her discreet attentions, Hessler had barreled at top speed through the village of Mutters and traveled down the curving mountain road to Innsbruck. More precisely, he had traveled to birch-lined Kresslerstrasse where he had parked along the street and entered a nondescript office identified with a bronze plaque as T&K IMPEX GMBH. What have we here, Sabine wondered.

She opened the leather handbag on the passenger seat beside her, extracted a thin black notepad, and jotted down the address and name of the firm, along with the time Hessler had entered its premises. She would check public records on the company in the commercial register back at the police *zentrale*. Still, the company name revealed something already. "Impex" was business shorthand for import-export, identifying the firm as one that moved goods of some sort to and from Austria. "GmbH" stood for *Gesellschaft mit beschraenkter Haftung*; a limited liability company in English. Perhaps Hessler had a commercial stake in the firm.

As she replaced the notepad in her bag, Hessler's lanky form exited the office building. Returning to his car, the NDF politician removed the jacket of his tailored, unvented olive suit and tossed it on the passenger seat. He checked his hair in the rearview mirror, teasing at it with both hands until satisfied with its effect. Hessler revved his Jaguar for a moment, executed a U-turn, and headed back in the direction of Mutters. Sabine engaged the transmission and followed at a distance, long enough to satisfy herself that her target was returning home. The visit to the import-export company might mean nothing more than that the well-heeled Hessler was pursuing mundane business interests; he was, after all, a wealthy man. Or perhaps there was more of interest to be discerned, something to help clarify the death of Forster. She most assuredly intended to find out.

NEAR GAMSDORF, BAVARIA

Driving the rented black Opel sedan at eighty miles an hour along the broad ribbon of the A8 autobahn from Munich toward Gamsdorf reminded Robert Hirter of his first excursion to Bavaria in the aftermath of the murder of his brother, Charles. That surprising, violent episode had also led to Robert's first encounter with the detective in charge of the investigation, the flinty and occasionally ill-tempered Kommissar Franz Waldbaer. Despite some initial friction, Hirter had, with time, come to appreciate Waldbaer's consid-

erable virtues. The detective was, above all, passionate in his investigatory duties. He had a voracious appetite for justice, for the crime
solved, for the malefactor exposed and brought to ground. Waldbaer
regarded crime as an affront to the natural order, and violent trans-
gressions offended his vision of a civilized, serene world shaped by a
reasoning humanity.

They had discussed these things quietly one evening, Hirter recalled, as they strolled through the English Garden in Munich, its
winding footpaths, groves, and meadows carpeted with autumn
leaves of burnished gold and fading yellow. Uncharacteristically,
Waldbaer had been in a mood to hold forth, and had issued a sort of
personal *Weltanschauung*. It had impressed Hirter sufficiently that he
retained a sharp recollection of the detective's soliloquy. "Our species
was born into a state of nature long ago, Hirter, so long ago that even
dim primordial memories of that epoch no longer remain. Since
then, we've moved to a point where we have imposed our presence,
and our will, on the world. We accomplished that with our minds
more than with our sinew. Our achievements carry us forward like
waves toward a distant shore. There are peaks and troughs in our
voyage, periods of discovery and of decadence, but we are impelled
forward. We've formed tribes, societies, civilizations. All of these
communal institutions, though, are fragile vessels. Their existence
depends on civility, and its twin, tolerance. Those citadels are under
constant assault from their polar opposites, rapacity and self-interest.
Disorder, crime, and murder represent a return to our primitive state,
and they threaten all progress and every finer thing devised by man.
Opposing the authors of chaos is, I expect, sufficiently important to
merit our time." Hirter recalled that he had wanted to ask Waldbaer,
Toward what distant shore are we impelled? And what awaits? But, for
whatever reason, he had remained mute.

Hirter's reveries were interrupted by the sudden appearance of a
red Porsche that seemed centimeters behind him, flashing its headlights impatiently. Hirter had forgotten that most of the German autobahn had no speed limit. With a tug at the wheel, he pulled the
Opel into a slower lane and the Porsche tore past in a flash of rap-

idly disappearing color against the asphalt highway. Hirter checked the digital clock on the dashboard. Nearly noon. His appointment with Waldbaer at the Alpenblick was in thirty minutes.

Hirter glanced at the attaché case on the passenger seat. It contained a concealed pocket, within which was secreted the CIA file on Georg Forster, cleared for passage to Waldbaer. The thin dossier with its clipped writing style was the reason for Hirter's travel to Bavaria. Hirter was familiar with the contents, and anticipated with a smile that the rumpled kommissar of police would find them of considerable interest as well. A large blue sign at the edge of the autobahn announced that the exit for Gamsdorf was two thousand meters away.

Above the sweeping expanse of tall pines on both sides of the highway, Hirter could see the distant necklace of the Alps, the peaks white with a dusting of snow. He felt happy to be back here. And excited that he and Waldbaer seemed, once again, to be probing at secrets concealed, at activities covertly underway, perhaps threatening the civil and orderly world that the kommissar so prized.

HAMBURG, NORTHERN GERMANY

Otto Tretschmer was content, his temperament undampened by the relentless downpour visible through his villa window. Had he been feline, he might have purred. Safe and comfortable within the spacious embrace of his late nineteenth-century Wilhelmine brick home in the exclusive Eppendorf section of the city, he considered the sequence of events that required his attention. Seated at the antique, claw-footed oak desk that dominated his library, he grasped a thick, black Mont Blanc pen to put words to paper in a rolling scrawl. The notations were intended for himself only, a device he employed to organize his thoughts.

Sample proven authentic, need to acquire more, he wrote. Tretschmer paused a moment, set his jaw, and considered. His well-paid technical specialist had just this morning confirmed that Jahanghir, whatever his other personal flaws, had been as good as his word. This represented a considerable success. It remained now to organize for the delivery of larger amounts of the substance, and Tretschmer was certain that this could be arranged. He nodded to himself and again moved his pen against the paper.

Equipment stowed on board in sealed containers, he scratched in black ink. Zellmann, captain of the *Condor Fury*, had confirmed the secure status of the cargo in a terse, cryptic phone booth call the previous evening.

Perfunctory customs check completed. Zellmann again. He had suborned some venal harbor official to ensure that the cargo would not be subject to any intrusive check by the *Zollamt* upon the ship's departure from Hamburg harbor. The sealed containers were marked as "oil drilling equipment" on the bill of lading, and the freight had not been opened.

International wire transfer successfully accomplished. Jahanghir had been paid for services rendered to date. The considerable funds provided by Tretschmer's client had made their way in a series of small amount transactions to Jahanghir's Baku account via a series of intermediary banks including Guernsey in the Channel Islands, and an ask-no-questions financial institution in Cyprus. This procedure ensured that the payments did not come to the attention of "due diligence" government organizations monitoring suspicious funding transfers.

Tretschmer placed the pen on the desk with a precise motion, arched his eyebrows, and gazed out the window at the display of turbulent North German weather. What else? Ah, yes. He retrieved the writing implement and applied it again to the stationery.

Next step: Contact client to make detailed delivery arrangements. It remained for him to provide an update to the end user. This needed to be accomplished with care. The customer had made it clear that security and discretion were critical considerations. The precise details of getting the shipment into the client's hands needed to be established. Tretschmer knew that this meant arranging a personal meeting with the customer's representative. The rendezvous would take place outside of Hamburg to provide another layer of security and mask to the extent possible any connection between the client and a maritime shipment originating in Hamburg. Turning his gaze again to the driven rain beyond his comfortable nest of a study, Tretschmer frowned. He would need to venture out into the angry gale and make an international call from a phone booth. No sense delaying, he counseled himself, the meeting should be arranged as soon as prudently possible. He felt a renewed surge of energy at the prospect of moving the transaction toward completion. He crossed the parquet flooring of the room with a bounce in his step and lifted the Burberry trench from an antique bronze coat stand.

Gamsdorf, Bavaria

Robert Hirter swung the rented Opel into the gravel parking lot at the side of the Alpenblick restaurant and turned off the ignition. The beer garden where he was to meet Kommissar Waldbaer stretched out directly behind the three-hundred-year-old establishment. Walking toward his destination, attaché case in hand, Hirter could make out the murmur of conversation and clinking of glass.

A moment later he stood at the edge of the beer garden and surveyed the scene. Hirter could not restrain a fleeting smile as he took in the typically Bavarian tableau. It looked, he thought, like a Carl Spitzweg painting from the 1880s. The scene was framed by broad chestnut tree branches, thick clusters of deep green leaves providing a tapestry of shaded relief from the robust noonday sun. Rude wood tables braced by long benches were placed throughout the garden, occupied by small clusters of customers in animated conversation, many of the men wearing worn lederhosen and a number of the women in traditional dirndl. Hirter detected the accented sound of rural Bavarian dialect. A waitress stepped from the back door of the Alpenblick clutching six mugs of beer, three in each hand. She dispensed these to thirsty visitors as she made her voyage around the tables. The final glass of lager was placed before a familiar figure in a rumpled jacket. Hirter smiled again, having spotted Kommissar Franz Waldbaer in his natural surroundings.

The kommissar of police lifted the krug of foam-capped golden beer from the table in front of him and indulged a long swallow. His features were sharp but the face lined and furrowed. Waldbaer's broad frame was garbed in a navy blue linen trachten jacket with horn buttons, the lapels and sleeves overlaid with forest green. As was often the case, Waldbaer's countenance displayed a look of mild annoyance with the world, or mankind, or both.

"*Gruess Gott*," Hirter intoned as he neared his host.

The kommissar slipped free of his silent discontent and raised a hand in greeting. "*Gruess Gott*, Herr Hirter," he replied, signaling for Hirter to take a seat on the bench directly opposite him.

"Good to see you again, Kommissar. Especially in such pleasant surroundings. I remember this place from my last visit. And that beer looks attractive to someone who just flew across the Atlantic and then drove here from Munich Airport."

Waldbaer nodded. "I'll get you a beer, Hirter, I wouldn't want you to dehydrate. They serve Schoenram beer, very fine, from a small brewery not far from here. You might be interested to know that the *braumeister* is a conational of yours, an American who learned the craft in Bavaria and decided to stay. We'll have something to eat, too. The specialty today is roast pork with onions and a *knoedel*, potato dumpling. I recommend it."

Hirter placed his hands flat on the table. "Sounds perfect. How could anyone turn down the invariably light and healthy fare of Bavaria?"

"Joke if you must, Hirter. We have no sushi bar in Gamsdorf, let me assure you. At any rate, the meal will provide us the energy we need to examine the death of the lamented Austrian politician Georg Forster."

Hirter provided a quizzical look. "Lamented by whom?"

"Well you might ask, Hirter. Forster certainly had a following; just look how well he did in the last Austrian elections. Still, he was not universally loved, being a man of extremes. The Israelis, to name one party, were not among his admirers. Which brings us to the Kirscheim killing in Munich, and how that seems somehow connected to Forster. We will be discussing these things, you and I, and it's my hope that you can provide additional pieces of the puzzle."

A waitress passed by with a tray of oversized buttered pretzels and Hirter ordered a half liter of beer.

"Kommissar, I brought along privileged information, cleared for passage. You can do what you want with it, as long as you don't attribute it to CIA. How useful it is, we'll have to see."

Waldbaer was about to reply when the tinny Mozart *Kleine Nachtmusik* tone of his cell phone intruded. With a grumble, Waldbaer plucked the device from a deep pocket of his jacket. "Waldbaer," he said, then listened silently, his eyes narrowing, his features settling into a mask of dissatisfaction.

"Frau Reiner, always a pleasure to hear your voice," he said without conviction. The detective paused, taking in strings of words from the other end. "Yes, we will get together, as I said earlier. But we're not at the police station. We're having lunch in the garden of the Alpenblick nearby. Just ask anyone in Gamsdorf for directions." Waldbaer shifted his narrow gaze to Hirter. "It will be a pleasure to introduce my colleague. I expect you'll be here in about half an hour. *Servus.*"

With a low sigh, Waldbaer deposited the phone back into his pocket. He studied the table for a moment and lifted his beer glass for a short sip. "That was Kommissarin Reiner, the police official from Innsbruck. I told her the other day that an American colleague would be joining us. She's on her way."

Hirter nodded, turning his glass of blond lager slowly in his hands. "Right. She's cleared for passage as long she understands CIA's role is unofficial and we'll deny involvement if word gets out."

Waldbaer pursed his lips and nodded. "I expect it will be a functional arrangement. As I mentioned, I have little choice in the matter. I'm sure I can keep her under control."

It was Hirter's turn to take a swallow of beer, his eyes not leaving Waldbaer's. "That's fine, Kommissar. I'm happy to see you with the lead in this case. What Frau Reiner's view of that is doesn't interest me. The fact is, I'm mainly here to work with you. That hasn't changed."

Waldbaer nodded assent. "Fine. I'll take care of things. But let's talk about the information you've brought to share."

Hirter raised his glass. "*Wunderbar*. All right, Kommissar, let me give you what I have. We'll discuss it with Frau Reiner when she arrives."

The two figures huddled closer together across the rude beer garden table, their postures conspiratortial, in the ancient manner in which men have traded secrets for centuries.

Sabine Reiner arrived at the back terrace of the Alpenblick a half liter of beer later. She quickly located Waldbaer in the shade of a chestnut tree and she assumed that the dark-haired, younger man seated across from him was the American.

"*Gruess Gott*," she offered with a slight smile, approaching the table.

Both men rose in a traditional display of courtesy, and each took her hand. Waldbaer beckoned for her to sit next to him. "Frau Reiner, permit me to introduce Robert Hirter, who flew in this morning from the United States."

She turned her head in a questioning gesture. "All the way from America? You must be tired."

Hirter gave his head a single up-down shake. "From Washington D.C., to be precise. The jet lag will hit me this evening, I expect, but I'm fine so far."

"Herr Hirter is a representative of the United States government, but is here informally," Waldbaer interjected. "He has an interest in the Forster case and might be able to provide us assistance. I can attest to his discretion. We've worked together before. I wanted to introduce him to you, Frau Reiner, as soon as he arrived."

Frau Reiner continued to smile slightly, if in a more brittle manner. "It's a pleasure to meet you, Herr Hirter, but I must express some surprise. Forgive me, but I don't quite understand your role in what is a German-Austrian investigation, I'm afraid. Are U.S. interests involved?"

Waldbaer began to reply, but Hirter interrupted with the wave of a hand. "I'm sure it seems a bit odd, Kommissarin," Hirter said, striving to employ his most disarming tone. "The fact is, frankly, it's not yet clear whether or not U.S. interests are involved. I'm interested in establishing what might be behind the Forster and Kirscheim incidents, that's the reason for my unofficial status. Let me add that I'm not here to be a complicating element for either you or the kommissar."

Frau Reiner folded her hands on the table and set her pale blue eyes directly on Hirter. "Thank you for that explanation, Herr Hirter, but permit me to say that I still feel rather uninformed. What part of the U.S. government did you say you represent? Are you from the legal attaché's office in the embassy in Berlin?"

Hirter unintentionally dropped the mask of a smile from his visage. "I didn't specify my affiliation. I'm not from the attaché's office. I'm from the Central Intelligence Agency."

Frau Reiner widened her eyes. "A spy?"

"An intelligence officer is the preferred argot of the trade, Kommissarin."

Waldbaer grumbled an assent and addressed his Austrian counterpart. "I'm sure we can work together. At any rate, as long as we're in Germany, I'm the lead authority, and I invited Herr Hirter here. Frau Reiner, you are at liberty to keep our guest from participating in investigative matters on Austrian soil, that's your call. But I suggest we allow joint collegiality to rule." He flashed a manufactured smile at Frau Reiner, which she returned with equal insincerity.

"Well, gentlemen," she replied, "I'm sure we can accommodate one another. As for your rather mysterious appearance, Herr Hirter, I only hope it contributes something to what has been a frustrating investigation, as I'm sure Kommissar Waldbaer has advised you. And I see no need to disinvite you to Austria, if our attentions turn again in that direction."

Waldbaer slapped a hand to the table. "Good. Said with typical Austrian charm." He knew that the feigned accolade would be a mild annoyance to the sensitive female detective and was pleased to see that her features were momentarily distressed. Wise to keep her a bit off balance, he counseled himself happily.

"Glad that's settled," Hirter said. "What do we discuss next?"

"The new information you've brought with you, Hirter, and where it might take us."

Hirter nodded. "Kommissarin Reiner, I can't provide you the sources for this, please understand, but let me give you a sense of the information CIA has developed about Forster." Hirter lifted the attaché case from the bench and placed it on the table next to his beer mug. Opening it with an audible click, he extracted some sheets of paper, consulting them. "Herr Forster was involved in significant commercial ventures before his death. These dealings might not have been strictly illegal, but he was, at the very least, involved with dubious undertakings. Forster was in contact with individuals who are considerably dirty. Most of these characters reside outside of Austria."

"What individuals?" Reiner inquired.

"Business types from the former Soviet bloc and Syria with a track record of illicit international activity like exporting proscribed goods to the Middle East, that sort of thing. I have some names that I'll share in written form."

Waldbaer joined the conversation. "The salient point is that up to now we've looked at a political motive for Forster's death—the Israeli angle. We need to consider an additional possibility—an illicit business transaction gone bad, with people not reluctant to employ violence."

Reiner drummed her nails on the tabletop. "So, Kommissar, you're saying we need to expand our investigation."

"Quite right."

Hirter spoke. "This is where I can be of assistance. Our intelligence community expends considerable resources tracking illegal international commerce. I might be able to pursue some leads and provide facts Germany or Austria don't unilaterally possess."

A mischievous smile returned to Reiner's features. "My, my, Herr Hirter, I hope you aren't talking about gathering information through illegal means, such as intercepting communications without a court order, but I suppose that's your matter. This talk about unsavory business people is interesting, but unless we have specifics— something that will stand up in a court—I'm not sure how far it takes us toward solving Forster's death."

Waldbaer took another sip of warming beer. "All in good time,

Frau Reiner. We at least now have additional pieces of the puzzle laid out before us. What else do you have, Hirter?"

The American ran a finger down the sheet of paper in his hand. "Well, Forster had curious travel patterns. He was underway a lot to the United Arab Emirates. We know he traveled to Amman, Jordan, and met there with a Syrian who is associated with that country's weapons procurement program. He also flew to Moscow several times in the last two years. None of these trips were publicized, even though Forster was a relentless self-publicizer. Closer to home, Forster was often in Vienna, which makes political sense, of course, but he had commercial meetings there as well."

"Has your organization turned up information that these trips involved illegality?" Reiner inquired. "Traveling to the Emirates or Russia is hardly a crime under Austrian law, Herr Hirter."

"No. Nothing illegal. But some of Forster's connections and behavior were suspicious. At least from an intelligence point of view. Let me find substantive examples." Hirter shuffled through the papers in the attaché case and silently read through a piece of paper. "Okay. Here's something you can retain. You might want to read it yourself." He handed the English-language document to Waldbaer, who ensured that Reiner could read it along with him. The Bavarian detective held the paper at arm's length and narrowed his eyes, wanting to avoid the small humiliation of reaching for his reading glasses, his flawed vision another unwelcome signal of incremental corporeal decline. The written words came into focus.

Georg Forster visited the Vienna offices of the firm Verbindung Ost KG on several occasions over the last two years. Verbindung Ost is registered as a Russian-owned company established in Moscow in 2007. Its owners, according to public documents, are Bogden Karniev and Sergei Ershov, former colonels in the Soviet KGB. Karniev and Ershov were active in the Middle East during their tenure as intelligence officers. Following the collapse of the Soviet Union, both

men partnered in commercial arrangements to provide excess AK-47s, RPGs, and other small arms and munitions
from Russian military stocks to a variety of Middle Eastern
contacts. Apparently, based on these initial successes, the
men founded Verbindung Ost in Moscow. Subsequently, a
second office was rented in Vienna, Austria.

The Vienna branch of Verbindung Ost would seem to
serve several purposes, in the analytical judgment of this
agency. First, it provides a reputable Western European address for a firm owned by former Russian intelligence officers
with a background of suspicious commercial activity. Second, given Austrian neutrality, Verbindung Ost is not subject
to the scrutiny it might be in other European locations.
Third, Vienna's central location and relatively lax travel visa
requirements make the Verbindung Ost office a convenient
and discreet meeting place for clients wanting anonymity.

Verbindung Ost activities are not transparent. Registered
as an enterprise to attract venture capital, the firm keeps a
low profile and is not active in Austrian commercial circles.
Based on information from our sources, we believe Verbindung Ost is primarily used to identify Western firms and individuals willing to provide technological products to clients
for whom such purchases are proscribed by national export
laws, such as the German H List. Verbindung Ost has hosted
dubious businessmen from Germany, Belgium, Switzerland
and Austria, and the office has connected them to customers
from Syria, Iran, Azerbaijan, and select African nations.

Waldbaer placed the piece of paper on the table and turned to
his Austrian partner. "Do you follow this?"

Reiner regarded the kommissar with a fixed smile, as delicate as
porcelain. "Just as well as you do, I'm sure. Why do you ask?"

Waldbaer shrugged and let his eyes roam the beer garden scene
around them. "Because some of this commercial stuff is rather eso-

teric for me. I presumed the same might hold true for you, Frau Reiner, but perhaps you are better schooled in such things. I do know the H list identifies what countries are prohibited from receiving specific products manufactured in Germany. For example, we won't export Leopard tanks to Turkey, out of concern that they might be used against the Kurdish minority. That sort of thing. Still, I confess unfamiliarity with commerce, not to mention the vagaries of Austrian export law."

Reiner's voice tinkled out a brief laugh. "I expect that Austrian export laws are in fact no vaguer than the German ones, Kommissar."

From across the table, Hirter watched the interplay between the two Europeans with a touch of unease and decided it might be wise to intervene. "I know something about international export, and the methods utilized to circumvent regulations. I can probably answer questions you might have, or get clarification from my colleagues."

Waldbaer and Reiner nodded in unison, grateful for the offer.

Frau Reiner reached over and with pinched fingertips took the document from the table, where it had been dampened by a spot of spilled beer. "Gentlemen, there is clearly much more of interest here and in the other items that Herr Hirter has so graciously brought with him. I have new information as well, regarding Forster's successor, Herr Anton Hessler. But might I suggest that we continue our discussions in a more private environment? Perhaps the kommissar's office. I appreciate that beer gardens are a central pillar of Bavarian culture, but we might leave their undoubted charms for another time."

Waldbaer's mouth turned down in an incipient frown and his face took on a degree more color. "Of course, Frau Reiner, as you wish. I was simply playing proper host for Herr Hirter's arrival. A beer garden, after all, is without pretension and seemed to me a suitable place for the three of us to get acquainted. But then, it perhaps lacks the civilized touch preferred by Austrian officialdom." He offered a predatory smile. "We head to my office. After my roasted pork arrives, of course."

Hirter considered that his time in Europe might not be, as initially anticipated, a happily uninterrupted episode of serene harmony.

CENTRAL INTELLIGENCE AGENCY HEADQUARTERS,
LANGLEY, NORTHERN VIRGINIA

A small and nearly luminescent lime-green square of paper with an adhesive back was fixed to Caroline O'Kendell's blank computer screen, ensuring that it would command her attention as the first item of her work day. She deposited her bag and cardboard cup of coffee on her desk and read the brief missive.

Caroline—Call me when you get in.—Saul Morgenstern

Standing beside her desk, she inhaled a quick sip of vanilla-scented coffee and punched four digits into the secure phone, wondering what her contact at the Israel Desk had to impart. The receiver at her ear transmitted two rings and then a reedy voice.

"Saul here."

"Good morning, Saul. Caroline. Got your note; what's up?"

There was a brief smoker's cough on the other end. "Carolyn, glad you called. I picked up some info last night that relates to your inquiry about that dead Austrian politician, Forster. Here's how it goes: Our station chief in Tel Aviv was engaged in a talk with Mossad about Syrian activities. Standard liaison stuff. But one of the Israelis mentioned Mossad has for some time been tracking a Syrian businessman from Aleppo named Sayed al-Khalid. The Israelis think al-Khalid is up to his neck in proliferation activity, specifically, trying to acquire nuclear technology items."

Caroline interrupted. "Trying to acquire nuclear technology for Syria, Saul?"

"That isn't clear. Maybe for the Syrian government, maybe for another unknown client. The Israelis don't have sufficient information to assess whether al-Khalid is working for his regime or whether he's a freelance, strictly-for-profit dealer. Anyway, the reason this might be of interest to you and your friends in Germany is that al-

Khalid met a number of times with this guy Forster. Mostly in Amman, Jordan, at the Hyatt, but also twice in Vienna. Al-Khalid has an apartment in Amman and resides there on and off, but the meetings were in the Hyatt, probably for anonymity. Mossad is convinced Forster was working a proliferation deal with al-Khalid, probably right up to the time of Forster's death. One of the Israelis allowed that proliferation was Mossad's real concern with Forster, not his anti-Semitic politics in Austria."

"That's interesting," Caroline replied, making a notation.

"Something else. Mossad was surveilling Forster all right, to try to establish who Forster was working with. In fact, the Israeli who was chatting with our chief of station admitted they were tailing Forster the night he died because Mossad believed Forster was on his way to meet someone in Germany associated with the nuclear technology deal. They wanted to clandestinely photograph the meeting and ID whoever Forster met. The Mossad surveillant saw Forster's car crash on some mountain road in Bavaria and got the hell out of there for the obvious reasons."

Caroline seized the pause in Morgenstern's monologue. "Which means Mossad didn't run Forster off of the road, or otherwise kill him."

"Right. They wanted him alive, to connect the dots and get a picture of Forster's procurement network."

Caroline paused for a moment. "Of course, Saul, this might be what the Israelis want us to believe, right? Wouldn't be the first time."

"Right again, Caroline. Mossad is out to protect Israeli national interests, period. If that means lying to CIA, they'll do it in a heartbeat. But in this case, I think they're telling the truth. Their narrative makes sense."

Caroline rested her lithe frame against the desk and brushed a strand of hair from her eyes. "Does Mossad know CIA is interested in Forster and is working with the German police?"

"They didn't give any hint of it. Forster just came up on the margins of their Syrian discussions."

Caroline glanced out her long, narrow window and watched a tractor trailer pull up to the crate-laden loading dock below. "That's good, Saul. I don't want to have to get the Israelis involved in this, too. Dealing with the Germans is sensitive enough; we don't need a three-ring circus. By the way, did the Israelis say anything to the station chief about the murder of their officer in Munich?"

Caroline heard Saul snicker.

"I was wondering when you'd get around to that. Mossad is convinced their officer was killed due to his involvement in the Forster investigation. In fact, the murder effectively stopped their investigation. First, the main target, Forster, is killed and then the on-site Mossad officer. That's pretty much the end of the story, especially given German police involvement and their suspicions about the Israelis."

"Saul, this is valuable. I'll ask our officer in Bavaria to focus on Forster's business contacts with an eye on nuclear technology. One question though, about al-Khalid. It sounds like he would have to know at least part of the story about Forster's dealings. Any way we can exploit that?"

Saul hacked out a cough again, longer this time. "Get in touch with the Jordan Desk. They have solid relations with the Jordanian intel services, civilian and military. Maybe the Jordanians can be of assistance."

"I owe you a coffee, Saul."

"Cappuccino. Large."

Caroline rang off, straightened her azure business jacket and watched two workers unload cardboard cartons from the docked truck two stories below. She mused that at CIA headquarters, such a delivery could contain anything from disposable coffee cups to encrypted communications devices. She glanced at her wristwatch. Nine a.m., which meant it was now three in the afternoon in Germany. A perfect time to pass the latest information to Robert. And to explore whether Jordanian intelligence might be able to clarify the dealings of Forster's commercial contact, al-Khalid. Perhaps that was something she could accomplish herself. She decided to stroll over to the corridor housing the Near East Division of the Clandestine Service, and pay a visit to the chief of the Jordan Desk.

BERLIN, GERMANY

Berlin, Tretschmer thought, his features assuming a look of mild distaste as he contemplated his current geographical location. Tretschmer had always considered the German capital city of Berlin with its gritty working-class quarters and acres of gray concrete apartment blocks to be a much less elegant metropolitan city than Hamburg, that prosperous, unabashedly haughty center of Hanseatic commerce on the banks of the Elbe. To be sure, with its four million inhabitants, Berlin was twice the size of Hamburg. But in Trestchmer's view, Berlin's scale was irrelevant—the city lacked flair, whereas his home residence of Hamburg enjoyed a distinctive atmosphere as the country's premier port, the "Gate to the World" as it was called. Hamburg was replete with an international array of boutiques, hotels with pedigree, restaurants with Michelin stars, and imposingly aristocratic dwellings along the well-tended shores of Alster Lake.

But, alas, he found himself unavoidably in Berlin. Tretschmer gazed through heavy-lidded blue eyes around the noble lobby of the Hotel Adlon and tipped a porcelain cup of espresso to his lips, savoring its robust, invigorating taste. The Adlon, he conceded, was something even a refined Hamburg resident had to respect. Located on Unter den Linden, steps away from the Brandenburg Gate, that eighteenth-century calling card of martial, imperial Prussia, the hotel was indisputably world class and wore its status with understated grace. There was nothing ostentatious about the Adlon, unlike the extravagantly garish five-star hotels in the Middle East. It was a redeeming oasis of refinement in the midst of proletarian urbanization.

A bow-tied waiter with a receding hairline passed by, and Tretschmer signaled him for another espresso. Tretschmer consulted his pearl-faced Rolex for the time. His contact should be arriving any minute. At least this contact, unlike the coarse maritime captain

Zellmann, was a man of cultivation. Just then, a voice addressed him from behind, its tone friendly and bordering on unctuous.

"Herr Tretschmer, it's always a distinct pleasure to meet you."

The Hamburg businessman turned and looked up at the tall, lean, and attentively attired figure of Anton Hessler. The Austrian had chosen to wear a jet-black, double-breasted blazer, its austere color offset by a bright pink shirt with white tab collar, and an intensely colored yellow tie. Hessler's hair was impeccably cut, every strand in place.

Tretschmer stood and shook hands. "Welcome to Berlin, Herr Hessler. I trust your flight from Innsbruck was uneventful. We haven't seen each other in months, as I recall."

The Austrian politician offered a sardonic smile. "Indeed, Herr Tretschmer. Lamentable, to be sure, but prudent, given the sensitive nature of our joint enterprise."

"Exactly," Tretschmer replied. "Best to be discreet. God knows, there are enough prying eyes to be wary of these days." He motioned for the other man to take a seat opposite him. "I doubt our little rendezvous will be noticed."

Hessler sat ramrod straight in the plush lobby chair, adjusted his onyx cufflinks, and straightened his cravat. "We should be unnoticed. I took the train from Innsbruck to Munich and then flew out of Franz Josef Strauss Airport there. Just a precaution, but it should enhance our anonymity. I fly back to Munich in a few hours and should be back in Innsbruck this evening. I doubt anyone will notice such a brief absence."

A waiter appeared with Tretschmer's espresso and Hessler ordered a mineral water.

Tretschmer opened the attaché case that he had brought with him from Hamburg. "Fine. In the interest of keeping our chat brief, we can get right down to business." He flashed an artificial smile at his guest that was returned in kind. "Let me provide an update. The cargo ship is getting ready to depart. Everything's covered. We've suborned a harbor official to ensure we don't run into inspection difficulties. The captain knows the drill, of course. The cargo is now safely on board. It's manifested as oil drilling equipment, a sufficient cover. And something else. I acquired that special substance and had it tested, as we discussed earlier." Tretschmer paused for effect.

Hessler leaned forward. "And?"

"It's legitimate. The real thing. Success again."

Hessler sat back again in his chair, folding his hands in his lap. "So it would seem. Thanks to the well-connected Jahanghir, I presume."

Tretschmer nodded agreement. "Just so. He does have entrée into the, shall we say, arcane circles we require. Now that we've established the material is what we need, Jahanghir has been instructed to acquire it in volume."

"Perfect," Hessler allowed. "Of course, the rest of the substance in the required amount will have to be delivered in a follow-on shipment. Our client understands the precautions we have to take."

The waiter made another noiseless appearance and deposited Hessler's bottle of mineral water and a small glass before gliding off again across the lobby.

Hessler steepled his long fingers. "Well, Herr Tretschmer, I will report these positive developments straightaway to our client. I also need to provide word as to how soon we might expect the *Condor Fury* to depart Hamburg. What do you suggest I advise?"

Tretschmer glanced upward for a moment at the ornate ceiling of the Adlon. "A fair question. We all want to get that ship underway in international waters as soon as possible. I'm certain we're talking about a few days. Let me get in touch with our good captain when I return to Hamburg and get back to you with a firm date. I need to see him in person anyway, to tie up final details. Is that sufficient?"

Hessler smiled and looked Tretschemer in the eyes. "Quite satisfactory. But please do hurry. We need to get this resolved very soon."

Tretschmer nodded. "Of course. I'm taking the express train back to Hamburg right after we conclude here. I'll call you tomorrow with the ship's departure date."

"Splendid, Herr Tretschmer. I don't need to tell you the sooner we deliver the cargo to its destination, the sooner we realize our profit. One other thing. Don't call my cell phone or the number at party headquarters. It's best at this stage if you ring me up via Skype, it's hard to trace."

It was Tretschmer's turn to smile. "Of course," he replied, placing the card into his wallet. But his mind was already elsewhere, contemplating the imminent prospect of a major addition to his bank account in Zurich.

GAMSDORF, BAVARIA

Waldbaer's ascetic office in the basement of city hall was windowless, illuminated by a plain Ikea floor lamp in one corner, and, on the heavy ball-footed desk, a small, antique lamp consisting of a bronze Mercury holding a lightbulb aloft, its exuberant glow largely tamed by a salmon-tinted lampshade. The object had belonged to his mother. At home in this chamber of light and shadow, the kommissar had provided his two guests with police station coffee in Styrofoam cups, something Robert Hirter happily accepted, but which had caused Frau Reiner to offer a wan smile, suggesting vague disapproval at the quaint ways of provincial Bavarian law enforcement.

Waldbaer, standing behind his desk, registered the implied rebuke from the woman seated on the cracked leather couch next to Hirter. He was annoyed that the modest courtesies he could offer the Austrian kommissarin seemed always to be judged inadequate. Frau Reiner had found the Alpenblick beer garden meal déclassé, and the workaday coffee cups proletarian. Well, he thought, let the Innsbruck police waste its budget on dainty porcelain cups and saucers. He had more consequential things to deal with. Not the least of which were the unresolved deaths of Forster and Kirscheim. Matters to which he now intended to redirect Frau Reiner's attention.

"I received a call yesterday afternoon from the chief medical examiner from the pathology lab in Munich. Forster's corpse was transferred there because our local morgue has limited capabilities and this is a high-profile case. With the examiner's permission, I recorded the call, which you will now hear." Waldbaer pressed a button on his desk phone. A moment later a voice emerged from the speaker.

"Here's what we have, Kommissar," the disembodied voice began, "and it's the best we can do. Forster had certainly been drinking in the hours before his death, no question. The blood tests make that incontrovertible. Normally, that would suffice for us to conclude that intoxication while driving was the cause of the crash. But, given that the deceased is Georg Forster, I ordered further tests. And found something else. We checked Forster's residual urine and picked up the presence of gamma-hydroxybutyrate, or GHB. It's in the written report, Kommissar, you don't need to memorize that. Anyway, GHB is odorless, colorless, and mixes well with alcohol. It's a strong sedative and increases the effect of alcohol and slows metabolism. Someone ingesting it unawares might notice a salty taste. But we also found that Forster had eaten a large pretzel not long before his death and perhaps that made the saltiness of his drink unremarkable, if the GHB was placed in his alcoholic beverage in tablet form. At any rate, we estimate Forster had about seven grams of GHB in his system, enough to ensure death, especially at the wheel of a car. Now, I have to tell you, GHB is a biological precursor to the neurotransmitter gamma-aminobutyric acid, or GABA, and the human body naturally produces both GHB and GABA. This makes detecting foul play difficult, especially in a corpse. GHB is naturally excreted in the urine. Still, our tests revealed seven grams of GHB, as I said. That's a lot by any measure. In my professional view, Forster was murdered by GHB mixed in his drinks. That will be the conclusion of my written report."

Waldbaer clicked off the speaker, rested his hands on the desktop, and addressed his visitors. "The operative word is murder. Now let's consider exactly where we are."

"Well," Frau Reiner responded, "the autopsy establishes that Forster was purposely killed. But who is the killer? That has to be our focus now. The Israelis, members of Forster's political party, business associates, all of them are logical suspects."

Waldbaer issued a primordial grunt of approval. "The business angle intrigues me. Especially following the information that Herr Hirter has provided." The detective nodded toward his American guest. "It seems we now have a better sense of Forster's activities aside from his efforts running the Nationalist Front. If Hirter's intelligence colleagues are correct, Forster was engaged in suspicious activities with dubious individuals and commercial firms. Verbindung Ost, for example."

Frau Reiner opened her leather bag and extracted a pen and pad of paper. "Verbindung Ost has an office in Vienna, according to Herr Hirter's friends in Langley. I'll see if I can come up with further information through our own police channels or the Chamber of Commerce."

"Good idea," Hirter said, folding his hands in front of him. "Being closer to the scene, you might get details that CIA doesn't have."

Waldbaer signaled agreement. "I have a feeling that Forster's commercial activity, not his politics, is the key to his death. If we can develop a picture of Forster's business connections and ventures, I think we'll be on to something important."

Frau Reiner looked at the kommissar and arched her eyebrows skeptically. "Perhaps you are right, Kommissar, but I have doubts. How would business enterprises, however dubious, account for the murder of the Israeli, Kirscheim? Not to mention Israeli surveillance of Forster? These things suggest a political motive."

Waldbaer stood and paced the floor slowly and rubbed a hand against his chin. "Do they? One thing stands out, Frau Reiner, at least for me. The Mossad agent Kirscheim was murdered. For reasons unknown, as the investigation currently stands. I have a bit of new information on that. Our forensics lab has established that Kirscheim was killed by a single round fired from a Dragunov, which is a Russian-manufactured sniper rifle. There are Chinese copies, but our people are satisfied that this particular weapon is of Russian origin. Anyway, it makes no sense to think the Israelis murdered their own representative. If the Israelis had some sort of internal problem with Kirscheim, they simply would have recalled him to Tel Aviv and dealt with the problem there, quietly. And although we've established that Kirscheim had Forster under observation, there is no shred of evidence to indicate this was tied to Forster's death. All of which, taken together, says to me there is nothing to suggest a political motive to Forster's death, which should encourage us to look with great detail at the commercial dimension. Even the partial information we have is sufficient to establish that Forster was in touch with some bad characters."

"Kommissar, I think you're right," Hirter said from his place on the couch. "Speaking as a case officer, I can tell you that there is a hell of a big difference between placing a subject under surveillance and killing him. It's true Mossad has conducted targeted killings on occasion. But those actions are few and far between, and the victims are almost always terrorists who have killed Israelis, like the Black September personnel for the Munich Olympic massacre. Frankly, I can't imagine Forster would be judged sufficiently dangerous to Israeli interests to merit assassination. He was an annoyance, maybe an anti-Semitic rabble-rouser, but that would hardly suffice to put him on a hit list. Doesn't make sense. Recall what my colleagues at CIA noted: Mossad believes Forster was involved in proliferation matters and also believes Kirscheim was killed because he was discovered investigating these matters. I agree that the commercial dimension is the key to all of this."

Frau Reiner shook her head slowly sideways and tapped her ballpoint pen lightly against the coffee table in front of her. "I'm not convinced. If Mossad was concerned about Forster's alleged proliferation activities, wouldn't that provide sufficient motive for them to kill him? Don't forget, surveillance is against the law in European countries, and the Israelis were willing to engage in that criminal act."

Hirter fixed the Austrian with a broad smile. "Kommissarin Reiner, intelligence services violate the law all the time, it's the air they breathe. It's the reason they are formed by governments; to perform extrajudicial acts that can be officially denied. But again, I don't see any reason that would impel the Israelis to kill Forster. Sure, Mossad was interested in his proliferation connections. But the service was trying to figure out what was going on. The last thing they would want to do, at such a stage, would be to kill one of the players in their investigation. I can assure you as an intelligence operator, Mossad would focus on connecting the dots, on trying to build a picture of a proliferation network, if one existed. They would use link analysis to chart the moving parts in such a network. Killing Forster doesn't fit."

"Perhaps you are correct, Mr. Hirter," Frau Reiner conceded. "I acknowledge that assassinating an Austrian politician, regardless of how unappetizing he might have been, would risk a huge international incident for Israeli interests."

Waldbaer stretched and registered concern at the sound of his elbows issuing a brittle snapping sound. What causes that? he worried to himself. "Well, where does this leave us? We need to establish our course of action. I suggest that all three of us focus on the same goal and not go running around examining separate pieces of this incident. Let's establish what commercial ventures Forster was involved in. And his political successor."

"Anton Hessler," Frau Reiner added.

"Precisely," Waldbaer agreed. "Let's dig as deeply as we can into Forster and Hessler's commercial interests. We already have initial information."

"That's fine," Hirter said, rising from his seat. "We have three countries represented here: Germany, Austria, and the United States working in combination, we should be able to gather quite a bit of information. Let's get to work and assemble again in three days with what we turn up."

"Agreed," Frau Reiner replied, standing as well and placing her bag over her shoulder. "By the way, regarding Hessler, I have something for you both. Three days ago I tracked him visiting a firm in Innsbruck named T&K Impex, GmbH. It's an import-export company. Maybe you can turn up something on it and Hessler's interest in it."

Waldbaer smiled. Perhaps things were finally falling into place. He had the feeling of forward motion, of an investigation making measured progress. He hoped that the pace was sufficient to prevent further violence.

CENTRAL INTELLIGENCE AGENCY HEADQUARTERS,
LANGLEY, NORTHERN VIRGINIA

Caroline O'Kendell stared at the information displayed on her computer screen. Under the boldface title T&K Impex, GmbH, were the words "Holdings and Physical Assets." The document provided a list of properties owned by the Innsbruck-based company.

The information had been assembled by a small commercial investigative firm located in Baltimore. The CIA was the firm's sole customer. The company's staff consisted of only four people, all with extensive private-sector experience, each of whom had been polygraphed and signed secrecy agreements. Some of their information sources were business services such as Dun & Bradstreet, supplemented by more aggressive information gathering by the four investigators themselves, sometimes involving the payment of bribes in exchange for business secrets.

This was, Caroline remarked to herself, a twenty-first century sort of intelligence operation, where private companies and individual businessmen were targets due to their suspected involvement in proliferation, money laundering, narcotics trafficking, or some other transnational offense. The decades when CIA and other intelligence organizations had been solely occupied with stealing the protected secrets of other nation-states, such as the Soviet Union, were quite extinct. The post-Cold War world was less tidy.

Caroline considered the array of information suspended electronically before her eyes. It had been gathered in response to Robert's request for trace information on the Innsbruck firm. Caro-

line noted the information snippets as potentially significant. The
limited-liability company was well capitalized and in good financial
health. The main activity was the export of industrial machinery
from Austria to other countries in Europe and beyond. On the surface, at least, much of this business activity seemed prosaic. T&K
had, for example, recently arranged for the purchase and transfer of
rum distillery equipment for a customer in the Caribbean nation of
Trinidad and Tobago. No harm there, Caroline thought, except perhaps to the livers of the Trinidadians, but that was rather beyond
the purview of the CIA.

She read further, scrolling the text. Ownership. The registered
owners of the Innsbruck company were listed as Otto Tretschmer, a
German citizen, and Sayed al-Khalid, a Syrian. Al-Khalid had the
majority share in the firm. The name formed a rhyme, and Caroline
paused at its familiarity. Of course! It was the name mentioned by
Saul Morgenstern. A Mossad official in Tel Aviv had claimed al-
Khalid was an acquaintance of Forster and had met with the Austrian in Jordan. Caroline smiled broadly. Here was something solid.
She also made a mental note to request follow-on traces from the
agency's central database on Tretschmer, the other owner.

Continuing her survey of the information, Caroline learned
that, in addition to an office building and warehouse in Innsbruck,
T&K Impex owned two seagoing cargo vessels, the *Harbor Seeker*
and the *Condor Fury*. They were listed as capesize, dry cargo vessels.
Both ships had been built in South Korea and were of Belize registry. Both ships were involved in international transport, with routine ports of call in Asia, Africa, and Europe.

The *Harbor Seeker* had been detained by Canadian authorities in
2008 for having a corroded engine room door in addition to defec-
tive gyro and magnetic compasses. More recently, the *Condor Fury*
had been fined in Hong Kong for inoperative navigation lights. Caroline was unsure what these infractions meant, but intuited that the
vessels were not maintained to the highest standard. She decided to
run additional traces on the two ships.

Caroline sat back in her office chair and closed her eyes for a moment, in temporary respite from the harsh overhead lighting. What had she discovered relevant to the Forster and Kirscheim investigation? The al-Khalid connection, surely. The Syrian partner in the Innsbruck firm was associated with Forster. Additionally, the Austrian politician Hessler had visited T&K Impex. His reasons for doing so were unknown, but might be interesting as it established a connection between Hessler, al-Khalid and Forster. As well, the Tyrolean company was involved in exporting heavy equipment.

Caroline knew that machinery export could involve the movement of what was called "dual-use" equipment; items that had an ostensibly innocent use but that could be easily altered or employed for weapons-related or other prohibited activity. That the firm owned high-seas vessels might also prove relevant. Especially if either ship had a record of engaging in suspicious deliveries.

All in all, Caroline thought, the information she had screened might help clarify why Forster had ended up wrapped around the sodden trees of a Bavarian forest and why Mossad had lost an officer bicycling through one of Munich's residential areas. She opened her eyes again and set to work filling out a central database trace request.

Hamburg, Northern Germany

Horst Zellmann exited the tiny shower stall in his hotel room, toweled himself dry, and pulled on the thick terrycloth bathrobe marked with the logo of the Hotel Atlantik. Entering the adjoining bedroom, he indifferently took in the clutter of empty liquor bottles and glasses littering the coffee table and beige, carpeted floor. The scene was suffused with anemic gray light filtered through a curtained window facing the Alster. Zellmann moved his gaze to the unmade bed and the covered shape of the sleeping Asian female. He moved to her side with an ungraceful gait, shaking her shoulder with considerable force.

"Wake up. You've already been paid, and don't whine for more. Get up and get out. I've got work to do."

The woman stirred and ran a hand tipped by false pink fingernails through her long, sleek cascade of black hair. She muttered something to herself that Zellmann could not understand, but there was brittleness to the tone.

Speaking that Tagalog shit, no doubt, he concluded, having heard the syllables of the Philippine language in many ports around the world. She's probably calling me a cheap bastard or something. If this was the bar district of Manila, he seethed, I'd punch her in the face; break her cheekbone. He flexed his hand and formed a fist, but a whisper from deep in his brain cautioned him to calm down. He knew his current enterprise was far too sensitive to permit a brush with the authorities. He exhaled a burst of sour breath and moved back toward the bathroom. "I'm going to shave. Be out of here by the time I'm done."

The woman loosed another singsong string of foreign words but sat up and, with eyes that looked infinitely older than her body, glanced around for her clothes.

Returning to the bathroom, Zellmann stared at his image in the mirror, focusing on the net of small, erupting blood vessels in his nose, the cavernous, discolored circles beneath his eyes, and a visage that betrayed a look of worn decline. Well, he thought, those are the necessary wages of free time and a thick wad of euros in a city like Hamburg, offering its full array of vices. Well worth the price, he concluded.

The sea captain registered two sounds in succession. The first was the unmistakable report of the hotel room door opening and slamming firmly shut on its hinges, signaling the departure of the nameless prostitute he had picked up in the gaudily lit Saint Pauli district the night before. The second sound, a moment later, was the tinny and insistent tone of his cell phone. What now, he wondered, reentering the chaos of the bedroom and searching for the device. He located it on the dresser next to his belt and socks. He put the phone to his ear and barked a clipped "hello."

The voice that responded was soft, but the manner direct. "Good morning, Captain. I expect you know who this is. I'm calling from a pay phone on the other side of the Alster. I think that it would be judicious for us to get together. It needn't take long, mind you. We should go over a few points regarding our transaction. I suggest the waterfront bistro on the Jungfernstieg. I'm sure you'd welcome a cup of coffee."

Zellmann frowned, taking this as a veiled rebuke to his drinking habits. "Whatever you want is fine with me. I know the place. Tell me when."

The velvet voice replied, its tone redolent with the cultivation that Zellmann both resented and envied. "Shall we say in about forty minutes? That should provide us both sufficient time to get to the bistro without hurry. I recommend you take a taxi from the hotel to somewhere on Ferdinandstrasse, and then walk the remainder of the way. Just to complicate things in the unlikely event that you have any uninvited observers. I'm quite sure you understand."

"I understand," Zellmann replied. "I'll see you in forty minutes." He rang off and placed the phone back on the dresser. He considered the brief conversation. This was the final phase. A last coordination meeting to see what remained to be done. It also meant that his run of excess in Hamburg was nearing an end. He did not mind. He wanted to feel exhilarating physical movement again, to luxuriate in strong engines propelling his vessel forward across an endless panorama of rolling waves. He wanted the sensitive cargo success-fully delivered, ensuring the final, generous tranche of his payment. Time to move on, he concluded, searching the room for his soiled undershirt.

Otto Tretschmer had chosen a small table away from the street, of-fering a fine view of the Binnenalster, the inner lake in the heart of the Hamburg business district that was linked by a narrow canal to the harbor on the Elbe. The noble sandstone edifice of the city hall and its imposing clock tower were behind him. The lake was slate gray on this day, mirroring the lowering sky above, intervening spots of white provided by the seagulls that floated on, or circled above, the water. Tretschmer had ordered and received a pot of coffee and two cups, to abbreviate the time he would need to spend with the coarse sea captain. He searched momentarily for the precise word to describe Zellmann. Unappetitlich; unappetizing. Exactly, he thought.

The subject of Tretschmer's contemplations entered the bistro, the open door momentarily filling the establishment with the invasive sound of urban traffic from Jungfernstieg. The figure, clad in a dark cotton windbreaker and jeans, cast an unsmiling survey around the establishment. Tretschmer raised a hand, which the captain acknowledged with a curt nod of his bullet head.

"I've taken the liberty of ordering you a coffee," Tretschmer said as Zellmann pulled up a chair.

Zellmann grunted. "Thanks. You sure it's all right to be here in public like this?"

Tretschmer presented a smile that he did not feel. "Of course. Trust me, we are perfectly anonymous. Anyway, there's nothing illegal about our chatting together. And, as I mentioned on the phone, this get-together can be brief. We just need to coordinate a few points."

Zellmann slouched his heavy form into a more relaxed sitting position. "Fine with me. Just tell me what you need to know."

"Indeed. I need to know this: is the cargo safely stowed aboard and ready for the voyage?"

"Yes. Everything is on board. I made sure it's secure against bad weather. No problem."

Tretschmer raised his chin a degree. "Excellent. Exactly what our valued client will want to hear. Do you anticipate any complications with the customs police or the harbormaster or anything of that sort?"

Zellmann shook his head with a dismissive gesture. "Nope. I've got it worked out, using a personal contact of mine. He's been paid good coin and knows what to do. Trust me, the *Condor Fury* won't have trouble clearing harbor and getting underway."

The businessman clasped his hands in satisfaction. "Nicely done again, *Herr Kapitan*. Always a wise precaution to purchase assistance. Now, how soon can you depart Hamburg?"

Zellmann hunched his fireplug frame over the tabletop and furrowed his brow, reaching for the cup of coffee. "How soon? Not long.
We're already fueled. We have to file some paperwork, notify the
harbormaster, get provisions, but we can be underway quickly."

"How soon?"

Zellmann took a prodigious gulp of coffee and wiped a sleeve
across his brooding slash of a mouth. "Two days. Two-and-a-half at
the most."

"Excellent," Tretschmer replied, his satisfaction genuine. "Our
enterprise is not without some element of risk, after all. The sooner
we are beyond the ministrations of German authorities, the better.
I will pass along the good news to our client. In the interim, Captain
Zellmann, take care of the provisions and paperwork. We shouldn't
need to meet personally again before you sail. We'll talk by phone
just before the *Condor Fury* is ready to depart." Tretschmer lifted his
coffee cup with both hands and took a careful sip.

Zellmann nodded agreement and coughed into his hand. "What
about the rest of my payment? We have an agreement."

Tretschmer winced slightly and fastidiously returned the coffee
cup to the table in front of him. Suspicious, uncultured dullard, he
thought as he chose his words. "We do indeed have an agreement,
Captain, and I assure you it will be honored. You received your initial payment as planned, didn't you? When you get underway, a second deposit will be made to the offshore account established for you
in Cyprus. The third deposit will, as we agreed, be paid in full once
the cargo safely reaches its final destination. No need to worry. I anticipate we will require your maritime services in the future and our
dealings will be accomplished with businesslike propriety."

Zellmann considered the words for a moment and muttered a
guttural "okay." He turned his head to the gray expanse of the Alster
and the avian choreography of the gulls. He realized that he was not
at home in the refined coffee shop or the precious urban surroundings of the city. He felt a stranger to the cultured and genteel am-
biance of Hamburg, and was comfortable only in its coarser,
voluptuary districts. Yes, he thought, with a tinge of bitterness. High

time to get underway, to feel the pulse of engines below deck and again be at sea.

ABOVE AMMAN,
CAPITAL OF THE HASHEMITE KINGDOM OF JORDAN

The black mass of land five thousand feet below the passenger plane was host to small clusters of lights, illuminated islands in a dark sea. Caroline O'Kendell knew that the flight path swept in from the Mediterranean and passed over Israel and Jordan on the way to Amman. She recalled from previous visits to the region that the duller, yellow lights marked Arab villages, the more incandescent illumination signaling Israeli settlements. Seen from above, the scene appeared to be one of uninterrupted tranquility. Caroline shook her head. Space and distance served as a cosmetic, conceal-ing the scars of enmity and violence that had seethed for decades across the landscape below. And seethed still.

"We are now on our final approach to Amman Queen Alia In-ternational Airport. Please fasten your seat belts in preparation for landing." The voice of the flight attendant was pleasant yet bored.

The engines secured to the wings emitted a deep metallic yawn and Caroline felt the aircraft slow as it descended. Her visit to the Middle East would be brief, two days only, but long enough to ac-complish her task. She had asked for and received Langley's permis-sion to travel to Amman to meet with a representative of the Jordanian General Intelligence Department, or GID, an organiza-tion with a long history of cooperation with the United States se-curity services. Caroline had never dealt with the GID, but her colleagues at the CIA Jordanian Desk gave assurance that her Arab partners would be helpful. Upon departing Amman, Caroline was to return to Langley and assemble any new information the Jorda-nians provided and transmit it immediately to Robert.

Before departing headquarters, Caroline had placed a call to the operational branch of the Office of Medical Services, OMS. She had inquired if they had any medication that might facilitate an inter-rogation conducted by the Jordanians. She had considered it a long shot, and was pleased to have received a positive response after a flurry of initial questions. The result was carefully nestled in her shoulder bag.

She stifled a yawn into the recycled air of the cabin and watched as the bright points of illumination on the ground gained definition and size. Caroline had been advised by a CIA cable from Amman that she should expect to be met at the gate by a GID representative, otherwise unidentified.

The landing was uneventful, like every landing that Caroline had to date experienced. After deplaning and making the short trek with the other passengers through the modest-sized terminal to customs, Caroline extracted her diplomatic passport for examination. As she was not a regular visitor to the region and did not need to have her identity exposed to the Jordanians, Central Cover Staff had provided her with documentation in alias. Her time in Amman would be spent as Helen Cienfuegos, her naturally dark hair lending credibility to the Hispanic surname. This was the identity that had been provided to the GID. As she approached the customs counter, Caroline heard a male voice from immediately behind her.

"Excuse me, please, but are you perhaps Miss Cien-fu-eg?"

She turned to encounter a dark-haired and mustached man defined both by middle height and middle age, wearing a navy blue suit of European cut. He smiled disarmingly and held a hand to his heart in a typical regional greeting.

She returned the smile. "Yes, that's right. Helen Cienfuegos. And I would guess I have the pleasure of addressing my official Jordanian contact?"

"Cienfuegos," the man corrected himself, with a shallow bow of his head. "Yes, I am your contact during your stay in the kingdom. Hamdi al-Bakhit." He moved a step closer and lowered his voice. "I am from the Dairat al-Mukhabarat al-Ammah—GID." In a fluid motion, he pulled a laminated identity card from the inside pocket of his jacket and displayed it to his guest.

The Arabic script meant nothing to Caroline, but she recognized the logo of a brown eagle surrounded by olive wreaths and clutching a snake in its talons. "I'm pleased to meet you, Mr. Bakhit. Thanks for bothering to come all the way out here this evening. I'm certain there are other things that you'd rather be doing."

The Jordanian's smile expanded and he loosed a laugh. "Actually, there is nothing else in particular I would rather be doing. It's important we get you out of here without any inconvenience and see you to the comfort of your hotel. Your agency colleagues here have reserved a room for you at the Grand Hyatt, and I have their permission to take you there. Please follow me."

Caroline followed as instructed. Al-Bakhit flashed his identification and said a few words in Arabic to the customs official, gesturing at Caroline. The portly and balding customs man saluted and waved them through automatic doors to the luggage area.

Caroline saw her single, forest-green suitcase already resting on the tiled floor and retrieved it immediately. Her host insisted on pulling it for her. She did not object. She had never taken offense at courtesy.

They emerged from the terminal into the coolness of the desert evening. The scene was a jumble of yellow taxicabs, most of them Japanese manufactured, and familial knots of Jordanians in animated conversation, welcoming the returning or soothing the departing. Some of the women were casually dressed in the Western style: blouses, blue jeans, and heels. Others were veiled votaries of traditional Islam. The GID man cleared a path with a few authoritative gestures and guided Caroline to a parked black BMW sedan. Al-Bakhit placed the piece of luggage in the trunk, opened the passenger door for his visitor, and seated himself behind the wheel. "We take the highway to Amman. Your hotel is downtown, on the third traffic circle, a nice area. We should be there in forty minutes, in normal traffic conditions. We have a formal meeting arranged for tomorrow, but in a restaurant, not an office. If you are here for such a short duration, we thought you should at least enjoy yourself a little."

Despite herself, Caroline felt flattered. "That's very thoughtful of you, Mr. Bakhit."

The Jordanian maneuvered from the airport access road onto the long, straight expanse of highway. "It would perhaps be easier if you call me Hamdi; Americans are at home with first names. I studied at your National Defense University in Washington, D.C., and I learned not to stand on formality. Okay with you?"

"Fine with me, Hamdi. Call me Helen." She decided that she too was more at home with a familiar form of address, even in alias. Her escort had an instinctive feel for these things, not unusual for a professional intelligence officer.

The sedan moved at seventy-five miles an hour over the rolling terrain. The darkness obscured the landscape. Here and there lights winked from distant dwellings.

"Farms," al-Bakhit said, as if reading Caroline's thoughts. "Small farms with olive trees and a few goats or cows, mainly. Not too prosperous, but one can make a living. Farther out, we have other agriculture; fruit orchards and vegetables. The problem here is water, there is not enough of it. We use water from desalination plants and from the Dead Sea. Some people say that the Israelis steal our water from underground, what do you call that, the aquifer? But I don't really know about those things. If CIA ever invents a device to alter the weather, please send us rain." He laughed genuinely and Caroline did too.

"Hamdi, will you be at the restaurant meeting tomorrow?"

The GID man engaged his blinkers and overtook a vintage Volkswagen van. "Yes, I will be there; I chose the location. It's out of town a bit, near where I live. A colleague of mine will be there too. It's our understanding that you are interested in Sayed al-Khalid, is that correct?"

Caroline nodded. "That's right. He's the reason I traveled here. I'm looking at some suspicious developments in Europe and al-Khalid might be involved. If GID can enlighten me about this fellow, I'll be grateful."

A moment of silence passed between them as al-Bakhit considered the information, and there was only the subdued murmur of the engine and the sibilance of tires cruising over asphalt. Then he said, "Helen, GID is interested in al-Khalid, too. And in his activities internationally. He is a most interesting man; to use an American phrase, a real son of a bitch."

"Well then, it sounds like we have something to talk about tomorrow," Caroline said with an amused lilt to her voice.

Al-Bakhit nodded in agreement, only his profile visible in the pale illumination of dashboard lights. "I'll do some homework before we meet. My colleague and I should be able to provide you something. In exchange, perhaps you might indicate to us the nature of CIA interest in al-Khalid. He's Syrian, but he does maintain frequent residency in Amman, and we don't want him using our country as the launching point for criminal activity. We should speak as frankly as possible tomorrow."

"Agreed, Hamdi. I'll be as transparent as the rules permit me to be, rely on it." A certain degree of candor was, Caroline knew, the required soil for a fruitful intelligence exchange. The car crested a low hill, revealing the universe of colorful shop lights and herds of traffic marking the approaches to downtown Amman. She knew her hotel could only be minutes away, and was pleased at the prospect. The trip from Washington had been tiring, and she longed for a bath followed by hours of sleep. Despite her increasing languor, she remained excited about the information she might acquire the next day. She wondered how the investigation into the Forster and Kirscheim murders was progressing in Germany.

GAMSDORF, BAVARIA

Waldbaer stood in an embracing circle of dim light in his office, staring at the whiteboard affixed to one wall, slowly rocking on the soles of his scarred loafers. It was evening, and he was now the sole nocturnal resident of the police station and, for that matter, of the entire city hall building within which the police spaces were located. Silence was kept at bay by the small CD player on Waldbaer's desk. His contemplations were accompanied by the stirringly vivid orchestral colors of Sibelius; *Night Ride and Sunrise*. Despite the title of the piece he had selected, Waldbaer did not intend to remain in his office until dawn, and expected to drive home within the hour, after

reviewing the investigatory picture one final time. He had discovered
long ago that his best insights into a case often occurred after hours,
absent ringing phones and the intrusions of the outside world.

The whiteboard was emblazoned with words written in disciplined script. Some of the words were in blue, others in green, still
others in red. Blue denoted items related to the Forster death, green
indicated a relationship to the Kirscheim murder. The words scribed
in red were those that seemed to have a general relationship to the
events under investigation, but could not be neatly catalogued.
Waldbaer rubbed at the circles under his eyes and considered what
he had written about the Forster incident.

> *Immediate cause of death: internal injuries due to car crash.*
> *Car crash caused by sedative placed in Forster's drink in Inns-*
> *bruck.*

Waldbaer had taped the autopsy results to the side of the whiteboard.

> *Forster departed Innsbruck, driving direction Garmisch. Final*
> *destination: ?*

Waldbaer sighed, unhappy with the number of unanswered questions. He dropped his gaze lower on the board and thought about
possible motives for seeing Forster off from the visible world.

> *Cui bono? Who benefits?*
> *Family members?—No indication of this.*
> *Israel-Mossad?*

Waldbaer shook his head sideways. How? Killing Forster for his
right-wing activities or anti-Semitic sympathies didn't make sense.
The Israelis would have realized Forster would simply be replaced in
the NDF by another party functionary sharing the same views. Nothing gained. Would the Israelis kill Forster over dubious business
transactions detrimental to their interests? Perhaps, Waldbaer conceded, but he was skeptical.

Cui bono? Anton Hessler?

Waldbaer's eyes fixed on the Austrian name. The detective did not take to the politician on a personal level. Hessler struck Waldbaer as effete and indolent, opinionated, conceited, and arrogant, none of which fit into the detective's inventory of virtues. Still, Waldbaer was aware that these were his own prejudices, based on limited exposure to the man. Perhaps, Waldbaer analyzed self-critically, he envied Hessler's evident wealth. Resentment is a poor ally to an objective investigation, he knew. Waldbaer accorded a degree of trust to his intuition, and there was something about the elegant, self-regarding Innsbruck resident that whispered to him of deceit. In terms of benefiting from Forster's demise, Hessler had already taken over the reins of the party and enhanced his political status and profile. Clearly a benefit for those who cared about such things—as Hessler certainly did. Waldbaer lifted a marker from the tray below the whiteboard and put a blue asterisk next to Hessler's name, adding the words "Pursue further."

Cui bono? Sayed al-Khalid?

There was a frustrating lack of information on the Syrian contact of Forster. Over to Hirter and the CIA to provide details. Waldbaer knew the Middle East was a tough neighborhood and that violence was often a preferred solution to perceived problems. Forster might have gotten involved with a severely humorless league of people. Stay tuned, Waldbaer thought to himself.

Waldbaer placed a finger absently to his lips and surveyed the board further.

> *Verbindung Ost KG: offices in Moscow and Vienna. Owners: Bogden Karniev and Sergei Ershov. Connections: Middle East, Iran, Azerbaijan, Africa—Americans regard firm as suspicious.*

As do I, Waldbaer concluded, in deference to his investigatory instincts. Forster was clearly involved with the firm and had met some of its international customers. But why? The answer to that query remained presently elusive. The Russian angle intrigued the detective. Members of the former security services had established a bad reputation as unscrupulous or worse, often involved in international arms deals or other criminal enterprises. A preference for clients from Iran, Azerbaijan, and the Middle East hardly eased concern about the activities of Verbindung Ost and its Russian proprietors.

Waldbaer could not shake a vague, intuitive sense that the firm had a link to Forster's death. He would ask his Austrian counterpart to try to gain access to the company's records; whether this was accomplished in an orthodox manner or otherwise was immaterial to him. Waldbaer next turned his attention to the words inked in green.

> Kirscheim: Murdered? Yes, single shot from Dragunov rifle. Random? No. Targeted.
> Suspects: Israeli service or associates for reasons unknown? No indication; unlikely to kill their own overseas.
> Other intelligence service? No indication, no suggestion of motive.
> Forster supporters? Why? Due to Kirscheim surveillance of Forster? No indication, but pursue.

Waldbaer stepped back from the board, stretched, and slouched against the side of his desk. The Israeli Consulate or Mossad would be conducting their own investigation of Kirscheim's murder. They might possess background information that could prove illuminating. Still, Waldbaer decided, exhaling a long sigh, the consulate had been singularly taciturn since the consul's death. He did not expect any cooperation from that quarter; their sole fixation was in protecting Israeli national interests. Waldbaer stared again at the names of Forster and Kirscheim etched in their respective colors. Was there any connection to link the two deaths?

The thought hit him suddenly. The Kirscheim murder weapon

was a Russian-manufactured sniper rifle. Russian. Like the two owners of Verbindung Ost. A very thin link, Waldbaer conceded, but
nonetheless a thread to be clutched. Had Verbindung Ost ever been
linked to an arms transaction? A Dragunov, after all, was a specialty
weapon. Not something that could be purchased on any street corner in Europe, and surely not designed for hunting Bavarian mountain goats. Waldbaer realized that the possible Russian link merited
attention. The detective pushed himself away from the desk, rubbed
at his back with both hands, and moved the few feet to the whiteboard. He regarded another set of letters emblazoned on the surface
in blue.

T&K Impex GmbH, Innsbruck

Yes, he recalled. The company Frau Reiner had observed being visited by the indecipherable Anton Hessler. The kommissarin was currently digging for additional information on the firm and its
activities. Another thought began to gestate in Waldbaer's mind.
Was the Innsbruck import-export company somehow linked to
Verbindung Ost, the Russian-owned commercial entity? Verbindung
Ost, after all, also had offices in Austria. The fact was that two import-export trading firms were written there in front of him, one with
a connection to Forster, the other linked, however tenuously, to
Forster's political successor.

Waldbaer found himself developing an unshakable sentiment
that commercial activities were more than incidental to the case.
Even though he felt a renewed surge of investigative energy, he was
aware of a growing heaviness about his eyes. It was time to head
home and sink into a welcome sea of sleep. He would keep a pen
and pad of paper at his bedside. The nocturnal world, he knew from
occasions past, sometimes whispered of hints and clues undetected
during the tumult of more animated hours.

Amman, Jordan

The breakfast buffet was enormous and enticingly exotic. Eggs and
omelets of every preparation were provided, as were hash brown po-

tatoes and fried tomatoes. There was no bacon as it was a form of pork and thus forbidden, *haram*, in the Muslim-majority kingdom. Curled, fried strips of lamb were presented as a suitable substitute. As a signal of local tastes, there were heaps of olives, trays of stuffed grape leaves, mountains of goat cheese, deep bowls of spiced hummus, and plates of hot, soft unleavened breads. A separate serving table held a colorful explosion of fruits: mandarins, pomegranates, pears, and melons from the Jordanian countryside. Strong, steaming Arabic coffee and unfiltered, unsweetened orange juice were delivered to Caroline's table by a silent but smiling waiter clad in a spotless white shirt and black vest.

Caroline was seated at a wall of glass overlooking the back terrace of the hotel and the jumbled, earth-toned expanse of Amman beyond. The cast of the buildings revealed an admixture of wealth and poverty. Perhaps a mile away, on the distant ridge that defined the horizon, a gigantic Jordanian flag rustled with stately languor in the torpid breeze. Most of the banner was composed of three broad stripes, one black, one white, and one green. Closer to where the flag was secured to its mast, a white star was centered in a triangular field of red. Caroline recalled that the imagery was a reference to ancient caliphates, to which the Hashemite dynasty traced its origins and on which rested its legitimacy and fiercely defended independence.

Caroline consulted the wristwatch at the sleeve of her yellow silk business jacket. There was time for a final glass of juice before meeting Hamdi in the opulent, marbled lobby of the Hyatt. She had breakfasted sparingly, aware that her meeting with the GID was to take place in a restaurant somewhere outside of the city. She ran through the points that she hoped to cover with the Jordanian intelligence officers. Her agenda was simple and direct.

Most importantly, she wanted the Jordanians to paint for her an information portrait of Sayed al-Khalid. What were the details of his background that CIA did not possess? She wanted to acquire as well a sense of the man's personality—what motivated him—politics, profit, jihad?

With whom was al-Khalid connected? She did not intend to raise al-Khalid's connection to Forster; she was curious to see if the Jordanians were aware of it independently. She was prepared to raise the Syrian's part ownership of the T&K Impex firm, but she would first give the Jordanians the opportunity to raise it themselves. Finally, perhaps there existed the possibility that the GID might meet directly with al-Khalid and interrogate him on his activities.

Caroline's instructions from Langley were clear on one point: do not request the GID to engage in operational activity on behalf of CIA. If the Jordanian service unilaterally decides to detain or otherwise deal with al-Khalid, fine, but the initiative must come entirely from the GID. The fact was both Caroline and her superiors at Langley were uncertain whether bracing al-Khalid would be a good idea. Might it somehow complicate Waldbaer's investigation in Germany, or tip off others in the dubious T&K Impex that they were being watched? Better to let the Jordanians go their own way on how to proceed with al-Khalid.

Orange juice consumed, Caroline took her shoulder bag and exited the hotel breakfast room. In the lobby she quickly spotted Hamdi, attired in a dark suit and foulard tie. With a wave of his hand, he beckoned her to follow him into the sovereign, reigning heat of the Jordanian sun and the waiting, air-conditioned GID limousine.

An hour later, Caroline stood on an arid precipice called Mount Nebo and gazed out at the shimmering image of the Dead Sea in the distance, its waters surrounded by an unrelieved mauve landscape that struck her as wild and unforgiving. Like the long march of history here, she thought, a chronology of conquests, crusades, wars, and massacres, ancient and modern. In these parched valleys and stark heights, peace was always a process and never an achievement. Enmity, eternal and uncompromising, seemed the dominant force, as if it sprung like a malignant weed from the dry terrain.

"The pope was here," she heard Hamdi's pleasant voice intone and she turned to the sound.

"The pope was here and held a Mass, because it is believed that this ridge is where Moses died before he could enter the Promised Land. You can see a stylized staff of Moses just above us on the summit. It is a plea for peace, I think, which is always the main theme here." He smiled as if embarrassed.

"An elusive theme, it would seem," Caroline replied, regretting the harsh judgment as soon as she had spoken. She felt a blush cross her cheeks.

Hamdi kicked a cascade of small, white pebbles over the cliff in front of him and nodded. "Yes, peace between Arabs and Israelis, between Moslem, Jew, and Christian does not have a history of success in these parts. But maybe someday we will surprise ourselves and establish an arrangement satisfactory for all. Perhaps I will see it, or my son. I don't want jihad. I want peace. I want my son to grow up to be an engineer, not a martyr."

Caroline could read personalities sufficiently well to know that her liaison partner was sincere. "If enough people share that hope, Hamdi, I think a solution will be found. People will demand it." She did not feel as unshakably certain as she sounded, but wanted to buttress Hamdi's sentiments.

Hamdi issued a slight smile, but the mirrored sunglasses obscured his eyes. "It is getting hot now. Even with the breeze, midday is not the optimal time to visit Mount Nebo, but I wanted to show it to you as it's on our route. The restaurant where we are meeting my colleague is ten minutes away. " As they turned back toward the waiting limousine, he gestured at the horizon past the Dead Sea. "Those are the hills of Jerusalem. Everything is close here. Except the people, of course."

They were seated on the roof terrace of a venerable, dusty brown stone building in the center of the little town of Madaba, famous for its production of mosaics. Their oval table was placed in the shade of a wall and protected by a rude wood overhang, and a slight breeze contributed to the comfortable temperature, a contrast to the languor-inducing heat prevailing in the parched landscape just beyond.

Hamdi had introduced his GID associate, Taher Mulki, a thin wisp of a man with piercing light blue eyes, dramatically beaked nose, and receding, reddish hair. Caroline guessed that he was in his mid-forties. Although the matter of hierarchy was not raised, Caroline noted that Taher was deferential to Hamdi, and she guessed that Taher was lower in the Jordanian intelligence service pecking order.

Hamdi and Taher were drinking tea as they consulted the menu, while Caroline, cocooned in her Helen alias, sipped at an ice-jammed glass of Coca-Cola. Hamdi had offered to order for Caroline, a courtesy to which she gladly acceded, being unfamiliar with Jordanian fare. The owner of the establishment appeared, took their order, and disappeared.

"Helen, perhaps it would be best if we let you explain what you would like from us," Hamdi said in a voice that was both deep and soothing.

"Sure. That's easy. I don't want to burden the GID with some complex request. I know how busy you all must be with the security threats in this neighborhood."

Taher loosed a staccato burst of laughter. "Neighborhood? A euphemism, I expect, Helen. But you're right. Our service is always busy with the goings-on in Israel, with which we enjoy a, shall we say, coolly correct and sometimes strained relationship. Then we have the more poisonous situation with Syria, not to mention Iran and the Shiite crescent. Lebanon with its warring factions is always a tinderbox. The Saudis are hardly close friends to the Hashemite Kingdom either. So, you are quite right. It's a tough neighborhood."

Hamdi intervened once his colleague had finished. "Helen, you said your request is not complex. Your interests, I take it, based on your past remarks, do not extend beyond Sayed al-Khalid?"

Caroline responded with an energetic, affirmative nod. "That's basically right, Hamdi. Al-Khalid is the reason I'm here. If you and Taher can help me out, I fly back to Washington a happy woman."

Hamdi indulged a modest sip of tea and looked his CIA counterpart in the eyes. As his jacket moved slightly with the motion, the holstered butt of an automatic pistol was visible beneath his shoulder. "We can help. Our relationship with Langley is good and you people have helped us in the past with information on terrorist plans against Jordan. We want to keep the intelligence flow a two-way street. Taher joins us because he is the GID officer most familiar with the elusive al-Khalid. So, over to you, Taher."

The smaller, wiry Jordanian hunched forward in his chair, and placed his manicured hands flat against the tabletop. "Right. We know quite a bit about Sayed al-Khalid, but not everything. He is a person of discretion. He keeps to a limited circle of contacts and maintains a low profile in Amman. He is self-disciplined and security conscious."

"For a reason," Caroline interrupted.

"Yes, most surely. We have traced his travel as best we can. We know when he enters Jordan and when he leaves our kingdom and where he is going, at least when traveling by air. He spends time in Damascus, Syria, which we would expect as that is his homeland. But he travels to Iran too, which is rather unusual. And he visits Vienna, Austria, with some regularity."

A waiter arrived with bowls of large green and black olives coated with garlic and herbs and slices of warm, unleavened bread. He departed wordlessly. Caroline reached for an olive with two fingers and turned it slowly as she spoke. "Taher, you characterize al-Khalid's travel to Iran as unusual. Why?"

Taher responded with a smile. "Because al-Khalid is a Sunni and the Islamic Republic of Iran is ferociously Shiite. No love lost between the two persuasions. We can't discover any personal reasons that might oblige him to journey to Iran, which leaves business reasons. But what? Iran's exports revolve around two products, Persian carpets and pistachios—Iranian gold, we call them. But there is no evidence that al-Khalid deals in these things. As for imports to Iran, we can discern no trace of that either. So there is something going on beneath the surface that we do not yet see. Which is why I call this connection unusual."

Caroline withdrew her notepad from the shoulder bag at her side and scribbled a series of words. "Point taken."

Taher continued, his voice registering just above a whisper. "There is more. Al-Khalid has met here in Jordan with a European named Otto Tretschmer. It would seem that Tretschmer is a businessman from Hamburg, Germany. He is involved in importing and exporting machinery, heavy equipment mainly. He and al-Khalid have established a company in Innsbruck, Austria, called T&K Impex. That would be Tretschmer and Khalid Import-Export. I would advise CIA to look carefully at that company to determine what Khalid is up to. I expect it is something illegal."

"Why do you say illegal?" Caroline asked. "Is there something irregular in the way the company was founded?"

Taher shook his narrow head from side to side. "No. T&K is legally registered and perfectly legitimate under Austrian law. I am speaking with the perspective of a professional intelligence officer. Consider: Why would a German businessman from the remote, northern port of Hamburg found a company in land-locked Austria, with someone like al-Khalid as his partner? And, by the way, in Innsbruck, a rather provincial city, more renowned for tourism than commerce. Doesn't make sense. But it does make sense if you are trying to cover your tracks. To make it harder for the authorities to figure out what you are doing. And that's what I think you have here, Helen. Another thing. T&K is linked via business deals to another dubious firm, this one in Vienna. It's called Verbindung Ost, which means 'Connections East.' The main office is in Moscow."

Caroline dabbed at her lips with a napkin. "And what kind of business is Verbindung Ost?"

"A dirty one, in our assessment. Its activities are not transparent. We know that in one instance Verbindung Ost was the conduit for a shipment of Russian-made rocket-propelled grenades and precision small arms to a client in Yemen. The weapons were documented as fishing equipment. Before you ask, let me tell you that our source for this information is an agent we had in Yemen at the time. Anyway, we think Verbindung Ost has likely engaged in other illegal shipments. And al-Khalid is tied to the firm, at least indirectly, through his Innsbruck company."

Caroline reflected for a moment before making an additional query. "Can you clarify the reason Verbindung Ost is linked to the T&K firm in Innsbruck? Why should they be working together?"

"Quite right, why should two import-export firms cooperate on business deals, when they are natural competitors in the private sector? This too is suspicious. The best reason for this cooperative arrangement is that it helps conceal the tracks of illicit activity. Look at it this way. Verbindung Ost moves goods from its Moscow office to its subsidiary in Vienna. Once in Austria, the consignment is moved by truck to T&K in Innsbruck, about four hours distant. This can even be done 'black'—with false consignment papers and end-user certificates. The goods can subsequently be reshipped by T&K to its contacts in, say, Germany, and from there to some other point in the world. The more moving pieces are involved, the more difficult it is for customs authorities to figure out what's really going on."

Hamdi's voice joined the conversation. "So, Helen, now you see why I invited Taher to join us today. But there is more, isn't there, Taher?"

"Yes. Sayed al-Khalid is an interesting man. In addition to his commercial activities, we know something about his personal contacts. I expect, Helen, that you'll find this information noteworthy as well. Al-Khalid hosted an Austrian right-wing politician named Georg Forster here in Amman. Al-Khalid paid him money for some sort of services rendered, details unknown. We also know for a fact that al-Khalid, who still retains Syrian citizenship, has high-level official contacts in Damascus. Our intelligence links him to the Syrian armed forces and the Ministry of Energy. As well, al-Khalid is connected to some rather interesting Iranians, including a positively identified senior member of the Quds Force—the special operations arm of *Sepah Pasdaran*; the Revolutionary Guards Corps. Al-Khalid also has met here in Amman with two members of the Iranian Defense Industries Organization. Their last get-together was three weeks ago."

Caroline scribbled key words in her notebook. "That's really interesting, Taher. My organization pays lots of attention to the Quds Force, which has a long history of involvement in weapons trafficking and terrorism, as I'm sure you know. And the Defense Industries Organization—the DIO, as we call it—has representatives in Iranian embassies overseas purchasing dual-use goods for the Iranian military. Al-Khalid is keeping bad company."

"Yes, undoubtedly. And we also know that al-Khalid is engaged in purchasing something on behalf of the Iranians and Syrians. They have discussed this in al-Khalid's apartment in Amman."

Caroline allowed a smile to trace across her face. "I wonder how the GID knows the contents of conversations made in the privacy of al-Khalid's apartment?"

Taher appeared flustered for a moment, but Hamdi returned the CIA officer's smile. "The same methods Langley employs against the targets of its attentions. When al-Khalid first came across our intelligence screen, we made a surreptitious entry of his apartment and installed some listening devices. They are still in place. There you have it, another signal of our transparency with your agency." The Jordanian nodded his head in a modest bow.

"Thanks for your candor, both of you. What kind of business activity has al-Khalid engaged in on behalf of his Iranian and Syrian friends?"

Taher reached for a piece of warm pita bread, dipped it in a bowl of hummus and resumed his narrative. "We don't know much about what al-Khalid is up to with these contacts. Even in his apartment, he and his guests speak guardedly. They practice operational security when discussing their dealings, which only makes us more suspicious about its legality. It's clear the Iranians and Syrians have paid considerable money for al-Khalid to work on purchasing equipment of some sort from outside the Middle East. But we don't know what kind of equipment. In conversation, they use the words 'extruders' and 'lathes' when referring to the items they want to acquire. A simple word substitution code, but effective. And they haven't slipped up yet. As I say, they are disciplined and professional. This suggests whatever activity they are engaged in is sensitive."

"Anything else to convey?" Hamdi asked his colleague.

Taher pursed his lips and moved his gaze to his partner. "Just a few things. Judging from the conversations overheard in al-Khalid's apartment, the deal with the Iranians and Syrians is progressing well. Listening to our audiotapes, one gets the impression the transaction is in its final phase. It's clear from comments made that some of the items acquired have been produced in Europe. And, although we don't know for certain, Europe is logically the place where these goods are currently stored. The word 'shipment' has been used, which suggests the material of interest has been acquired and only awaits transport. Probably to Iran or Syria, but that's speculation. Probably by sea, one would think, but again, not knowing the type or size or weight of the consignment, this is a guess. Perhaps, if the material is not large, air freight would suffice. As good as our information is in some respects, there remains much we do not know. That is the nature of intelligence work."

Caroline laced her fingers together and rested her chin on her hands, a contemplative look capturing her features. "This has been a big help, gentlemen. Even with lots of unknowns, it's clear al-Khalid is worthy of CIA attention, and GID's. Frankly, we're interested in the European angle of Khalid's activities. Maybe we can turn up information on that end of interest for both our services. A final question: in addition to the technical penetration of al-Khalid's apartment in Amman, is there anything else your service might do to collect more intelligence on al-Khalid's dealings?"

Hamdi cast a cryptic glance at Taher before turning his attention to Caroline. "There might be something we can arrange. I will be in touch when you return to Langley."

Caroline murmured her appreciation and reached into her shoulder bag, extracting a small metal pill box. "Hamdi, this is for you, if you choose to use it. It's something from our medical staff, a CIA creation, you might say. Let me explain."

Following her elaboration, and Hamdi's evident satisfaction with the information, Caroline felt ready to end her Jordan visit. Things were looking up. Whether or not the mysterious commercial conspiracies of al-Khalid were related to Georg Forster's death remained to be seen. But at least she felt confident that she had acquired considerable details for Robert to reflect upon in their investigation. She would process and forward the intelligence to him upon return to the States.

INNSBRUCK, TYROL

Sabine Reiner felt pleased to be hosting the meeting with Waldbaer and Hirter in the familiar, high-ceilinged confines of her police station office. The host always commanded a position of unspoken control. She expected that this sociological subtlety was not lost on Franz Waldbaer, who presently regarded her, arms folded defensively over his chest, forest-green loden jacket bunched at his shoulders. Hirter's features, on the other hand, were arranged in a serene mask, betraying nothing. The self-discipline of the trained intelligence officer, she concluded.

"Gentlemen," she began, standing at the window overlooking the street below and regarding the two seated figures with a smile, "I'm grateful you accepted my invitation and I appreciate your traveling here. I think I've been able to pull together some information that should be of value to all of us, and I wanted to share it as quickly as possible. It has to do with Anton Hessler. You might recall that I followed him to the offices of an import-export firm here in Innsbruck called T&K. Well, I've done a bit of digging and we now have more to the story."

Waldbaer waved a hand theatrically, a sardonic tone evident in his rumbled words. "Please don't keep us in suspense, Frau Kommissarin. We eagerly await the results of adept and proficient Austrian investigative work."

Frau Reiner sighed. "No need to be sarcastic, Kommissar Waldbaer. I think even you will find this new information of interest. It moves us forward, I am quite sure." Her voice was confident.

Robert Hirter let loose a toothy grin and leaned forward. "We are entirely your captive audience, Frau Reiner."

Frau Reiner perambulated slowly across the room, hands loosely linked behind her back, eyes fixed on the floor in front of her. "I've taken a close look at T&K Impex. It would seem that T&K is a rather strange firm. I talked to the Austrian *zoll*, the customs police, and they said they've had their eyes on the company for some time. According to customs, T&K doesn't seem to do enough business to be a profitable enterprise. That taken alone might not mean much. Perhaps there's a capital investor in the background prepared to take a financial loss for a period, hoping for eventual profitability. But there's more. T&K has been mentioned three times by customs informants who report on dubious business deals. These sources are Eastern Europeans with whom the customs service has an arrangement. All of the sources claim T&K traffics in controlled items originating in Russia."

"What exactly do you mean by controlled items?" Hirter queried.

"Goods that require a special export license and documentation identifying the end user and how the equipment is going to be used—dual-use equipment. For example, a specific type of metal tubing that might be used for water pipes but also has utility for rockets or artillery. That sort of thing. According to customs, their sources allege the company falsifies documentation on items it is transhipping, and has arranged, where necessary, for false end-user certificates, concealing the real final destination for shipments. Customs also suspects the firm has moved precision small arms out of Russia to the Western market, but again, no proof. "

Waldbaer placed his hands on his knees as he spoke. "Has Austrian customs brought T&K to court or arrested the principals?"

Sabine Reiner frowned and shook her head. "No. No court cases or arrests to date. Customs has never been able to prove the allegations. They've made official inquiries at the company and checked the books. One order of goods that allegedly had weapons application had already been moved from Austria by the time the authorities could act on the tip; too late. In another instance, the customs service lawyer said there were insufficient grounds for a search warrant. T&K has been lucky. Austrian customs also suspects the firm is using two sets of books to record business. Again, customs is convinced that is the case, but they lack proof. So, legally, T&K is clean.

The important thing for us is that experienced customs officers believe the company is dirty and they hope—with time—to be able to demonstrate it."

Waldbaer stood up and moved from the couch, causing an audible cracking sound in his knees and evoking a wince. "I'm willing to give credence to a *bauch gefuehl*, a gut feeling. If your customs officers regard T&K as engaging in illegal business, that carries weight for me. It was wise of you to get in touch with them, Frau Reiner."

The kommissarin smiled brightly at the unexpected compliment. "There's more, Herr Kommissar. Perhaps something you can pursue. Commercial information clarifies that the first initial in the T&K company name refers to one of the two owners, a German citizen. His name is Otto Tretschmer. Place of birth and current registered residence is Hamburg. Tretschmer owns forty-nine percent of T&K. He's in his fifties and has been commercially active in Austria for decades. Tretschmer has an arrest record here, if an old one.

During the Cold War, Tretschmer was caught by Austrian authorities smuggling goods into the Soviet Union. Not dangerous stuff, but things the Soviet apparatchiki had trouble getting their hands on. High-end stereo equipment and shortwave radios made in Western Europe, for example. Tretschmer would get a wish list from his Soviet contacts and purchase things in the West, not declaring them and obviating the need to deal with customs or pay tax. He would transport the items undeclared through Austria, a neutral country with less rigorous border controls than West Germany at the time. Not a huge deal, but it establishes that Tretschmer has been involved in crime, willing to break the law to turn a profit."

"It demonstrates more than that, I'd say," Hirter added, speaking slowly. "It means Tretschmer has a decades-old history of involvement in illegal shipments. And now he's associated with a company Austrian customs suspects is papering over major dual-use shipments. It sounds like Tretschmer has graduated to the big leagues. And, interestingly, we have Hessler visiting Tretschmer's company here in Innsbruck. I don't know if any of this is related to Forster's death, but the connection is worth exploring. Kommissar Waldbaer, since Tretschmer is living in Hamburg, can you pursue this further?"

The stocky detective plunged his hands into the pockets of his loden jacket and nodded. "I can make inquiries through police channels. We may have more dirt on him. Still, unless he's the subject of a police investigation, we probably won't have records of his travel and that sort of thing. But the German intelligence service, the *Bundesnachrichtungdienst*—BND—just might. Hirter, perhaps your CIA friends can query them."

"Easily done," Hirter said. "CIA has a solid relationship with the BND. I'll check with my colleagues and get back to you. But I have something as well. Details, Kommissarin Reiner, that I think complement the information you've provided us."

"Indeed," the kommissarin replied. "Well, don't keep us in suspense, Herr Hirter."

Hirter pulled a folded piece of paper from a trouser pocket and lifted himself from the couch in a fluid motion. He unfolded the item and glanced at it a moment before speaking. "This is from CIA headquarters. I have to ask that the information stay with us; it can't be used in court proceedings because of our need to protect the source. But it confirms we are moving in the right direction by looking at T&K. Kommissarin Reiner told us about T—Tretschmer—and I want to talk about K. That initial stands for Khalid; full name Sayed al-Khalid. The Syrian partner of Tretschmer, and just as dubious a character, if not more so. Al-Khalid owns fifty-one percent of T&K, making him the majority owner. According to our information, al-Khalid keeps bad company. He is in contact with the IRGC—the Iranian Revolutionary Guards Corps—and the Syrian military. CIA believes al-Khalid has provided these clients with prohibited items in the past and serves as one of their most important covert commercial contacts. Our intelligence suggests al-Khalid is currently involved in a major transaction on behalf of the Iranians and Syrians."

Waldbaer fixed Hirter with his eyes. "What kind of major transaction?"

Hirter exhaled audibly. "We don't know yet. Al-Khalid speaks in code when discussing the deal with his customers, but it sounds like he's dealing with some sort of machinery."

A wry, self-satisfied smile crossed Waldbaer's lined features. "Meaning your information comes from a concealed listening device in al-Khalid's office or somewhere."

Hirter frowned and narrowed his eyes. "Don't go there, Kommissar. Like I said earlier, I can't reveal the sources or methods employed. You know the operating rules for information sharing."

Waldbaer barked a staccato, guttural laugh. "Quite so, Herr Hirter. The eternal and secretive rules so beloved by professional intelligence officers. All right, I won't ask again about your sacrosanct sources."

"Please continue, Herr Hirter," Frau Reiner prompted, returning to her position by the window, her form backlit into silhouette by the sun.

"Sure, Frau Reiner. CIA believes that whatever al-Khalid is currently engaged in, involves acquiring and transporting sensitive equipment on behalf of both the Iranians and the Syrians. That's interesting in itself. Al-Khalid would seem to have two clients, not just one. CIA judges that the acquisition stage is now nearly complete, and the goods will be shipped to an unknown destination shortly. It's also likely that the items of interest—probably some sort of machinery—are of European origin, possibly with some sort of weapons application. Which, in turn, means that the stuff will have to be moved out of Europe without arousing any suspicion. And that might be where Tretschmer plays a role. If what Kommissarin Reiner says is correct, Tretschmer would be experienced in concealing the nature of international shipments, and exactly that type of shipment would seem to be the area of T&K expertise. Something else. T&K on occasion works together with the Vienna-based company Verbindung Ost. You might both recall that Verbindung Ost has been linked to the late Georg Forster."

Waldbaer clapped his hands together with reverberating force. "*Sehr gut!* Now we're finally getting somewhere. I see it this way: Al-

Khalid and his partner Tretschmer are both unsavory types and vet-
erans at violating the law. They own T&K. The Austrian politician
Hessler has visited T&K in Innsbruck, so he's somehow connected
to it, possibly to one or both of its proprietors. T&K in Innsbruck has
a link to Verbindung Ost in Vienna. We also know that the subject
of our investigation, Forster, also had some sort of interest in that
Vienna firm and had visited its offices."

Still animated, Waldbaer tugged at the flesh beneath his chin
and navigated a slow circle around the room. "None of this, of
course, clarifies the reason for Forster's death. But it suggests Forster's
involvement in criminal dealings. Working in that environment is
a risky pursuit, taking the wrong step with the wrong people—people
like Tretschmer and al-Khalid—can get you killed. A taste for dirty
money, filthy lucre, call it what you will, often leads to a bad end. We
now have an avenue to pursue, and I intend to put Tretschmer in my
sights."

Reiner addressed Hirter. "You've provided information on al-
Khalid that neither Kommissar Waldbaer nor I would have come up
with, and I thank you. Is there anything else?"

Hirter's eyes narrowed as he considered. "No, that covers it. I
agree with Kommissar Waldbaer. Al-Khalid, Tretschmer, and their
link to Hessler is where we should focus. They're involved in something they want to conceal, and Forster was involved too. If we can
find out what kind of transaction is underway, we'll break this open."

The Austrian woman's features suggested that she was not convinced. "How does any of this explain the murder of the Israeli official in Munich? It's hard to believe his death is not connected to
Forster's. Forster was his quarry, after all."

Waldbaer issued a grunt of impatience. "We'll clarify the Israeli's
death in time. I'm certain of that. We can't expect to have every detail illuminated at once. Life is never that neat, and neither are investigations like this one. I want to get at Otto Tretschmer. The CIA
and BND might have background on him, but I would dearly love
to get a fix on what he is up to on a daily basis."

"That's easy. Put him under surveillance," Hirter offered.

Waldbaer lowered his chin and frowned. "Tretschmer's living in Hamburg. I don't have jurisdiction. And besides, it's by no means clear that we—or even the Hamburg police—have sufficient legal grounds, under German law, to follow him."

Hirter smiled. "Well, maybe I can be of some modest assistance."

Waldbaer's frown did not dissipate. "Why do I have an unsettled feeling, Hirter?"

Hirter's features took on a cast of innocence. "I'm sure I don't know, Kommissar. Look, I can have my CIA colleagues talk with their German intelligence counterparts. Maybe they can conduct joint observation activities informally. Without, shall we say, getting mired in troublesome bureaucratic requirements. "

The detective saw from the corner of his eye that his Austrian host, like Hirter, was grinning. "Intelligence officers! Never assiduously correct in their approach to legality and dismayingly cavalier with regards to the rigors of jurisprudence. Still, Hirter, what you say makes sense. If your spy friends and German intelligence are able to learn more about the mysterious Otto Tretschmer, I would surely be grateful. Do what you can."

"I will," Hirter replied, producing a Bic pen and making a note on a small square of paper.

Reiner's softer voice replaced Hirter's. "We've made progress. If the both of you follow up on Tretschmer and al-Khalid, I'll pursue our friend Anton Hessler. Kommissar, I might arrange another meeting with him. I'd like to conduct it alone, unless you object. I expect you'll have your hands full with the Tretschmer angle."

Waldbaer was pleased that his permission was being solicited by the woman he still regarded as the junior partner in the investigation. He felt expansive. "Quite all right, Kommissarin. Why don't we give you the lead in the Austrian part of the investigation? Hessler is in Innsbruck, after all, and you know best how things work here in Tyrol. Feel free to conduct a solo debriefing of Hessler. Let's get together in two days. You can brief Hirter and me at that time. If you'd like my input on what questions to ask Hessler, just let me know."

•   •   •

Sabine Reiner clasped her hands at waist level and wondered at her ambivalence about her German partner. He had solid investigative traits, surely, but also seemed invincibly unaware that he often sounded like an arrogant, domineering ass. She kept her voice controlled, coating it with civility. "Thank you for your offer, Kommissar Waldbaer. I'm certain I can tackle Hessler on my own. As for briefing you in two days, I will. Just as I'm certain you will brief Hirter and me on Tretschmer." Her smile spoke of winter.

HAMBURG, NORTH GERMANY

Otto Tretschmer felt the taste of copper suffuse his mouth as he read the brief article in the Hamburger Abendblatt newspaper. The coffee he had just sipped suddenly turned acrid as he read the headline a second time, hoping that his first interpretation of the words had been incorrect. No, he saw with a sinking feeling, there was no misapprehension at play. He uttered a sigh that was nearly a moan, and closed his eyes. Even with eyes closed, he could clearly see the headline accorded the little article at the middle of the page in the section called Harbor News, which recorded items of commercial maritime interest.

Crewman Feared Drowned in Atlantic Incident; *Condor Fury* Reports Man Overboard During Voyage

Tretschmer felt a throb of anger rise from his chest and take up residence in his head. His stomach, at the same time, was suddenly queasy and threatened to expel the just concluded repast of eggs Benedict, sunflower roll, and veal sausage. "Imbecile, moron, fool," he pronounced aloud before forcing his eyes open again. Around him was the comfortable and familiar lair of his leafy garden terrace, but the image fixed in his mind was of a bullet-headed fireplug of a man in a peacoat. Zellmann did this; that animated pile of seagull shit called a ship's captain is responsible.

The tall, spare businessman cinched his patterned-silk morning

gown more tightly around his seated figure and rubbed long, pale fingers against his temple. What in God's name had the man been
thinking? Why hadn't Zellmann said something to him upon arrival
in Hamburg? What did it all mean and, of vastly more pressing im-
portance, what were the likely consequences for the current transaction? Tretschmer unleashed another toxic stream of vituperation,
leaned back in his wrought-iron garden chair, and willed himself to
breathe evenly and deeply. A moment later, he decided to read the
article again in its entirety.

Crewman Feared Drowned in Atlantic Incident; Condor Fury Reports Man Overboard During Voyage

Hamburg Harbor Police records note that a crewman
aboard the cargo ship *Condor Fury*, of Belize registry and Austrian ownership, was reported missing by the vessel off of the
Angolan coast. The crewman is presumed to have fallen
overboard one night during the *Condor Fury*'s voyage to
Hamburg, laden with a shipment of Asian rice. The missing
man, identified as Mr. Arturo Reyes, thirty-seven years old,
is of Philippine nationality and is now presumed dead. Police
interview of *Condor Fury* captain Horst Zellmann produced
an indication that the deceased had been depressed and
withdrawn during the voyage, and suicide has not been ruled
out as cause of death. Zellmann has in recent years captained
both the *Condor Fury* and its sister ship, the *Harbor Seeker*,
both owned by T&K Impex, GmbH, of Innsbruck, Austria.
The missing man's next of kin, residents of Manila, have
been advised.

Tretschmer felt a grimace of a cold smile cross his face unsummoned. The next of kin have been advised of the death, but Zellmann's employers have not been provided the same courtesy by the
good captain. Folding the broadsheet, Tretschmer placed it at the
center of the heavy glass table in front of him. He reached for the

coffee contained within the delicate, egg-blue contours of an early twentieth-century Meissen porcelain cup, but the liquid still tasted acidic. Tretschmer knew that he needed to immediately determine his next step.

He would have to advise Anton Hessler, of course, and soon. There could be no attempt at deceit on this point, especially as T&K and Hessler's home city had been mentioned in the article. It would not be a pleasant conversation, especially as he had just told Hessler in Berlin that all was well. But talking to Hessler, urgent as it was, would not be the first step. Tretschmer knew that he had to establish as many facts as possible beforehand, and there was only one source that could provide the required information, Horst Zellmann.

He would have to meet that feckless idiot of a captain again, confront him, and force him to reveal what had transpired on board the *Condor Fury* during the voyage to Hamburg. He wondered what had happened. Was it a simple incident of a man falling overboard, accidentally or on suicidal impulse? If so, why had Zellmann withheld this information? Or, was there something more sinister at work?

Tretschmer did not doubt that the powerfully built cretin Zellmann was capable of murder. Indeed, ability to murder if instructed to do so had to be viewed as an asset. But Zellmann had not been instructed to murder anyone, least of all a crewman aboard the ship that would soon be employed to transport a highly illegal sensitive cargo out of Hamburg. If Zellmann had killed the Filipino, what was his reason? Some personal quarrel, perhaps, over women, or men, or boys, or gambling debts? Tretschmer was well aware of the debased and often depraved nature of those who made their living on the sea, and viewed the mariner lifestyle with enormous distaste. But perhaps the death had not been some sordid personal quarrel. Had there been some other reason for Zellmann to kill the crewman, if indeed he had?

Tretschmer pulled himself from the table, the legs of the black iron chair scraping irritably against the flagstone. He picked up the newspaper and walked the few steps to the house, entering through the open French doors of the study. He would dress and immediately head to a phone booth located in the Alster park, half a mile distant. He would need to arrange another personal meeting with the deceitful Zellmann and it would have to be accomplished soon.

PULLACH, NEAR MUNICH

Hirter drove at modest tempo down the quiet residential street, taking in the array of homes on both sides of the well-paved road. Without exception, he noted, the houses were stately, most painted in Italianate ochre or vanilla white, and the word "villa" would readily apply to most of them.

This suburb of Munich near the banks of the Isar River exuded a supercilious haughtiness, the homes and exquisitely manicured lawns and flawless terraces playing their role as physical expressions of self-regarding success. Most of the houses were surrounded by stucco walls, some four feet in height, some taller, making the neighborhood appear to be a series of compounds, defensively private.

Hirter could not imagine that the people living here side by side interacted either often or well. As if to underline the point, an elderly wraith of a man with a patch of white hair opened a wrought-iron gate and retrieved mail from a bronze letter box. He glanced up as Hirter drove past, his face a mask of frowning suspicion and condescension. After all, Hirter was driving a mere Opel Insignia, far too proletarian for the streets of Pullach. He could not stifle a staccato laugh; the foibles of men did not vary much from Pullach to the privileged enclave of McLean, Virginia, or the effete Kensington section of London.

In deference to the sound-sensitive ears of Pullach inhabitants, the permitted speed limit was a languorous thirty kilometers an hour and Hirter did not stray from this, not wanting to earn a recorded and expensive violation from some concealed police camera. After all, he knew from the Opel's GPS that his destination was only minutes away. The imposing residences in their pastel hues slowly fell away, replaced by rows of oak trees on both sides of the road and, moments later, by a long, unwelcoming gray wall on the driver's side.

Eventually, the wall gave way to an entrance area. A sign affixed with a stylized eagle announced the headquarters of the *Bundesnachtrichtungsdienst*, or BND, the German intelligence service.

Hirter pulled the car over to a cobblestone parking apron, turned off the ignition, and surveyed the scene. Ahead of him was a small, squat gray structure, bunker-like in its design. A uniformed security official peered at him from behind a plate of bulletproof glass and Hirter noticed the man squint at the Opel's license plate and speak into a phone. Hirter pushed up the sleeve of his white oxford shirt, checked his wristwatch, and waited.

Two minutes later a silver Mercedes sedan exited the walled compound, navigated a U-turn, and pulled up in front of Hirter. An athletic man in his thirties exited the vehicle and approached, the sun washing over his shaved head and wraparound sunglasses. Hirter lowered the driver's window and nodded. "*Gruess Gott.*"

The mouth below the sunglasses smiled. "*Gruess Gott.* You must be Herr Hirter. Welcome to the BND. My name is Neureuth. Just follow me into the compound, please. We've arranged a private meeting venue."

Hirter signaled agreement and engaged the engine. The Mercedes proceeded at a regal pace, the BND driver waving to the guard in the gatehouse, the Opel following in its wake.

Hirter glanced around at the surroundings once the gate receded behind him. The scene was pastoral, with stands of trees and expanses of mown grass predominating. It appeared more like a university campus than the headquarters of an intelligence service. A brace of solemn ravens in a pine tree regarded the vehicles with taciturn avian indifference. Hirter stayed on the tail of the Mercedes as it navigated a series of winding streets, past rows of architecturally prosaic two-story buildings. Hirter noted an array of tall antennae receivers and parabolic dishes in the distance, indicating that signals intercept activity, the monitoring and mining of electronic communications, took place in this benign landscape as well.

Hirter followed the sedan in front of him as it turned right and passed through a gap in a tall concrete wall. On the other side of the wall, the street debouched into a broad parking lot, largely empty. The Mercedes pulled to a stop and Hirter edged his vehicle beside it. Both he and Neureuth exited their vehicles simultaneously.

The man with the shaved head pointed to a building adjoining the parking lot. "That's our meeting place, Herr Hirter. It's the formal reception residence of the BND president. We will be his guests."

Hirter cocked his head in surprise. "We're meeting with the president of your service? On a minor operational request?"

Neureuth uttered a soft laugh and dragged a foot along the ground, moving some pebbles. "Not as minor as you might think, Herr Hirter. But I should permit the president to explain that himself. I am what you would call the relevant case officer for your request, but it seems you've stumbled onto a matter of political sensitivity, thus the president's personal involvement."

Hirter mumbled an inchoate sound deep in his throat and ran a hand through his thick hair. "Political sensitivity? That doesn't sound good. To my ears, that sounds like a complication. Do we have a problem, Herr Neureuth?"

Neureuth plucked the sunglasses from his face, revealing pale blue eyes.

Like an Alaskan husky, Hirter thought.

The German guided Hirter across the parking lot toward an oversize brown wooden door. "I wouldn't say we have a problem, Herr Hirter. But I would say we need to consider the implications of what BND President Gagner is about to tell you." Without another word, Neureuth opened the door and ushered the American into a formal lobby with an ascending staircase. A large, gilt-framed portrait of a fiercely mustached, gruff-looking Otto von Bismarck dominated one wall.

"Is that painting a Lenbach?" Hirter queried.

Neureuth nodded and seemed to assess his guest anew. "Very good, Herr Hirter. Quite right. The portrait was indeed done by

Franz von Lenbach, Bismarck's contemporary. It belongs to the German government and is on permanent loan here. You are schooled in art?"

Hirter placed his hands in his pockets and shook his head sideways. "No, just an avocation. But I like historical portrait painting and nineteenth-century scenes. I've been to the Lenbach gallery in Munich. I'm impressed that BND art is not just an anarchic riot of colors tossed on canvas, which seems the preferred style at Langley."

Neureuth revealed straight, white teeth as he smiled. "Perhaps we're more traditional here, for better or worse. I rather like seeing the painting hang here. It suggests continuity in German affairs of state, despite the terrible, wrenching episodes of the last century. But we should move on, we are meeting in the garden." Neureuth strode through an open doorway and Hirter followed.

The garden was small, formal, and pleasing to the eye. A long, rectangular reflecting pool served as the centerpiece, embraced by a stone terrace. A copse of thick, trimmed bushes and a few mature trees provided a verdant background, the broad leaves providing shade from the afternoon sun. The overall atmosphere was one of timeless tranquility. A bronze statue of a female nude added to an overall air of classic style. Standing a few feet behind the nude, a fully dressed man in wire-rim eyeglasses, yellow bow tie, and a charcoal gray suit stood silently with folded hands. "Welcome to Pullach, Herr Hirter. I am Dr. Thomas Gagner." The voice was deep and self-confident.

"It's a pleasure, sir," Robert offered.

The tall man laughed. "Is it? Perhaps we should hold such judgments until we've had our conversation, *nicht wahr*? I understand from Herr Neureuth that you are involved with the Bavarian police in an investigation. An investigation in which the name of a German businessman has surfaced."

"That's right, Doctor. A Herr Otto Tretschmer. A resident of Hamburg."

The BND chief bit his lip, linked his hands behind his back, and began to stroll the garden, Hirter and Neureuth flanking him. "Yes, Otto Tretschmer. It is doubtless obvious to you, Herr Hirter, that the BND has information on Tretschmer, or we wouldn't be here today. So let me cut to the chase, as you Americans like to say."

"I appreciate your candor," Hirter interjected.

"The candor is required by events, Herr Hirter. It's like this. My service believes that Tretschmer is a thoroughly bad character involved in illegal trade activities, possibly weapons proliferation. We have information from sources on this, but cannot demonstrate it in a German court. To be frank, we've picked up conversation between Tretschmer and suspicious persons overseas. I won't play games, as long as you understand this conversation is off the record.

"Tretschmer has been dealing—and is dealing still—with a certain Jahanghir Karimov, an Azeri criminal located in Baku. Karimov is a thug, probably a murderer, if rumors in Baku are to be credited. But he's protected in Azerbaijan. Corruption is rife there, and he's bought himself immunity. Our intelligence interests in Karimov uncovered his connection to Tretschmer, something we hadn't expected. This Karimov has solid ties to people in Russia with access to certain nuclear materials. He's willing to sell such material to interested parties with enough cash, and we believe that is the basis of his link to Tretschmer."

When Gagner paused, Hirter raised a hand for emphasis. "This is solid background, Dr. Gagner, thank you. It confirms suspicions we have."

"Fine. There's more. You are aware that Tretschmer is in Hamburg, Germany's largest port. We've established that Tretschmer is dealing there with another German citizen, Horst Zellmann, captain of a vessel called the *Condor Fury*. We know there is a connection, but that's about all we know. Tretschmer is tricky; he's security conscious and deals with Zellmann in a conspirative manner. This, of course, only makes us more suspicious. More than likely, Tretschmer is using Zellmann and his ship to move illicit goods out of Hamburg, and this may all be tied in with Karimov in Azerbaijan.

BND interest in Tretschmer and Zellmann goes deeper than this, however. But my colleague Herr Neureuth is here for a purpose, and I ask him to provide the necessary details."

Neureuth moved his gaze to the reflecting pool as he spoke. "Yes. As I mentioned earlier, Herr Hirter, I am, like you, an operations officer. One of the operations I've been responsible for involves the *Condor Fury*. For some time, we've had unconfirmed reports from human sources that the ship has been involved in moving weapons and undeclared items internationally. Perhaps true, perhaps not. As you know, human sources can be wrong, or can be repeating unsubstantiated gossip, or can have an axe to grind. Be that as it may, we are determined to try to find out, as the *Condor Fury* often berths in Hamburg and is thus something of a German problem. Several months ago, I recruited a Filipino crewman of the *Condor Fury* and secured his agreement to report on the ship's activities in exchange for money to be paid into an escrow account. Name of Arturo Reyes. Clear so far?"

Hirter nodded. "Entirely. A classic agent recruitment operation. Go ahead."

"We provided Arturo with requirements and asked him to inconspicuously listen in on any of Zellmann's conversation that he could, without endangering himself. We also provided him with a satellite linked burst transmission device and trained him in its use."

"I have some familiarity with the technology," Hirter said with a thin smile. "So, this Arturo transmitted information to you from the *Condor Fury*?"

Neureuth exchanged a glance with his superior, who, with a nod, signaled permission to continue. "Yes. We could have waited until our source got to Hamburg, but we were anxious for real-time intelligence, in case any of it could be acted upon immediately. Remember that the BND is an external intelligence service, meaning it's legally easier for us to engage in activity overseas than it is inside Germany. At any rate, something went very wrong in the shipping lanes off the African coast. Arturo initiated a transmission and that's the last we heard from him, even though he'd been instructed to transmit a 'sign of life' message every three days. When the *Condor Fury* eventually docked in Hamburg, Captain Zellmann claimed to the authorities that Arturo had fallen, or jumped, overboard. As with most 'man overboard' cases, it's nearly impossible to prove otherwise, even if foul play is involved. The fact is, our agent is dead and it surely is no accident."

Hirter exhaled and shook his head. "I know how you must feel. I lost two sources in South America years ago and will never forget it. You obviously think Zellmann is responsible. But how about Tretschmer? Do you think the ship's captain was acting on Tretschmer's instructions? And have you gone to the Hamburg police?"

Neureuth opened his mouth to answer, but Gagner placed a hand on his shoulder in a restraining gesture and picked up the narrative. "Those questions are perhaps easier for me to answer, Herr Hirter. This is where things get complicated and why I am talking to you today rather than leaving it to Herr Neureuth to explain. If the BND approaches the police, we have to reveal that the dead man was a clandestine source of our service. That's German law. This information, in turn, would come up in any legal proceedings that take place. In other words, our secret intelligence operation would become public. The government of the Philippines would protest that we had recruited one of its citizens and placed him in danger, which would cause a diplomatic incident. Grieving family members would demand we make compensation for the death. The owner of the *Condor Fury* would ask to know on what basis we were spying on their vessel and lodge an official complaint. The press would get involved in its usual dilettantish way and this, in turn, would prompt some of our preening, leftist politicians to demand a formal inquiry into BND activity. In other words, a feeding frenzy. This is what I want to avoid. So, there will be no approach to the police and no hint of our involvement with the deceased. Such things are the price of intelligence work. I suspect the CIA can well understand such a sentiment."

Hirter found himself sympathetic. Every intelligence agency in a democracy faced the same dilemmas, the CIA not least among them. "I understand, Dr. Gagner, perfectly. I know where this is leading. The information you've just given me can't be made part of an official investigation involving the German police, such as the investigation I'm engaged in, correct?"

Gagner pointed a finger at Hirter's chest. "Correct. We just had a confidential exchange between intelligence services. Law enforcement authorities must not be involved."

Hirter moved a few feet to the reflecting pool, bent, and dipped in a hand, testing its temperature before turning again to his hosts. "A question. May I share your story with two law enforcement officials, if I guarantee it remains entirely off the record?"

The BND president frowned and pulled at the folds of his bow tie. "Accepted. As long as you can attest to the discretion of your police friends. They need to understand that the contents of our chat cannot be used in legal proceedings, period. You are responsible to ensure they play by our rules, Herr Hirter."

"Understood. One other thing. It's clear from what you've said that the BND doesn't have legal grounds to conduct surveillance on Tretschmer and Zellmann. But would you object to someone else informally observing them? It could establish what these two are up to, and what items they might be moving out of Germany, and when."

Gagner narrowed his eyes as he regarded Hirter. "If you are asking my permission for you to conduct surveillance against German citizens, Herr Hirter, I fear I must disappoint you. Especially in Hamburg, which is sovereign German territory. On the other hand, I can only prohibit things I am actually aware of, if you follow me."

All three of the men smiled. Hirter extended a hand and shook Gagner's, then Neureuth's. "Very good, Doctor. That will suffice. I understand."

Gagner moved to a nearby bush and plucked off the curled brown form of a dead leaf. "One more thing, Herr Hirter. Regarding the results that might be obtained from the surveillance that I am unaware of. I would expect to be kept apprised. Informally and orally, of course."

"Of course. I won't trouble you any longer. You've both been most generous with your time and information. I've enjoyed our walk in your garden."

A contemplative look crossed Gagner's features. "It's not my garden, really. It long predates my time here. Unfortunately, the garden's pedigree is National Socialist. This compound belonged to the Wehrmacht during the war. Some of the Nazi Party leadership used these spaces as well, especially when Hitler traveled from Berlin to his home at Bertchesgaden, which isn't all that far from here. It is said that this garden was designed for that fanatic, beer-bellied lout Martin Bormann, who strolled it frequently in polished brown jack-boots. God knows what kind of conversations these silent stones and trees must have witnessed during those times."

Hirter nodded, always surprised at how history seemed to lie just beneath the surface in Germany, its spoor too often a malevolent imprint. "Well, Doctor, with any luck, our conversation today could save lives and disrupt some nasty activity. Maybe that will help dispel some of the ghosts of that era." But, Hirter thought to himself, it is less the apparitions of the past that worried him than the demons of the present.

AMMAN, JORDAN

Sayed al-Khalid savored a mouthful of marinated lamb and tucked his fork into the heap of couscous on his plate. The restaurant was middle class, of no particular distinction and too brightly lit, but it was clean and the fare invariably good. More importantly, it was in al-Khalid's Amman neighborhood, just a few minutes from his apartment. He frequented the establishment at least twice a week. Al-Khalid was reaching for his glass of Coca-Cola on ice when he noticed a shadow fall over his table.

"Good evening," a voice above him said. "May I join you?" The query was pro forma, as the man who had so unexpectedly appeared at tableside slipped without hesitation into the chair opposite the diner.

Al-Khalid stared across the white tablecloth at a tall, mustached man with earnest features wearing a dark suit with an open collar shirt. The man was a stranger to him. His fork of couscous was suspended in midair as he tried to assess the situation. Sayed decided on a courteous approach. "Excuse me, but who are you?"

The stranger smiled in a revelation of perfectly white teeth. "That is quite unimportant. Considerably more important is who you are."

Al-Khalid dropped his fork back to the plate. He felt confused and uncomfortable, a cold talon of incipient fear dragging lightly along his skin. "I'm sorry, I don't have the faintest idea what you're talking about. I would be quite appreciative if you would respect my privacy."

The visitor's smiling white teeth vanished, a more somber cast defining the man's features. He placed both his hands on the table in a gentle clasp. "Sayed al-Khalid, it is unwise of you to assume a haughty manner with me. You are not in a position to dismiss me. Perhaps you've forgotten that you are a guest here in Jordan. You might say that I, for my part, am one of your hosts." The man moved a hand to the inside of his jacket and drew out a laminated identification card.

Al-Khalid stared at the document long enough to make out the distinctive symbol of the GID. His mouth felt unaccountably dry. He was unsure what to say.

The guest did not wait for a response. "So, al-Khalid, let us not waste time with theatric protestations. I am in a position to take your Syrian passport and invalidate the visa. That is not a course of action I choose to take, but it is most surely within my powers, understood? I can also see to it that your apartment is confiscated. Perhaps that provides a better basis for our conversation. Let us speak frankly. Your business activities are of some concern to this kingdom. What you do in Syria or elsewhere might not interest us, but you conduct some of your activities here in Amman. This we know absolutely, so do not waste your breath making meaningless protestations. I am here to discuss your commercial dealings. Based upon what you say, we'll determine what is to be done. Clear?" The man smiled again at the Syrian, but the set of his visage was without any hint of warmth.

Sayed al-Khalid raised a tremulous hand and massaged his forehead. A sigh escaped his lips and his eyes roamed the placid restaurant scene as if he were searching for allies. "All right. We can talk. But I am feeling unwell. I need to visit the men's room. When I come back, I can tell you some things. The last thing I need is to lose my visa and apartment."

The visitor regarded al-Khalid neutrally. "Go to the men's room. If you are thinking of making an escape, that would be exceedingly unwise. My people are posted outside and they know who you are. Don't take too long."

Al-Khalid nodded and rose, heading with a slow gait across the restaurant toward a white door bearing the stick-figure image of a man. Once inside the lavatory, he glanced around, confirming that he was alone. The Syrian stood at the sink, glancing in the mirror at his pallid face. He noted that he was still shaking slightly; a representative of the GID was not his idea of a welcome dinner guest. Reaching into his trouser pocket, he extracted a Nokia cell phone and punched in a series of numbers, struggling to control his trembling fingers. He heard the phone emit five rings. "Please answer," he implored. The phone rang a sixth time before being replaced by a voice, tinny and distant.

"Yes? Who is this?" The metallic-sounding inquiry carried an undertow of suspicion.

"Yes, yes, hello. This is your friend from Amman. I have to alert you. We have a problem, big or small I don't yet know. The secret police are nearby and they want to talk to me about our dealings. I have no idea what information they might have assembled, but they obviously know something. I can't talk to you for long, they're waiting for me." Al-Khalid licked at his parched lips. "I'm scared. These are not nice people."

Otto Tretschmer's voice was soothing. "Stay calm, Sayed, don't panic. They can't possibly know much. Perhaps they've picked up some rumors or even seen you meet me over there. Maybe they have found out the places you've traveled to. But that doesn't tell them anything important."

Al-Khalid issued a vibrato sigh into the phone. "I am confused. What do they want from me? I have to tell them something. I don't want them to hurt me."

The disembodied voice in the distance remained dispassionate, absent discernible emotion. "Sayed, relax. I doubt they will hurt you, I doubt they are that crude. They're fishing for information, trying to frighten you into telling them things they don't know. It's important that you not reveal our enterprise. Lie to them. Act like you are being cooperative, come up with a plausible story. It's all right if they think you and your contacts are corrupt, they would expect that, and it is of no interest to the security services. But you must conceal the nature of our transaction. I'm certain a man of your talent can persuade them that you are not a threat to the Jordanians. I understand that you have to go. I'll call you in a few days and perhaps we can arrange to meet in Europe. Good luck. This will blow over, I am sure of it."

"I hope so, Allah willing. At least now you are informed. I will try to leave Jordan if it is possible. Goodbye." Al-Khalid pressed a button, turning off the device. He splashed a handful of water from the sink on his face, wiped it with a paper towel, and left the lavatory, returning to his table and the waiting intelligence officer.

"Feeling better now, al-Khalid?" Hamdi al-Bakhit had decided to employ a solicitous tone, at least initially.

Al-Khalid seated himself and pushed away the plate of half-eaten food. "I am feeling unhappy. I don't know why you are interested in me. I have done nothing against the kingdom of Jordan, I swear by the Prophet." He took a long sip of the icy cola to cool the hot spot that had nestled behind his forehead. "I am willing to leave Amman, if that's what you want."

The GID officer regarded al-Khalid clinically. "It doesn't work that way. It works this way. You tell me what you know about the business you are currently conducting and who you are dealing with in Europe. Names and addresses and phone numbers. What products are you moving and to what destination? Who is the end user? When I am satisfied that you have been truthful, I might allow you to leave the country and scurry back to Syria. But not before I am satisfied. Those are my rules. I am willing to let you go if you cooperate, al-Khalid. If you dissemble, or play games, the consequences will not be to your liking. Clear? Are you ready to talk to me?" Al-Bakhit arched his eyebrows.

Al-Khalid rubbed the soft drink glass slowly across his forehead and closed his eyes. "Yes, I will talk, damn it."

"Go ahead."

Al-Khalid cast a nervous glance around the restaurant, but registered only disinterested customers and a waiter underway with a carafe of tea. "It's true that I am dealing with some Europeans. In Austria. One of them is a Herr Thiel from Vienna. The phone numbers and e-mail address I can get you, but that stuff is in my office in Syria, not here. For security reasons. I admit that what we're doing is illegal, but how much business in this region isn't?"

The intelligence officer's features betrayed no reaction. "What kind of business, al-Khalid?"

The businessman looked at the tablecloth and exhaled loudly. "Weapons. Automatic weapons. I'm purchasing Austrian-made Glock weapons and some Russian-produced stuff for my Syrian contacts. It's a big order, a shipping container full of guns and ammunition. Between us, it's destined for Hezbollah in southern Lebanon. The Syrians would kill me if they knew I told you this; they'd cut my head off. I'm supposed to fly to Austria and facilitate the payment to Herr Thiel and use a false end-user certificate to move the items from the European Union to Cyprus. The Syrians will pick up the goods by boat in Cyprus. I get a ten percent cut, which is normal under the circumstances." Al-Khalid paused, trying without success to assess his interlocutor. Frustrated, he continued. "The deal is ready now. Once I arrive in Austria, we proceed and shipment can take place within a few days, Allah willing. If you pledge not to confiscate my apartment, I'm willing to make the journey and report back to you. I can even meet some of your people in Vienna, if you want, at the Jordanian Embassy perhaps. But you will decide that, I expect."

The GID man nodded slightly. "Anything else you want to tell me?"

"I'll check my apartment to see if there are any other details that might interest you. But now you know the facts about the deal. This puts me in considerable danger, and I hope you use the information with discretion."

"Of course," al-Bakhit said absent emotion. "It grows late and I have an early day tomorrow. Let us leave here."

Al-Khalid eased a clutch of dinars from his wallet and tossed them on the table. He followed a few steps behind the intelligence officer as they exited the restaurant and stepped into the coolness of the Jordanian evening. He bought the ruse, al-Khalid concluded, overcome with a frisson of relief and self-confidence. At least the legend is plausible enough that he isn't putting up a fuss. He had to force himself not to smile.

The intelligence officer turned to al-Khalid in the darkened parking lot that opened onto the street with its necklace of street-lamps. "You will be walking home from here, I suppose?"

The Syrian nodded. "Yes, I will walk. It clears my head. You un-derstand that this is not a pleasant evening for me. I have given you valuable information that I am pledged to protect. And I expect that I will be seeing you again, unfortunately for me."

Al-Bakhit frowned, the facial motion caught imperfectly in the shadows. "Whether we meet again is up to you, really."

Khalid did not mask his surprise. "Indeed? Up to me?"

Al-Bakhit shrugged his shoulders in a dismissive gesture, as if contemplating a trifle. "Yes. But I should explain. While you were in the men's room—where I presume you made a phone call to one of your cronies—I took the liberty of adding something to your Coca-Cola. To be crudely unscientific, it is a poison. Invariably lethal for humans in the dose that I administered. I was surprised that you didn't notice the extra effervescence in the glass. But there you have it. I did warn you that there would be unhappy consequences to lying, and you lied. If your story had been more credible, I would have stayed your hand before you reached for the glass."

Al-Bakhit paused. "Here's what happens next. In about an hour you will begin to feel a bit queasy. Uncomfortable, but tolerable. This will change, of course. The intensity of your stomach complaint will increase incrementally. You will begin to sweat, although, I am told, you will feel unaccountably cold. I don't understand these things, I'm not a doctor. The irritation will turn to severe cramps over the next few hours and your system will react by trying to expel the poison. This is an exceedingly unpleasant process, and you will forgive me for not elaborating. Anyway, after this involuntary systemic reaction, which will fail to halt the spread of the poison, your internal organs will begin to weaken. Indeed, they will begin to slowly liquefy because the poison acts as a sort of powerful acid. As your insides assume the consistency of lamb stew, the internal bleeding will reach hemorrhagic proportions. Death will follow in all of its moaning, screaming, incontinent intensity. But not as quickly as you will like, Sayed al-Khalid."

Al-Khalid stared at the shadowed shape before him in a wordless stupor. This cannot be happening, he thought. It was a moment before he detected that he was passing urine in his trousers, the material moistly matted to his left leg. "You son of a dog," he whispered, wondering where his voice had gone. "You would not do this."

"I tell you, it is already done. The process has begun."

The Syrian inhaled, whimpered, and pressed a palm to his cheek, wet with tears. "I want to live. I don't want to die this way, not like this."

Al-Bakhit pulled his suit coat tighter against the cool intrusion of the desert night. "An understandable desire. If nothing else, it demonstrates that you have some fragment of humanity after all. If I were you, al-Khalid, I would hasten home and go through this process in privacy. Spare yourself the humiliation of a death like this in public."

"Help me." Al-Khalid noticed that both his legs were shaking. Was this a purely nervous reaction or was it a signal of the onset of the poison? "Help me."

Al-Bakhit extracted a small rectangle of paper from his jacket and passed it to the weeping Syrian. "I need to think about it. Here is my business card and telephone number. As I said, you lied to me, which was most unwise. It's true that I do possess an antidote to the poison. But I am not a fool and will not be taken for one. If I give the antidote to you, you would probably just begin to lie again."

Al-Khalid emitted a plaintive groan and raised a hand in a gesture of denial. "No, only the truth, I swear."

Al-Bakhit moved a few steps away and paused, lifting his head to inspect a desert sky rampant with stars. "Here is what you can do, al-Khalid. Go back to your apartment. Do not hesitate, you will soon feel the onset of the poison. But while you are able, write down for me everything that you know that might interest me. Everything. When you think that you have written a useful narrative, call me. I will drop by and read your report. I will bring the antidote with me. If I am satisfied with your offering, I will administer it. If not, well, we already know what will occur. If I were you, I would get to work in a hurry. You need to understand that once the organs begin to disintegrate, even the antidote cannot help. I am not your enemy, al-Khalid, time is your enemy. Go quickly."

Al-Bakhit turned on his heel and walked across the parking lot toward his car. He heard behind him a groan and a rush of feet as al-Khalid scurried home, but he did not turn, did not want to indicate interest. Good, he thought with a note of satisfaction. There was a good chance that he would have the information he required within a few hours. He would head to his home in a village outside of Amman, sip a cold tin of Jordanian-brewed Tuborg and wait for the inevitable whining, pleading phone call from al-Khalid. It would, he felt certain, be a productive evening.

HAMBURG, GERMANY

"You have betrayed my trust in you. From the moment you arrived here on the *Condor Fury*, you were concealing things from me. And this was no inconsequential deceit, it was an important matter that I had every right to know. You have placed our entire activity in jeopardy through your lies."

Otto Tretschmer stared unblinkingly at Horst Zellmann. They were standing in the shadows provided by the concealing branches of a willow tree in the Alster Park, out of earshot from the passerby on the gravel footpath several yards removed. The morning air was gray, with a tubercular dampness, and both men huddled inside of their jackets.

"I never lied to you," the ship's captain mumbled, hooded eyes searching the ground at his feet.

"That's just another lie. By concealing from me that someone died on board the ship, you in effect lied to me. You knew that such an occurrence was something I should know. So stop trying to defend the indefensible. That I had to find out about this incident through a chance reading of the newspaper infuriates me. I demand the truth right now or, believe me, I will find another captain for the onward voyage of the *Condor Fury*, regardless of how difficult that might be at this stage, understand?"

Zellmann continued his careful observation of the grass near his feet and grunted a guttural "*Ja.*"

With a fluid motion, Tretschmer brushed a thick shock of hair back from his forehead and endeavored to rid his voice of anger. Seeking a dispassionate tone, he forced himself to look out at the broad expanse of the Alster. Tretschmer let himself breathe deeply of damp air before continuing. "I need to know about the death of the Philippine crewman—the truth this time. Did he really kill himself as you suggested in the press article?"

Zellmann raised his eyes and squinted at Tretschmer. "*Nein.* That piece of shit didn't kill himself and he didn't accidentally fall overboard either. I killed him. At night. On deck, when he was alone, with a screwdriver. Don't worry, no one saw a damned thing."

Tretschmer felt a surge of fury return and start to take hold in his chest, but forced it away. "Why did you kill him?"

Zellmann raised both of his thick hands and let them fall by his side in a gesture of resignation. "I had to do it. No choice at all. The little Asiatic bastard was a *spitzel*, a spy. I had my suspicions for a while. He always seemed to be trying to see what I was up to, or listen to my conversation. One time, trying to sound casual, he asked me what consignment we would pick up in Hamburg after we offloaded the rice. But it wasn't a casual question, I could sense it. So I began to watch him, and I found him out." A crease of self-satisfied smile traced its way across Zellmann's doughy features.

"What exactly did you see that convinced you he should be killed?"

"I saw that piece of garbage try to contact somebody electronically. He had some sort of communication device and was trying to use it starboard. The little bastard was trying to hide, but I had my eyes on him. Before he could speak into that thing, I got him. Took him from behind, fast. I ripped his guts up with a screwdriver from the engine room and he whined like a swine. It was all over in a minute, and I tossed his worthless carcass overboard. I knew there'd be nothing for anyone to find, like in most 'man overboard' cases."

Tretschmer continued to glare at the captain, nodded slowly, and tugged lightly at his chin. "And what did you do with this communication device?"

Zellmann shrugged his shoulders, making his bull neck seem even shorter. "Tossed that overboard, too. Didn't want evidence around when the Hamburg police eventually got on board to do their cursory investigation."

Tretschmer could not keep the exasperation from coloring his voice. "I would have dearly liked to have seen that equipment. Did it have a receiver, a microphone?"

Zellmann furrowed his brow, squeezing his eyes into small creases in his fleshy face.

God, he looks every bit a Neanderthal, Tretschmer thought. *What kind of genetic heritage do these people have?*

Zellmann hacked and spit into the grass. "No, I don't recall seeing anything looking like a mike. But that doesn't matter, you don't see them on cell phones either. There were just a couple of buttons and LEDs on this thing. The important point is, I'm certain he didn't get to talk."

Tretschmer rubbed the bridge of his nose, feeling unwell. "Has it occurred to you that the fellow might not have had to speak? I expect that what you saw might have been a text-transmission device. Almost certainly encrypted to keep the contents from prying eyes."

Zellmann shifted his stance and seemed uncertain. "It could have been something like that, I guess. I don't know. One thing struck me, though. There was no logo or brand name or anything written on that chunk of black plastic. Not a damn thing. I thought that was strange."

Tretschmer's mood was not improving with Zellmann's revelations. "That's not good news," he said, "not good in the least, Zellmann. What it suggests is that your Filipino friend was in the possession of a sophisticated device. Which raises the next unhappy question. Who gave him such a device and why? He was surely in the employ of an organization with considerable means. I suspect a police department, or naval force, or similar. In other words, 'the authorities'—somehow defined."

Zellmann grunted and cocked his head. "Well, it doesn't matter anymore. *Tot ist Tot*; dead is dead. And that shitty little device, no matter how sophisticated, is lying on the ocean floor miles from the African coast. I made sure of that." He loosed another crooked grin at the taller man.

Tretschmer did not return the smile. "Actually, Zellmann, what you made sure of is that we will never know what type of communications gear that Filipino was using, or whether he successfully transmitted a message to his masters, whoever they are." Tretschmer exhaled and forced himself to glance out again at the placid Alster scene behind the hulking form of the ship's captain. "All right. At least now I know what happened on board and why. This is not welcome information, Zellmann. You do realize, don't you, that the man you murdered was there for a reason?"

Zellmann jerked his head up and then down. "Sure. He was there to spy on me."

Tretschmer shook his head sideways as if disappointed in a small child. "Not on you, Zellmann, don't value yourself too dearly. The spying was directed at the *Condor Fury*. But why? What could have excited the attention of the authorities to the extent that they placed an informer on board?"

The ship's captain assumed a more combative tone. "How the hell should I know? I just steer the ship and make sure that we get your goods from one place to another without anyone being the wiser about what's on board. That's what you pay me to do, and I do it. Maybe the harbor police in one of the ports got suspicious. This isn't the first time that *Condor Fury* has been on a voyage with illegal consignments, falsely declared. You know that as well as I do. Remember those Russian RPGs that we ran to the Ivory Coast the other year? And the C-Four explosives we designated as industrial chemicals that made their way to Sana'a, Yemen? I just captain the ship. You make the deals and finds clients."

Tretschmer had to concede that on this point the repulsive sea mariner was right. The *Condor Fury* had been employed to move illicit goods around the globe for quite some time. It was a much more lucrative pursuit than moving normal freight. Anyone in a series of such voyages could have alerted some authority along the way. It would be foolish to deny it. Illegal international transport was an inherently risky business. A risk worth running, to be sure, but still a risk. And Zellmann was right, it was a risk that had little to do with the captain's responsibilities.

"Anything else I don't know?" Tretschmer regarded Zellmann carefully.

"No. That's it," the captain responded sullenly.

Tretschmer contemplated the lowering Hanseatic sky. "Here is what we do. I have to advise my partner about these developments, but that's nothing to do with you. I want you to get the *Condor Fury* out of this harbor and away from prying eyes. You said the cargo is on board, that means there's no reason to delay. The sooner you're underway in international waters, the better. Now that things are clarified, there's no reason to meet again. Once you sail, once you are moving down the Elbe toward the Atlantic, call this number from your cell phone." He extracted a small rectangle of yellow paper from his trench coat and passed it to Zellmann. "This is a phone I seldom use. All you have to do is say one word: 'underway.' That's all I need to know."

Zellmann enclosed the strip of paper in a paw of a hand and shoved it into his trouser pocket. "You'll hear from me soon," he mumbled.

Regarding his partner with ill-disguised distaste, Tretschmer said, "Our conversation is concluded." He offered no word of farewell and watched in silence as Zellmann trundled off to the pebble footpath on the bank of the Alster and made his way toward Hamburg harbor.

Tretschmer did not relish his pending telephone call to Anton Hessler in Innsbruck, but it had to be done. He would recommend that, following this voyage, they offer the cretinish Zellmann a plump severance to keep him quiet and seek a more reliable captain for the cargo vessel. Still, one question bothered him enormously. Who had recruited the Philippine informer and what was the nature of interest in the *Condor Fury?* Unleashing a frustrated sigh into the damp air, Tretschmer thrust his hands deep into the folds of his coat and turned toward Harvesterhude Way and the comfortable, civilized confines of his town house.

CENTRAL INTELLIGENCE AGENCY HEADQUARTERS,
LANGLEY, NORTHERN VIRGINIA

Caroline O'Kendell stood by the window in her office and contemplated the flat, leafy Virginia countryside stretching off toward the George Washington Parkway. She waited long seconds for the encrypted mobile phone to establish a secure link with Hirter's device, which was an exact copy of her own, designed to highly classified agency specifications by a Washington Beltway communications firm. She listened to the dissonant, atonal symphony of electronic notes until it was replaced by a distant ringing from the other end. There followed a loud click and a slightly distorted version of Hirter's voice, as if he were speaking through a pane of thick glass, the result of the encryption process.

"Hello, Robert Hirter here."

"Hi, Robert, here's your favorite case officer. Just back from Amman." She considered offering a more personal message to the man for whom she felt considerable affection, but decided that sentiment should wait for a less official venue. "The GID people were really helpful. I'll keep this call brief and hit the main points of what they had to offer. The GID confirmed a connection between their Syrian target Sayed al-Khalid and this German businessman Otto Tretschmer. The GID is dead sure al-Khalid and Tretschmer have met in Jordan and discussed some sort of shipment, probably to originate from Europe."

There was a pause on the line as the encryption resynchronized, followed by Robert's voice. "Why are they so certain about the connection between these two guys?"

Caroline stifled a laugh. "It's pretty clear they have al-Khalid's apartment in Amman nicely bugged. And I expect they've run discreet surveillance on him too. The GID says that al-Khalid is connected to the Iranian Pasdaran and the Syrian Intelligence Service. So it seems likely that al-Khalid is serving as middleman between these Middle Eastern bad actors and your friend Tretschmer. The Jordanians also know that Tretschmer's company is linked to Anton Hessler's firm in Vienna."

"That's good, Caroline. It means we're on the right track over here. We've come to the conclusion that Tretschmer had at least an indirect role in the Forster death, one way or another. We'll be paying attention to him. Tell me, did the Jordanians have any idea what it is that al-Khalid and Tretschmer and their Middle Eastern contacts are up to?"

Caroline consulted the notepad that she had brought back with her from Amman. "That's still vague. But it's some sort of shipment.

GID speculates that, given Tretschmer's location, the point of departure will be Europe. The destination might be Syria or Iran, but that's less certain. I think we might learn something shortly though. Our Jordanian colleagues are going to make a call on al-Khalid, and I anticipate we might acquire useful details from him."

Even the flat transmission of the encrypted phone did not disguise Hirter's tone of surprise. "You think that a character like al-Khalid is inclined to be cooperative?"

"We'll have to wait and see, Robert, but before I left for Amman OMS provided me with a little something that might prove of utility in questioning al-Khalid."

Caroline heard her friend's robust laugh, thousands of miles distant.

"Caroline, I don't want to know. But I hope al-Khalid sings. If the GID can provide enough details to prove a violation of German export law, Waldbaer can arrange for Tretschmer to be arrested. And if Tretschmer and al-Khalid, and maybe Hessler, are planning for illegal cargo to be shipped from Germany, the stuff can be interdicted. And, once in detention, Tretschmer might have something to say about the death of Forster or the Israeli. So with luck, we could be looking at a case-closed scenario not long from now. Wouldn't that be tidy?"

"Tidy indeed," Caroline allowed, "in fact, too tidy to be probable. Cases like this in my experience are always messy, with lots of loose ends. Let's first see what the GID brings us. So, what's the next step on your end with Tretschmer?"

A brief hiss of static coughed across the line before surrendering to Hirter's voice. "Already have that worked out, Caroline. I have something to do in Hamburg tomorrow. The BND gave me a wink and a nod to conduct observation on Tretschmer, as long as I don't get caught. Which I won't. Hamburg is several hours from here, so I travel this afternoon. With any luck, I'll find something for our friend Waldbaer to follow up."

The two CIA officers exchanged a few more thoughts on how

the case might progress, until the conversation wound down to its conclusion. "Be careful," Caroline said to her counterpart, the half-whispered words not meant as an empty rejoinder.

AMMAN, JORDAN

Hamdi al-Bakhit stood on the narrow concrete balcony of his apartment and surveyed the enchanted sea of streetlights and neon signs that defined the boundaries of Amman by night. The scene soothed him. Seen from a distance, the illuminated city with its brightly lit minarets appeared chaste and orderly, darkness obscuring the metropolis's enduring failings of poverty-wrenched neighborhoods, substandard housing, flawed sanitation, and interrupted electricity. Not to mention the more invisible failings seething beneath the surface—the fissures between native-born Jordanians and Palestinian refugees, smoldering divisions between those who favored accommodation with Israel and those who rejected it, the subterranean presence of violent Islamists who detested a monarchy they viewed as a lackey of the infidel West.

Hamdi swept a hand through his brushed-back mane of thick black hair and lifted the chilled and sweating can of Tuborg to his forehead, luxuriating in the contact of cool metal to skin. He considered his circumstance. Although he was in the familiar surroundings of his home, he remained on duty. He was a Jordanian intelligence officer trying to deter immoral, vicious men, and to accomplish this, he was himself employing methods that were hardly exemplary. He took a short sip of beer and judged that the techniques intelligence officers employed to ply information from the unwilling were sometimes sordid, no more noble perhaps than the means car salesmen used to beguile the credulous. He could not suppress a slight smile at the folly of men.

The cell phone in his jacket pocket emitted its familiar purr. He knew who the caller must be. "Yes, al-Khalid, what is it?" he intoned in a voice like velvet.

Sayed al-Khalid was still crying, the evidence of it transparent in his voice. "I have done as you wish, as you instructed. Allah forgive me, I have put everything that I know on paper for you. Please meet me immediately, I will clarify any point you desire. Please. I do not think I have long." The words were followed by a very audible whimper.

The GID officer had prepared for this moment and this inevitable litany and uttered his response as if from a script. "Sayed al-Khalid, what you say may be true, or may not be true. Why should I interrupt my evening for an uncertainty? Explain this to me."

The cell phone exuded another whimper, louder this time. "I tell the truth, this you must believe. You have set my death in motion, I am already gravely ill. I admit it, I am not a brave man. I want to live. Give me back my life and everything else is yours. I have no more secrets. Please help me. I am at your mercy."

It was the response Hamdi had anticipated. But there was the final line of the script to follow. "Perhaps. But tell me, al-Khalid, will you betray your friends and business partners? Without exception?"

There was no pause on the other end of the line, no instant of hesitation. "Yes, I will do it, have done it already in writing. I am no longer a person of honor, I know. But there it is. Please, please let us meet."

Hamdi nodded to himself and entered his living room from the balcony. "Luckily for you, your humility persuades me, al-Khalid. We will meet within the hour. In view of your condition, it is best if we have our discussion in your apartment. I expect you are in no condition to travel. Wait for me." Hamdi rang off. He was certain al-Khalid would hold nothing back. In Arab culture, a man who has so abjectly humiliated himself to another has nothing to lose. Al-Khalid had degraded himself, this Hamdi knew. Far more importantly, al-Khalid knew it as well.

Al-Khalid's apartment was more richly appointed than Hamdi's. Silk Persian carpets seemed to be scattered everywhere, and the furniture featured imported British antiques. Hamdi did not resent these signals of success. Businessmen were often rich, especially those like al-Khalid, who specialized in breaking the law. And yet, breaking the law had proved to be al-Khalid's ultimate vulnerability. The pale, tremulous, and hollow-eyed form across from Hamdi hardly spoke of worldly contentment. Hamdi detected an acidic undertone of vomit in the air of the apartment, testimony to al-Khalid's physical distress.

Hamdi flipped again through the sheaf of handwritten papers placed on his lap. The information on the pages was both detailed and damning, precisely what Hamdi had wanted.

"It would seem you have done well, al-Khalid, I must admit. You have an organized manner of writing. A few questions."

"Anything you wish." Al-Khalid's voice was parched and weak, barely audible.

"Yes. What I wish is to know more about the name written here, one of your associates. Otto Tretschmer. And also another name here, Georg Forster."

Al-Khalid clutched at his stomach and winced as he spoke. "Both of them have visited me here in Amman. Forster was earlier, he died in a car accident in Germany a while ago. He was in at the beginning of the transaction that Tretschmer later became involved in. Forster said he was a friend of the Arabs, and I think that's true. He despised the Israelis, said they had tried to ruin his political career in Austria. And so he was pro-Arab, perhaps by default. Forster had heard of me due to my previous business dealings in Austria, and wanted me to connect him to the Syrians. I did. Later, the Syrians put him in touch with Iranian representatives too. The deal described in the papers you have was meant to provide funds to Forster's political party, and to damage Israeli interests, both at the same time. Forster said he could facilitate use of Austria as a safe place for us to conduct the European side of our business, including processing the required paperwork. I must add that I liked him."

Hamdi scribbled a notation on margin of the papers. "And Tretschmer?"

"My partner. I like him rather less." Al-Khalid made a gagging sound and doubled over in his seat. His breathing was loudly labored. "I am dying," he whispered.

Hamdi nodded. It was time. He tugged a tin pillbox from the breast pocket of his jacket and popped it open. He extended his arm and held the receptacle to al-Khalid. "I am a man of my word. You have restored my trust in you. Take two of these tablets. Swallow, do not chew. They will interrupt the progress of the poison in your system, and reverse the damage. You will begin to feel better, bit by bit. Take them."

Al-Khalid darted a palsied hand to the container and, with effort, plucked out two small white pills. He ingested them and it was a moment before he spoke again, his eyes uncertain and inquiring. "You are sure? This will save me?"

Hamdi issued a solicitous smile. "You will live, al-Khalid, be assured. It is not in my interest, or Jordan's, to lie to you. We may decide to invalidate your visa and perhaps make you persona non grata, maybe even take this fine apartment from you, but your life is spared. Rely on it."

The Syrian businessman choked back a sob, eyes moist. "I am in your debt. When you have finished with me, if you wish, I will return to Damascus and refrain from visiting Jordan again, whatever you command. But for now, let me tell you some more things about Otto Tretschmer."

Hamdi could not restrain a feeling of self-satisfaction. The ploy had worked superbly. The chemical that Hamdi had covertly administered to the recalcitrant al-Khalid might have possessed ugly qualities but had, in fact, acted as a truth elixir. He would have to pass his congratulations to Helen, the CIA woman, who had provided the substance. She had explained that the medication would make its victim feel ill by increments. Queasy at first, followed by more violent stomach cramps and spasms. At its worst, the chemical would lead to vomiting and a degree of incontinence. The physical discomfort would be no more than that, an inconvenience, and the effects of the medication would disappear within twenty-four hours. Combined with a plausibly hideous story, however, the effects of the medication were notably greater.

The narrative about a poison that devoured internal organs was a chimera, utter fiction. Al-Khalid, however, had been seduced by Hamdi's tale of malevolent consequences. The Syrian's imagination, not the medication, had transformed al-Khalid into a quivering wreck of a man. A more stoic individual might have weathered the discomfort and found Hamdi to have been a deceiver. There was no percentage, of course, in ever revealing the ruse to al-Khalid; it was much better to let him labor under the illusion of his redemption, and the life-saving debt he owed to his benefactor. The pills just offered to al-Khalid as an antidote were simply powder, purely for show. Al-Khalid's affliction was nearing the end of its natural course on its own.

"And so, al-Khalid, let us turn to this Tretschmer and his pursuits," Hamdi said in a voice as dry as a desert wadi. There would be much of interest to pass along to Helen via her associates in Amman.

MUNICH, NYMPHENBURG CANAL

The choice of meeting venue had been at Waldbaer's suggestion. "There is something of interest I would like to show you both," he had truthfully explained in phone calls to Hirter and Frau Reiner.

And so they found themselves on the verdant banks of the Nymphenburg canal, the mile-distant, stately profile of the eponymous palace visible as a pearl outline in the morning haze. Waldbaer, Reiner, and Hirter were huddled together at the rear of a green *polizei* van. A uniformed Munich police officer with a bodybuilder's frame stood nearby, hands clasped behind his leather-jacketed back. The arching embrace of a linden tree cosseted them in shadow, shielding the group from the glare of an assertive sun.

Frau Reiner, casually garbed in an earth-tone tweed jacket and jeans, glanced out at the shimmering surface of the canal, just yards away and separated from them by an expanse of untended grass. A pair of swans paddled by at a leisurely, regal pace, as if aware of their elegance and station. "These are pleasant surroundings, Herr Kommissar. I personally prefer this to a beer garden, if you don't mind my saying so. I've never been in this part of Munich. But I confess to a bit of confusion as to why we are here. Not to see the sights, I presume?"

Hirter bent to the ground, retrieved a stone from the pavement, rose, and skipped it into the canal. "Doesn't bother me. I haven't had time to jog as much as I do in Washington, so anything that keeps me outdoors for a spell has my full approval."

Waldbaer nodded happily at the banter and moved to the back doors of the police van. "We are, in fact, here for a reason related to our joint pursuit, and not to admire the architectural splendors of the Bavarian Wittelsbach dynasty. Allow me to make my meaning clear. Officer, if you please."

The silent hulk of a policeman opened the double doors of the van and extracted a long object encased in a plastic sheet. He passed it without remark to Waldbaer, and returned the plastic to the back of the van.

"What you see before you is the weapon that doubtless fired the bullet that killed the unfortunate Israeli official, David Kirscheim. You may recall that he died on the opposite side of this canal, a few hundred meters closer to the palace. One shot was fired, and our ballistics people determined it was a 7.62-millimeter cartridge from a Russian-manufactured Dragunov sniper rifle. This would be that rifle."

Hirter and Frau Reiner murmured collectively and drew closer to Waldbaer to inspect the weapon.

Hirter ran a hand along the length of the barrel and traced the synthetic butt. "Kommissar, this weapon displays visible traces of rust. Why is that?"

"That's easy to answer, Herr Hirter. The weapon was found in the canal, just across from where you're standing. That's why I thought we should meet here, at the scene of Kirscheim's killing."

"How did it get there?" Frau Reiner inquired.

Waldbaer replied with a satisfied air. "That's easy to answer too. The assassin tossed the Dragunov into the water after he fired the fatal projectile. His assignment completed, he had no further use of the weapon, and every moment that he possessed it carried risk of disclosure. So, he tossed the weapon into the water, knowing that the bottom of the canal is a thick bed of mud, quite able to fully conceal an object of this size. The killer then drove away from the crime scene, slowly, I expect, so as not to attract any attention."

Frau Reiner nodded, and bit at her full, lower lip. "But if the canal bed is as muddy as you say, why do we have this weapon at all? How was it discovered?"

"Fate, Frau Reiner. Random chance. Or the beneficent intervention of the deity, whatever explanation suits you. What the murderer could not have known is that the public works department drains and dredges the canal every few years, to keep it from emitting any brackish odor in this established and finicky neighborhood. That dredging activity, as luck would have it, took place a few days ago. Imagine the surprise of the city workers in orange overalls when they pulled this weapon from the encasing muck. They had the common sense to call the police and here we are. This rifle killed the Israeli."

"Any fingerprints?" Hirter asked.

"As you probably anticipated, none at all. This was no amateur murder, no spontaneous crime of passion. It was a carefully planned act. Not many scraps for us to feed on, other than this weapon, the result of a miscalculation. But not a sufficient miscalculation to identify the assassin."

Hirter grasped the rifle for a closer inspection, turning it slowly in his hands like a prized work of art, tracing the stylized stock. "Assassin is the right word. I know the Dragunov. I've fired it on the range at the Farm where CIA officers are trained during weapons familiarization. It really is intended as a sniper rifle, not a normal infantry weapon like the AK-47. The Russians created a winner with this one. The Dragunov can take rough handling, it's accurate and reliable. For a specialized weapon, it's relatively common. Quite a few of them were produced during the Soviet era. Which makes any individual copy hard to trace." He passed the sleek shape of the rifle to Frau Reiner, who winced in evident distaste before returning it to Waldbaer.

Waldbaer held the weapon in one hand, judging its heft. "We know how Kirscheim was killed. We do not know why, which is a far more important question. What purpose did the death of the Israeli serve?"

Frau Reiner looked up at the features of the rumpled kommissar, half a foot taller than she. "Perhaps Kirscheim was killed by someone who believed him to be involved in Forster's death. Vengeance is hardly an unknown motive for murder. We might not be the only ones aware that Kirscheim was following Forster that night near Garmisch."

Waldbaer grunted and replaced the rifle in its plastic blanket inside the van. "A powerful motivator, indeed, Frau Reiner. Not everyone pursues the biblical injunction, 'vengeance is mine, sayeth the Lord,'—quite true. But still, I wonder, in this case. Who would be seeking to avenge Forster's death? An obsessed member of his political party? Wouldn't it make more sense to do what Forster's successor, Anton Hessler, has done—make public accusations against the Israelis and seek to reap political capital from it? Hessler is no fool and certainly knew his press statement would be sufficient to initiate a police investigation, the investigation we are now engaged in. Within that context, gunning down Kirscheim does nothing to discredit the Israelis. Quite the opposite. If anything, the murder of the young official can be expected to increase sympathy for Israel. Anything is possible, of course, but something tells me revenge was not what caused Kirscheim's death."

Frau Reiner moved her head slowly from side to side.

Hirter spoke up, his voice a monotone. "I agree, Kommissar. When I think of revenge, I think of passion. A long-distance, single shot with a Dragunov does not speak of passion. This was an antiseptic killing, cold, professional, emotionless. My intelligence officer instincts tell me something else was at work here. What motive was at play, I don't know."

"Wait a moment, perhaps we do know something relevant." Frau Reiner tapped a hand lightly on Waldbaer's arm. "This rifle is of Russian manufacture. And falls into the category of small arms."

Waldbaer regarded her quizzically. "Yes. So what?"

She returned the kommissar's gaze and nodded. "Where did we

hear about Russian small arms previously? From information provided me by Austrian customs, remember? Customs believes that
T&K had engaged in covering shipments of specialized small arms to
the West. And I recall, Herr Hirter, that your CIA friends have said
something similar about T&K and the Vienna firm Verbindung Ost.
No solid evidence, nothing that would be compelling evidence in
court, but suspicion. This Dragunov would fit the description of specialized small arms, wouldn't it?"

Waldbaer gave a quick jerk of his head. "Yes. And I've wondered
about that connection too. No proof, as you say, Frau Reiner. But it
brings us back to the name that seems to be occupying our thoughts
increasingly. Otto Tretschmer."

"Quite right," Hirter interjected. "And I was about to tell you
both that I'm driving up to Hamburg tomorrow to find the dubious
Herr Tretschmer and follow him around a bit. See what he might be
up to, or who he might be connected with. The BND gave me an informal nod of approval for that."

Waldbaer narrowed his eyes and rubbed at his forehead. "Is nothing ever straightforward with intelligence officers? An 'informal nod'
for an American to surveil a German citizen not yet accused of any
transgression. Still, I wish you luck."

HAMBURG, EPPENDORF DISTRICT

It had been light for almost four hours, and Hirter had been parked
on the residential side street long enough to witness the nocturnal
world relinquish by degree its grip on the urban landscape. Dawn
was a process, not a moment. The line of streetlights seemed to lose
its intensity as diffused sunlight insinuated itself into the background. As Hirter watched in silence, sipping cooling coffee from a
thermos, the visible terrain seen through the dashboard window assumed structure and texture, until spectral, nocturnal shapes were
fully banished, replaced by the familiar, banal contours of the everyday world.

Hirter enjoyed the feel of surveillance; he had taken to it ever
since his first exposure to the technique during CIA training at the

Farm. It was a game of sorts, a contest. To observe someone covertly, without the subject of this attention becoming aware that he was observed. And through discreet surveillance, to discover something about the person being observed. At its core, surveillance was like most espionage tradecraft; it was intended to uncover secrets. Hirter smiled to himself, aware of how seductive that enterprise was—the lure of uncovering things that others wanted to keep concealed. And so he found himself slouched behind the steering wheel of his rental sedan, parked half a block from the noble brick town house belonging to, if municipal records were credible, Herr Otto Tretschmer.

Tretschmer, however, had yet to make an appearance. Hirter tugged up his shirt cuff and consulted his wristwatch. It was shortly after nine. Most businessmen with an office job would have been well on their way by this hour but, Hirter knew, Tretschmer apparently conducted much of his work from home. After another slow sip of coffee, Hirter opened the glove compartment and withdrew a pair of Steiner binoculars that he had purchased the previous day in Munich; an authorized expenditure of CIA operational funds. Checking the rearview mirror to ensure that no passerby might notice him, Hirter placed the olive-drab device to his eyes and focused the lens on the elegant symmetry of Tretchmer's dwelling. He detected that lights had been switched on on the ground floor. The quarry was likely either breakfasting or conducting some initial business in his study. Hirter sighed and pressed his head back into the supple beige leather of the driver's seat. There was nothing to do but wait. Surveillance was no pursuit for the impatient.

Hirter returned the field glass to the glove compartment and withdrew a small digital camera, placing it on the passenger seat beside him. He yawned into his hand and watched a middle-aged woman in a red jacket pass by on the other side of the street, a skipping young boy tugging at her hand. The area was coming alive, Hirter noted to himself, no bad thing for a surveillant, as the normal, unremarkable activity of everyday life helped to mask an unusual presence.

Thirty minutes later, Hirter began to wonder if his plan had not been sound. What to do, he considered, if Tretschmer decided to remain inside his residence the entire day? It was a depressing thought, but a possibility, especially in an age when so much commerce could be conducted by cell phone and Internet. The prospect of returning to his hotel room for a few hours of uneasy sleep followed by another prolonged bout of street surveillance did not amuse him. Still, he was at a loss as to another course of action.

Pondering alternatives, Hirter did not immediately notice the initial flash of motion at the front door of the town house. The door swung halfway open and a form emerged, tall and gaunt. A shock of light hair was swept to one side over a face lined enough to betray a man of around sixty. The figure pulled the door shut behind him and locked it. The man turned toward the street in front of his home and gave a cursory glance in both directions. Hirter huddled more deeply into his seat, although he knew that he was obscured from the man's vision. With a quick step, the man marched to a forest-green Jaguar sedan at the curb.

Hirter knew that he was looking at Otto Tretschmer. The BND had been gracious enough to provide him with a copy of a passport photo. *Let the games begin*, Hirter thought with a smile, engaging the transmission of his sedan and hearing in reply the subdued murmur of the engine. He would be obliged to pursue Tretschmer at a distance, he could not chance alerting his target. Tretschmer was the type of individual who probably checked to ascertain if he was being followed. Hirter was determined Tretschmer would notice nothing.

The Jaguar maneuvered from its parking space and proceeded down the tree-lined residential street at a stately pace. Hirter permitted two cars to take up the road space between him and Tretschmer, providing sufficient cover while still keeping the target within eyeshot. Hirter noted that Tretschmer drove at a steady speed, neither slowing nor accelerating, a sign that he had not detected his pursuer.

After pausing at a red light, the Jaguar turned left onto Har-

vestehuderweg, a long, winding avenue that braced the bank of the
Alster. The silver-gray expanse of the lake was intermittently visible
through thick stands of moss-encased elm and willow trees that lined
the shore. Given the direction, Hirter calculated that Tretschmer
was headed downtown, possibly to the harbor.

The Jaguar stopped to let a troop of school children with back-
packs cross the road at a zebra-striped pedestrian crossing. Hirter
could see through the windows of the intervening two cars that
Tretschmer sat ramrod straight in his sedan. He hasn't noticed a
thing, Hirter concluded. The children took to the sidewalk and the
column of cars moved ahead. The perfectly tamed green lawns of
the residential section surrendered to gray concrete and commercial
structures as they approached downtown Hamburg. The Jaguar
swung out of traffic and pulled up to a magazine stand. True to training, Hirter drove past and observed Tretschmer in the rearview mirror. He watched the businessman purchase a magazine and return to
his car. Hirter furrowed his brow. Was this just an innocent move, or
was Tretschmer executing a countersurveillance stop, trying to flush
out anyone pursuing him? There was no way to know, but it reinforced Hirter's decision to exercise caution.

A moment later, Tretschmer pulled back into traffic and drove
past Hirter's parked car without giving it a glance. Hirter remained
parked until Tretschmer's vehicle was nearly out of sight, pulling out
behind the concealing bulk of a bakery delivery truck. More traffic
appeared as Tretschmer and Hirter continued downtown, past the
Dammtor train station and Gaensemarkt, the Geese Market Square.

Hirter kept a discreet distance from his quarry and found himself
entertaining doubts about his plan. What if Tretschmer simply
parked his car and entered one of the large, prosaic office buildings
that defined downtown Hamburg? Hirter might check the list of
firms with offices at the address for later tracing, but that would
hardly reveal much about Tretschmer's activities. Still, Hirter knew,
there was no immutable law that surveillance would yield results.
Much rode on luck, a whimsical goddess.

The two cars drove on, only one aware of the presence of the

other. Traffic thinned as the Jaguar left the concentrated commercial
district behind and headed toward the chaotic series of access roads,
warehouses, wharfs, and bridges that defined the harbor. Hirter noticed that there were fewer cars now visible; most of the vehicles underway in the district were trucks. He worried at the reduced traffic
flow and slowed his speed, letting Tretschmer pull away.

The Jaguar moved toward the sullied water of the Elbe, and
Hirter saw a panorama consisting of tall metal cranes and seagoing
vessels riding high in the water. Things were getting rather more
interesting. As he watched, Hirter was surprised to see his target park
next to a small abandoned building of neglected cinderblock and
broken windowpanes. A second later, Tretschmer pulled himself
from the vehicle and stood next to it, surveying the waterfront.
Hirter pulled into an abandoned rectangle of weed-ravaged parking
lot, made sure that it afforded a clear view of Tretschmer, and turned
off the ignition.

From Hirter's concealed vantage point, Tretschmer stood mo-
tionless. The man was alone and there was no approaching vehicle
or pedestrian to signal a rendezvous. But Tretschmer had journeyed
across town to come to this place, and Hirter could discern no evident motive. He again extracted the binoculars from the glove compartment.

For several seconds, the stationary image of Tretschmer revealed
nothing. His was a solitary figure, disconnected from everything
around him. Hirter made a noise of dissatisfaction deep in his throat;
the scene made no sense. And then the thought hit him. Tretschmer
was not just idly standing there without purpose. He was focused on
something, staring at some object in the distance. Hirter used the
binoculars to try to determine Tretschmer's line of sight. What was
the businessman looking at so intensely? The harbor, clearly. But
what exactly?

Hirter moved the binoculars farther from Tretschmer's figure, following a straight optical line. He took in the cracked concrete of an
aging wharf, an oil-slicked expanse of gray water, and a small harbor
tour boat guiding its twenty or so passengers through the watery

labyrinth of one of Europe's largest ports. On the far bank of the harbor, perhaps a quarter-mile distant, Hirter noted two large stationary cranes, a docked ship, and a mountain of stacked containers. The scene was unremarkable.

Then he turned his field glasses back to the figure of Tretschmer. A moment later, a touch of motion animated the man who had been as still as statuary for several minutes. Tretschmer's tall form drew a cell phone from his jacket pocket, entered some numbers, and pulled the piece to his ear. Tretschmer turned a degree and Hirter determined that he was talking. A second later Tretschmer moved forward a few feet and moved a hand to his head as if blocking any intrusion of sunlight that might hinder his vision. Hirter again swung the binoculars upward until he fixed the object of Tretschmer's interest.

The seagoing vessel across the harbor was lumbering into motion, its unheard engines stirring the fouled waters into a flurry of effervescent agitation. The ship, dirty black with long seams of rust, pulled away from its berth and entered the harbor's main channel. Hirter turned his attention to the ship's prow and adjusted the binoculars to read the vessel's name. Two words, the white lettering stark against the dark surface, identified the ship as the *Condor Fury*.

"Bingo." It was the ship the BND had been interested in, the ship linked to the death of their Filipino spy. The connection to Tretschmer was confirmed.

A glance back at Tretschmer revealed that he had finished his cell phone conversation and stepped back into the Jaguar. The sedan returned the way it had arrived, heading back toward the Hamburg city center. Hirter remained in place for a while, watching the sullied shape of the *Condor Fury* head down the Elbe, which would flow into the North Sea, fifty miles distant. Whatever illegal consignment was being sent out of Germany was aboard, and was now underway to some foreign destination not yet revealed.

"I guess we're a damned bit late," Hirter mumbled to himself as he started the ignition. Still, there were actions that could be initiated. He would drive back immediately to meet Kommissar Waldbaer and Frau Reiner. But first he would employ his encrypted cell phone to alert Caroline in Langley. Perhaps she could secure satellite coverage of the *Condor Fury*. The pieces were falling together at last, if not necessarily in advantageous circumstance.

Central Intelligence Agency Headquarters, Langley, Northern Virginia

It was ten in the morning when Caroline O'Kendell's sleek gray operational cell phone issued its rasping tone. A glance at the incoming number revealed that the caller was Robert Hirter. She was supposed to be at the weekly division staff meeting in five minutes, but knew that whatever Robert had to impart took priority. She removed the phone from its charger, activated the transceiver, and spoke her name.

"Glad I reached you, Caroline," Robert's distorted, enciphered voice said, an edge of tension nonetheless alive in his words. "I need you to try to do something for me, and in a hurry, please."

She reached for a bright yellow pad of paper and a government-issue Skilcraft ballpoint pen. "I'm set to copy, Robert."

The malformed aural parody of Robert's voice reached out from a distant continent.

"Okay. I need you to see if the agency has technical assets that can track a ship. A vessel that has left Hamburg heading for the Atlantic. Destination unknown. The ship is the *Condor Fury*."

"That name sounds familiar. I have it! The *Condor Fury* and another ship are owned by that company T&K. I remember it from my trace request."

"That's right. It's involved with our shady German businessman Tretschmer. A lot of things aren't clear, but Tretschmer has some connection to the *Condor Fury*, and the *Condor Fury* has been plying dark waters for a while. I'm sure whatever items Tretschmer is trying to move out of Germany are on board. If we can track that ship, maybe we can get a fix on where it's headed. And it's not too early to start thinking about whether we can interdict it."

"Slow down, Robert. One step at a time. I have to see what sort of tracking capability we have for something like this, if any. And if we have the technical capability, we'll have to make a case that tracking the Condor Fury is worth the commitment of resources. I'm not even sure where to start in our organization. But I'll find out. How sure are you about there being something illicit on board? Someone is bound to ask that question."

Robert sighed into the phone. "You're right, I can't guess as to what's in the cargo hold. I ran surveillance on Tretschmer. It's a long story, but I followed him to the Hamburg harbor and it was apparent he was ensuring himself that the Condor Fury was getting underway. He was using a cell phone. My guess is he was talking to someone on-board, but that's a surmise. I'm certain my instincts are correct about there being something on that ship. I'm going to tell Waldbaer too, but I doubt there's much the Germans can do at this point, with the ship in international waters. I don't like it."

Caroline nodded and wrinkled her features. "Robert, I'm not sure what we can do. But I'll get back to you soon." She slipped the phone into its charger, a missed staff meeting less important, replaced by forming thoughts of maritime targets, a circle of unsavory international businessmen, and the uncertain, deeply shadowed terrain of operational possibilities. She glanced at the pad of notepaper where she had scrawled two words. Condor Fury.

THE NORTH ATLANTIC

Zellmann luxuriated in quiet contentment. He was at last in motion again, standing on the bridge of a solid ship that heaved and bucked into the deep, gray waves of a moderately turbulent sea. The ocean was his oxygen and his lifeblood. He was sated with the carnal enticements of Hamburg, yet restless and becoming nervous. The necessity of dealing with the prissy and effete Tretschmer had not helped his mood. Tretschmer had cunning, a commodity that Zellmann feared as much as he admired. More to the point, Zellmann did not trust Tretschmer.

The ship's captain exhaled a grunt as he surveyed the prow of the *Condor Fury* slicing through the endless maritime seascape. Trust was a scabrous word, he knew, and almost always a deceit. The world of sordid, illicit international commerce, just like the biosphere of sailors, prostitutes, and gamblers, was held together by stronger glue than trust. Self-interest ruled supreme, of this Zellmann was unshakably persuaded. There were alliances, of course, like his temporary connection to Tretschmer. But the prevailing force was raw self-interest, not some fantasy of trust.

He was well aware of the special nature of the cargo secured in the hold. And despite the fastidious Tretschmer's bitchy comments and case of nerves, Zellmann saw no problems looming ahead. The *Condor Fury* was safely plying international waters, beyond the authority of German customs. The voyage on which he was now embarked, like the blue, cloudless horizon stretching out before the bridge, betrayed no hint of danger. He again breathed deeply of the salt-flecked air and relaxed, felt the rhythmic pulse of the ship's engines vibrate beneath his feet, and permitted a comforting wave of satisfaction to embrace him.

GAMSDORF, BAVARIA

Waldbaer walked with a plodding gait along the earthen path braced on both sides by lush alpine meadows. His eyes wandered over the rich green sweep of grass punctuated by hundreds of wildflowers in exuberant cascades of yellow, blue, purple, and white. He had felt uneasy, and had persuaded himself that a stroll would prove salutary. Stopping at a broad chestnut tree, he leaned against the trunk with one arm, his hand caressing the bark. Breathing in deeply, he smelt fresh mown hay and a trace of pungent fertilizer. It was a calming sensation and helped restrain his restlessness. Waldbaer considered his phone conversation of twenty minutes ago with Hirter.

It was not welcome news that the American had related. At least, Waldbaer could not escape the sensation that events were moving at a tempo considerably faster than their investigation. It was this sentiment that caused his current frustration. Hirter had confirmed that the ship most likely carrying the cargo tied to Tretschmer's activities had sailed from Hamburg unimpeded. By this time, almost certainly, the *Condor Fury* was on the high seas, well beyond German territorial waters and jurisdiction. The nature of the cargo on board remained entirely a mystery. Waldbaer was at a loss to conjure up a solution to get control of the vessel and clarify what it carried; frustrated again.

As Waldbaer continued on his way, he realized that the Forster case had become the Tretschmer case. Tretschmer was clearly their most active lead. There were other strands to be pursued, but again, none in any apparent way related to the demise of the Austrian politician.

There was Anton Hessler, for one, Forster's successor in the party. Connected by business interests to Tretschmer. Whether these connections spoke of illegality or mere mundane commerce was uncertain. He would have to leave that question to Kommissarin Reiner. And then there was the murder of David Kirscheim, the Israeli consul. That had been a coolly planned and well-executed assassination. But why? Kirscheim had placed Forster under close surveillance and was following him the night of the car crash, that much was established. But casting the Israeli as Forster's killer was not established, and Waldbaer, for his part, did not believe Kirscheim was responsible. Whatever the consul's role in Forster's demise, it did not solve the issue of who murdered the Israeli. Nor was there any visible motive for that killing. But some unknown party did not simply take it into his head to kill Kirscheim. There was a reason for it.

Waldbaer sighed and stopped in his tracks. The landscape was darkening now, distant strings of streetlights flickering on, announcing the imminent arrival of night. The North Star shone low in the sky, the first sentinel of a celestial legion yet to be revealed. It was time to turn back, he knew, it would be a good twenty minutes or more before he was home. His stroll had calmed him a bit. There were disparate points in the investigation to be clarified. At present, Waldbaer had no sense as to who might have doctored Forster's drinks before the fatal journey to Garmisch. Still, Waldbaer was certain the confusing array of individuals and events turned up by the investigation were ultimately connected. And, as he turned toward home, he knew that it was he who intended to do the connecting, in concert with his Austrian and American partners.

Innsbruck, Austria

Sabine Reiner felt certain that Austria was key to the Forster investigation. After all, Forster himself had been an Austrian, and a prominent one. The political party he headed was also Austrian, as was its new leader, the enigmatic and elitist Anton Hessler. In addition, Hessler was tied to a business located in Innsbruck with a history of dubious commercial activities, and which, in turn was linked to another suspicious enterprise in Vienna, the Austrian capital. As if that wasn't enough, the cargo ship that had excited the interest of Robert Hirter, whose brief phone call update she had just received, was of Austrian ownership. All of which meant that Sabine enjoyed considerable jurisdiction over crucial elements of the investigation.

She had been savoring a cup of cappuccino on the terrace of La Mama, an Italian restaurant directly on a bank of the Inn River when the American CIA officer had reached her and advised about the departure of the *Condor Fury* from Hamburg harbor. Hirter confirmed that he had brought Waldbaer into the picture as well. Well, there was little she could do about the peregrinations of a vessel on the faraway Atlantic. But there were other worthy targets closer at hand, and she intended to move on them. The self-confident Hirter and the annoyingly smug and patronizing Waldbaer would learn not to underestimate her contribution to the case.

She looked out for a moment at the river, and rejoiced in its primordial wildness. Sabine loved the natural splendor of Tyrol and endeavored not to take its beauty for granted, even with the demanding press of police work. Turning back to the Forster investigation, she glanced at the open, leather-bound notebook on the bistro table in front of her and studied what she had written.

> *To do: Need insider information on T&K activities. Need same on Verbindung Ost in Vienna. How to get it? Can we get a search warrant? T&K office has been placed under temporary surveillance. Check with surveillance chief for results. Interview this afternoon with former Hessler close friend. Dig for items on Hessler's commercial dealings.*

Rather thin gruel, she thought, but a start. Hessler interested her. As she had learned long ago at the Austrian Police Academy in Gnadenwald, the first question to ask in a murder investigation was always—who benefits? Hessler had clearly been the beneficiary of Forster's death. Hessler had inherited Forster's position as leader of the Austrian Nationalist Defense Front, the political fortunes of which were surging. Hessler had profited as well from a wave of sympathy for Forster, a normal phenomenon following the death of a prominent personality. And Hessler, a talented orator, knew how to play the Forster card to advantage, as he had in his press conference alleging an Israeli role in Forster's demise.

Sabine was pleased that her digging for background on Hessler had turned up an association with another Innsbruck businessman, Peter Lingen. Hessler and Lingen had been close friends for years; some mutual acquaintances suggested that they had been more than friends. Lingen and Hessler had fallen out about a year ago, reason unclear, and now shunned one another. Sabine had secured Lingen's agreement for an off-the-record, discreet chat in a few hours, on the grounds of the Alpine Zoo on the heights above Innsbruck, reachable by cable car. If she could win Lingen's trust, and if he was willing to speak candidly, something might come of the interview. Sabine had also scheduled a meeting with her police colleague, the surveillance chief, for late afternoon, and hoped for some snippet of information to pursue. As for a search warrant on the T&K office and warehouse, she would make the best case possible. She would be aggressive, a commodity on which neither Waldbaer nor Hirter enjoyed a monopoly.

A brief, intense thunderstorm had left the concrete of the massive building wet and dark, and the Northern Virginia sky remained metal gray, as if the storm was considering an encore. Caroline viewed the scene through the cafeteria windows and sipped at a tin of Diet Coke. A taco salad was on the table in front of her, the delicate flour shell as yet untouched. She consulted her wristwatch, confirming that her lunch companion should appear at any moment.

"Hi, Caroline. I didn't see you at first, it's crowded in here today."

Caroline looked up at the familiar, solid form of her friend Laura Castleman. They had gone through CIA training together a few years ago and had remained on good terms, both of them currently assigned to offices at headquarters. They lunched together occasionally and chatted about mutual acquaintances and world affairs, the common conversational affliction at Langley. But Caroline had today invited Laura to dine with her for a specific reason. Laura, who had worked on the German Desk for years, was currently assigned to a branch of the Clandestine Service that tracked ships globally. The branch was located in the vast, windowless basement of the Langley headquarters.

Laura placed a plastic tray on the table and let her substantial bulk fall with an involuntary grunt into the chair opposite Caroline. The tray contained two cheeseburgers slicked with a tsunami of mayonnaise, an order of french fries, and another of onion rings. A generous wedge of cheesecake abutted a can of Fanta.

Caroline observed her compatriot dispassionately. Laura had some time ago crossed the line from stocky to fat and was a contender for obesity. Her waistline had disappeared, a development that she sought to conceal with a wardrobe of shapeless clothes. Laura did not wash her hair daily, and brushed it indifferently, leading Caroline to wonder whether her friend might be suffering in-cipient depression. Should Caroline at some point call Laura's at-tention to her appearance, or would such candor end their friendship? She deferred a decision. Not on the agenda today; there was work to be done.

After an exchange of small talk, and with Laura deep into the consumption of her first cheeseburger, Caroline maneuvered the conversation to her area of interest. "I need to talk about tracking ships, Laura. Maybe you can make me smart about our capabilities and limitations and how things work. Is that okay with you?"

Laura swallowed and nodded consent. She cleared her throat, placed the cheeseburger remnant back on the tray, and rubbed a pudgy hand across her chin. "Fine with me, Caroline. I'll tell you what I know, which isn't much. I've only been involved with mar-itime tracking for six months. Why your interest?"

Caroline toyed with her taco salad. "It's a case we're working with the Germans. The genesis is the death of an Austrian right-wing politician. It's complicated, but it seems a German citizen con-nected to the case is linked to a ship. The ship is the *Condor Fury*, and I've got the background on it. Anyway, the ship was at Hamburg and might have loaded dubious cargo, otherwise unidentified."

Laura slipped a glistening onion ring into her mouth. "I don't think you need me. If you're working with German authorities, just get them to board the vessel, check the manifest, and make a phys-ical inspection to find what's on board. That shouldn't be hard to accomplish."

Caroline moved her head sideways. "Too late for that. The *Con-dor Fury* left Hamburg a short while ago. She's underway at sea, in in-ternational waters, out of the reach of the Germans."

Laura frowned. "That makes it more complicated all right. Let me guess. You want to know whether we can track this ship's progress by satellite, right?"

Caroline placed both her hands flat on the table. "Exactly."

"Theoretically, we can do it. We have the technical capability.

Since you have the ship's identity we can get open-source records and photos and more than likely locate it at sea. It's not easy; there are thousands of major vessels underway at any given time. But we can probably do it. And maybe provide an informed guess as to its likely destination. We can possibly even determine what sort of cargo is stored on deck, if any. Naturally, we're blind to whatever is concealed in the hold or sealed in containers. But I'm speaking theoretically." Laura retrieved her cheeseburger.

Caroline leaned toward her friend. "You keep saying 'theoretically.' Theory doesn't help me. What's the reality? Can you help or not?"

"It depends. Something like this wouldn't be my call. That's for senior management to decide. Here's the problem. Assigning a satellite to cover a ship is no trivial matter. It can mean reorienting a satellite. And most of those high-altitude birds already have assigned priority targets. We can't cover everything we would like to, that's the reality. And it costs money. Using these orbital assets isn't cheap."

"Which means?"

"Which means someone pretty high up in CIA, maybe the DDO, needs to agree that the *Condor Fury* is worth the candle. That decision could go either way, but you need to make a case for committing the resources for tracking that ship. Do you have an idea of what this dubious cargo actually is?"

Caroline took a sip of Diet Coke and sighed lightly. "No, I can't say we do. It's all circumstantial. The cargo could consist of proliferation-related items, but that's a surmise at this point. The individual tied to the ship seems to be a bad character though."

"To be honest, Caroline, I think you'll have trouble selling this unless you can get more detail on the cargo. The *Condor Fury* isn't the only ship out there that gives us pause. We're tracking all sorts of vessels. Some linked to North Korea, some to Venezuela or Cuba, some to Middle Eastern interests with jihadi sympathies. Your ship has lots of rogue competition, sorry to say. I don't mean to be negative, but that's the reality."

Caroline did not attempt to filter her disappointment from her voice. "Thanks for the assessment, Laura. I'll think about how to proceed. I'll try to make the best case possible to management. If you can back my request up, I'd be appreciative."

"I'll do what I can, but I think the decision will ride on the case you make that the cargo is of real interest."

The conversation changed trajectory and moved on to other, more social themes. In contrast to her exuberantly hungry friend, Caroline found she had lost her appetite. Most of the salad was left uneaten. After saying her goodbyes, Caroline made her way down the long, broad Langley corridors and back to the office, a cloud dampening her mood. She would talk to Robert. Maybe he or Waldbaer had acquired some useful details about the cargo. But she could not shake an encroaching feeling of pessimism.

Returning to the familiar rectangular confines of her office, Caroline slipped into her chair, entered her password into the computer, and read the incoming classified traffic. One message caught her eye. It was from the CIA installation in Amman, Jordan. The text recounted information provided by her gracious GID contact Hamdi al-Bakhit. He had asked that the CIA chief in Amman pass it along immediately to Caroline. As she read through the narrative, she felt her mood lift. "Well now, wish I had known this before talking to Laura," she counseled herself aloud. "I expect these details will find an interested audience. Get ready to reorient that satellite." She read through the message carefully a second time, and prepared to forward it to Robert.

Mutters, above Innsbruck

Anton Hessler stood alone on his broad balcony and gazed across the Inn Valley at the darkening contours of the northern mountain range, miles away. Despite being mid-summer, the alpine air was bitingly cool once robbed of sunlight. A shiver coursed through his spare frame and he tightened the sash of his burgundy patterned-silk dressing gown. One hand held a slim black cell phone to his ear, the device unleashing a torrent of rapid-fire Northern High German that made him wince. How much more to be preferred, he thought to himself, were the softer, soothing enunciations of the ancient Teutonic language in its southerly, Austrian variant.

His face a mask of rigid displeasure, Hessler interjected, interrupting the stream of words.

"Hold on a bit, let me get this right. Our merchandise is in the mail, correct?" Hessler was certain that the man on the other end would understand the simple word substitution code indicating that the equipment was aboard the ship.

There was a burst of agreement from the phone. "Yes, it's definitely in the post."

Hessler nodded and his features relaxed a degree, his eyes fixed on the peaks beyond. "That, at least, is welcome news. I trust in the reliability of the postal service."

The northern German accent mumbled assent. "Of course. But that's not the problem. Not at all. As I just explained, the problem is the postman. He's proven to be impulsive. He's gotten press attention, which, as you are well aware, we hardly need. And I no longer have confidence in his judgment."

Hessler nodded his head slowly. "I understand. Perhaps he never was the right man for that postal route. But it's rather late to effect a personnel change at this point, I expect."

"Unfortunately true. But we need to do something once the mail is delivered. And I'll be honest, I'm nervous. This fellow's impulsiveness has already led to a death at sea, in a way that could result in an investigation."

Hessler gritted his teeth at the conversational indiscretion. Tretschmer needed to consider that their talk could be monitored. He sought to repair the damage. "I wouldn't be overly concerned at such stories, all fictitious in my view. We can discuss that some other time. But I take your point on reliable personnel. We are in agreement there. Is there any separate matter that we need to deal with?"

There was a pause on the line, followed by Tretschmer's careful pronunciation. "Perhaps not immediately. But we'll need to get together rather soon. I presume you will be speaking to the clients about the package being in the mail?"

Hessler nodded again to himself and walked back from the balcony toward the open doors of his penthouse living room. "Yes. I'll get in touch with them. But I don't want to trouble them with the other incidentals you've raised."

"That's up to you. You know those gentlemen best. I just want to ensure that you and I are aware of the facts. It's a good basis for business."

Hessler spoke with a touch of the unctuous in his voice. "Quite right, you've behaved correctly. I must say, it's a pleasure to have a real professional as a partner. That's one of the reasons I'm convinced this matter will work out to the satisfaction of all. We just have to keep our nerve." Hessler did not know whether Tretschmer required this motivational lecture, but decided it could not hurt. Illegal commerce on an international scale was, after all, a stressful enterprise. The conversation concluded, Hessler rang off.

The Austrian stepped from the balcony back into his penthouse living room, securing the glass door behind him and engaging the intrusion alarm system. Tretschmer was right about one thing. The impetuous Captain Zellmann would have to be dropped as soon as the *Condor Fury* had successfully fulfilled its mission. There was a whole universe of corrupt, criminally inclined maritime flotsam available to replace him. No worries there. The most pressing matter was ensuring the arrival of the shipment at its destination and receiving confirmation from the client that the transaction had been satisfactorily concluded. That, in turn, would ensure a major donation to the party's undeclared bank account in the Duchy of Lichtenstein, concealed via a cut-out front company located in Cyprus. Not to forget the promised foreign policy "coup" that the client would arrange for Hessler personally, a move designed to further his own political fortunes in Austria and, indeed, Europe.

Despite the complication with Zellmann, it would all work out, he felt certain. Moving to the antique Wilhelmine cabinet, he lifted a heavy crystal carafe, and poured himself a fine, well-aged double malt. He savored the first warming sip and judged that, on balance, he felt quite well.

BAKU, AZERBAIJAN

Jahanghir Karimov was glad to have returned to the familiar surroundings of home. He had come to dislike international travel, perhaps because he had been compelled to do so much of it over the years. Air travel lately tired and annoyed him, even though he flew business class. Flying had become especially burdensome since the terror attacks of 9/11, which had caused a global obsession with airline security. His just-concluded sojourn to Germany was no exception. Departing Baku at two a.m. and returning after midnight a few days later had been ruinous to his digestive clock and ability to sleep. At least the disagreeable episode was behind him now and he could relax in his spacious apartment with its calming view of the Caspian Sea. The sun had not yet set and the city was fiercely hot, the temperature hovering around ninety-eight degrees. He hoped for a thunderstorm and its cooling aftermath. Jahanghir held his wine goblet up to the sky and admired the deep red of the liquid within before taking a long mouthful. Yes, it was good to be home.

At least his business trip had been concluded with gratifying success. As he had anticipated it would. After all, he rated himself an experienced, consummate professional. His trade of the last two decades was a demanding one by any measure, but he had a talent for it, an instinctive sense of what and when, and where, and how. Jahanghir smiled, nodded to himself, and took another indulgent sip of wine.

The assignment in Germany was simple enough; it had been well prepared, and Jahanghir had been handsomely compensated for his services via a just-received wire transfer of funds. The task had not been particularly demanding, other than the requirement to positively identify the subject and find the right time and venue to conduct the business securely. All of this had been accomplished. It was true that increasingly sophisticated passport controls had meant that Jahanghir traveled on true-name documents; the use of forged alias papers had become increasingly problematic, at least in Western Europe. But no matter. The only thing an examination of travel records would reveal to the authorities was that an Azeri citizen and resident, one Jahanghir Karimov, had flown from Baku to Strauss Airport in Munich on a given date and returned to Azerbaijan five days later. Jahanghir had considered arriving at a German airport more distant from his mission location than Munich. Frankfurt or Berlin, for example. But upon reflection, he judged this additional precaution to be unnecessary. Munich was a city of a million and a half inhabitants, and the airport received thousands of international visitors daily. A lone Azeri traveler would hardly stand out.

At the Munich airport, Jahanghir had rented a black Volvo station wagon and set out for Innsbruck, Austria, ninety minutes distant. There, by prearrangement, he had picked up a package, indulged a quick lunch, and returned to Munich. His brief journey to Innsbruck would have been noted by no one, the advent of the European Union having eliminated border controls between Austria and Germany.

The remainder of that day, and the next, had been dedicated to familiarizing himself with a specific area of Munich, its traffic patterns, and level of police presence. Then, employing binoculars that had been provided in his Innsbruck package, he had identified the subject of his attention and confirmed the identity against photographs, also contained in his material from Innsbruck. Observing the subject's pattern of routine movement, Jahanghir selected the optimal time and location to conclude his business. His preparation, based on years of experience, left nothing to chance and ensured that everything went without a hitch. The matter concluded, Jahanghir had driven to the Munich Airport, turned in the rental vehicle, and purchased a ticket on the late afternoon flight to Azerbaijan. And now he was safely home.

Jahanghir's gaze wandered to the view of the Caspian and the gentle waves moving with languid deliberation toward the Baku shore. Perhaps it was time to consider retirement. He had over the years put aside considerable funds, some of it gold secured in his bedroom wall safe. The luxury apartment was paid for, and how much money did he really require to live the rest of his life in comfort? His current deal with Tretschmer and Hessler, once concluded, would make him even wealthier. Yes, he considered again. Retirement on the tranquil shore of the sea, without the need to endure long flights in fuselages full of sweating strangers, bad air, and worse food. He closed his eyes and drank again from the goblet, draining it.

INNSBRUCK, AUSTRIA

The ride to the zoo from Innsbruck center had taken only a few minutes, the red-and-white funicular train gliding serenely above the venerable tile roofs of nineteenth-century villas and the tops of countless fir trees before reaching its end station on the slope of the Hungerburg mountain. Kommissarin Reiner exited the conveyance, turned, and took a moment to regard the colorful city spread out beneath her and the winding sweep of the Inn River, its course tracing back to the alpine peaks embracing the valley. The zoo, at a higher elevation than any other in Europe, was a pleasant, nonthreatening, and inconspicuous location for a meeting. She had suggested it to Peter Lingen for these reasons.

The zoo itself was unusual. It was not populated by the more exotic denizens of the animal world, and visitors would have searched in vain for elephants, great African cats, hippos, crocodiles, or the like. This *Tiergarten*, or animal park, had been purposefully designed to house only fauna native to the alpine region. And so, the visitor encountered elk, deer, mountain goats, wild boar, eagles, and forest mammals in a replication of their natural surrounding. The zoo directors had given a nod to the past as well, and included animals present in former times but long extinct in the region, a few black bears and a pack of wolves enjoying pride of place.

Sabine paid the modest entrance fee and entered the park, heading for the section of hillside given over to a herd of elk. She had instructed her guest to meet her at the set of benches providing a view of the alpine herd. As she approached, she spotted a middle-aged man with reddish hair and an athletic build standing at the assigned place.

"Herr Lingen?" she inquired.

"That would be me," the figure said, extending a hand. "You are undoubtedly Kommissarin Reiner. *Guten Tag.*"

She returned the greeting and shook hands with Lingen, studying him with professional detachment. She reassessed her initial impression of Lingen's athleticism. The man in front of her possessed the vestigial signs of one who had worked out routinely in the past, but who had in more recent times abandoned the discipline. Lingen's shoulders were still broad and powerful, but his chest had softened and his biceps lacked tone. Although the boxy French blue shirt he wore served to partially conceal it, Lingen had a bit of a paunch. He seemed to be in his mid-fifties. He wore a disarming smile on his face, but there were concentric circles under his brown eyes.

"I'm glad you were able to meet me, Herr Lingen. I've no doubt that you're a busy man. I promise not to take too much of your time."

Lingen made a little bow, before gesturing for the detective to join him on the bench. "Not to worry, Kommissarin Reiner, I have time enough to answer your query about Anton. Otherwise I wouldn't be here."

Sabine nodded agreement. "Thank you anyway. As I told you on the phone, talking with me is purely voluntary. Let me make it clear that Herr Hessler is not a suspect in any crime. I'm interested in him due to his role on the margins of an investigation I'm involved in. To be frank, I'm examining the death of Georg Forster, and Herr Hessler is his successor in the NDF. I'm interested in whatever you could tell me about your friend. Atmospherics often move an investigation along."

Peter Lingen laughed and brushed a hand through his hair, which the detective noted had gray roots and was thinning in front.

"Kommissarin, you need to get your tenses right. Anton is not my friend, nor does he number me among his. Not anymore. We were friends for a long time, it's true, but those days are gone forever. Anton and I had a terminal row about a year ago. There's no going back to civility between us, I can assure you."

Sabine arranged her features into a display of sympathy and proceeded. "I see. But up until a year ago, you and Herr Hessler were good friends?"

Lingen fixed his gaze on the nearby elk, meandering slowly through the grasses. "Close friends, indeed. I believe the appropriate phrase, Kommissarin, would be intimate friends. I never moved into Anton's penthouse in Mutters, but was invited to do so. Even back then, I wanted a degree of independence. And Anton was always consumed with party matters. He had political contacts over frequently, endless meetings with Georg Forster and other party luminaries as well as his business contacts from around the globe. The penthouse is delightfully appointed, but it was all too hectic for me."

"You share Herr Hessler's political views, I suppose?"

Lingen raised his chin for a moment, closed his eyes briefly, and then shook his head slowly sideways. "Not entirely. I sympathize with some of the NDF platform, but I'm no ideologue. The NDF is against a lot of things, but I'm less sure what they are in favor of. And election politicking is so manipulative. Anton and Forster both loved that atmosphere, but it's an affection I just don't share."

Sabine moved the conversation to a central point. "Due to your falling out a year ago, you certainly weren't present at the celebration that took place the night Forster died. But how did Hessler and Forster get along in the past?"

Lingen turned his deep-set eyes on the detective. "They behaved correctly to one another. Respected one another, I suppose. They were not chummy, the association was purely professional. Forster was charismatic, Anton was not. Forster could appeal to all classes, had a knack for it. Anton is aristocratic by temperament and can't conceal it. Anton was well organized, Forster was not. They worked well as a team, but personal chemistry was lacking. You might say they were close collaborators, but not close friends."

Sabine nodded understanding. "I see. They formed a team for the good of the NDF, each bringing his talents to the table. Now with Forster gone, what do you think Herr Hessler intends?"

A perplexed look crossed Lingen's features. "Well, Kommissarin, I'm not certain, I must say. Anton is ambitious. Fiercely so, though the casual observer doesn't see it. He doubtless now revels in his role as NDF leader. Whether he has the personality to become a candidate who can win elections is another question. But it gives him a place in the sun, and Anton likes to feel in charge. Anton also has an appetite for international politics, and the NDF leadership position might be a platform for that. I always had the impression that Austria was too provincial to fully occupy Anton's attentions."

"That's interesting," Sabine allowed. "Did Herr Hessler have international contacts, to your knowledge?"

"Oh, yes. Again, it wouldn't have been visible to everyone, but, as I say, I knew Anton intimately. He's well traveled and speaks a few languages, including Russian and a bit of Arabic. I can recall guests from the Middle East and Eastern Europe being entertained in the penthouse or in exorbitant restaurants in Innsbruck."

"Do you recall their names?"

Lingen stretched his frame on the bench in a vaguely feline movement and laughed. "Just like a detective. Facts, names, places. I fear I must disappoint, Kommissarin. I can't recall names, I never paid much attention to those people. I can say that some of them seemed to be business contacts more than political ones. Related to Anton's various commercial interests, no doubt. That's how he makes his money, after all."

Sabine pursed her lips for a moment before continuing. "Herr Lingen, was there anyone who perhaps stands out in your memory? Anything that seemed a bit unusual? Or some occasion when Herr Hessler's behavior seemed out of character?"

A large elk with a magnificent rack of horns emitted a guttural bellow and marched across his patch of meadow. Lingen smiled at the display and returned to the detective's query. "Something or someone unusual in Anton's coterie? Let me think. Most of these business people were bores, at least to me. Endless talk over dinner about profit margins. Although, now that you mention it, there was something of an odd couple Anton entertained a few times."

"Yes?"

"Well, not a real couple. Business partners. But they acted conspiratorial. And so did Anton in their presence. They visited the penthouse twice, as I recall. Yes. They were introduced to me by first names, that much I recall. They were a strange match. One of them was a German named Otto. North German accent, respectable looking. The other fellow was unappetizing. Central Asian, I would guess, or some obscure East European type. I remember his loud suit, stocky frame, and ostentatious rings. Black hair slicked back like a time traveler from another decade. When he smiled it was like a visit to the goldsmith; all quite horrible. A gargoyle. And certainly not someone to Anton's tastes. This fellow was an aesthetic revulsion, absolutely repellent. But Anton was gracious to him and to this Otto. We had cocktails together and I recall the small talk was rather strained. And Anton invited me to leave them alone for dinner. He accomplished that with his usual suave courtesy, of course, but there was no mistaking it. That was unusual too; Anton generally had me take part in his dinners. But not with these two. They obviously had something sensitive to discuss that I shouldn't hear."

Lingen's voice became more distant. "Now that I think of it, it could be that the rift between Anton and me began that night. A first indication of a lack of trust, of secrets concealed. Wasn't I worthy of his confidence? Were his business contacts more important to Anton than I was? I asked him about it later, gently. He said it was nothing important, a mere social error on his part. The two visitors were just business contacts like any others. That was a lie." Lingen shuddered a sigh. "Who knows? It's history now."

Sabine sensed that she had uncovered something important. "And this Central Asian. Did he have a name?"

Lingen looked at her blankly. "Yes, a first name, at any rate. Anton and Otto both called him Jahanghir. I'm quite certain of that because it's a rather exotic-sounding name that I'd never heard before." Lingen shook his head and turned to study the herd of grazing elk. "Jahanghir."

Central Intelligence Agency Headquarters,
Langley, Northern Virginia

"Okay. Let's go over what we have. I've got to testify on the Hill this afternoon about the drone attacks in the Pakistani tribal areas. So, let's keep things brief. Who's first at bat?" Soren Jorgensen spoke softly but communicated authority, a trait appropriate to his position as deputy director of operations, chief of the CIA's Clandestine Service. His runner's body was slumped into the cherry-veneer conference room chair, exuding a look of fatigue. The knot of his paisley tie was pulled down and the collar button of his shirt open.

Caroline O'Kendell surveyed the room, her eyes moving from Jorgensen around the long, polished expanse of table. In addition to herself and Jorgensen, there were five other CIA officials in the room, located in the agency's seventh-floor executive area. They were representatives of the maritime tracking unit, Europe Division, Near East division and a note taker from Jorgensen's staff. It was crunch time. Jorgensen would give a thumbs-up or thumbs-down decision on committing CIA resources to tracking the Condor Fury. Caroline decided to make her case before one of the others initiated some soliloquy of objections.

She identified herself and began. "Well, sir—"

The deputy director held up a hand and intervened. "It's Soren. At least in here. Go ahead."

Caroline smiled and nodded, recalling that the agency had a long tradition of using first names among its own, a practice the highest level of leadership deferred to as well. An artifice perhaps, but it reinforced the bond of camaraderie. "Yes, Soren. What we're dealing with is a request to employ technical assets to track a dubious vessel underway on the Atlantic."

Jorgenson interjected again. "Is this feasible with a vessel that's already left port?"

"It's feasible. We've done it before," replied his staff assistant.

The tracking unit man across the table snickered and fixed Caroline with a set of hooded eyes. He had high cheekbones and a shaved head. "You say *dubious* vessel? Lots of those around. Every Third World shithole port is full of them. We can't pay attention to them all, my dear."

Jorgensen sighed and pulled his frame up from its languid pose, placing both his hands on the tabletop. "Don't interrupt. Let her make her case. You can have your say later. I don't have time for banter, not today. And she's not anyone's 'dear.' From where I sit, she looks like a case officer. Let's keep it that way."

The tracking unit man contemplated the tabletop and said nothing.

Caroline resumed her narrative. "The *Condor Fury* is central to a case we're running in Germany. Although we don't know what the vessel is carrying, the ship is tied to people linked to the death of Georg Forster, who you all may recall is the Austrian politician who died a while ago. The BND, the German external intelligence service, thought the ship suspicious enough that they had an agent among the crew. He went missing at sea, presumed dead under mysterious circumstances. Another intelligence service, the Jordanian GID, is investigating a Syrian they believe is a weapons smuggler. He, in turn, is linked to the people that own the *Condor Fury*, and met some of them in Amman. GID mentions a connection to Syria, Iran, and non-state actors. The Mossad, for its part, has told our station that they regard the Syrian as a proliferator, and someone who dealt with Forster. In addition, the Forster case seems tied to the assassination of a Mossad agent in Munich. So, although we don't have the clarity we would like, at least three intelligence services are interested either in the *Condor Fury* or the people who own it. It should be in our national interest to clarify what the ship is up to, what it's carrying, where it's going. Those are the grounds for the tracking request."

The tracking representative again found his voice. "An interesting story. In this business we hear lots of those. What we're talking about involves reorienting a satellite. Which means whatever target the satellite is currently covering will no longer be covered. Our resources are stretched. Does everybody know what's on our plate for priority coverage? North Korea. China. Lebanon. Russia. In addition, add narco-cartel facilities in Mexico, insurgent safe havens on the Colombia-Venezuela border, and Afghan smuggling routes. And since we're talking maritime targets, I should note we have over sixty vessels on our watch list. Trust me, business isn't slow. We can't do it all. And this *Condor Fury*, though probably up to no good, doesn't make the cut, in my view."

Jorgensen nodded and brushed a hand through his swept-back gray hair. "I agree our resources are stretched. We aren't like that paint company; what's their slogan, we cover the world? We can't do that. On the other hand, it's interesting that the Israelis, Germans, and Jordanians all sniff something rotten with this ship. Those are professional services. And I really don't like the word proliferation. Take a look at what's happening with Iran. Add Syria and non-state actors from the Middle East into that mix, and I get queasy. What else do we know?"

A blond man with handlebar mustache spoke up. Impeccably clad in a tailored double-breasted blazer and striped tie with matching pocket piece, he was the representative from Europe Division. Caroline knew him slightly. He had just returned from a three-year tour in London, which, Caroline thought, helped to explain his sartorial preferences.

"Since this case is largely taking place on German soil, Europe division is involved. We've run traces on the people under the microscope in this Forster investigation. In our view, there's something interesting here. Does anyone want to hear about Otto Tretschmer and Anton Hessler?"

Jorgensen frowned. "Nope. Let's not start with names. I'm not going to deal with that level of detail. Stick to basics. What's your point?"

"My point is, we have a network of companies linked to one another with a history of bad business. Allegations of arms smuggling and cross-border shipments. These sure as hell look like cover companies designed to conceal their transactions, serving clients trying to evade detection. Companies in Germany and Austria, links to Jordan, Syria, Russia. As to who the clients are, it's hardly transparent, which is alerting in itself. If Europe Division has a vote, we vote to employ tracking resources on the *Condor Fury*."

Jorgenson flashed a thin, tired smile. "You don't have a vote. I have the vote." He assessed each of the other officials one by one before continuing. "Based on a dispassionate reading of the facts, my inclination is to let this request drop."

Caroline felt a sinking, leaden feeling grip her abdomen.

Jorgensen adjusted his tie and buttoned his collar. "But in this line of work, facts aren't always enough. I don't want to reorient a satellite. But unless I do, I'm not going to sleep well tonight. If they had the technical assets—which they don't—the Jordanians, Israelis, and Germans would make the same decision. Given what we know, we can't permit that boat to make its voyage unobserved. We are caught: we know too much to disengage, and too little to disengage. I needn't remind anyone in this room that we are responsible for more than husbanding national resources, important as that is. We are also responsible for protecting the lives of our citizens. That might sound melodramatic, but it is, in the end, what we do. It's the reason we enter this enormous mausoleum of poured concrete every day. Instruct the Federal Orbital Assets Office to find and track that damned ship. And figure out where it's headed."

Jorgensen rose and smoothed his dark suit, signaling that the meeting was at an end. Caroline collected her papers and exited last. She could not suppress a broad smile as she anticipated her phone call to Robert.

ABOVE THE ATLANTIC

The composite frame of the Keyhole-12 (KH-12) satellite silently held its altitude and orbit against the equally silent pull of atmospheric drag. The platform was designed to provide its terrestrial masters below with photoreconnaissance and signals intelligence, and performed these tasks with a robotic efficiency devoid of sentience.

The device surveyed the earth below from a distance of six thousand miles, the precise objects of its high-altitude technical attentions dictated by a stream of encrypted electronic messages sent from the FOAO—Fedeal Orbital Assets Office—in Chantilly, Virginia. The FOAO was something of a hybrid organization, staffed by both CIA and Department of Defense officials. The organization was responsible for designing satellites, maintaining and tasking them in orbit, and sending up new ones to replace aged Cold War specimens that eventually succumbed to gravitational pull and plunged back to earth, consumed in a fiery, metallic death.

Older generations of the Keyhole satellite had launched their photographs and other data back to earth in special buckets. These were retrieved, often from the oceans, by U.S. military elements that then transported the secret product to the FOAO headquarters in the flat, relentlessly suburban Virginia countryside outside of Washington, D.C. More modern platform models, including the Keyhole-12, now transmitted data by electronic transmission directly to the FOAO compound.

The size of a large van, and weighing nearly thirty thousand pounds, the Keyhole satellite observed and recorded imagery of the blue-and-green globe below, providing the FOAO with digital photography from a set of high-resolution cameras. The detail of the photographs provided by the satellite was remarkable. Photo interpreters in Chantilly could read the script of billboards located at traffic circles in Kabul. Provided proper angle and light conditions, they could also make out the license plate numbers of a Russian official vehicle on a Moscow street. The Keyhole's optical capabilities, developed at tremendous defense intelligence budget cost, were, in short, the best in the world.

Silent and invisible, a communications stream of instructions coursed from an FOAO antennae in Virginia and reached the satellite's receiver. The orders digested by the onboard computer, the orbiting automaton rekeyed its array of photographic and signals equipment, and engaged its "maritime observation" software. The information sent aloft from Virginia included the length, configura-

tion, and other specifications of the *Condor Fury*. Apertures reori-
ented in the silence of space, and finely honed million-dollar lenses
moved their point of clandestine focus, concentrating now on the
rolling vastness of the ocean far below. Searching.

INNSBRUCK, AUSTRIA

Kommissarin Sabine Reiner was pleased that the querulous Franz
Waldbaer had not objected to meeting again in Innsbruck. She had
expected complaints about the primacy of Bavaria in the investigation. But, unexpectedly, the inspector had offered no resistance to
her telephoned request. He had sighed into the receiver, true, but she
was persuaded this was just a standard reflection of his perpetually
put-upon, peevish state of being. As she became accustomed to the
quirks of his personality, Reiner found that she could almost regard
the Bavarian kommissar with something akin to affection.

It was her call to Robert Hirter that had provided the surprise.

"Innsbruck is no problem," he had said, as she had anticipated.
But, he had added unexpectedly, "I'll be accompanied by a colleague
of mine who flew here from Washington with information of interest. If you don't mind, that is."

Taken off guard and slightly flustered, she had not found a reason to object. Only after the phone call had she experienced second
thoughts. Hirter was an American intelligence officer with no formal
role in the investigation, at least not in Austrian eyes. It was an
arrangement that made her mildly uncomfortable, and she had no
idea how to explain Hirter to her superiors, if they ever asked. She
could blame it on Waldbaer, she supposed, as the price of liaison
with the unorthodox German. But now there were two CIA officers
to contend with, involved in the investigation of the death of an
Austrian citizen. It was not what she would have wished.

But, she had long ago learned that wishes are not reality. Well
then, done is done. Let's get on with it. And so she accepted the fact
that her office was now hosting Waldbaer, Hirter, and Hirter's associate, a stylish young woman in a navy-blue business suit.

"Hello Kommissarin Reiner, Robert has told me about you," the

CIA woman said. "I'm Rebecca Skibiski. Please call me Rebecca. I'll be assisting Robert for a few days and then return to the States where I'll be his official point of contact. "

Sabine greeted the others and initiated the meeting. "Thank you all for traveling here." Standing in front of her desk, she looked at the trio in their chairs and noted Waldbaer's normal countenance of mild disapproval. She refused to let it annoy her. "I have new information to impart, and it's an opportunity for you as well to provide any details you might have developed." She saw Hirter and Rebecca nod their heads in agreement. Waldbaer stared at the floor.

"Well," she continued, "I can report that I located a friend of Anton Hessler and persuaded him to speak candidly. I should add that the two are friends no longer, but I don't believe there was any vengeful motivation at play in what I heard."

Waldbaer looked up, abandoning his contemplation of the parquet flooring. "This friend of Hessler's. Male or female?"

"Male," Reiner replied.

Waldbaer nodded and settled back into his slouch. "Then you're probably right about revenge not playing a role in his remarks. In my experience, that is far more often a motive behind a woman's comments." He paused and ventured a quick glance at the kommissarin. "No offense intended, of course."

"Of course," she said. "What Hessler's friend did say was interesting. He confirmed that Hessler is ambitious, involved deeply both in NDF politics and in international business. Among the contacts that Hessler maintained was a German businessman named Otto."

Hirter sat up. "Otto Tretschmer? From Hamburg?"

"Undoubtedly," Sabine replied. "Tretschmer was important enough to have dined in Hessler's penthouse and to have been on a first name basis with his host. Their shared interest is apparently commercial."

Hirter rubbed at his square chin. "Okay. Tretschmer and Hessler are tied together. If their common focus is business, they could both be involved with the *Condor Fury*."

Sabine nodded and clasped her hands in front of her. "Possibly.

But there's something else. Both Hessler and Tretschmer dined in the penthouse on at least two occasions with a third individual. He's shadowy. At present, I only have a first name. Jahanghir. Hessler's ex-friend says that this Jahanghir is a foreigner, possibly from Central Asia, almost certainly from one of the former Soviet territories. Jahanghir is apparently involved in the Hessler-Tretschmer business dealings as well."

Hirter extracted a small, black leather notebook from his trouser pocket. "That's an unusual name. I've heard it before." He flipped rapidly through the pages, examining the script. He stopped and stabbed a finger at the notebook. "Here we are. From my meeting with the BND in Pullach. According to the BND, a citizen of Azerbaijan named Jahanghir Karimov is a criminal plugged in to Russian circles that traffic in nuclear materials. Karimov lives in Baku. He's thrown enough money around there to have bought off the authorities. This means that we can't get the Azeri police to question him. And the BND believes this Jahanghir is linked to Tretschmer. Bingo."

Sabine nodded her head vigorously. "Excellent, Herr Hirter. I'd say that confirms it. Jahanghir Karimov is a person of interest. And he has a criminal record."

Waldbaer turned to Hirter. "Did the BND clarify what sort of crimes Jahanghir Karimov is suspected of, other than proliferation?"

Hirter briefly consulted his notepad. "Murder."

Waldbaer nodded, a contemplative look crossing his features. "All right. We now have established that a murderer from Azerbaijan has traveled to Europe, specifically Austria, and dined with Anton Hessler and Otto Tretschmer in Hessler's penthouse. We know the murderer's identity. I'll run his name with German customs and see what they have. Could be that Jahanghir Karimov has traveled to Germany as well as Austria. We also know from previous information that the firms Hessler and Tretschmer are involved with have smuggled small arms, including, allegedly, precision weapons." Waldbaer paused for a moment and surveyed the others. "Does anyone see where I am going with this?"

Hirter stood and stretched. "I think so. You think this Azeri traveled here, picked up a weapon, a Dragunov to be precise, from T&K stocks, traveled to Munich, and shot the Israeli official, Kirscheim. Am I right, Kommissar?"

Waldbaer clapped his hands tight together. "I suggest exactly that sequence of events as a distinct possibility. The pieces of information fit together. I can't prove it, but I'm inclined to believe that this Jahanghir character killed Kirscheim on instruction from Tretschmer or Hessler, or both. The Azeri certainly wouldn't fly to Europe with a sniper rifle, and probably didn't want to risk trying to locate one on the black market. Acquiring it by prearrangement with T&K would obviate those problems."

Sabine executed a slow circle around her desk, one hand at her chin. "But why? Why would Hessler or Tretschmer want to murder an Israeli diplomat in Munich?"

Waldbaer shrugged his shoulders, bunching the fabric of his worn jacket. "I can't answer that yet. Motivation is not transparent. But that alone does not make the scenario we've just discussed implausible. I'll get my German colleagues busy trying to track the travel of this Jahanghir Karimov. We may be able to establish whether he was in Europe at the time of the Israeli's murder. If not, my speculative musing is disproved. If he was here at that time, we may have identified our Munich murderer."

"Does any of this link to the shipment and vessel we're so interested in?" Sabine asked, wrinkling her brow. "I can discern no connection."

Caroline O'Kendell was employing the Rebecca Skibiski alias she had used with Waldbaer in their initial encounter a year previous. Her Clandestine Service supervisor did not want to expose O'Kendell's true name to the Europeans, as it might complicate her unilateral activities at some future point. The Slavic name matched the passport she had been provided in Langley. She spoke in a soft but authoritative voice. "You mean the *Condor Fury*. I can offer something useful on that topic. Off the record, at least for the moment. My organization is following that ship and trying to determine where it's heading. We don't know what's on board, but if the ship docks and unloads, we may have a chance of identifying what was on board."

Waldbaer issued a satisfied smiled. "The joys of satellite surveillance. Watching the *Condor Fury* from afar. Bravo. That's a significant commitment of resources toward what is, at present, still only a murder investigation. I'm impressed."

Caroline eyed the detective evenly. "I didn't say anything about satellites, Kommissar, that's just your interpretation of what I said."

Waldbaer nodded, the smile still marking his features. "Of course, as you say. But the bad news is that identifying the *Condor Fury*'s cargo after it has been off-loaded is not optimal. It would be far preferable to prevent illegal goods—if that's what we have here—from reaching the wrong hands."

"You're right, Kommissar," Caroline said. "But we don't always get optimal solutions. Finding out where that vessel is headed, and what's on board strikes me as a decent result."

Waldbaer pursed his lips and chose not to disagree.

Hirter crossed his arms in front of his chest and entered the conversation. "How about a division of labor? Let me think about what might be done regarding the *Condor Fury*. I have some ideas. Rebecca has provided us with a strong hand, maybe we can build on it."

Reiner agreed. "A division of labor makes sense. My area of pursuit is clear. Kommissar Waldbaer, if you can provide me a memo indicating that Jahanghir Karimov is suspected of murdering an Israeli diplomat in Bavaria, and that T&K in Innsbruck may have been the provider of a weapon to him, I should be able to parlay that into a search warrant of the company's premises. If my police colleagues and I can access the T&K records and hard drives, we might discover something."

Waldbaer stared at the figure of his Austrian counterpart for a moment, his eyes tools of neutral observation. "That is a request I can honor. You will have a memo electronically an hour after I return to my office in Gamsdorf. As for the subject of my labors, I'll be focusing on whatever German customs can provide me on the travels of our Azeri. And we might have enough circumstantial evidence to permit more active measures against Otto Tretschmer, who, after all, is a German citizen."

Tasks assigned, the small conclave broke up, the guests heading toward Kommissarin Reiner's office door and their separate ways. Door handle in hand, Waldbaer stopped in his tracks. "Oh, one other thing. Since we met this time in Innsbruck, I will be setting the venue for our next discussion. *Servus.*" There was no voice of objection and Waldbaer smiled to himself. He intended to keep a controlling grip on more than the door handle.

THE ATLANTIC

Moving on a bearing of sixty-nine degrees, the hulking black mass of a vessel sliced through the perpetual rows of waves, some of them occasionally breaking against the bow. Despite the surging of the ocean, old but powerful diesel engines propelled the ship implacably forward, their baritone grumble a constant background sound, day and night. The crew went about their tasks, their automaton movements betraying the languorous monotony of days at sea.

The ship's course was not unusual, and its progress along the shipping lanes off the African coast was no different from other oceangoing cargo carriers. The vessel was headed for the Cape of Good Hope, after which it would access the Indian Ocean. The ship would then proceed up the opposite side of the African continent to its final port of call, where it would be off-loaded.

Captain Horst Zellmann prowled the length of the *Condor Fury* with a plodding gait, inspecting the state of the vessel and its cargo. His experienced eyes took in every detail of how items were placed and secured, whether waves and wind had loosened knots or slackened ropes or cables, and whether anything on board needed adjusting. He was satisfied, judging that all was, as the saying went, shipshape. True, he allowed, the deck and hold were hardly visions of perfection. Some hull rivets needed attention and long streams of rust were detectable in many places along the walls of the cargo hold. The engines were more than adequate, but would require inspection and perhaps overhaul after the voyage. None of these things posed an immediate problem.

The jewel in the crown, Zellmann knew, was the cargo itself. The machinery secreted in the containers was the critical item, the reason for the complexities surrounding the voyage. False certificates of lading and other documents, the covert packing of the containers in a rented warehouse in Hamburg, clandestine meetings with Tretschmer, all of these things were necessitated by the cargo on board. Cash payments to Zellmann's corrupt customs official cousin had been invaluable in getting the cargo onboard without real inspection. It had been papered as oil drilling equipment; his cousin had taken care of the rest.

Then there was the matter of the package Tretschmer had provided him. It was an oversized aluminum attaché case, and Tretschmer had taken considerable care to underline that it contained something highly sensitive. In Hamburg, Zellmann had purchased a small but high-quality safe and had it secured to the wall of his quarters on board. He had placed the attaché case inside.

"No need to open it," Tretschmer had hissed, "just make sure it's in a secure space where no one can access it, other than you. And the contents are potentially hazardous and are in a special container. I'm telling you this in case you get curious and decide to take a look. It would be better if you don't."

Zellmann took Tretschmer at his word; the last thing he intended to do was play around with the attaché case. In fact, he didn't even like the proximity of having it in his quarters, but that was the most secure place on board. Zellmann entertained a momentary query—biological material? A lethal chemical? Radioactive nuclear matter? He shrugged resignedly. Speculation would bring nothing; best to leave well enough alone, it went with the job.

Pausing in his inspection routine, Zellmann scratched at the stubble on his face and glanced out at the swelling sea. The nature of his business had compelled him to kill a member of the crew on the way to Hamburg, the episode that had so enraged the skittish Tretschmer. But Zellmann was certain he had done the right thing;

there had been no alternative. Prying eyes and open ears could land him, Tretschmer, and others in a German prison for a very long time. This was not the sort of future he had in mind. If required, he would kill again to ensure that the cargo below his feet reached its destination and the contract was successfully concluded, ensuring the final wire payment into his Cyprus bank account.

A sudden blitz of pain raced across Zellmann's cheek. The damned tooth again. He pulled a bottle of aspirin from his trousers and popped two in his mouth. When he received his payment, he would have his teeth redone, perhaps replaced with implants. Pain, after all, was something he was more prepared to inflict than endure. He moved on again, toward the prow, his work boots dampening from the seawater that had washed aboard. Focusing on the sky in front of the *Condor Fury*, he frowned, the throbbing from his molar temporarily forgotten. The horizon in front of the ship was darkening. In the distance, gray skies surrendered to black which, in turn, betrayed a purple core. And the wind was picking up.

"Shit," Zellmann muttered to himself. A storm was developing unexpectedly and looked like more than a local squall. Its front seemed too broad to avoid. Turning on his heels, the stocky captain headed back toward the bridge. He would consult the latest weather information and marine forecast, but was certain from his years at sea, that the *Condor Fury* had a rough time waiting for it in the restlessly swirling darkness looming ahead.

CENTRAL INTELLIGENCE AGECNY HEADQUARTERS,
LANGLEY, NORTHERN VIRGINIA

A digital image scrambled by strong encryption was transmitted in an instant from a Federal Orbital Assets Office antennae compound near Charlottesville, Virginia, to the Communications Center in Langley. Upon receipt, the graphic was automatically decrypted by machine. Seconds later, the image was returned to its original state and downloaded by the CIA technical officers on shift. Following specific routing instructions, the image was forwarded to Laura Castleman in the Clandestine Service ship-tracker branch.

Upon the start of her workday at eight a.m., Laura slid her generous form into the chair in front of her office computer, savored a long taste of hot chocolate from her thermos, and entered a series of passwords to access her file of classified incoming mail. One message received overnight contained an attachment, which Laura opened. "Well, well," she murmured to herself, "a nice little treat for Caroline."

She surveyed the image displayed on the screen. It was a black-and-white photograph of a ship underway; the resolution revealed the slap of white-tipped waves against the dark hull. Below the photograph were lines of technical script. Laura recognized the arcane information. "Okay, now we have direction, bearing, and approximate speed. Probable course is around the Cape." Laura noted the rows of containers on deck and frowned. The *Condor Fury* seemed fully loaded, but the rectangular metal containers concealed what was within. The ship would expose no clue of its cargo to the surveillance satellite keeping its silent orbit miles above. Still, she concluded, the information received was at least another piece of the puzzle. She would transmit the information to a CIA operational facility in Germany, which, in turn, would have a case officer deliver it to Caroline and to Robert Hirter.

Laura took another swallow of creamy chocolate and opened a white paper bag, extracting a warm cinnamon roll. She enjoyed ship tracking, it was like a hunt. In this instance, the prey was a massive beast weighing thousands of tons and its brain was provided by the sentience of the men on board. A worthy target. She would continue to receive satellite updates on the progress of the *Condor Fury*. She again regarded the maritime image on the screen. Laura was set on determining the destination of the vessel before it reached port and off-loaded its secretive cargo.

GAMSDORF, BAVARIA

The mid-morning sun illuminated the pastel hues of the structures along Kirchweg, the principal street of the town. Most of the buildings were three-story structures, the ground floors housing shops and the floors above providing apartment space. Most of the structures were over a century old, some with a pedigree of three hundred years or more. Gamsdorf had been too insignificant a town to face bombing in the Second World War and the place was much as it had always been, except for the teenager-infested McDonald's located at the edge of town like a shunned exile, a gastronomical leper.

In view of the weather, Waldbaer had decided to convene the gathering across from the police station on the terrace of the coffee shop with the English-language name of The Brown Bean. Hirter and his female CIA compatriot sat side by side across from him, occupying a spot of sun, Sabine Reiner nearby, shaded by the overhead leaves of a chestnut tree. Automatically observing human interplay, Waldbaer wondered whether the banter and gestures between Hirter and his pretty American colleague signaled a relationship of more than a professional nature. None of my business, he cautioned himself, not relevant to the matter at hand.

After a waiter had served cups of rich coffee and a basket of fresh rolls and marmalades, Waldbaer rubbed at a stiffness in his neck and offered his opening remarks. "We move forward, *meine Damen und Herren*. Perhaps more slowly than we would like, but we know more now than we knew a few days ago, thanks to our concerted efforts. The question is, what do we do? What actions can we take? I see no grounds to arrest anyone for the murder of Georg Forster, and I doubt anyone here disagrees with me. On the other hand, we have developed indications of criminal mischief. So, I put the question to each of you—what next?" Waldbaer leaned back in his bistro chair and folded his hands over his stomach. The chair creaked with the movement and Waldbaer set his face in a look of reproachful disapproval. Modern furniture had become much too delicate.

Frau Reiner adjusted the bright, patterned-silk scarf that she wore with her beige Trachten jacket and skirt and took the lead. "My primary responsibility is clear, I expect. Solving the murder of Georg Forster and arresting any individual with a role in it. To date, there hasn't been much progress in that direction. Frankly speaking, the information about illegal shipments and the *Condor Fury* is at this stage almost a second investigation. Its relation to Forster is unclear to me."

Waldbaer wore a solicitous look on his features. "Quite right, Frau Reiner. We do seem to have developed information that the T&K firm in Innsbruck is involved in illegal export activities. And the politician Anton Hessler is, in turn, involved with T&K. But of course, all of that is, at best, circumstantial. We may well be looking now mainly at activities unrelated to Forster's demise. One hopes there is enough of relevance to keep you as part of our team. Nonetheless, if you feel you need to conclude your investigatory role due to jurisdictional reasons, I'm sure we would all understand. This may well have turned into another investigation altogether, separate from the Forster inquiry. You or your superiors might judge it inappropriate to continue the present arrangement. Regrettable as that would be."

Reiner suddenly understood. Waldbaer had been thinking along these lines in advance. That explained his unusually pleasant attitude of late. And his smiling countenance. He wanted her to opt out of the investigation and return to provincial Tyrol while he took over an uncontested pride of place. Well, she thought, he's underestimated the Austrians yet again. As he was about to learn. "Thank you, Kommissar. It's true events have developed along a trajectory that takes us away from the direct circumstances of Forster's death. You're quite right about that. Still, as an Austrian law enforcement officer, any illegality involving Austrian citizens or entities interests me, and is within my legal purview, *nicht wahr*? And our dubious Innsbruck company would seem to be engaged in illicit activities. That suffices to keep me involved. At least, that's the way I see it and I'm sure my superiors, as you put it, would agree. No need to regret my departure yet, Kommissar Waldbaer."

Waldbaer continued to smile, but his features had taken on a sour look, as if he had swallowed something unappetizing. He released a long sigh and glanced at the Americans. "Well, I'm certain we are all pleased to hear you remain part of our little circle. We would have missed you had you judged otherwise."

Frau Reiner offered her own exuberant smile. "No doubt. Not to worry, Kommissar, I am in this until the end." She took delight at his ill-concealed disappointment.

The American woman spoke up. "A question, Kommissarin Reiner. Hessler. Have you turned up anything new on him?"

"Yes indeed," she said. "It's my surprise for the day. Based on the link we made between Jahanghir Karimov, the Azeri criminal, and T&K, I was able to get a search warrant on the company. We conducted a search yesterday, just before the T&K close of business. I was there. Only two employees were present. They were surprised, but didn't try to interfere. We removed order books, boxes of documentation, and hard drives. We picked up some items in the warehouse attached to the office space. Night-vision devices and some sophisticated electronic devices that we think are intended to detonate IEDs. Our initial look at the documentation suggests this stuff was headed for Lebanon."

"That makes sense," O'Kendell interrupted. "Those are the sort of items Hezbollah would want to get its hands on, with the Israelis being the targets. Nicely done."

Frau Reiner resumed. "Yes, and it confirms T&K's involvement in weapons smuggling. We picked up other suspicious-looking things but we aren't sure what exactly they are. As I said, we just conducted the raid yesterday and need time to sort things out and exploit the hard drives. You'll get other details as we develop them."

"Good work, Frau Reiner, hats off," intoned Waldbaer. This time his smile seemed sincere.

"Thank you, Kommissar. Hessler has certainly gotten news of the raid by now. I have his residence under surveillance. That's about all I can do legally at the moment. But it might be interesting to see how he reacts."

Hirter chuckled. "You bet. He may do something stupid and provide us with another lead. But my guess is he'll keep a cool head. I wouldn't be surprised if he hunkers down for a while in his penthouse and figures out his next move. The *Condor Fury* is underway, out of harm's way. Hessler might want to contact his clients, whoever they are, and give them the bad news about the raid. That would be good, provided we monitor his phone calls. Are you listening in on him, Kommissarin Reiner?"

Reiner gazed up at the skies above the Gamsdorf street scene. "I'm afraid that is something beyond my authority. We got the search warrant due to the connection between Jahanghir Karimov and T&K. But getting a judge to permit intercepting Hessler's calls is a different matter entirely. We have nothing to tie him directly to any illegality. He's a public figure with a political following, so the bar is set high for getting permission to eavesdrop on him. To be honest, unless we convincingly link him to some major crime, I don't see an intercept happening."

"I understand," Hirter replied. "Rules are rules and we all have to face political realities."

Waldbaer drained his cup of coffee and interjected a query. "Herr Hirter, what do you and your associate see as your next move?"

Hirter glanced for a second at his colleague before responding. "To be honest, Rebecca and I were talking about that before our meeting here, and we've been in touch with Langley. You and Frau Reiner have the law enforcement front covered, Kommissar. So, let me suggest that I concentrate on the *Condor Fury*. While we sit here, that damned ship is closing on its destination, wherever that is. Unless we do something soon to interfere, that boat will dock and off-load its goods, which are probably weapons related. That is not in the interests of the United States, Germany, or Austria. And, without uncovering what's on board, I imagine it will be hard to make a case against Tretschmer, Hessler, or their associates. Let me see whether there isn't something we can do to change the game for the *Condor Fury*."

Waldbaer shot Hirter an earnest stare. "I'm not entirely certain I like the sound of that. Interfering with a cargo ship underway in international waters? When we don't know for certain what goods it is transporting? Makes me uneasy. I'm a simple policeman, charged with enforcing the law."

Hirter shrugged and smiled at the Bavarian. "And I'm a simple intelligence officer, instructed occasionally to break the law."

Waldbaer sighed, his face a mask of faux disapproval. "I grow concerned about the company I keep. I fear my personal standards are slipping. Do me and Frau Reiner a favor, Hirter. Relieve us of the burden of guilty knowledge. There are things related to your endeavors that we surely prefer not to know. We do not wish to hear the details of what you and your service might be considering, or doing, about the ship. I hope you understand."

Hirter regarded Waldbaer with a sympathetic look. "Not a problem, Kommissar. I understand entirely. We're used to conducting our pursuits in secret. Indeed, that is our instinctive preference."

BND Headquarters, Pullach

Dr. Thomas Gagner stood in the main lobby of his representational offices, the oil portrait of Bismarck on the wall behind him displaying a martial glower, the rendered Prussian face a mask of earnestness, betraying neither reproach nor approval. The face of the BND president, in unintended contrast, was a countenance of tranquility, the thin lips suggesting but not quite delivering a hint of smile. Gagner's posture was entirely straight, with hands lightly clasped behind his back, like a military officer in standing repose. The black wool suit he had selected that morning avoided the funereal due to the French-blue shirt and yellow patterned tie.

"You present me with a valuable summary of recent developments, Herr Hirter," he said. "I am grateful for that and will see that my appropriate subordinates are informed as well, according to the rules you and I set earlier. But I anticipate that you are here not simply to inform, but to make an inquiry, or perhaps a request. Am I right?"

Hirter regarded the German official with professional respect. Gagner had the instincts of a professional operator. There would be no delicate dancing around with him.

"President Gagner, you're exactly correct. There is something I want to ask of you, or of your service. The *Condor Fury* is underway on the high seas, in international waters, beyond anyone's jurisdiction. It seems clear that, in violation of German law, prohibited items are on board, most likely weapons related, based on the history of the people involved and the information from the Jordanians. My service is tracking the ship, real time. I'm advised by my colleagues that there is a good chance they will eventually be able to determine the port of destination. Still, the most likely scenario is that the *Condor Fury* will successfully off-load its clandestine cargo before we can interfere."

Gagner unclasped his hands and raised a finger contemplatively to his cheek. "Yes. In other words, Herr Hirter, the situation suggests that the vessel and its owners will succeed in its mission. Correct?"

"Correct. If we'd been able to board and inspect the ship in Hamburg harbor, it might have been different, but we lacked the evidence—and thus the legal authority—to do so. That hasn't changed. In terms of courtroom proceedings, we don't have much of a case that would meet a prosecutorial threshold."

Gagner nodded and closed his eyes for a moment. "I am a lawyer by training. There are valid reasons why the demands of the law are sometimes exacting. But I don't need to lecture someone like you on these things. I share your frustration and gather that you want me to do something. Perhaps I could ask our Foreign Office, the *Auswärtige Amt,* to issue a démarche to the country of destination, once the CIA has discerned it? Such a diplomatic request might prompt an investigation of the *Condor Fury* by the authorities once it has docked in port. Is that what you are considering, Herr Hirter?"

Hirter shuffled a bit in a display of discomfort and looked over Gagner's shoulders to Bismarck's penetrating stare. "Not precisely, Dr. Gagner. Frankly, my agency colleagues and I doubt that the receiving state—wherever it is—will cooperate in stopping a transaction it almost certainly is involved in. The authorities in the receiving port might make a show of inspecting the ship, but that would likely be pure theatrics, permitting them to report to us that they discovered nothing illegal on board. I don't think that diplomacy is what we require under the circumstances."

Gagner permitted his smile more latitude, and folded his arms across his shallow chest. "What exactly do we require under the circumstances, Herr Hirter?"

"What I am going to ask is complicated and sensitive. I can tell you that there have been discussions about this just yesterday at Langley. So I've been advised. Here it is, unvarnished: the CIA considered whether we could use our resources to interdict the *Condor Fury* in international waters and conduct an armed search. A search that might well be physically resisted by the crew. The goal would be to take possession of illicit cargo on board, especially if it is weapons or WMD related."

Gagner narrowed his eyes, casting his features in an almost Oriental appearance. "A bold proposal. Very bold. But I see many problems with it, not least the fact that you would be conducting a coercive action against a European vessel carrying goods of German origin. And that's just the legal consideration, not to mention the daunting requirements of carrying out such a maritime operation. You follow my concerns?"

Hirter shook his head vigorously and exhaled. "I understand perfectly, Dr. Gagner. So do the officers at Langley. Which is why, after considerable discussion, the idea was rejected."

The BND president relaxed his features. "Very wise of them, under the circumstances."

Hirter fixed Gagner with his gaze. "Quite possibly. And they requested that I ask your service to take on this assignment. Which is why I am standing here."

The German regarded the American with a look that migrated from confusion to disbelief. "You can't be serious. If the CIA has decided it makes no sense for them to conduct such a sensitive operation, why should they expect the German service should do it? You cannot possibly mean that the BND should do what the CIA refuses to do. This would be unreasonable, to say the least." Gagner's voice was calm but the suppressed irritation seeped through.

Hirter took a moment to articulate the CIA position carefully. "I understand your initial reaction, Dr. Gagner, but, with respect, the proposal might not be as unreasonable as you think."

Gagner shifted his feet, and Hirter held up his hands in a gesture of supplication. "Let me explain our reasoning. You are right to say it would be a big legal and political problem for CIA commandos to board a European ship from Hamburg in an armed operation that might result in violence. You are also right to point out the difficulties of organizing and carrying out such an operation on the high seas."

Gagner interrupted. "Which applies just as much to German forces as to American."

Hirter squinted and brushed a hand through his hair. "Perhaps not. Consider. If German forces board a ship directly connected to Germany—Hamburg and the businessman Tretschmer—doesn't that simplify things legally and politically? The *Condor Fury* was loaded with its cargo in a German port, a dubious German businessman is directly involved, and, not least, a BND source was likely murdered on this ship during its last voyage. You can make the case to the Bundestag intelligence committee that this is no violation of national sovereignty. It's a covert operation, certainly, but that's why countries keep intelligence services; Germany is no exception."

"You forget something, Herr Hirter. The *Condor Fury* may operate out of Hamburg, but its legal ownership is Austrian, not German. Why not approach the Austrian government?"

Hirter shook his head from side to side. "Austria is a small, landlocked country with no access to the sea and no navy. They lack the capacity to engage in an activity of this sort."

"Possibly," Gagner allowed. "But we still have the matter of the operation itself. Intercepting, boarding, and gaining control over a ship on the ocean is not child's play. Not to mention the search. The *Condor Fury* is not a small vessel. Where on board is the suspicious cargo? What implements do we need to open containers? Are they booby-trapped? Has the crew been instructed to resist? There is a host of practical problems to be considered."

Hirter shook his head sympathetically. "Complexity and uncertainty are the two words that apply to this proposal, I'm the first to admit it. But that doesn't mean that getting the *Condor Fury* under our control is impossible, only that it won't be easy. And there's another reason our German partners might be the right ones to take on this task."

Gagner raised his head a degree and arched an eyebrow. "And that other reason might be?"

"The German Navy has recently been involved in anti-pirate operations as part of a NATO mandate. Which means Germany has real-world experience in maritime operations against an armed foe. That's precisely the type of experience that would be useful in a mission like the one I've described."

Gagner stared at the polished floor tiles. "Well, it is true that many BND officers are members of the armed forces. Some are on loan, others spend most of their career with our organization. They don't wear uniforms while they serve with us, but they are active-duty military. Which means we have excellent relations with the military, including the *Bundesmarine*, the navy. And it's true, as you say, that the navy has engaged in successful, high-risk operations against African pirates of late, it's a point of pride with them. But why not go to the *Bundesmarine* directly, why involve the BND at all?"

Hirter nodded his head in a quick jerk, up and down. "That's a fair question. The fact is, CIA has no grounds to approach the German Navy. We don't have a relationship with the navy, we have one with your organization, the BND. And if this operation happens, it will have to be covert, not openly acknowledged. Neither the American or German governments are going to want to publicly reveal something as sensitive as this; there would be a firestorm of criticism from the UN and a hundred other organizations. All of which translates into this: an assault on the *Condor Fury* must be conducted as an intelligence operation under the direction, we suggest, of the BND. You would be at liberty to bring in whatever *Bundesmarine* elements you judge necessary for the job. The details are up to you, Dr. Gagner."

The German official said nothing for a moment, and Hirter offered a last volley. "We understand you may decline this request. It's sensitive, and to be honest, the BND does not have a record of engaging in covert action or paramilitary activity. My Langley colleagues and I realize this is entirely your call. We hope you agree to engage, but the CIA-BND relationship will remain strong whatever you decide."

Gagner placed a hand briefly on Hirter's arm. "You've expressed your position well. Perhaps this is an occasion where Germany needs to play a leading role and not stand in the shadows. But I cannot conduct an operation like this on my own authority. I need permission from the intelligence committee of the Bundestag. We would certainly want to use a Federal Police GSG 9 unit as the boarding party. They have law enforcement status and are legally easier to deploy quietly than a military team. You are a persuasive man, Herr Hirter. I'll fly to Berlin tomorrow, ask for a closed session of the committee, present the CIA's request, and see what I can do. Just realize that the politicians have the last word."

Hirter smiled. "It's no different in the States. Intelligence agencies don't set the rules; not in democracies. There's one other thing. Even though we're asking the German side to take the lead in this affair, CIA regards it as a joint operation and we'll provide whatever support we can. That includes access to satellite-derived information and supplying special equipment your service or the navy might not possess. We're not asking you to do this solo."

Gagner adjusted his tie and extended a hand, indicating that the meeting had concluded. "Of course, Herr Hirter. But the BND will be doing the heavy lifting and taking most of the risks, provided Berlin gives its approval. This will be a considerable weight on my shoulders. But I assure you, I do not lack the will." The spare-framed German bowed slightly in an old-school gesture, turned, and walked out of the lobby, his footfall reverberating on the tiles. Only Hirter and the scowling Iron Chancellor remained.

KIEL, NORTHERN GERMANY

Like the port city of Kiel itself, the *Bundesmarine* base was a collection of functional, prosaic architecture, most of the buildings simple, unimaginative postwar rectangles of dark brick. The protecting wall surrounding the base was somber brick as well, the grass periphery a deep, lush green, a signal of the frequent rainfall that moved over the region from the North Sea.

Frigattenkapitän Udo Kulm invested little time in considerations of beauty, either of Kiel or anything else. Those were reflections that would have to await his retirement. And since that was years in the future, Kulm could concentrate his mind without diversion on the pursuits that defined him, the navy and the ocean. At forty-seven years of age, black-and-silver hair complementing his white officer's uniform, Kulm exhibited the self-confidence of an experienced naval officer.

And there was salt in his blood, as he sometimes liked to say. His father had been an officer during the war, aboard the battle cruiser *Scharnhorst*. And his grandfather had spent his life at sea as well, for decades fishing the waters between Germany and the Baltic. But Udo Kulm expected that he was the last seadog of the line. His only son was interested in pharmacy, studying it at the university, and had expressed a desire to settle somewhere far from the waves. Kulm accepted this fact, and did not attempt to beguile the boy with tales of the sea; it was a demanding life even for those who loved it.

And there were days when the kapitän was hardly filled with affection for his profession. The present day seemed to be falling into that category. All of this had to do with the visitor sitting across the metal table from Kulm in his office. The visitor, a man in his thirties who identified himself as Herr Neureuth, was attired in a mustard sports coat and pale-yellow trousers. Kulm decided that he did not like the color combination and was for the moment suspending judgment on whether or not he cared for the visitor. Much would depend on how the conversation progressed.

"So, Herr Neureuth, you are here representing the BND; thank you for having shown me your credentials. We don't often get visitors from the intelligence service, though I do know some naval personnel who've been assigned duties with the BND. Some from our communications branch. You'll forgive me if I seem short on hospitality, but we have a major leadership exercise about to start here and my schedule is mercilessly full. I would have appreciated more advanced warning than the e-mail message I received last evening."

Neureuth sat forward in his chair in an athletic hunch, his elbows braced on his knees. His voice exuded apology. "Kapitän, I regret this meeting had to come about with so little warning. For what it's worth, I had to change plans too in order to fly up from Munich this morning. But developments required it, as I'll explain. Sorry for the intrusion on your time, but I think you'll understand the urgency once I brief you."

The naval officer regarded his younger guest with an unblinking gaze. "Brief me? That sounds pretty formal, Herr Neureuth. Not to mention unorthodox. Why would the BND be briefing a *Bundesmarine* officer?"

Neureuth glanced over his shoulder to ensure that the office door was firmly shut. Satisfied, he turned back to Kulm and spoke in a low monotone, almost a whisper. "It's unorthodox, you're right. And sensitive, and urgent. Which is exactly why I'm disrupting your plans today. I should add that I'm here as a personal emissary of Dr. Gagner, the BND president."

Kulm's voice was curt but professional. "All right. Now for the details, if you don't mind."

Neureuth nodded, tugged a folded sheet of vanilla paper from his sport coat pocket, and consulted it. "This is for you. It was written in the Chancellery in Berlin. It's a directive approved by a special committee in the Bundestag. The Naval representative to the Chancellery has also approved it. The top figures in your chain of command are aware of it, and a few naval officers who will be in a support capacity to your mission."

Kulm leaned forward over the table. "Mission?"

The BND officer extended a hand and waved it slightly, signaling for patience. "In a moment, Kapitän. I just want you to know that the appropriate officials approve this directive. It's a small group, due to the need for tight security."

Kulm steeled himself to remain calm. He folded his hands under his jaw. "I still don't know what it is I'm supposed to do, Herr Neureuth."

The visitor passed the document across the table to the naval officer, who read it slowly before placing it on the table in front of him.

"Kapitän Kulm, the federal government wants you to lead a hand-selected GSG9 maritime strike force to conduct an interdiction and seizure operation on the high seas. You select the equipment required to carry this out, it's your call. Assemble the personnel and weapons you need. I'm afraid there isn't time for precise training, other than what you can arrange on board. The BND will provide you with special encrypted communications equipment and two technicians who are naval personnel assigned to us; something you alluded to a few moments ago."

Kulm breathed in deeply, his barrel chest swelling. "I still don't understand. What sort of ship are we supposed to interdict, and why?"

Neureuth nodded. "A cargo vessel that departed Hamburg some days ago. It's called the *Condor Fury*. German captain. As for why, the ship is believed to be carrying illicit, sensitive cargo intended for another country. More than likely advanced weapons or equipment for producing weapons of mass destruction. At least some of the freight, if not all of it, is believed to be of German origin. It's the position of the German government that we do everything within our power to prevent that vessel from reaching its destination. That, in broad terms, is your assignment."

The naval officer squinted and rubbed both hands against his temples in a circular motion. "Well, this is something we haven't attempted before. We've engaged North African pirates. But those were operations against small craft. Only once did we consider boarding a large pirated vessel, but in the end, it was too complicated and the plan was scrapped. I expect the same complications that scuttled that mission to apply here."

"I understand, Kapitän. But we have to try. No one is minimizing the difficulty of what you are being asked to do."

Udo Kulm pushed himself from his sitting position and walked across the office to where a window afforded a view of the Kiel suburbs and the gray sea beyond. "This may all be academic. You mentioned that this ship left Hamburg days ago. Even though we can make more knots, it's hardly certain we'll catch her. And determining where exactly the *Condor Fury* is on the ocean is daunting. We may not even find her."

Neureuth remained seated, his eyes on the naval officer now silhouetted by the window. "Maybe I can give you good news in that regard. Our information is that the ship has not been proceeding at great speed and is approaching a storm front that should slow her down even more. That should help you catch up. As for tracking the vessel, we'll be able to provide you real-time data on location and bearing, and get overhead photographs of what things look like on deck. That will presumably be of assistance."

Kulm raised his bushy eyebrows and turned back toward the intelligence officer. "That would be of considerable assistance. I wasn't aware the BND had such impressive technical capabilities."

Neureuth smiled. "Sometimes we have friends."

Kulm returned the smile. "I understand. Friends who speak English, I expect. No matter, I'm grateful for any help we can get on a mission where the odds are stacked against success."

Neureuth's features clouded with a more somber cast. "I'm no naval man, Kapitän. Other than vacation trips to the Adriatic, I have no acquaintance with the sea. So let me ask you, presuming you can close in on the *Condor Fury*, what do you see as the most problematic element of this task?"

Kulm placed his hands in the pockets of his white service trousers and walked slowly back toward his guest. "Lots of things can go wrong in an operation like this. But physically boarding the vessel and bringing it under control is critical. If we lose the element of surprise, it could all fall apart. If the crew has small arms and is ordered by their captain to resist, we have a problem. We might prevail, but there will be casualties, including my people. How would the German government propose to keep that quiet? And if we stop the vessel in international waters, what are we supposed to do? Pilot it back to Hamburg? Load the cargo onto another vessel? Details, Herr Neureuth. Remember what the strategist Clausewitz said two centuries ago: war is simple, but in war the simplest things become very difficult. His phrase fits this mission perfectly."

"Understood. We'll get you more details as events progress. Don't worry, I'll keep you informed."

Kulm stood over his visitor. "You will indeed, Herr Neureuth. Because there is one point I intend to insist upon."

Neureuth frowned. "Which is?"

"That you will accompany me as my personal liaison to the BND. I want you on board my ship. You say you're the personal representative of the BND president. Good. If an intelligence issue arises, I want you to resolve it. Be so kind as to work that out."

Neureuth looked unhappy. "If you get your way, which you probably will, chances are I'll get seasick."

The naval officer nodded agreement. "Just remember: physical discomfort does not rob one of a clear mind."

Neureuth glared at him. "Would that be the estimable Clausewitz again?"

"*Nein*. That would be Udo Kulm."

CENTRAL INTELLIGENCE AGENCY HEADQUARTERS,
LANGLEY, NORTHERN VIRGINIA

Soren Jorgensen, deputy director of operations, read through the message that Robert Hirter had passed to a CIA facility in Germany for onward transmission. It seemed to be good news. The BND had gotten parliamentary approval for the interdiction operation against the *Condor Fury*, no small accomplishment. Moreover, the BND had reported back to Hirter that a German Navy officer had now been tasked with developing the operational plan and carrying it out. Personnel had been selected, most of them experienced in high-seas action against African pirates. The Germans were now preparing to depart Kiel in pursuit of the cargo vessel.

Nothing to second-guess, Jorgensen judged. The Germans were

operating with commendable celerity and efficiency. The BND was proving a reliable partner in a risky undertaking. And they were keeping the CIA informed via Hirter. That was fine too.

Jorgensen read the cable further. The BND had advised Hirter that BND president Gagner's personal aide would be aboard the naval vessel to ensure smooth coordination and to handle any dicey political issues that might arise. A sensible arrangement, Jorgensen concluded. He paused, placed the paper on the polished veneer of his desk, and thought for a moment. Yes, the Germans were right to realize that the operation could turn into an international incident if anything went wrong. All the elements were there. International waters. A civilian vessel and crew. Lack of clarity about what cargo was on board. An armed interdiction with the possibility of an exchange of fire and casualties. The BND was undoubtedly right to have someone on the naval vessel who could report directly to his intelligence chief, real time. There was only one thing absent. The CIA. The more Jorgensen considered, the more he became certain the agency needed a person on board as well, for the same reasons the BND did. An officer to keep Langley informed, and provide word on developing problems. Someone reliable and decisive.

He grunted to himself and lifted the receiver of the secure phone on his desk. Punching in a series of numbers, he waited for a voice on the other end and spoke. "This is the deputy director of operations. Send me someone from that shiptracking operation directed at the *Condor Fury*, and someone from the German Desk. We're going to have a lucky officer enjoying the sea in short order."

INNSBRUCK, AUSTRIA

Sabine Reiner stood in the cool, high-ceilinged space of the corrugated metal police station warehouse where physical evidence was stored. The place had the look of an upscale flea market. She took in a brace of recovered mountain bikes leaning against a wall, and a pride of televisions and DVD players arranged in an uneven stack nearby. Standing next to her was the wiry, young uniformed polizist who had led the raid on the T&K offices. The policeman had introduced himself, but she had immediately forgotten his name, absorbed by the sight before her.

"This was in the storage area behind the offices, you say?"

The young man jerked a nod. "That's right, Kommissarin. It was surrounded by other crates that contained high-end Bang & Olufsen stereo speakers, which, of course, are completely legal. But as you can see, the contents of this particular crate are rather different." He smirked to underline his point.

She could see indeed. The wooden crate open before her revealed three lethal-looking shapes separated by blue foam packing material. She knew immediately what they were. "Those are Russian-manufacture Dragunov rifles."

The uniformed officer jerked his head again. "Correct, Kommissarin. And illegal here without special licensing. We also turned up an e-mail indicating the weapons were shipped from Verbindung Ost in Vienna." He gestured to another crate across the room. "The carton over there contains the 7.62-millimeter munitions this weapon uses. All in all, I'd say that T&K has some explaining to do."

Sabine inspected the crate more exactingly, tracing a hand over a hollow space in the foam packing. "There was a fourth rifle in here originally."

The policeman shrugged narrow shoulders. "When we opened the crate we found it like this. Nothing has been removed."

"Of course. But one of the weapons was removed at some point before our people arrived. And I think I know where it is at present. I've seen it." She saw again in her mind a rumpled Waldbaer, holding the sleek metal and wood form, standing on the banks of the Nymphenburg canal in Munich.

The policeman gazed at her, a confused look suffusing his features.

The Kommissarin smiled. "Never mind, colleague. It's an investigation of which you are unaware. What else did you discover?"

"We found a lot of suspicious e-mails on the computers. We're

JOHN J. LE BEAU

still examining that, trying to figure out who the senders are. Some of the paperwork appears bogus. But some things are clear."

"Such as?" Sabine inquired.

"Well, there have been overland deliveries from Bosnia. Allegedly of small alloy parts for machinery manufactured in Sarajevo and Jajce. But that doesn't make sense; those items are readily available here in Austria. We checked with the ostensible Bosnian firms involved, and they claim to have no knowledge of deliveries to T&K."

Sabine slowly dragged a patent leather pump through the film of dust of the warehouse floor. "Bosnia is still an uncontrolled area, and has been since the war in the nineties. The fighting was terrible, and the country is still full of weapons from small arms to land mines. To say nothing about criminal gangs operating there. And Sarajevo is only twelve hours from Innsbruck by truck. I wouldn't be surprised if these Dragunovs originated in or transited Bosnia. And if the weapons were moved by van, there's a good chance they wouldn't have been stopped for inspection along the way."

"That's our thinking exactly, Kommissarin," the policeman said. "Anyway, we'll know more in a day or two. There are still crates unopened. I'll call you if we turn up anything."

Sabine nodded her agreement, and the uniformed officer snapped a salute before departing.

Her cell phone issued its familiar musical tone as she exited the storage building for the parking lot. She immediately recognized the voice of the telephone operator at the police station.

"Kommissarin, we've had two calls in the last twenty minutes from an irate gentleman who insists on talking with you immediately. He's on the verge of being verbally abusive. I said you are currently busy and would return his call later. He didn't like that answer and demanded your mobile number, which of course, I didn't provide. I'm sure he'll call again shortly. I know you're running around the city but I have his phone number and, considering who it is, thought you might want to return his call."

"Who is he?" Sabine asked, suspecting that she knew the answer.
"Anton Hessler. A decidedly unhappy Anton Hessler."

THE ATLANTIC

Zellmann stood in the open on the starboard side of the ship, just
outside the protection of the bridge, and surveyed the nautical scene
through eyes narrowed against the assaulting wind. The entire horizon was a festering pastiche of deep purple and funereal black, ragged
tendrils of cloud shifting and expanding in an angry, tropospheric
waltz. Slashes of lightning, silent in the distance, traveled from the
roiling sky to the water, illuminating the tableau. The sea too had
turned black. The storm front was broad; Zellmann's visual observation confirmed the latest weather charts. The storm had developed
quickly, taking the weather routing office in Hamburg by surprise.
The very size of the storm meant that no amended routing was possible. There would be no outflanking this weather. The *Condor Fury*
had no choice but to pass through it as best it could.

He turned his attention to the ship itself. Outwardly, all seemed
well enough. He had personally inspected the stacks of containers on
deck and knew that they were as secured to the deck as he could
make them. He would check the material below deck shortly. Zellmann's concern was that extremely rough seas could shift the cargo,
the unevenly dispersed weight rendering the vessel unstable. If severe enough, this weight shift could sink the *Condor Fury*.

With a glance at the bow, Zellmann could see that the ocean
storm winds were driving the waves higher, their amplitude accelerating as well. How high the waves might get no one could really
know. Still, the *Condor Fury* should be able to take considerable
weather abuse. True, she was hardly the best-maintained container
ship underway on the high seas. Expenditures on overhaul and maintenance had been minimal the last few years. The owners seemed
content that the *Condor Fury* could ply the waters from port to port
and pass the maritime inspection requirements. Anything beyond
that they regarded as an excessive expenditure that cut into profits.

Zellmann had never argued with Tretschmer about maintenance issues, other than to insist that the ship be seaworthy. As a result of this neglect, the diesel engines needed an overhaul, there were some hull rust issues, and the compressors and seawater piping required attention. Zellmann concluded that once the cargo had been successfully delivered, he would insist that Tretschmer drop some money on the *Condor Fury* before she sailed again.

Zellmann felt the first drops of cold rain scratch at his face, driven by the accelerating wind. He heard the metallic clang of footfall behind him and turned to see one of the Nigerian crewmen in a yellow sweatshirt stained with machine grease. The crew member was a tall and perpetually dour man. Perhaps, Zellmann, thought, the fellow had assessed his station in life and correctly concluded that it was unlikely to ever improve.

The Nigerian approached closely and yelled to be heard above the rising gale. "Captain, weather getting worse. Some water coming in below, from around some of the rivets. The bosun said to let you know."

Zellmann grimaced. "How much water?"

The Nigerian shrugged his broad shoulders. "Not much. Not yet. Just sort of tricklin' in. But the bosun said to tell you about it."

Zellmann turned and spit toward the deck, trying to rid his mouth of its acrid taste. His tooth was throbbing again. "All right," he responded gruffly, "you've told me. I'll check it out myself. Anyway, it's nothing to worry about."

The Nigerian nodded, rain pouring off his brow, and retreated the way he had arrived, gripping railings to stay balanced in the wind.

The *Condor Fury*'s captain felt sure the water did not signal a major problem. Some corrosion around the rivets, probably, and the invasive rust that was visible on the hull. Nothing to cause real difficulty. But the wild card was the intensity of the storm.

"Screw it," he said to himself. Instead of moving inside to the bridge to enjoy the warmth and protection from the weather, Zellmann hunched his shoulders and headed into the slamming pellets of rain, making his way forward along the slick deck to access the hold. He judged that the wind was stronger than it had been fifteen minutes ago. The waves would be higher too. He could feel the ship shudder underneath him as the massive engines propelled it toward the unleashed furies of the storm ahead.

AMMAN, JORDAN

GID intelligence officer Hamdi al-Bakhit luxuriated in the feel of early morning sunlight that washed against his face. It was not yet oppressively hot and he enjoyed the opportunity to stroll outside and escape the confines of his government office space. He had selected a small, neglected park near al-Kindi Street for the meeting with Sayed al-Khalid. It would suffice. Located near respectable residential areas, and far from al-Khalid's neighborhood, the park offered the anonymity and privacy so prized by espionage officers.

He had left his jacket in his car, which he had parked a quarter mile away so as not to betray his presence, and walked the dry earth of the park in his shirtsleeves, to give the appearance of a businessman seeking a few moments respite from urban stress. Although only a precaution, Hamdi had placed a small Walther pistol in his trouser pocket along with the car keys. He consulted his wristwatch. Al-Khalid should arrive in ten minutes; he had been instructed to be punctual. As he walked through an old orchard of parched olive trees, Hamdi reviewed the status of his relationship with Sayed al-Khalid .

Hamdi had reason to be pleased. Not only had his ruse with the sickness medication moved al-Khalid to provide detailed information on his business contacts and dealings, but, exploiting his position of strength, Hamdi had persuaded al-Khalid to accept a formal relationship as a reporting source. Al-Khalid had even signed a document stating that he was a GID agent, in exchange for a pledge from Hamdi that al-Khalid would not be forcibly removed from Jordan. Although the topic was never raised, both Hamdi and al-Khalid knew the implications of the document now kept in a safe in Hamdi's GID office. If the memo were ever made public or passed to the right individuals, al-Khalid would be a dead man in short order. And so, al-Khalid belonged to Hamdi, the junior partner in a very uneven relationship of convenience.

A shape moved deliberately in a zigzag pattern a hundred meters away. Hamdi recognized the form of the Syrian businessman. Hamdi lifted an arm and waved, signaling al-Khalid that it was safe to approach. He smiled at how al-Khalid, a born and raised city dweller, crunched uncertainly over the clods of dry earth.

"A *Salaam Alaikum*," al-Khalid intoned the ancient Moslem greeting as he approached.

Hamdi repeated the convention and shook hands with his agent. "Al-Khalid, I need not detain you long today. I have a few points to clarify, based on things you said earlier."

Al-Khalid offered a thin smile, wiping a handkerchief over his sweating forehead. "As you wish. I am always at your disposal."

Hamdi nodded, his intelligence officer training compelling him to continually assess the state of mind of a recruited agent. "Al-Khalid, do you recall what you told me earlier about Tretschmer and his dealings with the Syrians and Iranians, with you as middleman?"

The Syrian nodded affirmatively. "Yes, I met with Syrians and Iranians on Tretschmer's behalf."

The Jordanian intelligence officer crossed his arms. "Exactly. You gave me the names of the people you met, and I checked those names without result. This does not surprise me. They were using aliases, no doubt. But you have been around, al-Khalid. Do you think those guys were commercial types?"

Al-Khalid sought out a narrow spit of shade provided by an olive tree, tracing one of his loafers through dry earth. "No, not business people. I'm sure they were officials. Representatives of their governments. Like you."

"Like me?"

"In the sense that they were at home with secrecy, discreet meeting places, not trusting telephones. That sort of thing."

Hamdi nodded with apprehension. "Intelligence officers."

"Yes. I've dealt with such people before. They have a certain vocabulary, a way of expressing themselves. I dealt with two Syrians and one Iranian, as you know. They were intelligence operatives but they also had a military manner about them."

Hamdi eyed his sweating conversation partner. "You mean military intelligence representatives."

Al-Khalid offered a weary smile. "Yes. If I had to guess, I would judge the Iranian was from Sepah Pasdaran, the Revolutionary Guard Corps, and the Syrians associated with al-Amn al-Askari, the Military Security Department. From their small talk, I'm quite sure the Syrians are from Damascus and the Iranian from Tehran. The Syrians struck me as more pragmatic, the Iranian as a real jihadi, talking about 'the Great Satan' and martyrdom for the sake of Allah. A typical, bloody-minded Shiite."

Hamdi returned the smile. "I know that type. Fanatic and dedicated. Now, al-Khalid, tell me again about their dealings with Tretschmer and Forster. Just in case you forgot some detail in your earlier account."

Al-Khalid breathed a resigned sigh and dragged the handkerchief along the swath of neck above his collar. "As you desire. Forster and later Tretschmer were supposed to arrange for the production in Germany of a specific, high-quality type of centrifuge for the Syrians and Iranians. The centrifuges are designed for uranium enrichment."

Hamdi held up a hand. "But the Iranians already have centrifuges. It's public knowledge. Why would they need to deal with Europeans to get what they already possess?"

Al-Khalid placed his hands in his trouser pockets and moved his head sideways. "What the Iranians have are P1 or G1 centrifuges. Functional, but not state-of-the-art. What Tretschmer has produced is apparently much better, more reliable. I gather from remarks he made that Tretschmer employs some Russian scientists who worked on nuclear programs in the Soviet Union. They assisted with centrifuge design."

"That makes sense," Hamdi allowed. "And the centrifuges are the items to be shipped by Tretschmer via cargo ship?"

"Correct. Tretschmer was to arrange all of this."

Hamdi rubbed at his eyes. "Al-Khalid, are the centrifuges presumably heading to Iran? Some of them perhaps overland from Iran to Syria?"

Al-Khalid furrowed his brow. "No. I admit to finding that confusing. I never heard mention of the final destination for the centrifuges, and it wasn't my business to ask. But it was clear from what the Syrians said that they weren't headed to our region."

Hamdi brushed an insect away from his cheek with a swift flash of his hand and let his gaze wander to the cloudless sky above. "Centrifuges manufactured and purchased in Europe for covert clients in the Middle East, but not being shipped to the Middle East. Nonetheless, the machinery is being shipped somewhere. Destination unknown. This is very curious indeed. But someone knows where the centrifuges are supposed to end up."

Al-Khalid eyed his intelligence handler carefully. "Of course. The ship captain must know where he is sailing. Tretschmer probably knows. My Syrian and Iranian contacts obviously know as well."

"Yes, al-Khalid, undoubtedly true. The question of destination is not trivial. Tretschmer is beyond my reach, and so is the captain of the ship. Which leaves—" Hamdi turned toward his recruited agent.

Al-Khalid looked at Hamdi, his eyelids fluttering nervously. "Theoretically, that leaves the Syrians and the Iranian. But they are unavailable to us."

Hamdi grinned, perfectly white teeth glinting in the sun. "Ah, perhaps that is not true, al-Khalid. Perhaps they can provide us with the information we require. It's worth an attempt."

Al-Khalid did not like the direction the conversation was taking. "I don't follow you, I'm afraid."

Hamdi continued to smile. "No? Consider the situation. You have been the middleman between Tretschmer and his Syrian and Iranian customers. You know these people. More importantly, they know you. They have some degree of trust in you. We need to exploit that situation. Do you follow? I want you to get back in touch with your clients and try to get them to reveal the end destination of the centrifuges. We will have to craft this inquiry carefully, but with luck, we will get the answer we want. If you can do this, I assure you the gratitude of the Hashemite Kingdom will be generous." Well formulated, Hamdi congratulated himself. He was offering al-Khalid a sum of money, without rubbing the agent's face in the mercenary transaction.

Al-Khalid began to sweat again, despite the shade of the olive tree. "I don't know. My part in the transaction is over. I have no reason to recontact those people. And anyway, they aren't in Jordan, they are in Damascus and Tehran."

"True, al-Khalid. We have to be creative. Out of concern for your safety, I don't propose that you travel to them. I want you to get one of them to travel here for some reason. Tell me what that reason might be."

"I have to think. These people are suspicious by nature. Could smell a rat."

Hamdi placed a hand paternally on the smaller man's shoulder. "Don't worry, al-Khalid. We will work together. Even a suspicious man can be deceived. Is there one of these people who is easier to talk to than the rest?"

Al-Khalid bit his lip absently and nodded. "Now that you mention it, one of the Syrians, who calls himself Rafi al-Diri, seemed less guarded than the others. And he enjoys wine. I would choose him. As I think of it, I have some documentation from Tretschmer concerning how the centrifuges—documented as brewing equipment—were transferred from Vienna to Innsbruck to Hamburg, transport receipts, that sort of thing. Nothing important, but I suppose I could offer that for Syrian files."

Hamdi clapped al-Khalid on the arm. "Excellent. And the Syrians would probably prefer that you don't retain documentation, for security reasons. That should be a pretext to get this fellow to Amman. Call him, talk conspiratorially, and lure him here."

Al-Khalid's features edged toward a frown. "If he tells me where the centrifuges are headed, what will you do with him? If you arrest him, somebody will eventually suspect me."

Hamdi released a deep laugh. "Al-Khalid, we are not stupid.

Nothing will happen to your Syrian. If you get him to your apartment, we will record what he says. Other than that, no interference. He returns to Syria unhindered, unaware of our interest in him. I don't care about him, I care about those centrifuges."

Al-Khalid exhaled a breath, his frame more relaxed. "Thank you. I will call him once I leave here and report back to you. This might work."

The two parted company, al-Khalid exiting the park first. Hamdi followed him at a distance, ensuring that neither he nor his agent had attracted any attention. The sun's grip on the landscape remained relentless and the fading footfalls of Hamdi and al-Khalid were replaced by the scratchy scampering of small, sharp-eyed lizards.

INNSBRUCK, AUSTRIA

"You have no right, no right at all to interfere with legitimate business. I will not accept harassment from the police. You forget who you are dealing with." The sharpness of Anton Hessler's angular features was accentuated by the livid red that suffused his face. He raised his head a degree, lip slightly curled, and regarded Kommissarin Reiner with unalloyed disdain.

Aware that it would provoke him, the detective returned Hessler's baleful look with one of smiling tranquility. "But, Herr Hessler, you are quite mistaken, I fear. I am entirely aware of whom I'm dealing with. It is you who is laboring under a misapprehension."

Hessler's lidded eyes flared. "You test my patience, Kommissarin. Very unwise."

Sabine retained her pleasant demeanor. "I expect I will test more than your patience, Herr Hessler. I will test your veracity. That is, after all, my professional duty, don't you agree?"

Hessler said nothing.

"I should add something else, Herr Hessler. You used the words 'legitimate business.' From what I've seen, that is not the phrase I would employ to describe T&K. Our inspection uncovered illegal weapons, doctored paperwork, and other information indicative of criminal activity. If I were you, I'd drop the show of indignation. As an associate of the firm, you have much to answer for."

Neither Hessler's voice nor countenance had lost its poison. "If you uncovered anything illegal, I assure you I knew nothing about it. And there's probably some explanation, misshipped items or something like that. T&K is a firm involved in international trade. Perhaps goods were received that weren't ordered. It happens."

Sabine set her features in a look suggesting sympathy. "Perhaps. But let me advise you of something troubling. A crate of weapons was on the premises. One weapon was missing. It appears the missing weapon has been recovered in Munich, where it was used to commit a crime. That suggests something more sinister than receipt of a mistaken shipment." She watched in interest as some of the color drained from Hessler's face and he wet his lips. Good, she thought, he's off balance now.

"Kommissarin Reiner," Hessler began, his tone less aggressive, "if what you say is true, I am astounded. Perhaps there were rogue activities underway at T&K that I am unaware of. I can assure you, I would never engage in criminal activities; the very thought is vulgar. And you will admit, the seedy underworld hardly goes with my established position here in Innsbruck."

Sabine shrugged her shoulders. "It's precisely your position that might be at risk. God knows, the last thing we need is for this to leak to the press. You know how irresponsible the media can behave. Just for the sake of a sensational story they would gladly link you to weapons dealing and crimes in Germany. One can imagine the political price to be paid." She flashed a sadly innocent smile.

Hessler's features were now pallid and he unbuttoned the collar of his starched shirt. "The press? Surely you won't allow an investigation like this to get to the media?"

Sabine opened both hands in front of her and nodded. "Well, Herr Hessler, I can try to see that our investigative proceedings remain discreet. Of course, I could guarantee that with more ease if I knew that you would cooperate with me."

Sabine watched Hessler's serpentine eyes harden. Yes, she judged, he knows that a trap has been sprung.

Hessler pressed a hand to his forehead and exhaled a whisper of breath. "Of course, Kommissarin, whatever I can do to help the authorities. Presuming you can keep the media at bay."

She leaned forward conspiratorially. "Tell me about Otto Tretschmer and his friends in the Middle East."

The Baltic Sea, off Denmark

The sky was uncharacteristically cloudless as the German Federal Navy frigate *Luebeck* made way from the Baltic Sea in the anemic and tenuous first light of morning, moving through Kattegot Bay and the narrows of the Skagerrak Strait toward the Atlantic. The ship was a newly commissioned F 125 model, its sleek gray form displacing over five thousand tons. In addition to the crew of one hundred and ten sailors, the *Luebeck* hosted a group of fifty hand-selected GSG 9 special-action troops and officers. The vessel was armed with deck guns of various calibers and two quadruple missile launchers amidships that could fire an antiship projectile at a target well over fifty miles distant.

Frigattenkapitän Udo Kulm stood on the forward deck of the ship with his two civilian guests. All three clutched sturdy plastic mugs of coffee, emblazoned with an image of the black-yellow-and-red German flag. Kulm observed how the two men, Neureuth and an American named Robert Hirter, continually eyed the sea, their vision drawn magnetically to the endlessly undulating water. They'll get over their aquatic fascination in a few days, he thought, and the ocean will become for them something routine, like the air they breathe. It was always like that for those on their first long sea voyage. Kulm, however, never treated the sea as routine. That conceit rested poorly with the duties of commanding a naval vessel, responsible without respite for ship and crew. He forced himself to be perpetually alert, even to the point of sleeping only lightly while on the waves. He savored a mouthful of strong, unsweetened coffee and decided to learn a bit more about his guests.

"Herr Hirter, I understand you're an American intelligence offi-cer, you've told me that much already. It's not my responsibility to in-quire further about that, but a few details about what precisely you'll be doing aboard my ship, if you please. You brought aboard commu-nications gear. Based on Herr Neureuth's request as a German offi-cial, I permitted my technicians to install it in the commo shed. But perhaps you can explain to me how you intend to use that gear. I want to make sure it doesn't interfere with our own ship-to-shore communications."

Hirter swept a hand through thick hair, tousled by the wind. "Fair question, Kapitän Kulm. Let me lay out what it is I'm supposed to do—with your and Herr Neureuth's permission—and that should clarify the role my commo system plays onboard the *Luebeck*."

Kulm nodded his agreement and tipped his coffee mug again to-ward his mouth.

"The mission I've been given by CIA is simple, Kapitän Kulm. This task is of interest to my country as much as it is to Germany, as explained earlier by Herr Neureuth. Just as Herr Neureuth is ex-pected to be linked in real time to his BND superiors, I'm expected to be in touch with Washington. As a German federal official, Herr Neureuth can employ your encrypted naval communications and patch through to his chain of command. I have no right to use your communications and, anyway, couldn't efficiently reach my people that way. So, I've been provided an encrypted transceiver linked di-rectly to CIA. As Herr Neureuth reports on something via your sys-tem, I do the same with my gear, parallel."

Kulm pursed his lips and ran a hand across the incipient stubble along his cheek. "*Sehr gut*," he allowed. "But tell me, Herr Hirter, pre-suming we catch our target, this *Condor Fury*, how do you see your responsibilities? Do you remain here for the duration of the inter-diction and send out reports based on what I tell you? Or do you ac-company the boarding team? This is not clear to me."

Hirter considered. "Well, Kapitän, I guess you probably have the last word on that subject. From my prism, I need to be in a position to let my superiors know how events develop. If that means I stay on board the *Luebeck*, so be it. I don't want to get in the way of your commandos when they move into action. That said, if you give me permission to accompany them, I'll get a damn good view of things. Presuming that seizing control of the *Condor Fury* will occur quickly, I suppose I could be back in the commo shed within an hour or so. That would be soon enough to keep Langley in the loop."

Kulm furrowed his brow. "All right, Herr Hirter. I guess I have time to consider the best course of action. That cargo ship has quite a lead on us. We may not catch her, that's a real possibility. If we get that scow in our sights, we'll work this out. *In Ordnung?*"

Hirter flashed a brief smile. "*Ja. In Ordnung.* But tell me, Kapitän Kulm, do you think we'll catch her?"

The German naval officer raised his head and sniffed the salt in the wind. "One thing is certain—the *Condor Fury* is entering one hell of a storm front. That will slow her down. The weather will have changed by the time we traverse that area, and won't affect our speed. And the technology integrated into this warship gives us a reduced radar and acoustic signature, which will significantly blind the *Condor Fury* to our pursuit. My sailor's gut tells me our chances of intercepting her are good."

The dull gray form of the frigate moved past the narrows into the broadening sweep of the North Atlantic, the Danish and Swedish coastlines falling away on both sides. The *Luebeck*'s two distinctive pyramidal superstructures and forward-mounted deck gun gave it an earnest look. Like the thresher sharks searching the waters below, the frigate was on the hunt, alert to the scent of prey.

Gamsdorf, Bavaria

Waldbaer sat alone with Frau Reiner at a table in the Alte Post. The table was positioned flush against a stucco wall and set for two. A large, age-darkened oil painting of an elk hung above them, the animal's antlers embracing a luminous cross, the symbol of Saint Hubertus, patron saint of hunters. *Kommissars are hunters too,* Waldbaer had thought with a smile upon viewing the picture. Other diners casually examining their surroundings might have mistaken the two detectives for a married couple on an evening out. With Hirter on the Atlantic and his female CIA counterpart coordinating with colleagues in Berlin, the two kommissars had decided to assess the status of their investigation. A tea candle burned in a gray clay cup at the center of the oaken table, Waldbaer's half-liter mug of Spaten beer facing off the more delicate shape of Reiner's glass of red Franconian wine. The stolid, eternally grimacing waitress had taken their order, and Waldbaer awaited his *schweinshax'n*, knuckle of pig, and Reiner her fresh trout with boiled potatoes.

Waldbaer grabbed a small wicker basket containing a clutch of pretzels and offered it to his dinner partner, who declined with a smile. He shrugged and took one of the doughy, salted forms, tearing out a substantial bite. "You know," he said after chewing for a moment, "we're making progress on the Hessler and Tretschmer angle, and Hirter and his friend are moving against the *Condor Fury*."

Reiner cupped her wine glass and moved it slowly across the tabletop. "Yes, it would appear so. But I wonder if we aren't losing our way. Chasing a ship across the Atlantic isn't our primary interest, is it, Kommissar? It might be the main concern of the CIA and BND, but does it take us any closer to establishing who killed Georg Forster? Investigating his death, after all, is the main reason we're working together."

Waldbaer took a mouthful of beer and swiped a hand across his lips. "I haven't forgotten. I still remember standing in the rain and mud that night near Garmisch, looking at that ruined sedan. We have the photos taken before the crash, of Forster's car and the vehicle rented by the Israeli. We know Forster had been drinking. We know that GHB was used to drug him. But there is something we haven't asked ourselves."

Reiner toyed with her wineglass, holding it by its stem. "And that question is?"

"That question is: where was Forster going that night? He didn't

drive through that thunderstorm for the alpine view. What was his
reason for taking that road toward Garmisch?"

Reiner sighed. "We don't know and Hessler doesn't seem to
know, nor does anyone else. We've uncovered no notation in
Forster's office or home to answer that. Nor will we, I expect."

Waldbaer's head shot up and, without thinking, he placed a broad
hand over her arm. "Garmisch. Yes. That was the likely destination.
Forster had already passed Mittenwald. And were he traveling to Munich, he would have taken the exit to Wallgau. My stomach tells me
he was going to meet someone that night in Garmisch."

Reiner delicately removed Waldbaer's hand from her jacketed
arm. "That makes sense. But it doesn't get us far. We have no idea
who he would be meeting there."

Waldbaer nodded, his voice animated. "No. But we do have the
names of people associated with Forster, *ja?*"

"Well, Hessler was at the party gathering in Innsbruck, that's established."

"I don't mean him, Frau Reiner. But perhaps Jahanghir Karimov
or Otto Tretschmer or Horst Zellmann. A long shot, but worth trying. I'll send a team to Garmisch in the morning and have the boys
hit the hotels, looking for any of those names in the registers. We
might get lucky."

"True. And by the way, I had a chat with Hessler in Innsbruck,
he was very unhappy about the search of T&K. More importantly, he
was worried about the details getting to the media, publicly linking
him to the firm, and damaging his party's popularity. Typical politician. So, in exchange for police discretion, quid pro quo, he volun-
teered a few details on Tretschmer and his activities."

Waldbaer raised his glass in a salute. "*Respekt*, Frau Reiner, nicely
done. Properly communicated, a subtly veiled threat is often effective in eliciting information. So, what did Hessler have to say about
the good Otto Tretschmer?"

A shadow engulfed the tabletop and the two diners looked up
to encounter the unsmiling visage of the solidly built waitress, who

wordlessly deposited the ordered meals, turned on her ankleless legs, and trundled back toward the kitchen.

"*Guten apetite*," Waldbaer mumbled, gazing in satisfaction at the massive knuckle of pork dwarfing the plate.

Reiner picked at her trout with a delicate, probing gesture. "Hessler is sly, and guarded in what he says, as you might expect, but he offered a few details on Tretschmer. For example, he said Tretschmer's connections in the Middle East go back some time. During the Cold War, Tretschmer served as a commercial intermediary between the East German Communists and the Syrian regime on transactions where goods transited Western Europe. Tretschmer's connection to al-Khalid dates to that time. Tretschmer also has a Syrian passport. After the Cold War ended, Tretschmer and al-Khalid went private, setting up T&K as a conduit for illegal business activities. Hessler now admits he knows Tretschmer and that Forster knew him too. Hessler denies he personally ever engaged in illegality. He doesn't know what Forster might have done with Tretschmer."

Waldbaer nodded. "That's useful information, Frau Reiner, thank you."

Reiner studied him for a moment before replying. "You know, we've been working together for a while now, and the end is not yet in sight. I was wondering if we might use first names. If you don't object. I know you Germans are more formal than we Tyroleans. Calling me Sabine would do just fine."

Waldbaer sat back in his chair, eyebrows arched. He felt warm at his neck and hoped that he wasn't blushing. "Of course. Sabine. Call me Franz. I should have made the offer myself, but, well, I've perhaps been too focused on the case and not enough on courtesy." It occurred to him, as it had from time to time, that the Austrian detective was not unattractive. *Perhaps the light in here shows her to advantage,* he thought before chastising himself for being so fiercely ungallant.

"Franz, I think we need to keep two questions in mind. First, what happened to Forster, and, second, who killed the Israeli? Solving those two deaths is our primary responsibility. I like your idea about checking the Garmisch hotels. But how do we move forward on Kirscheim's murder?"

Waldbaer placed his elbows on the tabletop and steepled his fingers. "Well, Sabine, we have the murder weapon. And everything points to this Azeri, Jahanghir, as the trigger man."

"True. But we have no motive. And we can't expect much progress with him safely nesting in Azerbaijan, with which we have no extradition agreement. I can't understand why the Israeli was murdered."

Waldbaer exhaled quietly and squinted. "I have some thoughts, but nothing I can prove. Forster suspected he was being followed, as you'll recall, and his private investigator identified the surveillants as Israeli. After Forster's death, Hessler made this information public. You and I have concluded that Kirscheim followed Forster around on Mossad orders, but not to assassinate him. It was an intelligence operation to gather information on Forster's contacts. The Israelis never intended to kill Forster, the risk of political blowback was too great. But Hessler had announced Israeli complicity to the world. Whether or not he believed it himself, I can't say. At any rate, I think someone seized on that public allegation, determined that Kirscheim was the man involved, and contracted Jahanghir to kill him."

Reiner offered Waldbaer a puzzled look. "But who would have given this order, and why?"

Waldbaer drummed his fingers against the beer glass. "As I say, I have no proof, Sabine. But I wager Hessler had a hand in it, probably in league with Tretschmer, who would have been the connection to Jahanghir. In view of his ambitions, Hessler would want to avoid direct contact with someone as sordid as the Azeri. Why kill Kirscheim? To keep attention away from themselves and their activity, and suggest an Israeli role in Forster's death. In other words, a red herring, a deception."

Reiner sipped from her wineglass and dabbed a napkin at her lips. "It's an interesting theory, Franz. But as you say, no proof. Nothing to justify an arrest. To be honest, I don't think we'll ever get enough evidence to bring Anton Hessler to trial."

Waldbaer looked at his counterpart unblinkingly. "Agreed. But Hessler's fear of negative publicity is interesting. Maybe our American intelligence friends can exploit that, I understand they're a creative lot. I'll get in touch with Rebecca. And let's see what our check of the Garmisch hotels reveals."

She was unsure what Waldbaer had in mind, but decided it best not to inquire.

They returned to their fare of fish and pork, and for all appearances were no different than the other diners at the Alte Post, enjoying a quiet evening of no particular consequence, as guests had been doing at the establishment for two hundred years.

Amman, Jordan

Even with three glasses of wine happily consumed, the Syrian was conscious of security requirements. Balding, narrow-jawed Rafi al-Diri was by nature and training a miser with words, measuring his comments with care. His conversation with Sayed al-Khalid was conducted with parsimonious economy.

Al-Diri collected the various sheets of paper that al-Khalid had provided him, documenting wire deposits to the T&K bank account. Al-Diri opened his black leather attaché case, and slipped a finger into the corner of the interior wall, pulling back the fabric and revealing a concealed compartment sufficiently capacious to store several documents. He placed al-Khalid's papers inside, resealed the compartment, and closed and locked the attaché case. "Good," he mumbled without elaboration.

Al-Khalid poured his guest another glass of wine before reciting the lines he had rehearsed. Make it sound casual, he had told himself. "Glad you have that stuff now, I don't want to keep anything. No paper trail means better security. And I hope to work with you and your associates in future. This has been a most profitable enterprise. I hope you've been satisfied with my role."

Al-Diri smiled and nodded, saying nothing and taking a sip from the glass.

Al-Khalid ventured his next comment. "Well, the goods are safely at sea. No need to worry any longer. I just hope everything is okay at the port of destination. You know, I've got reliable contacts in lots of major cities. Maybe I can provide someone at the destination point to offer assistance and facilitate things. And given the handsome profit I've made, I'm willing to offer this service gratis."

Al-Diri eyed him with a gaze that struck al-Khalid as coldly reptilian. "Let's go out on the balcony, al-Khalid."

The men walked through the open French doors and stood with hands on the wrought-iron railing, looking out at the hooting aural chaos of an Amman traffic circle below. "Do you have contacts in Somalia? Specifically, the port of Eyl?"

Al-Khalid improvised. "I know someone in Somalia, but in Mogadishu, not Eyl. Still, I expect he could travel there if I instruct him to do so. I'll have to check."

Al-Diri waved a hand in the air, his voice slightly slurred. "Don't worry about it. We're in good shape as it is. Everything is arranged. Deals have been struck, payments made. Local pirates will escort the ship to Eyl and provide protection. Al-Shabab militia will off-load the goods and bring them to a prepared location outside of the port. We started building the required structures two years ago, anticipating this delivery." He snickered and ran a forearm across his lips. "Of course, from the air, it looks like a few nondescript, flat-roofed warehouses. Larger than normal warehouses, it's true, but that should alert no one. Anyway, if you know someone reliable who can get down there, maybe we can use him. But we've already got a team of Syrians and others on the ground in Eyl. Thanks for the offer." He raised his wineglass in a toast, and al-Khalid smiled, bowing his head politely.

Al-Khalid knew not to pry further. It would suffice. He knew as well that the brief conversation had been captured. Hamdi and his GID comrades had installed tiny, concealed microphones on the balcony, where they expected al-Diri would go to impart any sensitive information. The Jordanian intelligence officer would be able to hear for himself the peculiar words uttered by the wine-loving Syrian.

The Atlantic

It was worse than he had anticipated. Worse than he had ever experienced in his years at sea. Waves battered the hull of the *Condor Fury* without pause, the hollow sound of their rhythmic assault a torment in itself, a threatening, malevolent symphony. He detected fear in the eyes of the crew, but made sure to keep his own face an emotionless mask. A sovereign attitude was a requirement of captaincy.

The leakage problem with the rivets had worsened. What had hours before been thin tendrils of invading seawater had now escalated to forceful streams. Sections of the hold were filling dangerously and the labors of the outdated pumps were insufficient to the task.

Just as bad, the heavy sea was slamming against the ship ceaselessly, like a liquid battering ram. The *Condor Fury* was acquiring a pronounced list. The abuse was exacting an increasing toll on the integrity of the vessel and Zellmann, standing on the bridge, swore again at the shortsighted parsimony of Tretschmer and the poor condition of the ship. We'll get through it, Zellmann assured himself, the storm will abate, no front lasts forever.

The captain watched one of the crew on the deck below fight the wind with crablike steps to vomit over the side. They were all miserable, he knew, but there was nothing to be done about it. More critically, they had lost time. The storm had slowed their progress to a near standstill and their arrival in Somalia would be days later than anticipated. That was a mathematical certainty. He would communicate this unwelcome news to those who needed to know, once the storm withdrew its talons. At least the cargo was unaffected by the surging anger of the sea. Care with packing and storage had kept the centrifuges secure. And the special material in his captain's safe was undisturbed as well. As long as he could keep the *Condor Fury* on the waves, and not under them, things would yet work out.

Zellmann wanted the voyage over, the cargo off-loaded. He felt fiercely unhappy, his contentment at the beginning of the journey now utterly dissipated. His teeth hurt. The aspirin that he took and the violent contortions of the ocean had made a ruin of his stomach. The din of the waves had instilled a dull, throbbing pain in the back of his brain. Perhaps it was time to retire after all. Time to end his servitude to Tretschmer. It was a liberating thought.

Zellmann's eyes surveyed the instruments on the bridge's console, alert to potential problems. He detected no new difficulties. He glanced through thick glass at the sky before the ship. It was still dark and vicious, the waves below it towering and merciless. He thought there seemed a marginal reduction in the fury of the assault, and a tinge of yellow barely visible on the horizon. We'll ride it out after all, he told himself, this time with grim conviction.

MUNICH INTERNATIONAL AIRPORT

The terminal was modern and airy, a successful architectural creation that married steel and glass harmoniously. The disembarked passengers from the flight from Baku walked the broad corridor toward the array of booths belonging to German immigration. Jahanghir Karimov moved at the pace of those around him, blending into the mass to avoid standing out. He glanced ahead and noted the uniformed German officials without concern. He knew his papers were in order. He joined the shortest line and pulled his passport from his blazer pocket.

Ten feet in front of him, a young, red-haired female immigration officer glanced from the glass pane of her booth at an elderly woman wearing a headscarf. She muttered "*Guten morgen,*" as she had been trained to do, took the woman's passport and opened it. Her motions hidden beneath a counter, the official entered the name into a computer linked to the German watch list of suspicious persons. A list that included the name Jahanghir Karimov. Seconds later, the notation "no match" appeared on a small screen. She returned the old woman's document with a mumbled "*Auf wiedersehen,*" and waved her through.

Jahanghir Karimov appeared next and wordlessly presented his Azeri passport. The woman took it, submitting the name to the routine search process. Jahanghir glanced with purposeful disinterest at the baggage claim area and terminal exit ahead. After a few moments, the immigration woman passed the document back to its owner. "Have a nice stay in Germany, Mr. Alekperov," she said, waiting with a bored look for the next passenger.

Jahanghir moved his head down to conceal a slight smile. The new passport he had employed was not forged, he had purchased it from a corrupt interior ministry official in Baku, in exchange for cash. Having reluctantly accepted the assignment to visit Europe again, he decided it would be safest to employ a new persona. He consoled himself that he would be back in Azerbaijan in a few days. After collecting his single suitcase, he would take the escalator down to the subway station below the terminal and travel to the Munich train station. There he would purchase a rail ticket in perfect anonymity and be on his way. His task was utterly clear, simple in its own way, and he anticipated no complications.

GARMISCH, BAVARIA

The Sonnenbichl Hotel at the edge of Garmisch looked out on the valley toward Partenkirchen like an aging, grand dame surveying her surroundings through fading eyes. The façade and structure of the hotel betrayed its age, even though the current owner had painted the building a bright, pastel yellow, and trimmed the windows in white. The effect was that of a woman in decline, trusting the deceit of rouge and paint to soften the implacable, unforgiving tyranny of time. The Sonnenbichl had been built on a small rise above the valley in 1890 and for decades reigned as the premier hotel of the region, dispensing the trappings of luxury to generations of wealthy tourists from the flatlands intent on viewing the mountains. The hotel had survived the Bavarian monarchy, the Prussian-led empire, the Great Depression, and two world wars, but the years had quietly extracted a price.

Waldbaer had coordinated his visit to the Sonnenbichl with the

Garmisch police and met one of its uniformed representatives in the small hotel lobby, its interior softly lit by a series of delicate lamps. The Garmisch policeman had the large build of a farmer and took the lead with the attractive, ponytailed young woman at the reception desk, displaying a search order with a flourish and explaining the requirement to check the registry. The woman acceded unquestioningly, turning the book over to the official. Some inconsequential banter ensued, followed by soft laughter. Stop flirting, for God's sake, Waldbaer wanted to hiss, but refrained, aware that regulating social customs was rather beyond his brief.

The policeman turned to him a moment later. "It's all yours, Kommissar."

Waldbaer grumbled a sound suggesting grudging thanks and focused his attention on the registry. "I'm interested in who stayed here the night Georg Forster died," he explained to his associate. "Any one of three or four names interests me. Your colleagues checked the hotels in Garmisch and said one of these people stayed here for one night. I need to confirm it." He flipped through the pages until he came to the date. Squinting, he traced his finger down the page of registered guests. His eyes took in a collection of letters in a familiar sequence, and a broad smile crossed his features.

"Looks like I'm a lucky swine," he said.

The Garmisch policeman regarded him quizzically. "What do you mean, Kommissar?"

Waldbaer turned from the book to the earnest face of the police officer. "Your comrades were right. A person of interest was here. Otto Tretschmer. A most helpful revelation."

The receptionist with the ponytail turned toward the officials. "Did you mention Herr Tretschmer? He's been a guest several times. In fact, he's here right now."

Waldbaer gripped the counter. "What? Tretschmer is in the hotel?"

"*Ja,*" the woman replied, nonplussed. "He arrived a few hours ago for a one-evening stay. I think he has a visitor; another gentleman asked about Herr Tretschmer around twenty minutes ago. Shall I ring him up?"

"By no means," Waldbaer growled through his teeth. "We'll welcome him to Garmisch personally. Room number please."

The detective and the local policeman took the stairs toward room 219. Waldbaer tapped his compatriot on the shoulder. "Is your handgun loaded?"

The Garmisch policemen nodded affirmatively, his eyes wide.

"Good. We might need it. I have no idea how Tretschmer will react to this intrusion. I'm not carrying a weapon myself."

The two men reached the hallway on the second floor and proceeded toward Tretschmer's room, the policeman with one hand molded around his checkered pistol grip. Standing directly in front of the door marked 219, they paused. Seeping under the door was the sound of voices, too muted to be understood, and a series of blunt thumps.

"Break it down," Waldbaer barked at the Garmisch policeman. The officer tossed his uniform cap to the floor and slammed heavily into the door with his leather-jacketed shoulder. There was the crack of splintering wood as the door separated from its frame. The policeman nearly fell into the room, propelled by the force of entry. Waldbaer was steps behind him.

Waldbaer's eyes took a snapshot of the scene confronting him. A European-looking businessman with a garrote around his neck, face purple. His assailant standing behind him, a swarthy, stocky man with a goatee, dark eyes wide in astonishment at the appearance of the police. Both men were lurching, partners in a violent waltz.

"Let him go and put your hands up," Waldbaer growled. He noted with a side-glance that his police partner had drawn his pistol and was trying to aim it at the attacker's head. The assailant yelled something in a language Waldbaer could not understand, and the detective caught the glint of gold teeth.

A moment later the attacker was gone. In a fluid movement, he flung the garrote at the policeman, turned and slammed his form through the French doors opening onto the narrow balcony. Before anyone could react, he pulled himself over the metal railing and dropped from view. His victim crashed to the floor.

Waldbaer was first onto the balcony, in time to see that the man had landed on a flat roof just below, and sprinted to its edge. Without a glance backward, he launched himself from the roof into the hedges that surrounded it. Waldbaer watched as the figure crashed through the brush and ran down the small hill at the front of the hotel, heading for the road.

"Damn it," Waldbaer roared, slapping his hand against the railing. He turned to the policeman and jerked his head toward the disappearing shape. "Get after him. Call in an alert and an ambulance for this fellow. I'll stay with him."

The policeman reholstered his pistol with a hand Waldbaer noticed was shaking slightly. "*Jawohl*," he replied to the kommissar, before exiting at a run.

Waldbaer swore. He doubted the assailant would be caught. The man's quick reaction had bought him a commanding lead and it would be easy enough to exit Garmisch unimpeded. He turned his attention to the moaning form lying on the floor. A quick survey of the victim revealed a ferocious, burgundy welt across the neck, but the man was breathing deeply and the windpipe seemed undamaged. Waldbaer assessed the wound as not life threatening. Had they arrived a minute later, the narrative might have been different.

"Herr Tretschmer, I presume," Waldbaer intoned as he dropped to his knees at the man's side. He unbuttoned the victim's collar but did not attempt to move him. Better to let the paramedics take responsibility for that, he thought.

The man on the floor groaned and looked up, eyes wild. A pungent smell assailed Waldbaer's nostrils and he knew the victim had soiled himself in fear. "You are Tretschmer, aren't you?"

There was a wheeze, followed by a graveled voice. "Yes. Oh, God."

"No," Waldbaer answered dryly, "just the Bavarian police. But nonetheless responsible for your salvation, Herr Tretschmer."

Tretschmer coughed out a barely audible "Thank you."

Waldbaer snorted. "I'd hold my thanks if I were you. We have much to discuss. But we'll get you to the hospital first. Just one thing. The man who nearly put you in a hearse. You know him. I want his name. Don't play games with me."

Tretschmer's face grew more disconsolate. "Jahanghir Karimov," he rasped.

PARTENKIRCHEN, ONE MILE FROM THE SONNENBICHL HOTEL

Jahanghir focused his thoughts on identifying the best escape route as he ran along a path through scrub pine, skirting a meadow. He was certain his split-second decision to plunge from the balcony had thrown the police off his trail temporarily. He congratulated himself for keeping his head. He was puzzled as to how the authorities had discovered his plot to kill Tretschmer, but would consider that later. He needed to exit Germany. A simple plan, he knew from experience, was invariably the best.

He felt his heart racing and a dull pain at his side, and slowed to a jog. There was time, he assured himself. There was no sound or sign that betrayed police in hot pursuit. Through the latticework of fir branches he saw a road ahead, perhaps four minutes distant. His plan evolved quickly. Locate a taxi and go directly to Munich Airport, about an hour and a half away. At the airport, purchase a suitcase and some clothes to fill it, to avoid being profiled as a passenger without luggage. Get a ticket for the next flight to Austria or Italy, whichever came first, to get him out of German jurisdiction. From there, arrange a connection to Azerbaijan. He would be gone before German law enforcement could react, especially with his identity concealed under the alias of Alekperov. Simple enough, he concluded.

He left the narrow dirt path behind and crossed a spit of grass to a sidewalk by the main road. He strolled casually along the sidewalk until he saw the beige form of a Mercedes taxi heading in his direction. Jahanghir lifted a hand and smiled as the car slowed and pulled over. Opening the rear door, he climbed in and settled into the seat, pleased to have his exertions behind him. "Munich Airport, please," he intoned pleasantly, noting the driver's confirming nod.

As the vehicle pulled away and increased tempo, Jahanghir let his thoughts return to Tretschmer, who was so unexpectedly alive. What had happened? What had led the police to Tretschmer's hotel room? Jahanghir glanced out the taxi window framing a moving tableau of craggy alpine terrain. The police must have been after Tretschmer, he concluded; they could not have known of Jahanghir's alias passport. Which meant that the authorities were on to Tretschmer's activities. Precisely the reason Jahanghir wanted to eliminate the effete businessman in the first place.

The Austrian, Hessler, had alerted Jahanghir to the security problem a few days ago, in an email sent anonymously from an Internet café in Vienna. Tretschmer was talking too much on the phone, and had lost control of the captain of the *Condor Fury*. Hessler feared Tretschmer would come to the attention of the authorities, with ruinous implications for them all. The Austrian underlined Jahanghir's vulnerability. International law enforcement did not take kindly to people who trafficked in fissile nuclear material, such as he had provided Tretschmer in Baku. Hessler closed his message with a vague blessing; he would endorse any course of action Jahanghir felt was necessary. Well, Jahanghir sighed, he had tried. And nearly succeeded. But nearly succeeding carried no water in an unforgiving world.

The taxi left the narrow mountain valley and took to the autobahn heading past Murnau to Munich and the airport beyond. Jahanghir had decisions to make. Should he return to Germany in a few weeks and find a way to kill Tretschmer? Or was it best to leave things as they were, retire from his craft, and merge into the sedate pace of a privileged life in Baku? The latter possibility carried appeal. He was tired, and the failure at the hotel might signal to someone superstitious that it was time to retire. Jahanghir did not consider himself superstitious, but prudent, and prudence dictated not playing a losing hand. He would look after himself. Hessler and the others were on their own.

Garmisch Clinic, Bavaria

Waldbaer sat on a metal stool, the pallid form of Otto Tretschmer prostrate before him, propped up in his hospital bed, body covered with a white sheet. The doctor who had examined Tretschmer had coated the deep neck wound with salve and bandaged a spot where the skin had broken. Tretschmer's face was an alloy of exhaustion and fear.

Waldbaer leaned forward on his stool and spoke softly. "So, Herr Tretschmer, I am advised you will survive. *Wunderbar*. Had my police colleague and I not been at the hotel, things might have turned out differently. Not to put too fine a point on it, but we saved your life. Unfortunately for you, Jahanghir Karimov has not been found. He's out there somewhere. He may be on his way to Azerbaijan, who knows?" Waldbaer leaned forward and glanced theatrically out the hospital window at the pine-covered hillside beyond. "Karimov could be nearby, even now. Waiting for an opportunity to finish what he started. Who knows?"

Tretschmer's ivory face seemed to pale even more and he tried to wet his dry lips. "Still out there? You have to protect me. I'm a German citizen, for God's sake. You're obliged to help me!"

Waldbaer knew where he wanted the conversation to go, and how to play it. "Herr Tretschmer, I am quite aware of my responsibilities. But I can only do so much. It's my intention to question you on your activities with the *Condor Fury*, the late Georg Forster, the very-much-alive Anton Hessler, and this Jahanghir Karimov. If it appears you have broken the law, you will go to jail. For a time. Upon your release, I can hardly guarantee that Karimov won't look you up. Of course, the police would do what they can."

Tretschmer's eyes were wide and one hand clutched the bed sheet. "That's not enough. Jahanghir is ruthless, a professional killer. He'll come back for me."

Waldbaer sighed and rubbed at his neck in a calculated show of resignation. "Herr Tretschmer, there are limits to what we can do. You have, it seems, gotten yourself in with bad company." He waited for Tretschmer to reach the logical conclusion.

"Kommissar, can't you relocate me? Give me a new name, papers? Anything to keep Jahanghir off my trail."

Exactly what I wanted, Waldbaer thought. The bait taken, he had to ensure the hook had solid purchase. "You must watch lots of television, Herr Tretschmer. True, that sort of thing is occasionally done in exceptional circumstances. But not often. It's a huge resource commitment."

Tretschmer's face clouded with distress. His voice became plaintive. "I'll make it worth the resources. I'll talk. Settle me securely somewhere with a new identity. Please, my life won't be worth a toss any other way."

Waldbaer was delighted, but concealed his satisfaction. "Provided what you say is significant, I might be able to do something. But for me to determine that, you need to answer questions. Now."

Tretschmer pulled himself up in the bed. "Yes, ask me anything."

"All right. The company T&K Impex. You are T, one of the owners. Who is K?"

Tretschmer did not hesitate. "Sayed al-Khalid. My partner, a Syrian operating from Jordan. He's in touch with our Middle Eastern clients. Meaning the Syrian government and Iranians from the Defense Industries Organization."

Waldbaer had known the answer to the question, but wanted to establish Tretschmer's truthfulness. He was pleased with the response. "Interesting clients. What services are you providing? I want details."

Tretschmer closed his eyes a moment before answering. "T&K owns a ship called *Condor Fury*. Our clients have contracted it to move material from Germany to Somalia. The material is documented as oil-drilling equipment."

"What is really on board, Herr Tretschmer?"

"Centrifuges. State-of-the-art. Advanced Zippe-type equipment for collecting uranium 235. Several hundred. Clearly for nuclear weaponization."

Waldbaer leaned back on his stool and placed his hands on his knees. "Very candid of you. And incriminating. You realize that is an admission of violating German export law?"

Tretschmer exhaled. "Yes. I told you I had valuable information in exchange for protection. There's more."

"Do continue," Waldbaer said.

"I was in Azerbaijan recently at the request of the client. Jahanghir provided me an item they wanted sent to Somalia with the centrifuges. HEU—highly enriched uranium. He got it through contacts in Russia. A relatively small amount, the first delivery, with more to come. It's on board the *Condor Fury* with Zellmann."

Waldbaer moved his legs, his knees issuing a brittle protest. "Nuclear material? For whom?"

Tretschmer shook his head. "I don't know. The Syrians and Iranians have contacts there, but they never revealed anything."

Waldbaer found the reply plausible. "All right. We'll talk about Zellmann later. Anton Hessler interests me more. As does the deceased Georg Forster."

Tretschmer eyed Waldbaer directly. "Hessler is part of this transaction. He took over once Forster died."

Go carefully, Waldbaer cautioned himself, now we move to the Forster murder. He chose his words with precision. "Herr Tretschmer, on the night of his death, Forster was on his way to Garmisch. You were registered as a guest at Sonnenbichl hotel on that evening. He was coming to meet you, correct?"

"Correct. Forster made the initial contact with the Iranians and Syrians and subsequently located me as someone who could service their needs. Forster met these people on trips to the Middle East. They trusted him due to his stance on Israel. And Forster wanted revenge on Israel; he thought they tried to sabotage his political ambitions. Forster put things in motion, using his firm Verbindung Ost.

He'd get a cut of the profits, but that wasn't all. Forster wanted a friendly arrangement with the Iranians and Syrians. It was political."

Waldbaer considered the information and rubbed his hands together. "So Forster believed his Middle Eastern contacts could make him look good, if he helped with their Somalia plans. Fair enough, it fits what we know about Forster. Why was he planning to visit you here in Garmisch?"

Tretschmer rubbed diffidently at the wound around his neck. "Forster's election victory changed things. We talked on the phone. He now had a real chance at political power in Austria. He thought involvement in an illicit nuclear transaction might jeopardize his gains, if word leaked out. I think he was going to tell me that he not only wanted out of the deal, but wanted me to find a reason to kill it, to tell the Iranians we couldn't deliver. Based on his call, I'm quite sure that was in the cards."

Waldbaer kept his voice a steady monotone. "Forster was murdered. His death was no accident."

Tretschmer evidenced no sign of surprise. "I wasn't involved. Why would I be? If I were you, I'd look toward Anton Hessler."

"Why would Hessler want to kill his party comrade?"

Tretschmer released a low laugh, as dry as sandpaper. "Why? Because Forster wanted the deal stopped and Hessler wanted it to go forward. Hessler's ambition meant he was willing to run more risks than Forster. Hessler was the man for foreign policy. I think he saw this transhipment as giving him great international leverage, if he could pull it off. Which meant Forster had to become a martyr, and Hessler his mourning standard-bearer."

"That is an assertion, Herr Tretschmer, not proof."

Tretschmer shrugged. "I have no proof. I have instincts, I've been dealing with people like Hessler for decades. Smart, successful, big ego, self-absorbed. And cold as a winter's night in Tyrol. I'm certain he killed Forster. As you say, supposition on my part. But there's another murder I can clarify more authoritatively."

"Please continue," Waldbaer said.

Tretschmer settled more deeply in his bed, a grimace briefly creasing his features. "Jahanghir is my source. He took pleasure in letting me know what was happening as he yanked that wire around my neck. He figured me for dead anyway. He was laughing as he tightened it, and I could smell his filthy, sour breath." Tretschmer paused and traced a finger lightly along the gash on his neck, as if to convince himself it had all really happened. "That fetid little animal told me Hessler ordered my execution. Because Hessler said I was unreliable, a security risk who talked too much. Bastards, both of them. I could barely hear him, the blood rushing in my ears, but I remember. And he said I was his second victim in Germany."

Tretschmer eyed Waldbaer, who remained a cipher, eyes unblinking.

"Yes, Jahanghir said he killed an Israeli on Hessler's instructions, that it was all the same to him. Just work assignments. Loose ends. He killed an Israeli and would have killed me, if you hadn't intervened. And that conceited Austrian ass Hessler is behind it. Now you know what I know. And you have to protect me."

Waldbaer leaned forward and gripped the side of Tretschmer's metal bed. "That's explosive stuff, Herr Tretschmer. But I wonder, is it true? Why would our Azeri admit to such a crime? No percentage in it for him."

Tretschmer paused before answering. "His ego, I suppose, hubris. Jahanghir holds himself in high esteem, believe me. And as I said, he thought I'd be dead in a few minutes. He probably derived cruel satisfaction from letting me know his power over life and death, an avenging angel. I have no reason to lie to you, Kommissar."

Waldbaer stood, rising slowly, one hand at the small of his back. "Agreed. The confident criminal often relishes taking credit for his deeds. All right, Herr Tretschmer, I'll see what I can do, in view of your cooperation. You may serve prison time for violation of export laws, that sort of thing. But we'll keep you out of Karimov's clutches. By the way, there's a policeman posted outside your door, just to put you at ease. I have to pass your revelations to some colleagues."

Waldbaer exited the brightly lit hospital room, entirely pleased with what he had divined. He would pass it to Hirter's CIA partner and to Sabine Reiner immediately.

CENTRAL INTELLIGENCE HEADQUARTERS, LANGLEY, NORTHERN VIRGINIA

Soren Jorgensen, deputy director of operations, was seated at the end of the polished oval table, facing the VCR screen and camera on the far wall. Half a dozen Clandestine Service officers were in the conference room with him. The VCR screen beamed the encrypted image and voice of Caroline O'Kendell into the room, speaking from a CIA facility in Berlin.

"Good morning, Caroline," Jorgensen began, sipping coffee from a cardboard Starbucks cup.

"Good afternoon, Soren. We're six hours ahead of you here in Germany."

Jorgensen smiled fleetingly at the attractive young woman on the screen. "Right. I forgot that, been stuck inside the Beltway for too long. Caroline, let's coordinate on the *Condor Fury* case."

"There are developments on this end, Soren. I have a request from our German detective, Kommissar Waldbaer. He's convinced that Anton Hessler, the successor to Georg Forster, is a bad character deeply involved in this case. But there's not sufficient evidence to prosecute. He asked whether we might be able to tarnish Hessler's reputation and sabotage his political career. I agree with him. Hessler's dangerous and it's in our interests to defang him if we can."

Jorgensen turned to a man on his left clutching a spiral notepad. "Make a note of the name. Caroline, I'll look into our launching a black propaganda campaign against this guy. We can get some innuendos about his proliferation activities onto some blog sites we control. From there, we'll have a tame journalist or two to pick up the story and give it broader circulation. I'll ask our covert action staff to do their best to ruin Hessler's reputation and political prospects. Now some news from our end. We received word from your Jordanian GID friends that the destination for the *Condor Fury* is Eyl, Somalia. You might let your German detective know that. We've advised Hirter."

Caroline shook her head quizzically. "Somalia? That's something I didn't expect."

Jorgensen nodded. "Neither did we. But it makes sense. The goods on board are high-quality centrifuges for nuclear weaponization. Ordered by the governments of Syria and Iran, possibly in league with non-state jihadist types. The stuff will be off-loaded in Somalia and delivered to a facility already constructed there."

Caroline interrupted. "But wouldn't the Syrians and their friends want the cargo delivered to Syria?"

Jorgensen shook his head. "Apparently not, for good reason. The Syrians were installing a nuclear capability in their country a few years ago, with North Korean assistance. The Israelis got wind of it and took it out. A high-cost learning experience for the Syrians. The Iranians aren't stupid either. What they've done is move their nuclear ambitions out of the Middle East to Africa, away from Israeli reach. They've found an ally in the Somali al-Shabab jihadists, and probably paid for security. The Syrians have dispatched nuke technicians to Somalia, built and camouflaged the appropriate facilities, purchased centrifuges and related equipment from Germany and Bosnia. Now they're ready to install everything and move toward a weaponization program. That's what we've stumbled onto. And that's what we'll stop."

Caroline furrowed her brow. "Stop?"

Jorgensen rapped his knuckles on the veneer of the tabletop. "Yup, stop. To fill you in, CIA has been handed a Presidential Finding authorizing a covert action to seize the *Condor Fury* and prevent the centrifuges from reaching Somalia. The German Navy has the lead, which is why your friend Hirter is on the *Luebeck*. This is hugely sensitive, Caroline."

Caroline leaned toward the camera. "It's about to get more sensitive, Soren. Kommissar Waldbaer just got in touch with me. He now has one of the businessmen behind the *Condor Fury* in custody. There are lots of details, but the most important is that the *Condor Fury* is carrying highly enriched uranium. HEU-235 to be precise. We don't know how much. Waldbaer is convinced the information is solid."

"You're saying that damned ship is carrying highly enriched uranium along with the centrifuges? That's a game changer."

There was a rumble of murmured conversation from the other Clandestine Service officers around Jorgensen. He raised a hand sharply and commanded silence. "Caroline, I believe we're going to need a new Presidential Finding. It will be the White House's call, but I doubt we'll play around with radioactive material. Too dangerous, too many unknowns. I'm going to head downtown now and ask permission to sink the *Condor Fury*. We'll have to sell it to the Germans, but the best thing to do is put that boat at the bottom of the sea. I'll get back to you and Hirter once our marching orders are signed. Things are taking a more dangerous turn."

Caroline's expression became more somber. "For Robert, too. We don't control events at sea."

Jorgensen had heard the corridor whispers that Caroline and Robert Hirter were more than just colleagues. "Right. For Robert, too."

The Atlantic

The *Luebeck* pounded through the waves at top speed, the mass of water retreating from the charging prow. Kapitän Kulm surveyed the frigate's progress from the bridge, taking in the monotonous, endless panorama of ocean. They had encountered no vessels in two days; Kulm had taken a course outside normal shipping lanes to keep the *Luebeck's* movements as covert as possible.

Kulm was satisfied with their situation. Hirter had provided satellite information on the location of the *Condor Fury*, and it was clear the frigate was steadily narrowing the gap between it and the cargo ship. At the current rate, if nothing changed, it was a mathematical certainty the *Luebeck* would interdict its prey off the African coast, before the *Condor Fury* could enter Somalian waters.

He heard voices behind him and turned to see Neureuth and

Hirter conversing as they entered the bridge. "Anything new, gentlemen?" he inquired.

A smile animated Neureuth's face. "Indeed," he said, pointing a thumb at his companion. "Herr Hirter's friends have intercepted a ship-to-shore message from Zellmann to some party in Somalia. But I should let him explain."

Hirter joined in. "Zellmann was informing his contacts in Eyl that the *Condor Fury*'s arrival will be delayed."

"Due to the storm," Klum interjected.

Hirter held up a hand. "Not only that, Kapitän. It seems the *Condor Fury* has problems. She's taking on some water. It's not critical, apparently, but Zellmann needs to reduce speed to keep things under control."

Kulm shook his head. "Excellent. For us, that is. It's time to finalize our plans."

Neureuth spoke up. "I've talked to the *Oberstleutnant*, the lieutenant colonel in charge of the GSG 9 commandos. His plan is simple. Assault at night with small boats."

Kulm frowned and stroked at his cheek. "We have a helicopter on board. I presumed that would be used."

The BND officer shook his head. "Not their preference. The helicopter is loud; it's hard to mask an approach. Remember the botched Israeli raid on that Turkish ship trying to break the Gaza blockade? The crew tackled the Israelis as they rappelled to deck. Our team wants to avoid that. With a coordinated small boat assault, they're convinced they can overwhelm the crew and take control of the vessel."

Hirter joined the conversation. "These guys know what they're doing, they're well trained. I expect their plan will work."

Kulm stared hard at Hirter and Neureuth. "I'm glad to hear you approve. I'm less comfortable with it. My responsibilities as kapitän give me a vote on this, no matter who else approves the plan. Let's walk through it, shall we? When we close on the *Condor Fury*, presuming she doesn't detect us, the commando team heads for the cargo vessel in small boats. As you noted, no role for the helicopter as its rotors would alert the *Condor Fury* crew to an impending assault. The small boats are dirtied up to make them look like African dohas. They approach the *Condor Fury* at night, to avoid detection. The team hits the stern of the ship with hooks and climbs up and on board, carrying small arms and explosive charges."

"Right," Neureuth interrupted, "for later use."

Kulm nodded curtly. "The commandoes are not wearing uniforms, a point which gives me cramps when I consider international law of the seas. Instead, they're in blue jeans and sports shirts and balaclavas, trying to look like pirates. Right down to the use of greasepaint to make them look African. Once on deck, presuming they haven't been spotted, the team moves point to point, seizing crew members, moving them to the galley, which will serve as a temporary holding pen. Correct?"

"Right so far," Hirter replied.

"The *Condor Fury* captain is to be captured or, if he resists, killed. Once the ship is under control, the crew is placed in *Condor Fury* lifeboats and cast off, supplied with provisions and radio."

Neureuth smiled. "Elegant, isn't it? On to part two."

Kulm retained his solemn demeanor. "Part two. With the crew safely dispatched, the commandos place explosives along the ship's spine. These explosives have high brisance and will take the vessel to the bottom. They will be command detonated once the commandos return to the *Luebeck*. Whatever is on board goes down without a trace. End of mission, *ja*?"

"*Ja*," Neureuth replied. "Exactly. The explosive is hexogen, the Americans call it RDX. It's made to shatter, and will crack open the hull of the *Condor Fury*."

Kulm shook his head from side to side and ran both hands slowly through his hair. "I have concerns about this plan. Everything at sea is more complicated than operations on land. The sea is in constant movement, unpredictable. Using small craft on the high seas can be problematic. This plan is full of uncertainties. Will *Condor Fury*'s radar pick up the boats as they approach, meaning they could meet a wall of small-arms fire? We don't know. Is the crew anticipating an attack, alert for it? We don't know. Will they really believe our commandoes are pirates? Again, we don't know. And why are we sinking this ship, not seizing it? Not clear to me. Why not have the *Luebeck* approach the vessel and threaten to sink it if the captain does not comply with our commands? That would be easier than the scenario you've described."

Neureuth pursed his lips and gestured to Hirter. "Over to my American colleague, he can explain better than I."

"Sure," Hirter said, looking directly at the *Luebeck*'s captain. "As far as the risks you describe, I won't disagree. As far as sinking the ship, both my government and Germany agree it is best to send her to the bottom, now that we know what's on board. Highly enriched uranium and sophisticated centrifuges are an undesirable combination. Both our countries agree we don't want dangerous nuclear material on this frigate, not for a second. And seizing the stuff has been judged riskier and more legally complicated than putting it on the sea floor."

The frigattenkapitän appeared unpersuaded. "No uniforms. German commandos in civilian outfits pretending to be pirates. Pure theater."

Hirter shook his head in disagreement. "No. Plausible deniability. An operational scenario to deflect suspicion from our countries for an action some would judge illegal. We don't want public inquiries and hand-wringing in the United Nations. A cargo vessel is attacked by pirates off the Somali coast. Regrettably, that vessel is sunk. That's a believable story, just read the headlines. Even if the crew of the *Condor Fury* suspect there is more to the seizure, they won't be able to prove it."

Kulm stared out at the waves for a moment and exhaled. "It seems this is more a political operation than a military one."

Hirter and Neureuth offered no reply.

The kapitän returned his eyes to the two men. "So be it. As an officer, I follow orders, providing they're legal. None of this seems illegal, only highly unorthodox. Gentlemen, whether or not you are religious, pray this action plays out as envisioned."

INDIAN OCEAN, ONE HUNDRED NAUTICAL MILES OFF SOMALIA

Zellmann watched as the sun slipped behind distant waves on the horizon, the uninterrupted expanse of ocean draining of color, a prelude to encroaching darkness. He ran his tongue over his offending tooth and considered its steady throbbing, the sensation hovering between irritation and pain. He considered ingesting two more aspirin, but decided to wait. He had last medicated three hours ago and didn't want to overdo it. Perhaps there was a dentist in that cesspool of a Somali port who could perform an extraction. *A bloody last resort*, he thought, contemplating with a grimace the likely degree of hygienic dental practice prevailing in Eyl.

The sea had calmed, the anger of the storm dissipated, like a child's tantrum. Still, its ministrations had left a mark on the *Condor Fury*. Most of the crew was dining in the galley and the bridge was quiet, providing Zellmann an opportunity to assess his situation. Not bad in aggregate, he concluded. The ship had negotiated the storm as well as could be expected; at least they were afloat, thanks to the pumps. They would have to improvise hull repairs in Somalia, enough to ensure a safe return to Hamburg, where more professional efforts could be accomplished. Importantly, the cargo had not suffered during the tempest, due to the efforts taken earlier with packing. The sensitive material provided by Tretschmer remained secure in Zellmann's safe.

Zellmann rubbed absently at his cheek and considered the course ahead. Two day's voyage would get them into harbor in Somalia, even at the reduced speed he had ordered for safety. They had encountered few vessels underway and none had evidenced interest in the *Condor Fury*. He anticipated no problems. The Somali clients had pledged to take care of everything in the port from paperwork to off-loading the centrifuges. As in much of the Third World, he might have to grease things with coin, but he had sufficient petty cash aboard. What the centrifuges were to be used for did not concern him. He wanted the cargo unloaded and an uneventful return to Germany, with a handsome payment to his offshore account.

The seascape had darkened, the horizon barely discernable. He could detect no ship navigation lights in the distance. A glance at the sonar revealed an empty green screen. The chief engineering officer would post watch for the next several hours. Zellmann intended to get some sleep in his cabin and was determined to wash down the next duet of aspirin with a soothing assist from a slug of Scotch.

INDIAN OCEAN, ONE HUNDRED NAUTICAL MILES OFF SOMALIA

Frigattenkapitän Kulm married up the information on the gray metal table in front of him. His communications officer had provided a satellite-derived sheet with the location and bearing of the *Condor Fury*. A technical officer had just confirmed a sonar contact ahead at the same coordinates. Kulm nodded to himself and pushed the paper aside. "All good things come to an end. It appears that our sea hunt is over and the target is within striking distance."

There were sounds of assent from the little group that huddled around him on the bridge, Hirter, Neureuth, and the *Luebeck*'s first officer.

"We are traveling at twenty knots," Kulm continued, "and our target at ten knots. The sea is calm. The *Condor Fury* doesn't seem to have detected our presence due to our masking devices. We should prepare to strike. As Shakespeare advised, 'We must take the current when it serves, or lose our ventures.' The current serves now, gentlemen. Let us begin the assault."

Neureuth turned to Hirter. "I'm going with the men. Are you planning to report to Langley from here?"

Hirter's features were unsettled. "That's what my superiors expect. But the issue hasn't arisen, so I won't be violating orders if I join you. As they say, better to beg forgiveness than ask permission. I'm going."

The group broke up, Neureuth and Hirter heading below deck, both silent in their contemplations.

Kapitän Kulm fixed his blue eyes on the first officer. "In case you're wondering, we remain on the bridge for the duration of the operation. No telling how long this will take, even if it works perfectly, and I've never seen a plan work perfectly at sea. Let's hope to God we succeed. It could be a long night. Order up coffee from the galley, we're going to need it."

One Nautical Mile from the *Condor Fury*

Hirter felt beads of water sting his face as the small craft made its way on open sea toward the meager lights of the otherwise dark, distant hulk that was their target. The waves were not high, but their motion was an unfamiliar sensation for him, small boats as alien to his life experiences as life aboard a frigate had been, until recently. He did not feel any incipient trace of seasickness but neither was he comfortable in the cramped posture forced on him by the confines of the dinghy. Before they left the *Luebeck*, the *Korvettenkapitän* who was the commando leader had pressed a compact Walther TPH semiautomatic pistol into Hirter's hand, muttering "you might need this if our plan falls apart." Not much comfort in that, Hirter reflected, and brushed a hand reassuringly against the weapon he had placed in his jacket pocket.

Hirter knew that there were two other craft underway along with the one he occupied. He glanced about but could not detect them in the darkness. All of the boats were the same make, a sturdy black neoprene frame with a motor capable of over forty knots. The frames had been covered with dirty cloth and oil-stained rags to give them the rough appearance of African fast boats. Each of the inflatable boats held seven commandos including Hirter and Neureuth, who was wedged up against the American. The German commandos around them were uniformly silent, clutching the severe contours of Heckler and Koch G36 assault rifles, barrels toward the sky.

"I'm starting to wonder whether we should have stayed aboard the *Luebeck*," Neureuth muttered to Hirter.

"Too late for that, my friend. Anyway, whatever happens, it'll be something you can tell your kids about someday."

"If we live long enough to have kids. But our navy assault friends here seem to know what they're up to."

Hirter nodded in agreement. The specially trained GSG 9 maritime commandos seemed disciplined and proficient. Hirter did not seek to converse with them, having decided it best to stay out of their way and let them perform their task undistracted.

The stolid shape of the *Condor Fury* grew larger, now and then made invisible by a large passing wave. Focusing on the cargo vessel, Hirter for the first time noted the looming height of its hull. He knew they were to board by some sort of rope device, but that task was taking on Herculean dimensions. His stomach growled.

As if reading his thoughts, one of the commandos leaned toward him and spoke in clipped North Sea German. "You and your friend wait on us, along with the navigator. We are climbing up, and we'll drop you the ship's ladder. Easier for you."

Hirter felt the momentary shame of the cosseted invalid, but the emotion was quickly swept aside by relief. "As you say."

The German who had just spoken stood up in the prow of the little boat, his frame steady through training, even in the pitch of the sea. "*Achtung*," he said, "prepare for boarding."

The commandos remained silent but shifted their position in a subdued choreograph of feline movement. Skitting over wave and trough, the small craft approached the stern of the *Condor Fury*, out of line of sight of the bridge.

Hirter noticed that his mouth was dry and wished he had brought a water bottle with him. He wondered what awaited on the silent decks far above. Up close, the hull of the ship was daunting, a metal cliff towering over them. There was no hint that the crew of the cargo ship had detected their presence.

Two commandos shouldered large, unwieldy objects with hooked snouts. Hirter knew from the briefing on board the *Luebeck* that these devices were pneumatically launched grappling hooks towing Kevlar lines, the means through which the Germans would board the *Condor Fury*. The grappling hook launchers employed com-

pressed air and were relatively quiet, the waves and breeze expected
to mask any trace of the launch from the cargo crew, many of whom
would be asleep.

The commando officer, a short, slim silhouette of a man, raised
a hand in the air and dropped it sharply, issuing a curt "*Haken los.*"
His two subordinates fired simultaneously and the savage-looking,
three-pronged hooks traveled eighty feet to the hull above. A muted
metallic clang signaled that the hooks had found purchase, and the
commandos pulled the lines taut. Wordlessly, their comrades lined
up, shouldered their weapons, and began the ascent.

Hirter watched them disappear into the enveloping darkness,
and thought the scene surreal. He glanced back at the half-visible
form of the navigator, who worked the motor to keep the small craft
steady and a few feet clear of the *Condor Fury*'s mountainous hull.
"Pretty damned impressive so far," he whispered to Neureuth.

"It needs to stay impressive," the BND officer replied.

A rush of sound commanded their attention. A portable ladder
had been dropped over the side of the *Condor Fury* by the Germans
who had just boarded. The ladder, soiled plastic and nylon, was just
beyond reach. The navigator maneuvered the small boat a degree
closer. "Everybody up," he muttered. The navigator alone would remain on the assault craft.

"Showtime," Hirter exclaimed, as he and Neureuth joined the
remaining Germans and moved forward.

ABOARD THE *CONDOR FURY*

The Ugandan sitting in the plush mock-leather swivel chair on the
bridge chewed a few leaves of khat, relishing the mild narcotic effect.
He had stashed some of the illegal shrub leaves in his duffel bag and
indulged the substance whenever he was alone. He knew that Captain Zellmann would disapprove, but with Zellmann asleep in his
cabin, the Ugandan assessed the chance of discovery as slight. And
chewing khat helped to endure the boredom of night watch and the
slow voyage to Somalia.

With eyes that could focus only with difficulty, the African stared through the large, rectangular windows of the bridge toward the bow of the ship and the dark arc of sea beyond. Illuminated sparsely by a few deck lights, there was nothing on the vessel to arrest his attention. Nor was anything visible on the ocean to suggest the presence of other ships.

A sound intruded upon his languor, and his listlessness retreated. He thought he heard a brief resonance of metal on metal. Listening carefully, he detected nothing other than the familiar background hum of the *Condor Fury*'s engines. Perhaps the sound had come from below decks via the ventilation louvers. Or maybe he had imagined it, khat sometimes had unexpected effects. He decided it was nothing that merited checking. After all, the seas were calm and the weather gave no cause for alarm. What threats could there possibly be?

Ninety seconds later two GSG 9 men in blue jeans and tee-shirts gathered outside the weather-tight metal door that led onto the bridge. It hung slightly open, revealing a crease of light from inside. Edging closer, the lead commando pushed the door gingerly with one hand, and surveyed the bridge. He raised a single finger in the air, signaling to his companion that there was one person inside. A second later he eased past the door frame in a fluid movement and approached the Ugandan from behind, unseen.

The African was big and broad shouldered, but disadvantaged by surprise and seated position. He could not comprehend what was happening as he was yanked backward, a strong arm gripping his neck. He flailed, but his fists found no purchase, his assailant behind him. Preparing to shout, he inhaled. The reflex propelled khat leaves into his throat, the ingested fiber blocking his windpipe. Eyes wide in panic, he wheezed loudly, vainly attempting to inhale air.

The commando pulled the crewman over the back of the chair, landing him on the bridge deck. The initial flash of resistance from his victim had ceased, the motions replaced by a desperate shaking of the torso. The German was confused as to what was transpiring. He watched in quiet horror as the African ceased all motion, eyes rolling back in his head.

The second commando joined him, grabbing his shoulder. "What's the matter?" he whispered to his partner.

"He's dead. I didn't do it. I just grabbed him. Maybe a heart attack. Shit, *Scheisse*."

"It doesn't matter. It wasn't in the plan but it can happen. You need to forget about it, we have things to do. We stick with the plan. I'll take control of the ship from here and keep her steady on course. Let the others know."

The first commando pulled a black phone from his trousers and whispered into it. "We have the bridge of the *Condor Fury* under control. Will maintain course and speed until otherwise advised. All elements proceed."

Divided into small groups, fifteen commandos and the two intelligence officers proceeded down narrow, anemically lit walkways, preceded by the muzzles of their weapons.

Hirter and Neureuth, armed only with pistols, followed behind a clutch of three commandos. After four minutes of searching, they had encountered no one.

"Where the hell are they hiding?" Neureuth breathed.

"Most of them are sleeping at this hour. Easier for us; that accounts for the timing of the raid. Wake somebody up unexpectedly and he's disoriented, not likely to offer effective resistance."

"Unless they're sleeping with their AKs," Neureuth replied.

Hirter left the remark unanswered and concentrated on the scene before him. He saw the backs of the commandos, all of them in casual clothing, right down to sports shoes instead of boots. The party passed through a bulkhead and was confronted by a series of doors on both sides of the corridor.

"Sleeping quarters, I wager," Hirter advised his BND companion.

Further progress halted with the sharp report of two shots in rapid succession from somewhere deeper in the ship. A third shot reverberated seconds later.

What had been prevailing stillness erupted into aural chaos. Several doors lining the corridor were yanked open from inside, the crewman occupants emerging in confusion and varying states of undress, accompanied by a cacophony of several languages. Tagalog, Hausa, broken French, and pidgin English filled the corridor. A chubby Indonesian, eyes squinting, noticed the approaching commandos and issued a high-pitched scream. The crewmen stampeded in panic, a human wave running down the hallway away from the intruders. In seconds they had crossed over a bulwark and disappeared. A solitary, powerfully built Nigerian remained, his face a display of defiance. With a guttural yell, he charged the commandos. The Nigerian was brought down with the strike of an assault rifle butt to his shoulder. He collapsed to the deck and moaned, and the lead German cinched the man's wrists together behind his back with a plastic band.

Another commando's portable radio emitted a rush of static and he spoke into it. "*Jawohl*," he said a moment later, replacing the device in his pocket.

"What's going on?" Neureuth inquired.

"Armed resistance by a crew member against our team searching the engine room. One crewman shot dead, one of our men with a leg wound, not serious. We're herding the crew into the galley, that's the collection point." He pointed to the prostrate Nigerian. "This one stays here for now. We need to collect his mates."

The group moved forward, swiftly checking the rooms for inhabitants, pursuing those who had fled.

Zellmann bolted up in his bed, instantly alert, shaken out of his Scotch-induced slumber by the shots. He had issued firearms to a few, trusted crew members, in the event of a pirate hijacking attempt. But Zellmann knew that pirates operated close to shore, and the *Condor Fury* was still some distance from the Somali coast. Besides, his contacts in Eyl would ensure the ship safe passage.

"Damned shit voyage," he mumbled, pulling on his clothes and chambering a round in his Walther pistol. Moving to the gray safe in a corner of the cabin, he spun the dial in a familiar sequence of numbers. He pulled the metal door open with a grunt and stared for a moment at Tretschmer's offering within. He calculated that if he needed to abandon the *Condor Fury*, he should at least take this incriminating item with him. "What a bitch of a business." He removed the attaché case and secured it to his wrist with a length of twine from his dresser.

Easing open the cabin door, Zellmann surveyed the corridor, satisfying himself that it was empty. He listened, but detected no sound. He imagined that a pirate boarding would be loud, undisciplined. Perhaps there had been an accidental weapon discharge, careless handling by one of the crew. No need to panic, he told himself. He would check the bridge, ensure the ship was safe, and then investigate the gunshots. If he detected boarders, he knew what to do. He would get to one of the covered lifeboats and abandon ship, taking Tretschmer's metal attaché case with him, striking out for Eyl. The crewmen would have to fend for themselves. He snickered as he recalled the saying, "No honor among thieves." Pistol in one hand and attaché in the other, Zellmann moved along the corridor, heading toward the bridge, forward and a deck above him. He had killed before and was prepared to do so again.

SIX THOUSAND MILES ABOVE THE ATLANTIC

In the perfect silence of a vacuum, the Keyhole-12 satellite responded to the directions issued by a ground station in Virginia, and relayed into space through the SDS, the Satellite Data System. A charge-coupled device engaged for electro-optical imaging, and a camera moved soundlessly to acquire a new target. A digital color camera with a Bayer mask began capturing images of the target every ten seconds. The camera shutter closed and opened in a regular sequence, reducing the effect of cosmic rays on image resolution. Even with the effects of atmospheric degradation, the camera was able to record a detailed image of objects far below.

The onboard satellite computer combined its resident information with the detailed guidance instructions sent from the Virginia countryside, locating and focusing on the port of Eyl, Somalia. The computer-linked camera was instructed to conduct a thorough photographic sweep of the city and its surroundings. The images captured by the metal-and-glass satellite would be relayed back to earth and analyzed by flesh-and-blood photographic interpreters. The specialists knew what they were looking for. A series of oversize warehouses on the outskirts of the port. The structures were no more than two years old, which meant that they should not be present in any inventoried images of Eyl taken before that time. Once the warehouses were identified, the images were to be relayed to a small CIA facility in Djibouti. That was all that the photo interpreters knew, or cared to know.

The cold optic eye moved slightly, blinked, and imaged, responding to the programmed impulses of its electronic brain. It continued this routine with the efficiency of an automaton, absent boredom, excitement, or any emotion.

ABOARD THE *CONDOR FURY*

Robert Hirter and Herr Neureuth stood against the wall of the galley, so as not to intrude on the commandos' activities. Captured members of the *Condor Fury* crew had been brought to the large bay area and were ordered to take seats along the long dining tables. Most of the crewmen wore terrified expressions. *Not surprising under the circumstances*, Hirter thought. They had been woken from their sleep, marshaled at gunpoint, and assembled here by a company of "pirates" wearing balaclavas and brandishing automatic weapons. The crew members were uncertain of their fate, having been told nothing by their captors.

Neureuth conversed with the bantam rooster of a commando leader, out of earshot of the crew, who might have found German an unlikely language for African-based pirates. He turned to Hirter and whispered. "Here's our status. The ship is in our hands. Two crewmen dead; one on the bridge, one in the engine room. One of ours wounded but ambulatory; he's been evacuated to one of the boarding craft and is underway to the *Luebeck* for further treatment. The boarding craft will return here momentarily. It looks like we have

all the crew. Except the captain, this Zellmann character. Don't
know where he is. The designated commandos are laying Composition C hexogen charges along the spine of the ship right now. It's all
science. They know how much explosives to place, and precisely
where."

Hirter eyed the crew as Neureuth spoke and kept his voice low
as he replied. "Good. That means what remains is finding Zellmann,
getting the crew into lifeboats, getting our own butts back to the
Luebeck and sending *Condor Fury* to the bottom. I'm worried about
the crew. Look at their eyes. They're scared, for good reason. I hope
they don't decide to rush us out of desperation. I don't want to tell
the commandos their business, but it might defuse things to inform
the crew—in English—that the ship is being pirated, and they'll be
put on lifeboats and permitted to leave unmolested."

Neureuth nodded. "Good point. I'll persuade our lead commando. My English is good enough to make an announcement to
the crew. The sooner we herd them to the lifeboats, the better. The
longer this takes, the more chance there is of a complication."

Hirter smiled. "You're starting to sound like Kapitän Kulm.
While you're doing that, I'm going to step out and find a toilet. I'll
be back in a moment."

Exiting the galley, Hirter turned left in the narrow corridor,
searching for some sign of a men's room. He turned a corner into another corridor, lined with doors both opened and closed, none of
them looking like what he wanted. He noted a stairwell at the end
of the corridor, leading upward, presumably to the main deck. *Maybe
up there*, Hirter thought.

A black, inchoate shape clouded the periphery of Hirter's vision,
partly obscured by his balaclava. The blow slammed into his shoulder and back, the burst of pain buckling his knees. As Hirter grabbed
at the wall to keep from collapsing, he saw a figure exit one of the
rooms at his side and run toward the stairwell. The assailant was a
fireplug of a man, Hirter saw, clad in a dark shirt and jeans, a metal
attaché case swinging from one arm. Hirter knew instantly that the
attaché case had been used to strike him. The shape clambered up

the narrow stairs and vanished. Hirter pulled himself to his feet with a groan, the pain making him wonder whether his shoulder was dislocated.

Hirter knew that his attacker was Zellmann; everyone else was accounted for. Pushing himself to his feet, Hirter moved in pursuit. A voice in his head told him to return to the galley and let the commandos conduct the hunt, but a primordial imperative urged him to deliver Zellmann himself. Hirter hobbled up the metal steps, and pulled his pistol from his trouser pocket. At the top of the stairs, the door to the deck was thrown open, and Hirter cautiously moved forward. He detected neither sound nor movement. Stepping onto the deck, he noticed the mild stir of breeze and the salt air. Hirter surveyed the scene before him, rows of containers in various colors and markings visible in the uncertain light, but no trace of Zellmann. Hirter turned and looked upward. He could make out part of the well-lit bridge, but some of it was obscured by the stacked containers. Looking toward the ship's bow, Hirter decided to move directly down the center, between the rows of cargo.

Zellmann had never made it to the bridge, didn't have to. Watching from behind a darkened bulkhead, he had observed several of his crew being herded to the galley by hooded men with automatic weapons. Apparently pirates. But there was something odd in the way they moved, their gestures disciplined, trained. And the intruders were toned and muscled, not thin and wiry like most Somalis or Arabs. An elaborate ruse? In the end, it didn't matter. The *Condor Fury* had been boarded and seemed under the control of the intruders.

From his hidden niche between two corrugated containers, Zellmann felt a momentary flash of pain from his tooth and moved a hand to his stubbled face. He would get to one of the outboard-equipped lifeboats, engage its lowering mechanism and make for the Somali coast. What awaited there was uncertain, but infinitely better than prospects on board. Whatever was in the attaché case might compel Trestchmer to rescue him, or perhaps he could sell it to Somalis for safe passage. At the very least, he was sure the contents of the case were incriminating, and did not want it in the clutches of the men who had seized his ship. Zellmann heard a subdued footfall and glanced down the expanse of deck.

A silhouetted figure was moving in his direction. It was the man he had hit below decks. "Stubborn bastard," he spat, pulling his Walther. He raised the pistol and prepared to fire a clip into the man's chest. Zellmann paused, and thought again. Gunfire would immediately bring a squad of the others after him, and his pistol was no match for the automatic weapons he had seen. He needed to get to a lifeboat. Zellmann edged between the containers away from his pursuer and moved forward, portside. He headed for the nearest lifeboat and its free-fall ramp. Zellmann knew how to handle the escape craft, and estimated he could be underway in minutes. He took care to walk the deck softly, so his footfall would not betray his location.

Hirter's ears detected nothing other than the whisper of breeze and slap of waves against the ship's hull. The vessel was coasting slowly to a full stop, as called for in the operational plan once the crew had been seized and secured. There was no sign of Zellmann, but Hirter was certain the captain was somewhere on the container-laden cargo deck. *What would he be doing up here?* Hirter wondered. The answer occurring to him seconds later. Trying to escape. Which would mean getting to one of the lifeboats Hirter had seen in the overhead photographs of the *Condor Fury*. Hirter changed course from the center of the deck, veering right toward the hull. He would check one side of the ship and then the other, hoping to discover Zellmann before he could release the lifeboat.

Hirter's shoulder emitted bolts of pain and he fought to concentrate. As he moved forward along the hull, the red-and-white shape of the lifeboat came into view. He wrapped his good hand tightly around the grip of the pistol and tried to detect some hint of movement in the lifeboat.

Zellmann's attack, as before, came from the side. Launching himself from a dark space between two containers, Zellmann again used the heavy attaché case as his weapon, not wanting to risk a shot. The blow struck solidly against Hirter's arm, slapping the pistol from his hand and sending it skittering along the deck.

Zellmann raised his attaché case anew but Hirter grabbed at his torso before he could bring the device down. Both men slammed against the hull and groaned. Zellmann pistoned a fist into Hirter's abdomen, slamming the air from his lungs. Hirter fell to the deck, the hard fall compounding the pain in his injured shoulder, putting him on the verge of unconsciousness.

Hirter willed himself to stay focused and saw Zellmann's enraged countenance above him, raising the attaché case for a final blow. The case, connected by its lanyard to the attacker's wrist, was at the level of Zellmann's chest when Hirter kicked both legs in a powerful arc. The blow drove the aluminum box forcefully into Zellmann's face, breaking his nose. He screamed. Hirter was up in a second and on him.

"You're dead," Zellmann screamed through bloody lips, managing to push Hirter a few inches back from the hull. Raising the attaché case above his head to deliver another blow, Zellmann overcompensated. The weight of the heavy object pulled Zellmann backward, and his feet lost purchase on the deck. Eyes wide in panicked comprehension, Zellmann pitched over the side of the ship in a free fall. He had the presence of mind to gulp in air before he hit the water. Dragged under by the weight of the object connected to his wrists, he struggled to undo the knot. He could not see in the darkness but felt the coarse twine between his frantically clawing fingers. He pulled, but it would not give. Zellmann felt himself descending, arms and head first. It occurred to him that he would not see the strip bars of Hamburg again. He noted that his tooth no longer seemed to hurt. But an excruciating pressure was building in his lungs as his body demanded oxygen. Make it quick, he thought. He opened his mouth and let the sea enter.

Aboard the frigate LUEBECK

Kapitän Kulm turned to his first officer. Hirter and Neureuth stood nearby with the lithe commando team leader, all breathing heavily from their recent exertions, having arrived at the bridge moments before.

"Status report, please." Kulm said without preamble.

The first officer held an encrypted phone to his ear. "All commandos safely back aboard *Luebeck*, everyone accounted for. RDX charges placed along the spine of the *Condor Fury*. Crew of the *Condor Fury* in lifeboats and life rafts. Radar images indicate they're now over a nautical mile distant from the cargo ship. Still on board the *Condor Fury* are two dead crew members."

"And the captain fell overboard," Hirter interrupted, "certainly dead too."

Kulm nodded and looked introspective. "All right. That's what we wanted. No need to delay. I want the *Luebeck* out of here, on a course for Kiel." He fixed the commando leader with a stare. "Is your ordinance officer ready to detonate those charges?"

"*Jawohl*, Kapitän," the man replied.

"Do it."

The commando leader turned toward the bridge window and spoke softly into his communications device. The others turned as well, gazing out at the distant navigation lights of the *Condor Fury*.

Hirter counted the seconds silently. Eleven seconds after the commando leader had issued his order, flashes of bright orange erupted from the hull of the cargo ship, silhouetting it. A moment later, the deep growl of an explosion reverberated against the *Luebeck*'s bridge. In quick succession, other explosions followed. The orange glow aboard the *Condor Fury* intensified.

"It won't be long before she goes down," Kulm muttered. "Those charges were placed to take out the bottom of the ship. That's the vulnerability of metal vessels. Once the hull is breached, there's no natural buoyancy. She's filling rapidly with water."

As they watched, the silhouette of the *Condor Fury* shifted, the prow and stern angling higher.

"Her back's broken," Kulm said absent emotion.

A moment later the cargo ship settled deeper in the water. The navigation lights disappeared. The outline of the ship vanished, leaving only sheets of flame upon the waves, until these were extinguished as well. Below decks, some of the commandos heard the haunting and unmistakable metallic cacophony of a major vessel breaking up and beginning its descent to the sea floor.

"Kapitän, we are now on a course for Germany," the first officer remarked.

Hirter and Neureuth left the bridge for the communications room, to send their respective messages to CIA and BND headquarters.

"From onboard *Luebeck*: 'All's well that ends well,'" Hirter began. "Target vessel destroyed in accordance with plan. Three crew killed, including captain. Others safely aboard lifeboats awaiting rescue. No delivery of centrifuges or HEU to Somalia."

Eyl, Somalia

The morning had broken sunny, as every morning, and the heat and humidity began their inexorable combined ascent, as every morning. By ten, the humidity exceeded eighty percent, and man and beast sought shade where they could find it. Abdi Abdullah Hassan leaned against the wall of the Syrian-built warehouse, enjoying the relative coolness provided by the roof overhang's shadow. As on many somnolent mornings, he gazed out at the arid, desiccated yellow terrain and the shimmering blue of the Indian Ocean beyond. He slapped without enthusiasm at a fly that landed fleetingly on his cheek.

Abdi considered his luck at being assigned to guard the building, along with a dozen other al-Shabab jihadis. It was boring, of course, but Abdi found boredom and routine to be considerable luxuries in the fierce, unstable environment of Somalia. He was fifteen, and had spent two years fighting Ethiopian infidel troops of the African Union in Mogadishu. He had been wounded in the leg by shrapnel from a mortar and walked with a limp. One day, he had been accorded the honor of beheading a captured, weeping Ethiopian corporal, and had accomplished his task with strong, unyielding strokes, one hand gripping the man's wiry tangle of hair. He recalled how his Shabab friends had jumped about, yelling "*Allah akhbar*," and how the Ethiopian had screamed until his windpipe had been severed. There were still traces of his dried blood on Abdi's rubber flip-flops. If Eyl lacked that degree of excitement, it also lacked Mogadishu's risks. And there was food here, stolen from captured cargo ships, including cartons of unsweetened Libyan orange juice, for which Abdi had acquired a taste. As for the warehouse he was guarding, it was true that he was not permitted inside, as the building was the exclusive preserve of the perpetually scowling Syrians and Iranians. What went on inside was equally a mystery to him. But it did not matter. He was content.

Abdi shifted his posture slightly, a worn AK-47 dangling loosely from his shoulder. He wondered what he and the other guards would be given for lunch, an hour from now. He stretched, yawned, and raised his eyes toward the cerulean sky. A few distant clouds that promised no rain hung listlessly over the ocean. But there was something else. He noticed a small metallic glint high above, like a tear in the azure canopy. The reflection was in motion, but too small to signify an airplane. What's that light, he wondered, without realizing that this would be his final, banal burst of sentience.

The Hellfire missile impacted the warehouse exactly at center of mass. The shock of the blast collapsed the steel-and-concrete roof of the structure, crushing the Syrians, Iranians and equipment inside, and initiating a series of fires that spread rapidly, fed by spilled generator fuel and ruptured tanks of industrial chemicals. A second missile detonated moments later at the main door, an intense wave of high pressure blasting it into particles and shredding into strips of blood and tissue the writhing, moaning forms of the technicians and guards who were not already dead. The flames continued their devouring work, and there was no one left alive to counter the fire.

The optical images were viewed in a whitewashed bunker in Djibouti, located on a French military base hosting a small American presence.

"Perfect targeting. No need to reengage. No movement, no more integrity to the structure. And it's burning out of control." The balding, blond man spoke with a slight New York accent.

The man next to him, an athletic Cuban-American, whistled softly. "Beautiful work. Classic. Let's bring these babies home."

Eyes focused on the monitors before them, both men tugged gently at joy sticks by their side. Hundreds of miles away, two Predator drone aerial vehicles turned in response, their metallic fuselages glinting in the remorseless sun. The outline of the port of Eyl, and the Gulf of Aden, far below, slipped away.

MUTTERS, ABOVE INNSBRUCK, AUSTRIA

Anton Hessler found that he could summon no more tears. He had been weeping for several hours, shuffling aimlessly through the finely appointed rooms of his penthouse and gazing with watery eyes at the distant Tyrolean Alps. Copies of Innsbruck and Vienna newspapers littered the parquet floor of the living room. Some he had ripped into pieces, as if to eradicate the information within. The stories were damning and, he knew, impossible to refute.

"Anton Hessler Linked to Murder of Israeli Diplomat, Confidential Source Says," ran one of the headlines. "Party Chief Tied to Organized-Crime Hit Man," screamed another front-page article. Perhaps even more damaging was the in-depth piece from the news magazine Profil detailing Hessler's association with T&K GmbH and Verbindung Ost. The article cited anonymous law-enforcement sources and listed various weapons smuggling deals the firms allegedly engaged in, along with the names of Russian and East European criminal contacts. As if that were not enough, some online blog was hinting that Hessler had ordered the murder of Georg Forster because the noble Forster had discovered Hessler's unsavory activities. The allegations had been picked up by the international press, and he had disconnected his phone to end their incessant calls.

"Lying little bitch," he pronounced, the image of Kommissarin Sabine Reiner appearing before his hollow eyes. He had given her just enough information to keep himself out of the line of fire, he thought, and now this. He wished that he could strangle her, feel her pulse beneath his hands as he squeezed that feminine little throat.

Worst of all, party representatives had informed him this morning that he was being relieved of his position as chief, and of all his responsibilities. "You're poison for us now, Anton, you've dirtied our reputation and we have to cut our losses as best we can," one of them had said. Feckless bastards. His political ambitions, commercial interests, and dreams of power were suddenly, incredibly in ruins. And the Austrian interior minister had announced that he was ordering an official investigation of Hessler. It was over, his future turned to ash. He wondered at how this could happen to him, a man of refinement, taste, and intelligence.

He moved to the bedroom and pulled the paisley covers from the eighteenth-century Parisian bed. He draped the material around his body, caressed the soft fabric and took the few steps to his dresser, mumbling in a steady, monotonic litany, "little bitch, little bitch." Pulling open the top drawer, Hessler extracted the heavy form of his father's old Wehrmacht pistol, a metal-blue Luger. Ensuring that a round was chambered, he placed the barrel in his mouth, tasting cold metal. He checked his image in the gilded mirror above the dresser, ensuring that his hair was combed. Hessler adjusted the blanket around his shoulders again, to catch the blood. It would be déclassé to leave a mess. He squinted against what he presumed would be explosive noise, and pulled the trigger.

The report disturbed the pigeons on the penthouse balcony. They flew off in a flurry of feathers for more tranquil accommodations.

Gamsdorf, Bavaria

He stood again in the garden behind his home and savored the stillness of an approaching Bavarian evening, the sun beginning its incremental descent behind the chain of craggy alpine peaks. He considered for a moment, frowned, sighed, and drew a cigarette from a pack tucked into his loden sports jacket. He had cut back to three cigarettes a day. Except on stressful days, such as when he had to deal directly with Hauptkommissar Streichner. Today had been such a day.

The press conference on the closure of the Forster case had been arranged for ten that morning. Waldbaer had invited Sabine Reiner to join him for the announcement and she had agreed to meet him in front of the police station. They had both written brief statements to read explaining their investigative conclusions. But it was not to be. Streichner was standing by the main door when they arrived.

An insincere smile formed a crevice beneath Streichner's thick glasses as Waldbaer introduced his superior to the Austrian woman.

"I kiss your hand," Streichner intoned in imitation Tyrolean accent, as false as his smile.

Sabine Reiner accepted the archaic greeting gracefully, and Streichner turned his attention to his subordinate. "Waldbaer, although I labor under the demands of other business, I decided to do you a favor. I want to spare you the perils of dealing with the media. They twist things, and always find a way to ask some question you aren't prepared for. And your photo in the papers or on television can only make any of your discreet future investigations more difficult. I won't have it. I told myself this morning that it's my duty to protect as capable a person as you from such hazards. Although I'm no fan of the press myself, I'll serve as your shield today and make the Forster statement myself. It's one of my responsibilities as hauptkommissar." He beamed and nodded sagely, the effect meant to suggest the considerable service he was selflessly rendering.

Waldbaer took satisfaction in finding his loathing for his superior once more confirmed. Streichner had nothing to do with the case in the least, but was prepared to grab credit for it and deny the stage to the detective who had handled its intricacies. Not that Waldbaer cared. His need for publicity was about as great as his need for Streichner. He decided to cede without resistance. "That's certainly big of you, Herr Streichner. Entirely in character, I might add."

Streichner shook his head in what he intended as a display of modesty and continued grinning obtusely.

The Austrian detective spoke up. "Well, if the event is proceeding without Kommissar Waldbaer, who has been my partner on this matter, I think it best if I absent myself from the proceedings. I expect you can speak for both of us, Hauptkommissar."

Streichner's weak eyes widened further behind his lenses. "Of course, Frau Reiner. I'm fully willing to help you as well. Anything to please our Austrian neighbors."

Waldbaer grinned at the unexpected solidarity from his Tyrolean counterpart. "Well then, Frau Reiner and I will be leaving. By the way, Herr Streichner, I understand there are some rumors going around that the information the Americans informally provided to our investigation was obtained in Jordan through, shall we say, methods illegal under German law. But I'm sure you can handle that. Good day."

Streichner rubbed his hands together in a rapid motion, and called after the departing couple. "What's that, Kommissar? What illegal methods? Which Americans are you speaking of? Waldbaer!"

Neither detective replied.

Waldbaer finished his cigarette along with his recollection of the morning's events and dropped the filter into the tall grass, pushing it into the dark Bavarian soil with the sole of his shoe.

"Dinner is ready, Franz," Sabine Reiner said from the terrace behind him. Following their departure from the police station, she had offered to cook him an Austrian dinner of *Tafelspitz*, boiled beef, as a celebratory cap on their collaboration. He had given her run of his kitchen.

"I am not without hunger," Waldbaer said, moving toward his guest. He considered again that the Austrian detective was not unattractive, in figure and features. The soft alpine light of evening is generous to us all, he reminded himself, not willing to surrender his happily self-contained solitude without a fight.

Sabine was wearing an apron she had found closeted in the kitchen. "Franz, will you be having a beer with your meal?"

"Yes and no. That I will be having beer, there is no doubt. That we are speaking of a single foray is considerably less certain."

She smiled at him, a look in her eyes conveying a silent message that he could not entirely decipher, nor readily comprehend.

Author's Note

This is, of course, a work of fiction. The story is nonetheless mindful of some of the troubling realities of the twenty-first century. There is broad agreement in intelligence circles that Syria was working on a nuclear weapons program until stopped in its tracks by an Israeli military strike. It is likewise true that the Pakistani scientist A. Q. Khan illicitly proliferated nuclear weapons knowledge, the extent of his international dealings unknown. As well, it is fact that there have been disturbing incidents of highly enriched uranium being offered for sale. One such incident took place in the republic of Georgia in 2006, discovered by a joint operation of the Georgian intelligence service and the CIA, according to press reports.

The German Navy has been involved in antipiracy operations off of Somalia, along with a number of other western navies. The German frigate described in the novel is from the 125 series, a state-of-the-art warship intended to come into active service in the next few years.

Somalia has for years been a failed state, home to pirates and terrorists. Al-Shabab is a real terrorist organization, linked by jihadist ideology and perhaps organizationally as well, to al Qaeda.

The author is aware of no indications that the challenges of nuclear weapons proliferation, transnational criminal activities, rogue state desire for weapons of mass destruction, or international terrorism are likely to recede in the near future.